INCONSEQUENTIAL TALES

Inconsequential Tales

Ramsey Campbell

Hippocampus Press

New York

Acknowledgements: See p. 251.

Published by Hippocampus Press
P.O. Box 641, New York, NY 10156.
http://www.hippocampuspress.com

Cover art and interior illustrations by Jason C. Eckhardt.
Cover design by Barbara Briggs Silbert.
Hippocampus Press logo designed by Anastasia Damianakos.

First Edition
1 3 5 7 9 8 6 4 2
ISBN13: 978-0-9793806-6-2

for Geoff and Lisa—

some disinterred indiscretions

Contents

Truth or Consequences

I hold Ted Klein responsible, at least for my title. Ted ascribes the name of his recent *Reassuring Tales* to me, but you must discover the reason by reading his book, as you certainly should. However comforting the title and the author may seek to be, let me reassure you that Ted continues to display his considerable talent for terror so quiet that its whispers may go unheard by the careless reader. He's one of the absolute masters of unsettling reticence, and I wish he were more prolific. Where's that second novel? He's unreasonable about his own work in the introduction to *Reassuring Tales,* and perhaps self-deprecation may be inhibiting his output. As you'll see from what follows, it never stops me. Nevertheless these tales deserve the kind of criticism Ted heaped on his.

"The Childish Fear" was written in 1963, immediately after I'd completed *The Inhabitant of the Lake and Other Unwelcome Tenants* (as it was meant to be called) and a tale that read less like Lovecraft, "The Stone on the Island." I'd intended "Fear" to fit into *Inhabitant,* but August Derleth thought not, finding that "it requires too much knowledge of certain films on the part of the reader to make it effective." He was right, and I should explain that Val Guest directed the first two Quatermass films. Too much of the tale is straight autobiography, even if my childhood habit of turning over stones in search of insects has some thematic relevance. I used to judge the effectiveness of horror films by how much they quickened my pulse, if they managed to. The narrator's opinions of films were all mine at seventeen years old. I disliked *Them* on a first viewing, although not now, and remain bored by *The Blob.* I shouted at noisy audiences, which would surprise them into silence the first time but not on repetition, and often sat through films twice: double bills allowed this as well as tempting some viewers to come in before the end (alas, my mother would insist on our doing so).

The tale does convey some sense of the period, when the Liverpool suburbs were still full of cinemas in their decline, and perhaps it vaguely prefigures "The Show Goes On" of fifteen years later. From the same year, "The Offering to the Dead" appears to echo Clark Ashton Smith's "An Offering to the Moon," though they have only their titles in common. Like "The Stone on the Island," and just about as awkwardly, the tale does convey a naïve sense of an unconsummated office romance. The clumsy introverted swain was of course the author, who did indeed pretend to be asleep if anyone (his mother) entered his room when he was abed. Alas, the prose is clumsy too, and holds the narrative at arm's length, although it has its inadvertent moments: "David found his way into a pair of her father's pyjamas," for instance, and what seems to be the thickest carpet in all literature. Radio Luxembourg was a pirate radio station of the time, and stop press reports in newspapers were printed in thick messy type. None of this took Derleth's fancy, and quite right too. "This one does nothing for me, I'm sorry," he wrote. "It seems to be in the tradition of the olde Gothick rather than in your better vein, though it's told well enough—I've no quarrel with its style, though I think you may be mixing your liking for [Henry] Miller and [William] Burroughs with your penchant for the weird, an insoluble combination, unfortunately."

"The Reshaping of Rossiter" (1964) is the first version of "The Scar." It and its much improved rewrite were both produced for Arkham House anthologies, although they could equally well have been destined for *Demons by Daylight* (in which both "Cold Print" and "The Cellars" would have appeared if they hadn't already found other Arkham homes). I completely rewrote several of the *Demons* tales, but this is the only ur-text that was eventually published. It reads as if it was written too soon in my life, given the unconvincing details of behaviour and dialogue. The influence of Alain Resnais may explain the change of viewpoint halfway through a paragraph (an effect better used for the temporal lurches in "Concussion"), and the viewpoint shifts again later on, twice too often for a short story, even if Ambrose Bierce brought it off. Like the protagonist of "The Moon-Lens," Rossiter at one point falls asleep because the author's imagination did, and the same can be said of the moment when Rossiter's wife faints. The urban wasteland where the finale takes place was the kind of blitzed Liverpool cityscape into which I would venture in search of cinemas, and I appear to have borrowed Rossiter's surname from the film *Circus of Horrors*. Initially Derleth told me that he "rather liked" the tale for *Travellers by Night*, although "would it not be improved by an interpolated clarifying paragraph? Many of our readers would find it written with such restraint as to be obscure to them, unmotivated, and fundamentally too puzzling." Having reread it a month later, however, he reported that he had "decided finally against using it in *Travellers by Night* . . . Little things about it continue to bother me—the change in point-of-view midway from Rice to Rossiter, the 'disgustingly familiar' and unmotivated liquid in the cup, and the like. I fear to you these are integral, but to me they are not." They weren't to me either, as "The Scar" eventually went to prove, but he rejected that version for *Dark Things* as being unpleasant rather than horrible. I assumed this meant he would refuse it for *Demons by Daylight* too, and learned my mistake too late.

Having completed *Demons by Daylight* in 1968, I felt directionless, and it shows in quite a few of the subsequent tales. Some experiments saw print, and some, such as "The Void," fell short. The French new novel hovers over this narrative, which is oblique to a fault. Shall I give a hint? Read on. There really are no simpler puzzles: literally, a Nabokovian textual secret.

1969 brought "The Other House." The grey protagonist lurking at the edge of drugs and sex was of course the author himself, and the character carried off my dropped first name. His sense of how he sounds and appears to other people was mine, and in other ways too the tale reports more than it invents. The Ingmar Bergman loudly found wanting by students (at Liverpool University) was one of his greatest films, *The Shame*. By now Brichester hardly bothers to disguise its resemblance to Liverpool, even if I'm not sure that you could find a Chinese restaurant serving sake. Surely the first time I drank that was decades later in Japan.

1969 was the year I became the film reviewer for BBC Radio Merseyside, and it may also have been when I appalled some of the staff at Quarry Bank High School with a lecture on horror. Among the teenage audience was none other than Clive Barker. My BBC producer Tony Wolfe had me invite several of the pupils, Clive included, to discuss horror on the arts programme, and I believe Clive and I did most of the talking. I wouldn't be surprised if this recording was at the back of my mind when I wrote "Broadcast," since I was still pretty nervous (unlike Clive, as I recall) of the microphone. Perhaps there's also a trace of the first radio interview I ever gave, soon after *The Inhabitant of the Lake* saw print. I was so befuddled to be asked why I'd used the Severn Valley as a location that I mumbled about "furtive little cottages," which became the caption under my photograph in a newspaper reprint of the interview. Of course even professional broadcasters can be panicked by the prospect of dead air.

That same year I wrote "The Urge" and "The Sunshine Club." In the first story I made the mistake Robert Aickman thought he made with "Just a Song at Twilight"—writing the tale too soon after the incident that suggested it rather than taking the time to invent. The actual encounter took place in a Liverpool coffee bar, the Masque. These days I would have used the name for its thematic relevance. A timid interest in drugs may underlie the tale, and perhaps paregoric had lodged in my mind from *Naked Lunch*. As for "The Sunshine Club," Tom Disch reviewed the anthology in which it appeared and marked the tale, I think, D-. It deserved no better.

The next couple of years were my lean ones. Two of the four tales from 1970 are here. "Writer's Curse" was suggested to me by a neighbour in my birthplace of Nook Rise, Hazel Carline. Her house overlooked the real pavilion, although it wasn't derelict. I can't recall whether any unpublished writers had approached me by then, although Dunn's embittered sense of entitlement rings all too true. The story belongs to the tradition of "The Suitable Surroundings" and "The Unnamable," but is it worthy? It was called "Talent" until I remembered that Ted Sturgeon had used the title.

"Property of the Ring" was rewritten as "Medusa," though you mightn't realise. I can only hope the dialogue was meant to sound pretentious. The sunlight that requires no participation may be a muffled echo from Beckett's novel *Watt*. The signet ring was mine, a twenty-first birthday present from my mother. Not long before her death I injured myself, and the ring had to be sawn off in hospital.

1971 was more productive—all of five stories. "Night Beat" suggests a first attempt to write a horror comic story with a twist in the tale. Later I discovered that Gahan Wilson had already dealt with the idea in a single *Playboy* cartoon. Perhaps I can comfort myself by reflecting that Steve King's "Lunch at the Gotham Café" reads like a nightmare variant on Monty Python's dirty fork sketch.

Later that year came "The Shadows in the Barn," eventually improved as "In the Shadows." It takes us back to my old Cotswold territory, although by now I'd visited the area; perhaps that shows. This was one of the stories I submitted to the Scott Meredith Agency when they sent me a strangely impersonal invitation—a booklet about their firm accompanied by a note saying "This will express interest in your work." Once I'd followed with the stories with the fifty dollars they'd neglected to mention they required, they responded with a letter listing reasons why they couldn't sell the tales. Certainly the narrative method of "The Shadows in the Barn" is ineffectually conventional.

We skip ahead to 1973. I'd set out to write fulltime, supported—propped up, more like—by Jenny. Retrospect demonstrates how untimely my decision was. Kirby McCauley, now my agent, had to tell me that the market for short horror stories was very limited. He tried Damon Knight with "The Companion," but Knight responded that he didn't know what was going on in it half the time. My solution was to lurch into science fiction as best I could. Little of it sold, but most of it is here.

"The Precognitive Trip" was my first attempt, and I appear not even to have sent it to Kirby. It may derive from a notion recorded in Lovecraft's commonplace book. "Berger's mind reverted, striking the present with an almost tangible blow." That's an overstated description of the kind of thoughtful trance I used to enter in my youth, when I became wholly unaware of my surroundings and would return to them with a shock. It's depicted better in my novel *Thieving Fear*. Elsewhere in "Trip" the prose gets still more out of hand: "Words she'd spoken tumbled through him, somehow linked." A car tramples someone, and "The whole of him smiled broadly" deserves a place in Thog's gallery of unfortunate writing in *Ansible*. The narrative traps a few potentially interesting ideas in its amber, but I've no idea why it was infected with a rash of colons. I used to lend my typescripts to my mother (most of them, anyway—not the *Scared Stiff* tales, which weren't for her), and I was disconcerted to find while transcribing this story onto the computer for this book that she'd revised one sentence in pencil. I enshrine her additions in square brackets: ". . . as if [it were] on the other side of a thin[,] almost invisible[,] plastic sheet." Is a ghost here?

"Medusa" followed, and then "Murders." The late Ken Bulmer bought this one, commenting that he liked it once he'd found his way past the style, which seems to have seized up whenever I was aware of writing science fiction. It may have been a pity that I hadn't read Brian Aldiss's observation that the prose of the genre was characteristically light and rapid. Whenever the tale is supposed to take place, the future is insufficiently imagined, since its people still send letters. The name Mounth was nothing but a mistyped word. I don't believe in wasting material.

The last tale of the year was "Point of View." Like "Through the Walls," it tries to depict the effects of LSD before I'd taken any; indeed, cannabis is far more prone to halt time. "I knew that the worst response to an acid flashback was paranoia, because that was self-perpetuating. If you rode the experience it would fade away eventually, integrated." Soon I was to learn how mistaken I was. Kirby had doubts about the story's commercial potential and showed it to another of his clients, David Drake. Dave thought it should have been about two thousand words long, and I think he was right. Coincidentally, the next bunch of tales I wrote—my EC Comics group—were each about that length. I should explain that on Merseyside, last is a slang term for useless; hence the line "Gases are last."

After the EC tales of early 1974 I had another fumble at science fiction. I can't find much to say about "The Grip of Peace," which suffers from too much expository dialogue, not all of it even speakable. Rereading my early work, I often feel as if it's someone else's, but I don't recognise myself anywhere in this tale, although the final scene seems unexpectedly authentic: years later Jenny and I had a blazing row as we tried to find our way around the labyrinth of Birmingham, but once booked into our room at Fantasycon we had some of the best sex we've ever had.

Later that year I tried to recapture the skills I'd discovered while inspired by EC, but they'd deserted me, or good ideas had. "Only the Wind" lives up to its title by containing little else, while "Morning Call" is a minor piece deriving from my mother's distrust of doctors, though she didn't pester them—quite the reverse. It was another tale I didn't let her read, not out of guilt but simply to avoid an argument. Did this pair dissatisfy me so much that I fled to another field? "Pet" was next—more floundering in the shallows of science fiction. I managed to lighten my style to some extent by using a youthful narrator, but the narrative voice is insufficiently naïve, and the predictable ending—weighed down by sentimentalism too—falls with a dull thud. I've recast one sentence ("He had a little pink face under the fur, that looked old and very peaceful") but otherwise I've restrained myself from some considerable editing of what looks like a transcribed first draft. "My father's voice sounded surprised and puzzled, like his expression"! Another quote for Thog, I think. Ken Bulmer bounced the story because of the ending, and quite right too.

It was immediately followed by a further lump of science fiction, "Hain's Island." It's vaguely ecological and vaguely psychological, with too little sense of character, which is obscured by stiffened dialogue. It was written by someone I no longer have any sense of having been, and so I've no idea whether I was aware of pinching a motif from *The Body Snatchers*, if it wasn't from *The Quatermass Experiment*. Perhaps the tale finally prefigures the central issue of *The Long Lost*—a fantastic element used as a scapegoat for behaviour that it was hardly needed to cause.

Although I wrote some better stuff that year, "Bait" mainly goes to show how little interest I had in vampirism, or at least how I felt there was little left to explore. The fissure in the wall might seem deeply Freudian, but I pinched the idea of being spitted on a sword from John Metcalfe. Rounding off 1974, "Snakes and Ladders" is somewhat more original, and gave rise to an interesting editorial disagreement. The tale was originally intended for Mike Ashley, who felt that it was undermotivated. He took "The Gap" instead, and I returned to "Snakes" five years later, reworking it as "Playing the Game." By now T. E. D. Klein (he of the highly recommended *Reassuring Tales*) was the editor of *Rod Serling's The Twilight Zone Magazine*. I heard from Kirby that Ted had bought "Playing the Game," but I only belatedly realised that he'd taken the first version. I offered the second, only for him to prefer the original. "When you rewrite," he commented, "you *really* rewrite, don't you?" In the cases of some of the contents of this book, not nearly enough.

At least "Snakes and Ladders" is more substantial than my final offerings, but chronology can't be denied. From 1979, "The Burning" is another story written too soon after the incident that gave rise to it, a firework display in Newsham Park in Liverpool. Like "The Stone on the Island," this one seems to have some roots in M. R. James's "Stories I Have Tried to Write." Up pops the scapegoat theme again, uninterestingly handled.

In 1990 a theatrical producer in, I think, Los Angeles contacted me for a contribution to his Grand Guignol revival. I'd just written a drabble—a story of exactly one hundred words for an anthology of them, which ultimately didn't appear—and it suggested itself as suitable for adaptation. "A Play for the Jaded" was the result, but the producer rescinded his initial enthusiasm after receiving a supposedly similar piece from someone else. Whether the revival ever saw a stage I have no idea. Here's the sketch to round off this book.

And perhaps it will do as a way of bringing down the curtain on this motley entertainment. Let these misshapen creatures of my superseded mind shuffle and stumble for your amusement as best they can—poor things but mine own, even if the brain cells that produced them may be long gone. Perhaps now it's the author who is losing shape, but he hopes his prose has grown shapelier instead. Besides, if this book sells just a single copy of *Reassuring Tales*, it will have justified its existence.

RAMSEY CAMPBELL

Wallasey, Merseyside
16 July 2007

The Childish Fear

In a way I suppose it began in Camside. That was where I was born, and perhaps when I was younger I realised things that I'd forgotten by the time I came to work in Brichester. Perhaps we're all aware of certain things when we're younger, and forget them later so as not to be ridiculed? After all, you and I—and everyone else—have lain awake at night and seen misshapen things peering out of the shadows. There used to be an ornament on the top of my bedroom wardrobe that cast an outline on the wall like a leering demon. I couldn't bear to look at it after dark, but during the day it was just an ornament—nothing more. Certainly not terrifying. It was only during the night that I used to think: suppose that face comes down from the wall at me? The night was the catalyst.

Well, maybe I was more imaginative than most. That's why I didn't care to join in the idiotic games the neighbourhood children played, but instead wandered into the woods behind Camside. I could lie for hours in the grass there in summer, staring into the water, watching the streams and the river rush by, or further into the woods just peering into the stagnant pools and watching the pebble-ripples glitter. But I didn't like the frogs. I didn't mind the croaking that drifted out of the night through my window, but those unblinking things that pulsed at me in the grass were somehow horrible. I kept watching them, though—always ready to jump back if they moved.

That was my trouble; I was fascinated by those moist scuttling, hopping things in the woods. Particularly, I noticed, they'd collect in dark places—in the marshy ground among the trees, or under the flat stones that lay around in the woods. I used to get a horrible sort of thrill from turning those slabs over and watching the white things stir slowly and scatter into the darkness under the stone again; then I'd wait for days and return to throw the rock back onto its original side, and tremble back as the many-legged horrors hurried out of sight. It was a perverted pleasure, too. I knew I'd scream if one of those things scrabbled onto me. They repelled me, but I couldn't keep away from them.

This sort of thing happened all the time during the school holidays, and even during term time I tried to spend a half-hour watching the inhabitants of the dark woods. Then I reached grammar school, homework began to pile up, and there was less spare time in the evenings. So I had to confine myself to looking at the woods from my bedroom window at night, and that was how I got to thinking about the crawling things from another angle. They had to stay away from the light, I thought—that was why they hid under the stones—but at night darkness covered everything. Suppose they crawled into the houses? Suppose armies of them were creeping through the grass down there? I couldn't keep the light on until morning, but I made sure the doors and windows were closed tight.

Meanwhile I was doing well at Ordinary Level, six passes, which would have been enough to get me a decent job had my guardian not been one of the biggest bastards I know. In 1955 he died, I moved out of grammar school into the Ministry of Labour and leaving his house to the rats I found myself a flat on North Abbey Avenue. I didn't have a great amount of money to spend, and most of that went on books and beer.

Then, one day in 1960, someone got me interested in films. I occasionally visited a cinema, but usually I preferred to read. Anyway, this winter morning I walked into the office with my nose in "Casting the Runes", and Bill Henty—one of my friends there—glanced at it as he passed me on the way to the washroom, and remarked casually on the title.

"Yes, it's very good," I said, having lost the thread of the story. "Have you read it?"

"No, but I've seen the film," he answered. "Excellent film."

"Didn't know there was one," I told him, not especially interested. "I can't recall seeing the title around."

"Oh, it isn't around under that title. The film's called *Night of the Demon*—I believe it's coming to the Capitol, and isn't that on your road?"

There was a cinema opposite my flat called the Capitol, a rather decrepit exterior that had always suggested to me one of those places where the audience take seats home for souvenirs. "Yes, the Capitol's just across from me," I confirmed.

"Well, I think it's on there next weekend. I would advise you to go and see it—it is most definitely recommended."

I hadn't finished reading the story, but when I got through with it I liked it very much and wondered about seeing the film version. The weekend came. Saturday night I'd intended to join a drinking party at the Queen's Arms on Bentley Road, but three of the party were in a car accident that afternoon, and the beer session was called off—out of sympathy, I suppose. So I was left in my room with nothing to do, staring out at the red neon Capitol and the procession of couples passing under it for 3/6, and before very long I slipped across the road with the wind slashing my ears and followed the rest out of the sleet into the cinema.

I was the only person in the front row of the circle, since I'm taller than most and could see over the too-high bar. The second feature came on and the audience (including myself) yawned, scratched and visited the ice-cream girl or the toilet. At the end of that there seemed to be a general rush in the stalls to get to other places. When the lights came up the stalls were about half as crowded as I had taken them to be in the dim light. Then the lights dimmed again, leaving a queue around the ice-cream tray, and the seats began to fill up again as the main film appeared.

I was very impressed, too. It brought screams from the stalls and a quickened pulse from me. I was determined to see if I could track down any others like this. The curtains drew together and the scramble to beat the National Anthem began, mostly in the stalls. However, the Queen briefly blinked at us from behind the curtains and vanished with a baleful growl from the soundtrack.

I hurried downstairs to the toilet, noticing that already the stalls were almost empty, although they had seemed crowded. Two students from Brichester University were standing against the wall as I entered, presumably drawn to this district by Jacques Tourneur.

"How about that fellow next to you?" one remarked.

"Yes, I know," said the other. "How could anyone fall asleep in a film like that—and I couldn't even hear him breathing."

"Maybe he was dead—of fright perhaps."

"Possibly," agreed the other, laughing. "He jumped up in the interval, anyway, and ran out somewhere—ran for it again at the end."

They moved toward the door, and I lost interest. Looking around, I thought how ignorant of human anatomy the amateur artists responsible for the surrounding murals must be—or perhaps this was their way of expressing their disgust for the female. Some of these outlined figures looked hardly human.

Next morning I made straight for Bill Henty's desk to agree about the previous night's film, and after that I quickly became addicted. Before, I hardly ever visited a cinema unless I'd made an appointment with someone who hadn't turned up; but now I wandered into the Brook Street–Cushing Avenue area at the centre of Brichester twice a week to catch some film at one of the five cinemas there. Henty gave me some guidance; but it was against his warning that I caught a bus the week before Christmas to the Granada, to see Terence Fisher's *Dracula*. I'd never been so terrified by a movie as I was that night. Wednesday night I visited Taylor Gardens to see it again.

Saturday night found me in a quandary. Either *Dracula* for the third time or a party at the Cock and Bottle down the road, and I couldn't decide which. But there were people at the party who I'd have liked to speak to over various matters and didn't normally see, and no doubt the film would turn up elsewhere. So I left about half-seven for the Cock and Bottle.

By the time I arrived the party had begun and four or five people were in the mood for buying acquaintances drinks, so I circulated around the bar a little and found someone who insisted on paying for my beer. Someone from the Customs who'd come to stay with friends in Camside was remarking about Ultimate Press books in the distance, and I struggled across the room to take this in.

"—pages of sheer obscenity," he was saying with a thick Lancashire accent as I approached. "I can tell you, it even shocked me. I mean, that's not art or anything—just damned filth—"

"Did you mention Ultimate Press?" I broke in.

"Yes, we had some of their things in the other day from Paris, in the middle of some other goods, and I was just talking about them."

"What did you do with them?"

"Threw them on the fire. I'm telling you, you wouldn't believe the sort of things that was in them."

"But for God's sake," I protested, "how do you know how these scenes fitted in if you didn't read them right through? It's people like you who make sure there's no future for art at all!"

"Aren't they trying to print a different sort of book soon?" said Bill Henty, coming up behind me. I suspect he interrupted on purpose—he knew how I was if anybody started defending censorship.

"Don't know—what book is that?" said the Customs officer's original listener, probably also glad to turn the subject.

"Oh, it hasn't got a title," Henty informed us, "but it's a black magic symposium which has been banned for hundreds of years—the publishers in Jena originally refused to print it. I've read extracts from another book by this man Henricus Pott, and that was sick as hell—sort of thing Ultimate might well do."

"What's this other one about?" I asked, giving up the argument.

"Well, I'm not too sure. But there is one idea running through a lot of it that I know about—you know the way insects crawl into damp places and under stones? This man's idea—bit twisted, I know, but still—his idea was that if dark places teem with insects like this—as they do!—mightn't it be reasonable to suppose that larger dark places might be inhabited by larger creatures?"

"What—giant slugs and things, you mean?" I put in.

"No, not necessarily—just larger . . . creatures. Things that'd keep to the darkness because it mightn't be pleasant for people to see them. Freaks, cripples, and worse, from what I can make out. They wouldn't do much—they might or might not be intelligent, but all they'd want would be to stay in the darkness. Only—they might venture out at night. But no, I don't think he meant insects."

"Somebody talking about insects?" a middle-aged man called, pushing through the crowd. "We've got ants at our place—the house is crawling with them. Anyone know what to do with the damn things?"

The month after Christmas was crowded with films to see, and I journeyed all over town to catch up on the Hammer films I'd missed. But I still hadn't seen *Dracula* again. Bill Henty and I argued violently over that one—he'd found it rather cheap with only a couple of good moments. I retaliated by hating *Them!* which he'd called a "damn good film" and which I thought was utter crap. The visitors at the other side of the counter frequently had to wait during office hours, as one of us was struck by a point in our respective favourite movies and cornered the other with "But surely you must have liked . . .?"

Then, in early February, *Dracula* reappeared; at the Capitol opposite me, in fact.

"Well," I said that morning, "I'm off to *Dracula* again tonight."

"Best of luck," he replied, and didn't speak to me the rest of the day.

Of course, if I confined myself to a snack at the fish-and-chip cafe down the road from the cinema, I could make the six o'clock performance and sit the film round again till half-ten. And I did. Of course there had to be a staff shortage at the café, and even my worried glances between wall-clock and waitress weren't effective; but finally I escaped and pounded up the road towards the cinema.

As I clattered up the steps a teenager with attendant mistress asked for two stall seats, was answered inaudibly to me, and wearily paid for entry into the balcony. The foyer walls were crowded with intimations of coming pleasures; but no time to examine these now, I thrust silver through the glass archway and had a ticket flicked back at me. I plunged up the stairs and into the darkened auditorium. "This film has been passed for exhibition when no child under 16 is present," remarked the screen. ("You mean there are children over sixteen?" an irate voice muttered behind me.)

The loudspeakers crashed and the camera tracked into the vault to a close-up of a blood-spattered inscription, which brought defensive laughter from higher up the balcony but no reaction whatever from the stalls. Wait for fifteen minutes, I thought, then you'll react. Apart from a couple of gasps behind me, however, the terrible entry of Christopher Lee fell flat. I wondered if the customers in the stalls had seen the film before—but of course, at this early hour the cinema would be almost empty. Satisfied, I sat back to watch and await the nine o'clock performance's effect.

But during a lull in the cinematic action, with Peter Cushing and Michael Gough creeping around the grounds of a house, I realised that the stalls were not empty. Somebody (perhaps the attendants—it wouldn't be the first time these people had annoyed me) was whispering audibly down there. I couldn't catch the words, but that sibilance filtering through the soundtrack was enough to distract me. Occasionally there came a faint scuttling and thumping—couples coupling on the back row, conceivably. At a fade to black I leaned over the rail, but only dark forms were visible, and small too, from what I could see.

The lights glowed at last and the rumble of people who "didn't want to see the ending first" began. Nobody I knew, however. A few tried to join me in the front row, muttered together and moved back, not wanting to risk a dislocated neck. The light withdrew as the last party thudded down the steps, and *The Mummy* began. Several seconds later the curtains drew belatedly apart.

I've never seen such an unreceptive audience. They didn't scream, they didn't even laugh—though there was an intake of breath somewhere further up the balcony at the tongue-cutting scene. And somebody was whispering again in the stalls, more of them by the sound of it.

Well, I sat the main film through again, and enjoyed it—but I'd have got pleasure from screams from the audience, which didn't occur. Afterward I lingered in the foyer to glance over the posters (*Quatermass II* was on its way, I noticed) and, out of curiosity, I watched the stalls exit to see what sort of people didn't react in any way to *Dracula*. But it looked as if the stalls had emptied before I'd reached the foyer, for the exit doors remained closed.

In the following week I went to the Superior in Binns Crescent to a double bill, the names of whose films I've fortunately forgotten. All I remember is seeing them because Bill Henty advised me against it. The next day the Magnet outside Camside closed down. On Saturday, passing the boarded-up front with its dead neon and peeling posters, for no reason I thought how little I'd like to be in the silence and darkness of that place. I thought of living among the rows of seats in blackness, feeling my way around dimly-glimpsed shapes, and abruptly I forced myself to think of something else.

Monday brought *Quatermass II* to the Capitol. I arrived in the interval at half-seven, and was immediately caught up in the unexpected twists of the plot. I was very impressed indeed. Then came *The Blob*, another Bill Henty recommendation, another load of rubbish. I yawned my way through it once the promising first scene was over. My spirits sank lower as Steve McQueen accepted a challenge to a backward car race, having no bearing whatsoever on the plot.

Then a girl screamed.

That rather woke me up. Had I missed something worthwhile on the screen? But no, McQueen was still acting moronically, and nothing terrifying had occurred. Then, as an altercation in the back circle became audible, I realised that perhaps the girl's boyfriend had explored too far. Whatever had upset her, she continued to argue hysterically, drowning the soundtrack.

The balcony doors swung open. "Will you be quiet there, please!" ordered the manager. But the girl had obviously had a pronounced shock; she went on babbling without answering him.

"Please keep quiet," the manager insisted, "or I'll have the film stopped. We can't have the audience disturbed by this commotion."

The girl's cries did not cease; and a few minutes later, to a chorus of protests from the balcony and a loud clattering from the stalls, the film flickered off and the lights went up. Looking back, I saw that the argumentative couple were standing in the aisle; apparently they had begun their clamour on reaching the end of the row. The manager and an attendant hurried down the stairs.

"Now, what's all the row about?" inquired the manager.

"Oh, it's nothing," the girl's companion replied uncomfortably. "She just put her hand on someone's ice-cream in the dark; that's all, and—well, she's rather nervy, and it upset her."

"I did not!" the girl cried. "I touched someone in the dark—but he's gone now. . ."

"I'm not sure I understand," interrupted the manager. "What do you mean, you touched someone in the dark?"

The girl was obviously becoming more hysterical. "We were on our way out," she gulped, "and I was going first—and someone was sitting between us and the aisle, so I said excuse me, but he didn't move. I thought he was asleep at first, so I asked him again, but nothing happened . . . so I put out my hand to shake him . . ."

"And then?" the manager had to prompt.

"I couldn't see him in the dark except a vague shape, but his head seemed to have dropped forward, and I touched him where his shoulder looked like it should be. And my hand slipped, and touched his neck—only he hadn't got a neck, and he hadn't got a head . . ."

"Come on," the young man said, "I'll take you home."

"Yes," she agreed breathlessly, "yes, let's get away from this horrible place—" and without another word to the manager they climbed the steps, she muttering what sounded like "all wet and slippery" as they passed through the exit.

The manager looked at the attendant; then he made a remark that struck me as very peculiar. "My God," he said, "they're coming into the balcony now!"

Thursday night *Suddenly Last Summer* arrived at the Odeon in central Brichester, and so did I. Though not a horror film, this terrified me as much as any I'd seen, and the rest of the audience seemed to agree. I leaned over the rail to discover if there were any acquaintances down there—and it hit me that practically nobody down there had gone out. Why, then, was the interval always the signal for the audience in the Capitol stalls to migrate? Well, I knew the audiences were different, but that didn't mean they had to act differently in the intervals. I'd noticed this before, but only now did I begin to wonder why it happened.

Friday I had a splitting headache. Saturday a cold had set in, and I spent the weekend and Monday catching up on some paperbacks. Tuesday I found out that Bill Henty hated Tennessee Williams. He wanted to know what the Capitol had to offer; I didn't remember (they were showing a season of horror films, I recalled, but the titles that night eluded me). As I turned away he called out. "Damnation, I'd forgotten!" he said. "I wanted to go to that radio shop next to the Capitol—there's a torch there that's in the sale—but I won't be able to make it. Hell!"

"Well, that's all right," I replied (perhaps I could persuade him to like *Dracula*). "Give me the money and I'll bring this torch in tomorrow if you can give me the details."

He scribbled the details on the back of a form; and that night I pulled the form out with my bus fare and remembered his request. The bus stopped outside the wireless shop, just past the cinema—and that was how, standing on the platform, I caught sight of a poster: for one night only—*Invasion of the Body Snatchers* and *Suddenly Last Summer*. Hell, I thought, jumped off the bus and hurried into the shop. The assistant squinted at the form; "Oh, I know—last one, too," he told me and insisted on unpacking the torch, demonstrating its efficiency, and wrapping it indifferently. It was just before six o'clock. I paid, fidgeted until the change arrived, ran out and clattered into the foyer next door. "You're all right, it hasn't started yet," I was informed. Above the pay-box a leering skull proclaimed that the management would not be responsible for deaths by fright during the night's performance. I rushed upstairs just as the lights began to dim.

Invasion was a splendid film, as good as my Val Guest favourite, but marred by one thing: the audience in the stalls. They were whispering again. The soundtrack was loud, luckily, and the film was so fascinating that I didn't unduly notice the whispers. The end came unexpectedly, but the lights didn't go up. There was a spate of switch-clicking behind me, but nothing happened. I heard the thud of people standing up in the stalls—and then they sat down again. For some reason, that worried me. They ran out every other night in the interval; why not tonight?

In a couple of minutes the balcony had filled up, and the second feature appeared on the screen. There were a few yawns from around me during the first scene, then interest began to rise—everywhere but in the stalls. Down there someone was as loquacious as ever, and the soundtrack was faint, so that I had to strain my ears. My face was getting hot. Suddenly I leaned over the rail and yelled "Shut up!" in a voice that must have carried to the foyer. There was a startled silence below me, then the whispering broke out afresh.

I'd had enough. I turned back toward the projectionist and shouted "Are there no attendants in this bloody place?" Apparently there weren't, for nobody answered my call. To some eloquent glances from the upstairs audience, I stumped up the stairs and down into the foyer. The manager was talking to the pay-box girl.

"Is it possible for you to keep the people in the stalls quiet?" I called from under the Circle sign.

"Very possible, I'd say," he answered laughing, and pointed.

I couldn't imagine what he found to laugh at till I looked where he was pointing. The double doors at the far end of the foyer were closed and hung with a sign: STALLS CLOSED—NO ADMITTANCE.

"It's the teenagers," the manager said. "They've been tearing up the seats—we've closed up the stalls, and we're only letting selected people upstairs. We may have to shut the place up for a few weeks for refitting, but if we do I'm getting a few more attendants. The audience upstairs are only just keeping us going."

"But there's someone in the stalls now," I interrupted.

"There isn't, you know," he contradicted. "It's all locked up."

"But I can hear them talking," I insisted.

"I'm afraid you're wrong," he said. "It may be soundtrack noise—I know it crackles sometimes. That's probably what you can hear."

It wasn't, but I didn't feel like arguing. I returned to my seat and tried to concentrate; quite impossible with the voices down there. I yelled again: "Shut up, I said!" but the silence was shorter this time. I fumed, kicked something on the floor, and had an idea. Watching the screen, I felt about in the dark and came up with Bill Henty's torch. The film had reached one of its less important scenes. I leaned over the edge of the balcony and switched on the torch. The disc of light wavered over the seats, and reached a seated figure. The man was asleep; his head leaned on his chest.

Then the figure looked up and turned around.

And I knew what that girl had touched in the dark. It had no head—it had eyes, but I won't say where they were located—it was white and terribly thin, and it had the wrong number of fingers, and there was no flesh on its arms and legs as it scuttled away sideways. And it was dressed in a man's suit and raincoat, but I've never tried to guess where it found them. Then the torch fell, and the manager and an attendant were barely in time to stop me following it.

The next few weeks I spent in hospital. Hardly anyone visited me—except Bill Henty, and he was more interested in his goddamn torch than what I'd seen down there in the dark. Anyway, there was only one visitor I wanted to see, and they finally brought him along.

"Do you remember that night a girl caused a row in your cinema?" I asked. He did. "Well, you said something to an attendant when she'd left—something like 'they're coming into the balcony now.' What did you mean by that?"

"Why, the teenagers," the manager replied. "They're always starting trouble in the stalls, and I thought they were trying it on upstairs."

"You're lying!" I cried. "You meant those things that live in the dark, and you know it."

"I don't know what the hell you're talking about," he said. "I meant the teenagers, and that's all." And he left.

So I said I'd had a fainting fit while leaning over the balcony, and pleaded amnesia about what had happened; and at last they turned me loose. And I might have believed my own story—even forgotten it—if it hadn't been that, as soon as I'd asked my question, the manager had looked away and not met my eyes again.

So now—especially on windy nights, or when the house is full of inexplicable creaks, or when I'm near an unlit street-lamp—I have a childish fear.

I am afraid of the dark.

The Offering to the Dead

Whenever he went to an unfamiliar place, David Maxwell always alighted at the wrong bus stop; and 19 November 1962 was no exception.

Being normally nervous, he was uncertain when, that night, he called at Iris Glendenning's home for the first time. He realised, of course, that the visit had probably been engineered by Iris's parents, to give them a chance to examine him; or rather her parent, for her mother had died some six months before. He had known Iris at that time and had been startled by her lack of distress after the first two or three days. Obviously, she had not liked her mother.

He crossed a blackly wet bridge over railway lines and entered a narrow alley between high brick walls. Four minutes to seven; seven o'clock being set for the meeting. Across a cul-de-sac yellow-lit by occasional lamps, he plunged into a second alley from which slanted others, unevenly paved. At one point the wall had collapsed into somebody's garden; and over the crumbled gap and a hedge he glimpsed a low building, shaped somewhat like a garage. He immediately knew that it was not a garage or shed; but no time for speculation about sheds, he had two minutes to reach his destination punctually. He hurried to the end of the alley; Brice Street, an askew metal sign informed him, and that was the road in which Iris lived. Now it only remained to locate her house; and here it was, no. 17, the first on the right.

The rusty metal gate squealed open. He crossed the concreted path, and behind the house glimpsed a looming oblong outline. He had seen it before, across the hedge, but still could not identify it. He reached the front step and rang the bell.

A warm dazzling hall received him, and he was ushered in by a thickset man, slightly beyond middle age. "You'll be—David?"

"Yes, that's right. And I suppose you'll be Iris's father."

"I am, but we'll be seeing each other a lot—so you just call me Bill. Iris tells me I have to entertain you in the living-room. Well, I'll be with you in a minute, so perhaps you'd like to make yourself comfortable in there." He hurried away down the hall.

The living-room door stood open on the left, but David did not notice it. He made for a heavy panelled door in the right wall.

"Not that one! The living-room's behind you." Mr Glendenning—Bill—had turned back, but too late. David had already had time to turn the knob and push against the door. It was locked, he found.

"That's, um, the dining-room," Mr Glendenning informed him. "We're decorating it. No, this is the room I meant."

They entered a chandelier-lit room, and David sat by the television. Mr Glendenning faced him across the fireplace. David glanced round frantically for a newspaper, but saw none. He began to trace the convolutions of the wallpaper design. Well, *say* something!

"I see Brichester won four-one," Mr Glendenning remarked. He had said something. Unfortunately, David detested all sports, and thought of football as the most inane.

"Oh, yes?" He continued to search for some conversation piece. He might ask, *did you decorate this room yourself?* . . . and might be answered, *why, does it look as though I did?*

"Where are you two going tonight?"

"Oh, the ABC Bowl," David answered, grabbing the bait, "the one they've just opened at the centre of town. Of course, we're not very good at it yet but better than when we started. I remember, the first time—" But by his listener's occasional pause-filling sounds, he realised he had overanswered. His roving gaze travelled along the mantelpiece and braked at an odd-looking ornament. He pointed. "What's that?"

"That?—Oh, just an ornament."

It was a triangular bowl on three short metal legs. "What do you use it for?"

"Why, as a—an ashtray. It's an old family possession, as a matter of fact."

"Well," David said, "it looks like—"

"Hi, Dave! Sorry I kept you waiting."

Forgetting what the triangular bowl looked like, he rose. "That's okay—we've plenty of time. Bowl doesn't fill up till about half-nine. . .

. Well, goodnight, Mr Glendenning."

"*Bill,*" corrected Mr Glendenning as they entered the night.

At nine o'clock they were sitting at a table inside the Bowl, drinking coffee from shallow glass cups and waiting for an alley to empty.

"Where shall we go Saturday night?" he inquired.

"Didn't we say we'd try the dance at the Locarno?" she reminded him. She looked away, stared into her coffee.

"Hey—is something the matter?"

"Not really. I was just thinking about that ornament you were so interested in—"

"Yes, what about it?" he prompted.

"Well, it shouldn't have been there. It was my fault—I put it there by mistake."

"But surely it's not all that important—"

"*Alley no. 9,*" a loudspeaker blared, "*your game should now be finished.*" They left the table and headed for the alley.

Saturday night, at the Locarno, they tired each other out and left about 11.30. Stopping occasionally, they progressed through the infrequently-lit alleys to her home; and there Iris realised she had left her key inside. What was she going to do, she wondered.

"Ring the bell," David suggested.

"I can't—I told you, Daddy's away in Severnford tonight. But I may have left a window open round the back. Let's go and see."

There was a small window open on the ground floor. He supported her while she reached in and, straining, knocked the lower pane open. She levered herself through, leaving him to experience her perfume and the glacial night air. "Hold on and I'll open the door," she called distantly. Glancing round, he saw a dark bulk nearby—that unidentifiable building. He hurried across the uneven grassy ground and stared at it.

The building was low, flat-roofed, shaped of stone with an iron-grilled gate in the side facing him. It had been unevenly painted in an obvious attempt to camouflage it as wood; in the other side there were even two clumsily painted "windows". Beyond the grille he could make out the beginning of a downward-plunging flight of steps, but nothing else inside was visible.

"Here we—" remarked Iris from the back door—*"Dave?"* He hurried back to the luminous rectangle and joined her inside.

"I think we both deserve a coffee for that," she said, and turned to prepare the drink.

His eyes flicked across hanging utensils, pale blue cooker and washing machine. "What's that building out in the garden?" he enquired finally.

"What? Oh, just the garden shed." There was no hesitation in her answer. "Daddy keeps gardening tools and things in there."

David wandered into the living-room, noticed a radio with its lid folded back atop a low table. "Could we listen in to Luxembourg while I'm here, do you think?" he called through the rooms.

"Well, we could normally," Iris replied over the bubbling of the percolator, "but that radio's blown a fuse or something and it'll have to be fixed tomorrow. Tell you what, there's a portable in my bedroom, if you'd like to get it. First door across the landing."

He clambered up the stairs, which doubled back on themselves between floors. Bathroom walls glared whitely at him from the top. He crossed the landing and opened a door. Wrong room: a football rattle proclaimed Brichester's colours from the seat of a chair, an orphan electric razor lay on the dressing-table. He eased the door shut and moved on. The second bedroom was Iris's; dresses stirred faintly as he pushed the door wide open, lipstick and powder and perfume bottles were scattered across a glass surface, a paperbacked romance with its cover peeled back lay on the bed. David entered and found the radio sunk into the carpet, below a bedside table carrying a framed photograph. The same woman in a different pose stared from the mantelpiece with glazed eyes: obviously the late Mrs Glendenning. He swung the radio up by its handle and closed the door, its lower edge whispering over the carpet. He turned down the passage—

Two photographs? Of her *mother?*

He swung the door open again and entered, his footsteps muffled (the percolator still throbbing downstairs). Yes, the photographs were indeed of Iris's mother; a signature—Moira Glendenning—slashed the lower left-hand corner of each. Some detail essential to his understanding was absent, he thought. She showed no reaction to her mother's death, yet kept photographs of her in the bedroom? Of course he had heard of people "going into shock" in such circumstances, but not in the way Iris must have. No, there was something she was concealing—something besides the identity of the building in the garden.

The radio creaked from its handles as he descended the stairs. He entered the living-room, placed the portable on the low table, and glanced towards the mantelpiece. The triangular bowl had vanished. He stared at the empty spot for a few minutes, clicked the radio into life. Music rose into sound as Iris elbowed open the door, a tray between her hands, and distributed cups of coffee.

"Where to next?" he asked. He liked to clarify vague details as quickly as possible.

"I thought we agreed to see that film Kev recommended," Iris reminded him.

"Yes, sure, that's fine," he put in. He was wondering how direct a question she would be prepared to answer frankly; he considered that he knew her well enough to ask. He regarded her with receptive eyes.

"Iris," he plunged, "what's that thing in the garden *really?*"

There followed a few minutes of mutual gazing. "But I already told you," Iris said finally. "The shed."

"No, Iris, you didn't tell me," he contradicted. "I was up close, you know—that shed exterior's only painted on, and I saw those steps going down. That's no shed."

"Oh, why shouldn't I tell you, anyway?" demanded Iris. "You'd have to know sooner or later, it might as well be now. . . . It's a tomb."

"It's a—?"

"Tomb," she repeated. "It's the Glendenning vault, so to speak."

A throbbing silence commenced, thoughts crossing it in arbitrary arcs. David scrabbled frantically for a question. The pendulum of the wall-clock ticked back and forth. "Who's down there?" he ventured.

"The Glendennings—oh, way back into the seventeenth century. My mother was the last, about six months back, but you know that."

"Your *mother* is out there? But how can you—"

"'Get away with it?' We've patronised the same family of undertakers since the vault was built, so Daddy tells me, and they know about it—only they're paid not to talk about it. They put slate or something in the coffin. The person everyone thinks is in it never goes out of the house."

"You must wonder sometimes if someday someone will let it out—" He stopped. "No, about your mother, what I meant was—isn't it a little bit . . . hell, don't you think it's morbid?"

"Morbid? *Dave* . . . I prefer to know she's nearby. We don't think of—death—as apparently everyone else does."

He broke his gaze and turned to the clock: preferable to look at anything rather than the honesty in her eyes. "My God, my last bus has gone!"

"Oh, Dave, t . . . Well, there's only one thing you can stay here for tonight. You can't walk home."

What else could he do but stay? (And really he wanted to, anyway, tomb or no tomb . . .) He thanked her very much and wildly emitted something to push away that still-disquieting family vault. "Your father looks a lot like Ustinov," he remarked, which broadened into a discussion of the relative merits of Peter Sellers and Ustinov as they ascended the stairs, their arms vaguely linked. They said goodnight at last and David found his way into a pair of her father's pyjamas. He lingered in the bathroom (disinfectant and after-shave lotion cutting the air) and finally returned to his bedroom for that night. He pondered in front of the dressing-table, rattling his nails on the glass top ("You can use the electric razor if you like" Iris had remarked through the closing bedroom door) and turned to the door to switch out the light, throwing the furniture into vague visibility with sides of moonlight. His feet brushed through the carpet as he crossed to the bed.

He stayed a minute to peer out the window. A church spire poked upward beside the moon; a garage's neon sign spread crimson across the sky. He slid the sash open a little, and stared down at the burial vault, crouching in the darkness below him. No sound except the usual churning throb of night; no sound from the tomb down there—and indeed, how could there be? How could the tenants of that place move? He stepped back and slammed the window down.

The sheets had a keen cold edge. He stretched out and his feet entered areas of unqualified frost. From the bathroom came a gurgle as Iris unplugged the washbowl; she was crossing the landing and entering her room. A few confused sounds escaped the room as she tidied up, then the creak of a bed. David sank further into sleep.

Suddenly he stiffened a turn through the sheets and stopped

breathing. Iris's door had opened again; she had padded across the landing and was standing outside his door.

David had acquired the habit of pretending sleep when anyone entered his room; so that his breathing now deepened and slowed. The doorknob turned with a slow squeak and a thin blade of light opened along the floor. He sensed her gaze drawing along the bed, then the door clicked quietly shut.

What had she wanted? he suddenly wondered. Had she something important to tell him? He slid into a sitting position and listened, trying to locate Iris. A bedroom door—not her own—softly closed and she passed his room with a muted jingling of keys. She was slowly descending the stairs, probably supporting herself with one hand on the banister. He levered himself out of bed, left the room and crossed to the edge of the landing, unthinkingly imitating her silent tread.

Iris had reached the heavy locked door in the lower hall—to the room Mr Glendenning had explained they were "decorating"—and was easing a large key into its lock. She was holding something under her left arm that David could not see. She pushed the door wide and entered. Between closing door and frame he glimpsed what appeared to be an unfurnished room; then it was blocked from his sight.

For a long time he leaned on the landing rail, wondering whether to wait, go down, or perhaps return to his room and forget the whole thing. Metallic sounds came from the locked room. David redistributed his weight against the rail. The landing was freezing rapidly. He stared out the window as a car coasted by, trailing rectangular echoes of light; tightened his grip on the banister and turned to go at last. At that moment the locked door opened and Iris came out, turning the key behind her. The razor-sharp knife in her left hand split the light into fragments. Blood trickled from a knife-wound in her wrist.

He clattered down the stairs, thudded into the hall. "What have you done to yourself?" he demanded.

"What are you doing up, Dave?" She clasped one hand around the wound, but a thread of crimson escaped. "Oh, it's nothing—just an accident . . ."

"Is there any Elastoplast round here?"

"In the kitchen—cupboard on the left as you go in. But really, Dave, it doesn't matter—"

He urged her ahead of him into the living-room and stretched the plaster round her wrist. Spots of red burst through the dressing. "How did you manage to cut yourself, anyway?"

She glanced at a corner of the ceiling while he waited. Into the silence fell the sound of soft padding footsteps in the next room.

He held up one finger for silence. "There's someone messing around in there," he whispered. "I'm going in. Give me the key, quick." He slid the key from the mantelpiece.

"No, you can't go in!" protested Iris, leaping up. "It's all right, there's no need to go in."

"Of course there is!" he hissed, entering the hall. "It can't be your father, and who else could be in there for any good reason?"

She clutched his arm. The dressing had wrinkled and blood was beginning to trickle again. "Dave, this cut—" She pulled at his sleeve. "I did it deliberately."

He withdrew the key with a click and turned slowly. "What for?" he asked.

Iris stared between his eyes. "You'll have to promise," she told him, "that whatever I tell you—and this time I'm going to tell you everything—you won't try and go into that room. *Whatever* I tell you."

A scrape of metal and an odd liquid sound filtered from behind the locked door. "All right," he agreed, and followed her into the living-room.

"All right. Now why did you do it?" he asked, lowering himself into an armchair.

"I'll have to go back a bit," began Iris. "Everybody in the family's told this as soon as they can understand, so they won't be scared of dying. We've always lived on this site, only different houses have been built on it from time to time—we couldn't move away, you see—or at least you don't see yet, but you will . . ."

Flat footsteps receded down what sounded like a long corridor.

"It probably began when one of the Glendennings—don't know what relation he was to me—went to Hungary in the seventeenth century. I don't know why he went, but while he was there he picked up ideas he'd never thought of before. The Hungarians believe in things like that—they had inklings of the real nature of death, Daddy says. The story's got very confused by the time it reached me, but this ancestor of mine met someone who took him to some forest or other—took him down some steps, a long way, into this place where a race of people lived in the dark after they were supposed to be dead. When he came back to England he built the vault out there in the garden. It's been there ever since. I know you don't see what this has got to do with this cut, but you'll get it in a minute.

"After that all the Glendennings were entombed down there. We wouldn't be buried in an ordinary grave under any circumstances; there's got to be the connection with the house. I mean—there's a tunnel which joins the vault and the room next door, you know. That's because we still don't like to go down into their place; we'd rather do our bit in that room—it gives us the time to get out. Because I imagine they don't look very nice after they've been down there for some time. It's enough to know they're all right."

"But what are you talking about?" demanded David wildly. "What do you mean about the vault? What's it got to do with you?"

"Well, you see," Iris continued, her eyes cutting arcs between the fire and his face, "the people down there aren't really dead, as you understand the word."

"Not dead? You mean you bury them alive?"

"No, they're not buried alive either," Iris assured him. "They're not buried at all—there are alcoves in the walls where they lie. No, they're not alive as we are alive, but they are alive in a different way. They sleep down there until they're brought up, and if they're not brought up every so often they stiffen: don't move, just lie in the darkness trying to get up . . . They only come up to take blood."

"Take blood? You mean they *drink* blood?"

"Well, yes—that's what I was doing in there; you make a cut and fill the bowl. Oh, yes, the bowl that was the ornament you saw on the mantelpiece; that's what it's used for. You fill the bowl and call the name of the person you want to take it. Daddy does it more often than I do, but since he's away tonight I didn't want Mummy to go without . . . Only you have to call the person's name. The vault's much longer than it looks from above ground; the 'shed' used to be the only entrance to this long passage down there with all alcoves along it, but in eighteen-sixty-something someone went down by and they all started to paw him—he said he couldn't see anything, but he felt all these cold

slippery hands grabbing him. Moss grows on them after a bit, you see
. . . They don't usually attack people, but there were some rather nasty
types in the family in those days. So they opened up the tunnel again
and used that."

"And so this is why you cut yourself . . ." said David flatly. "Tell
me, where'd you get all this?"

"Why, Daddy told me," she reminded him. "So I wouldn't be
frightened."

"I see," he mused. "Will he be home tomorrow night? . . . Well, in
that case, Iris, don't cut yourself tomorrow night. You never know—
you might slip and hit an artery. Give yourself time to recuperate."

"Oh, I wouldn't cut my artery," she assured him. "I've done it too
often." And she pointed out the evidence on her wrist.

Surprisingly enough, David slept that night. Even the teeming
vault below his window faded into the vortex. But about dawn he
jerked from a dream in which he was pursued down subterranean tun-
nels by skeletal shrouded figures covered with a phosphorescent green
moss; and he lay after that, watching the sky break into day. He wondered how he could face Iris.

But at the breakfast table she acted as if nothing had happened;
because nothing *had* happened, he realised, as far as she was concerned. She had merely revealed a family secret to her friend; but the
secret seemed to her quite normal. He watched her numbly as she
made breakfast, small-talking, ate with him, and afterward conducted
him to the bus-stop. As the bus drew away he looked back and saw her
waving happily. The Elastoplast shifted with her movement.

That afternoon David set out on a walk in the country outside Brichester. He often strolled in the area beyond Mercy Hill, where the houses
gave out and only the road and telephone wires were unnatural. He slid
a cigarette from the packet and began to trail smoke. An occasional car
rumbled past. Wind rippled the moist grass, disturbed droplets in the
black branches of the trees; dripping out of a metal sky. He looked
down at his feet, monotonously levering him across the ground. He
stared toward the hills, above which birds fluttered. But he could not
lose himself. Inevitably the Glendennings vault intruded.

The worst thing was Iris's unquestioning acceptance of the whole business. She would have to be convinced that death was final, not just a transition to a less active life—but how to convince her? David's parents believed in cremation; perhaps that was the answer. Take her to a crematorium and force her to watch the whole process; did she hear any screams from these "living" corpses? Even, if necessary, cremate one of the late Glendennings—no cries of pain there, either. But first of all she must be removed from the atmosphere of that house on Brice Street; the whole building was saturated with belief. More important, her father must be out of the way. But how was his influence to be eliminated? Murder? By marrying Iris? Hardly! Perhaps the law could be called in to help. Surely this back-garden tomb was illegal; maybe Iris's father could be prosecuted for pretending that the coffins buried at the various funerals were occupied—or conceivably the Public Health people would have something to say about burying corpses so close to the houses. Yes, this was more feasible. He'd put in an anonymous telephone call to the police—Iris might suspect him, since she'd so recently told him about the vault, but he'd have to chance that. One day she might thank him.

He turned back toward Mercy Hill and began to hurry toward the glinting snake of the Severn beyond the hospital building. Monday morning he would lay some sort of foundation for this operation to convert Iris.

Monday morning, someone mentioned that Iris was dead.

David had reached his desk, noting the empty desk opposite him (Iris was late; good—it would give him time to frame some remark) and was sorting his files to discover why he had put them aside on Friday, when Jack Dixon—someone he had always passively disliked: trailed a swathe of sweat—approached rather awkwardly. Had David heard about Iris? No, what did he mean? Why, he said, "she had an accident last night; it's in the stop press." And he flapped open the newspaper before David, one yellow nail pointing with a crescent of dirt. David bent closer and there, behind the uneven print, was Iris, dead. Fallen on a knife. Died in the ambulance howling its way to hospital.

The sounds of the office seemed to jumble and retreat down a muffled corridor. David stared at the square of print until it lost all significance and was tentatively removed. Dixon obviously wanted to speak, but David did not look up. The other finally left, leaving sweat curling in the air, and David stared ahead at the files. He could not picture Iris as a skewered corpse, only as a lack. His eyes moved across the bare desk top opposite. He stared at the telephone.

He lunged at the receiver, dialled, listened to the throb of the bell at the other end. It repeated its sequence several times; then the line clicked open. A weary voice said "Hello?"

"Mr Glendenning? This is David Maxwell." This fact was vaguely acknowledged. "What happened last night, for God's sake?"

"It was an accident," Mr Glendenning began slowly. "She was cutting the Sunday joint, you see, and the knife slipped and went into her. The doctor couldn't save her."

But David's preoccupation cut through this facade. "I know everything, Mr Glendenning," he threw out. "I know about the vault and the tunnel to that locked room—everything, so you needn't be afraid of giving anything away. What really happened? She fell on that sacrificial knife, didn't she?"

Mr Glendenning's grief obscured any unease he might feel at David's revelation. He seemed glad of someone to whom he could speak freely; he plunged into an embarrassingly hysterical account. He had not arrived home until early Monday morning, after all. It had been past time to feed the things in the vault. Iris must have determined to give them blood, entered the room of the sacrificial bowl with the knife, and at that moment Mr Glendenning had rung the doorbell. She had run to admit him, had tripped over a hummock in the hall carpet and driven the knife into herself. She had died conscious. She had died, David realised, because of the legend of the undead Glendennings; the legend which he might so soon have disproved for her. The thought cut him open.

"You did it!" he screamed into the telephone. "You and your stupid fucking beliefs!"

Mr Glendenning's breathing cut off. The office had gone quieter, too. Some people twisted round to raise eyebrows; the backs of other heads moved slightly. David slammed the receiver down against them all.

He somehow fought through the rest of the morning. Nobody spoke to him; the sound of the whole office, in fact, was subdued. David closed files at intervals and raised them to a pigeon-hole in slow arcs. At ten past eleven Jack Dixon made a wide detour around his desk.

It was approaching twelve-thirty when David saw the writing on the file cover. It was Iris's usual thick pencilled script: "you wanna check for mathematical errors?" it inquired. She always wrote that type of direction on the cover; or at least, had always used to . . . The voices in the office were receding again; the pencilled note was blurring. Suddenly he slid the file cover away and stood up. His teacup splintered on the floor.

The week dragged by. David sat in various rooms in his home, staring at objects; trying vainly to lighten the shadow of Iris that was paralysing his thoughts, slowing his limbs. Wednesday he received and tore up a curt invitation to her funeral; what emotions was he supposed to feel while staring at an empty coffin? She was at home, with her father—her father with whom she had perhaps shared God knew what perverted relationship—indeed, only he could prove or disprove the manner of her death; how could anyone know whether he had not killed her himself to drag their relationship into yet more abnormal regions? But David could do nothing now. He couldn't see Iris again, therefore the only sane action was to forget. To that end he avoided the Brice Street area, prolonging his walks outside the town, and finally in desperation swept custom and opinion aside and began to frequent public houses regularly.

It was in one of these that he met Jack Dixon. At about nine o'clock that Saturday night, Dixon and a party of friends entered the bar; from overheard references David gathered that Dixon had cashed a bet and was celebrating. They noticed him sitting in the corner at once, and somebody offered him a drink. He accepted, joined them at a table, finished his pint, crossed to the bar for a refill. While he stood there muttered remarks drifted in and out of his consciousness: "You'd think he was celebrating it" . . . "bloody disgusting, if you ask me" . . . "and he reckoned to fancy her . . ." He could have attacked them, but he preferred to force politeness from them. He returned to the table and began to drink in earnest.

So it was that by ten-thirty he was determined to wake Iris.

After all, he mused as he unsteadily approached a telephone booth on the corner of Brice Street, she had believed it; she had died while resurrecting her mother to drink her blood, and she was down in that vault of half-life now. So it was logical that his blood would bring her back. And when she returned, she would recognise him, speak to him, perhaps leave the tomb altogether—that was logical enough. Or so it seemed to David as he thumbed through the directory after a number that had slipped his memory. He dialled, waited until the other receiver was wearily lifted.

"Is that Mr William Glendenning?" David inquired, deepening his voice with a Scottish accent (which Iris had always said he could do well). "I thocht I'd better warn ye that they're digging up yer daughter's grave at St Michael's. Something about 'investigation'. Mebbe ye'd better get down there quick." He replaced the receiver.

He watched no. 17. Soon the lights blinked out and Mr Glendenning hurried down the path, slamming the door behind him. He disappeared around the corner furthest from the telephone booth; and at that point David pushed himself away from the booth and swayed toward the house. The front door had locked itself, which he expected; but the window at the back was open again, and after some manoeuvring he succeeded in levering himself through the lower pane.

The house was silent except for the ticking of a clock somewhere in darkness. There was no time to waste. He entered the hall, switched the light into a brief flare and glanced from the locked door to the telephone—beside which flashed a key-ring. He plunged for the keys, knocked the telephone to the floor, and made for the door. In the darkness he fumbled for the keyhole and missed it, returned to the light-switch, finally selected the appropriate key and, opening the door, clicked on the room's light. He darkened the hall again and entered.

It was a small square room; uncovered plaster formed its walls, a light-bulb without shade hung from the ceiling by a dusty cord. An unsteady table stood in the centre of the bare tiled floor, between the door and an uncurtained archway in the opposite wall, leading into an arched passage of chipped red brick. The knife and bowl caught the light on the table. There was nothing else, and no sound at all.

David's heels fell flatly against the tiles as he approached the table and picked up the knife. The blade was quite clean, but there was a flaking brown ring around the inside of the triangular bowl. He looked away quickly and examined the weapon. Both edges of the blade had obviously been recently sharpened. The handle was carved with odd images, a black sea under a gigantic oval light (suggestion of some flickering shape inside it) and many heads rising from the water and long thin arms reaching toward the light with dripping fingers. He looked away from that too, glanced at his watch, and began to search for a place to cut. Veins throbbed in his wrist, but as he remembered a wound in the wrist often proved fatal. He noticed blue tendrils on the ball of his thumb, but this struck him as probably painful. At last he closed his fist, stuck out his thumb and sliced open the first joint.

Blood broke from the slit at once. Ignoring the cold pain, David dragged the bowl toward him and let the stream trickle down the side. A shivering reflection of the light-bulb formed in the pool. What else had he to do? He remembered, and called "Iris—Iris—it's me, Dave . . ." He resisted a drunken inclination to add "come and get it", and listened for some sound. His call returned muffled by the walls, but nothing else was audible. He waited, his thumb resting on the edge of the bowl. There came a faint shifting rustle, but that could have been one of many night noises. His thumb continued to stream. He leaned on the table and stared through the arch in the wall, but nothing moved beyond . . .

Suddenly he heard footsteps approaching. He strained toward the archway but though he was unsure, he thought the sound came from the region of the hall. Mr Glendenning must have returned! What would he do if he discovered David? David pinched the edges of the wound together; the pain rose and he bit down on the thumb. He peered again at the arched tunnel; no movement there. He hurried to the door, hesitated a last moment and switched the light off. At that moment the footsteps—bare feet slapping the tiles—entered the room from the other side.

He grabbed at the light-switch, missed, stumbled and fell, cracking his forehead against the edge of the door. The door slammed, and the key thudded outside on the hall carpet. The pain in his head faded, and David levered himself to his feet by the doorknob. He could see nothing in the darkness, but could hear; slow footsteps, a soft thud, hands brushing wood, then a metallic sound and a cat-like licking. He felt along the wall for the switch. His other hand clenched with concentration and a nail scraped open his thumb. Then he had the switch, pressed it down and turned round.

Iris had her back to him. She was thinner now, paler, and the hem of a translucent white dress stirred below her knees; but it was she. He knew the hair and the earrings that swung the light back and forth. "Iris!" he called, but she did not turn. She was holding the triangular bowl up to her face, and he caught a muffled sucking.

"Iris? Iris, it's Dave . . ." he told her, raising his voice. She did not respond. Her head was thrown back now; she had inserted one corner of the bowl into her mouth. Her inverted face was whiter than he remembered. The light-bulb glistened moistly in her eyes.

"*Iris!*" he shouted. "It's Dave—why don't you speak? Don't you recognise me?" and he swayed forward and shook her shoulder. It was cold and slightly damp, like moss. Something plunged into the pit of his stomach. She's dead, he thought numbly. Then she turned round.

If David had gone to her by means of the other entrance—that in the vault outside the house—perhaps he could have reached her. If she had awakened into that half-life of hers and seen him waiting for her, perhaps some vestige of affection, of memory, might have broken forth. Perhaps he could even have brought her up from the vault to stay with him. But she had not come up to stay with him; she had come up after the blood—to the exclusion of all else. Too late he saw that as he stared at last into her eyes; eyes that, although set in a face he knew, he could not recognise—eyes which brushed across his face and turned toward the line of red across his left hand; her eyes in which there was not a trace of recognition—only the all-excluding desire of a thirsty, savage, and quite unconquerable *animal.*

The Reshaping of Rossiter

Someone—probably the English master at school so long before—thought of the perfect word to describe Lindsay Rice: he was an "oblique" person. "Take his essays, for example," the English master used to say. They were excellently constructed, the smooth flow of their concepts was extraordinary, and the reader would be so caught up by the flow that he might read two pages before noticing that the whole thing had no connection with the title. The persistent reader would eventually uncover the topic, approached through this labyrinth of ideas. "It's very well written, but I don't think you quite do justice to your title," the teacher frequently remarked –while at the same time the mathematics master might be wearily tracing Rice's calculation of some problem through a maze of figures to— inevitably—the correct solution. Rice's name was repeatedly mentioned in the staffroom as "a borderline case".

"Oh, he gets there in the end," someone always remarked, "but the way he does it is useful only to himself. Any guesses what he'll be when he leaves school?"

Surprising those who swore he would never gain a worthwhile position, Rice entered the Brichester branch of one of the larger banks. His oblique approach carried over into his life there; his explanations to clients, for example, were intelligible only to those who had the patience to hear him out. If he wanted to speak to anyone otherwise engaged, he had a habit of watching the other in the lid of his cigarette case; and if someone entered the washroom while he was at the sink, his eyes would flick up to catch the passing reflection in the mirror. He had a special fixation about mirrors and mirror surfaces. The most notable example of this was on the bus which took him to and from the bank; for when he had nothing to read on the journey, instead of watching the streets and pedestrians flashing by, he would carefully spy on the other passengers in the glass of the window. "It's amazing what you get to see that way," he said once.

One day in February 1963 he boarded the vehicle at the usual tine and hooked himself along the upper-deck aisle to a midway seat. He leaned back in the seat to slide money from his pocket, and began to cough. He was unpleasantly ill with influenza; he had been coughing unhappily all night, and now felt only half-awake.

The conductor arrived, stood clicking change in his hand. Rice paid him, plucked the ticket from his fingers, and shifted toward the window. (Ask for eight, get a nine—hell, it's not worth bothering about.) He peered into the window. The seat opposite him was unoccupied. That ahead of him was filled by two old women, sporting headscarves and curlers, who were carrying on a loud conversation punctuated with shrill bursts of laughter. Ahead of them sat a young man and presumably his girlfriend, arguing—the question apparently being who should pay the fare, to judge from the way the young man pushed his friend's hand away from the conductor.

The bus slowed to a stop, several passengers were urged aboard by the conductor, and it moved into the traffic again. A patch of waste ground slid by beyond the window, so that momentarily the reflection was lost. Someone lowered himself into the seat opposite. The reflection returned, and Rice saw that the man seated across the aisle was Jack Rossiter, a friend who worked in a travel agency on Harrison Avenue. Odd, Rice thought; Jack always boarded this bus, but on every occasion he caught it three stops further on. He must have been visiting early. Rice decided he should put out some greeting, and turned toward the other. He stretched his arm across the aisle and tapped the man on the elbow.

Then he retreated to the window, reddening with embarrassment. The other had turned in his direction, so that his full face was visible; and Rice saw that it was not Rossiter at all. The left side of his face resembled Rossiter's, but a livid scar ran down the right side from temple to jaw—cut by something rusty, Rice deduced—and the man was paler and thinner than Jack. But from a distance—Rice peered at the reflection—yes, from a distance one would be deceived. The two men were not identical, but they could be taken for twins.

He found the resemblance more striking when Rossiter himself boarded the bus at his usual stop. Rossiter clattered up the aisle, not noticing his friend, and plumped into the left front seat. As he passed in reflection, for one moment Rice glimpsed the two men simultaneously; and realised that if Jack were thinner, paler, and scarred, he would look exactly like the man opposite. Rice's concentration moved away from the duplicated world of the window, toward this unusual fact.

A few stops towards Brichester's city centre, the streets darkened into an area of slum tenements and derelict houses. As the bus drew to a stop where stood a group of overalled factory-workers, the man opposite Rice hooked himself into the aisle and clattered down to the lower deck. Rice's gaze focused on the street below. The man strolled across the pavement and turned up an alley between two houses. The bus re-entered the traffic, and as it passed the opening Rice glimpsed the other hurrying up the alley, which was black with rain and walled by blackened houses as far as he could see. Then the view was behind him, leaving him with an odd feeling of depression.

The bus cruised down Harrison Avenue and Rossiter alighted, noticing Rice for the first time as he entered the aisle and remarking "Hello there—see you at lunch." The two men often met for dinner at the Queen's Restaurant, which was midway between their respective places of work and which they both patronised. That day Rice, having dealt with what few callers arrived at the bank, reached the restaurant first, and was thus able to prepare some opening remark. The appearance of the figure on the bus had been inexplicably troubling him all morning, and he felt he must mention it. Typically, however, when his friend arrived Rice did not refer to this; instead, he eased into a discussion of the *doppelganger* legend, and only when Rossiter showed signs of boredom did he mention the morning's incident.

"I saw someone this morning who looked very like you," he remarked finally.

"Oh, did you?" Rossiter replied. "Then, according to you, I'm going to die soon. Yes. Anyway, about that fishing-rod I bought . . ."

Rice could have steered the conversation back to his subject, but that was not his way. If someone chose to monopolise the conversation, Rice would accommodate him. So he merely agreed to visit his friend's house the following night to inspect the fishing-rod, and left the incident on the bus to itself.

The next morning, his cold was worse. He could think of little else except the cigarette-smoke which persisted in drifting toward him; but as riding on the lower deck inevitably brought on his travel sickness, there was no escape downstairs. At intervals he blew his nose hopefully. If there were no improvement during the night, he decided, the bank would have to manage without him for a few days.

The bus turned into the stream past a rectangle of waste ground, where, Rice realised, Rossiter's double had boarded the vehicle the day before. He squinted into the window; the seat opposite him was empty. He shifted and took in several more reflections; no sign of the other. He then did something unusual for him; he turned in his seat and quickly took in the faces behind him, then scanned the passengers ahead. None of them was the one he sought.

Rossiter arrived at the usual point along the route, noticed him and crushed him against the window. Rice coughed out answers to his friend's remarks as he stared at the glass, his eyes focused somewhere between the surface and the exterior. When they reached the slums and finally an alley that he remembered, he strained his gaze for scarcely any reason, and made out that the alley ended on a distant waste; nothing more. A severe cough at that moment cut through his throat, and he lost interest.

His cold thickened during the morning, and by lunchtime he had decided to break off the evening's visit. But Rossiter was not in the Queen's Restaurant, and Rice disliked breaking appointments without notice. So it was that he walked that night the length of Ferris Drive and reached the Rossiters' semi-detached.

"Yes, it's a very good buy," Rice commented nasally, spinning the fishing-rod's reel.

Julie, Rossiter's wife, glanced up in simulated interest. Her husband was not listening; he was standing at the window and holding the curtain aside a little. "Jack, you're not listening to Lindsay," she said.

"What? . . . Oh, yes, I heard," replied Rossiter, and let the curtain fall. "I was just watching that fellow under the lamppost. No, too late, he's gone now," he waved her back. "He's been there ever since I came how tonight, watching the house, I thought . . . Funny thing, I've felt all day as though I was being watched."

"What did he look like?" Rice asked, laying down the rod.

"Tall, about my height. Very pallid complexion."

Rice glanced round, opened his mouth, and Julie stood up: "I'll go and make us all some coffee."

"Oh, no, you won't," corrected her husband. "*I'll* go and make it. You stay here and entertain Lindsay. God knows we've been boring you all night. And if you don't feel more alive by the weekend, I'll cut out that fishing trip," and he was gone.

For same moments a smothering silence hung round the plush armchairs and walnut bookcase. "Happy home life," ventured Rice disconnectedly.

"Yes," Julie agreed, leaping into the opening. ". . . If you could be too good to someone, Jack would be to me."

The morning after, Rice's head felt as if it were swelling out of bed. He shivered in the cold of dawn, pulled himself further under the blankets and sank back into sleep. Waking past three o'clock, he telephoned the bank, tasted a cup of coffee and poured it down the sink, and finally crawled back into bed.

Sometime later—it must have been the following afternoon—a persistent doorbell arrested his drifting. He struggled into his dressing-gown, padded coughing into the next room, and opened the apartment door. Two people pressed in: an apologetic police officer following a distraught Julie Rossiter.

"No, I haven't seen Jack since Tuesday night," Rice told the officer. Here Julie broke in to explain. Jack had not come home the previous evening, there had been no phone message, no hint beforehand that he might be late, but he had not been home all night. It wasn't his way to do such a thing. "I've a feeling that something—I don't know—*horrible* has happened to him," she said.

Rice could only repeat his denial and stand awkwardly before her anxiety, until at last she turned away. He began to close the door, and she switched back to face him: "You'll let me know if he gets in touch with you?" Rice confirmed that he would and, closing the door, lurched back to bed.

Days passed before he was ready to return to work; but when he did, he began really to be affected by Rossiter's absence. An empty seat on the morning bus, an unoccupied place at his table at the Queen's Restaurant—these were sinister reminders and provoked speculation about the disappearance. The police had dismissed suicide as an explanation, so did he; nor did he think, as some passing acquaintances had suggested, that Rossiter had deserted his wife—his last visit to Ferris Drive convinced him against that. But his own suspicions were formless and menacing. He found himself looking in vague apprehension down an alley off the route into Brichester.

Toward the end of the third week since the disappearance, Rice left his Douglas Road apartment in search of the entertainments of central Brichester. As he emerged from the street door, a pale figure met him: Julie Rossiter in a white overcoat, breathless from running. He waited at the foot of the wide stone steps as she summoned her breath and gasped "They've found Jack—will you come?"

On the bus to Ferris Drive she sketched in details: how Rossiter had staggered out of the woods on the Camside-Clotton road and been driven home in a passing car; how pale and emaciated he had been as he strained out directions to the driver; how he had been the victim of some insane crime. And yet, after all this, he refused to—but perhaps Rice should hear it from Jack.

And Jack told his story at length, now and then leaning from his supporting mound of pillows to stress a point to Rice, sunk in the bedroom armchair. "It began the day after you came round here," Rossiter commenced. "Just when I was off to lunch I had a telephone call—said it was from you: it wasn't? No, I know that now—but at the time I wasn't sure, you with a cold and so forth. The voice was thick and forced, and it said I was to go to Potter's Crossing—said there was something very interesting there. No time to explain, or there wouldn't be time in the lunch hour to look it over. You know Potter's Crossing—that place on the Ton we went beyond Clotton?"

Rice remembered Potter's Crossing well enough. It was difficult to reach; one took the bus through the deserted remains of Clotton, dismounted at the first stop beyond, and followed the path that led to the Ton through a small tangled wood. The path was hard under Rossiter's feet, and frost penetrated his soles. He had rather expected Rice to meet him at the bus-stop, but he had not been visible there, nor did he appear through the marching trees. Rossiter could not make out the guiding gleam of water and, glancing back, he saw that the trees had closed off the road. He quickened his pace toward the Ton, and a blow on the back of his neck knocked him unconscious.

He found himself eventually lying in semi-darkness on damp boards, walls closing him in on every side. He drew himself up to survey his surroundings and one supporting hand sank into something spongy. He recoiled and frantically glared around; his eyes were not receiving details of the enclosure, but he could focus no looming shape of another tenant. The dimness of the room and a pounding agony in his head made him squeeze shut his eyes for as long as he dared; and at last they snapped open on the interior of a hut, mossy but stout-looking walls, opposite him a stubborn-looking door, above him a thickly-raftered roof with here and there a gap of sunlight, splashing its pool of radiance on a floor of muddy boards on which were isolated three dimly unappetising pieces of bread that he had earlier touched and near them a tin of some liquid.

Having oriented himself, he quietly approached the door. His trouser cuffs swung wetly against his ankles, and when he reached down to finger them his hand came away covered with grit and mud; he realised that he must have been dragged here. And perhaps his attacker—whoever he was, whatever his motive—was waiting outside the door; Rossiter's right hand closed round a cigarette case which might be used to lethal effect. His left caught hold of a flaking ring set into the door; he raised the case high and wrenched at the ring. But not this, nor repeated onslaughts with his shoulder, affected the immobile door.

Only when the night outside strengthened the hut's gloom did he become really worried. Until then his battering on the moss-softened walls and cries for help, while urgent in tone, had been soothed by a conviction that aid would soon arrive; but who would take the forest path after dark, and how distant might that path be? He could no longer see the wood against which he lay; the door might well be open but invisible against the forested darkness, so that he could not be certain that faintly audible creaks did not mark the progress of his unseen attacker toward him. And oddly enough, all at once it no longer mattered. He must close his eyes to relieve the pain in his skull. He was overpoweringly tired.

When he awoke the light was dimming again: the late afternoon of the following day. He examined the walls; there was no crack to be widened. There were those chinks of sky above him, but his fingers alone could not enlarge them. He kicked at the wood, called out hoarsely, but no sound filtered in from outside and nobody came to release him. He lay down again, staring at the door with eyes that grew heavier—and so it continued. Gradually he became hungry, but only one of the pieces of bread was palatable; the others were white with mould. The odour of the liquid in the tin was disgustingly familiar, and he tipped it out. Sometimes when he awoke he broke open the remaining pieces of bread and found that their untouched cores briefly numbed the gnaw of hunger. Once it began to rain, and he slid the empty tin under a dripping hole in the roof; but from the tang which persisted through the rainwater he knew he had been right about the previous liquid, and he spat it out revolted and lay down to catch the rain directly in his mouth. All too soon the drumming faded from the roof, and he wearily sat up again to watch the door or batter on the walls until sleep came.

Time had almost lost its meaning when he woke one afternoon to face an open door. Instinctively he clutched his cigarette-case as he tottered dizzily toward release; but the empty woods were silent save for the opposing notes of birds above him. Rejecting caution, he stumbled down the arcades, tripping over fallen branches and reeling against trunks until he fell into the road outside Clotton. As he slumped to his knees at the kerb, a car screeched stationary close by.

"But after all that, he won't go to the police," Julie complained as her husband went silent.

Rice stared at Rossiter, who returned the stare and nodded with weak obstinacy. "That's right," he said. "Whoever did it all, I think he's through with me. That sort of warped mind works in odd ways—if we called in the police, he might get enraged and do something worse. But if he intended to do something more violent even without provocation, why didn't he attack me while I was softened up? It might even be one of those teenage gangs the Severnford police are after who got the wrong victim. Anyway, I'm recovering—I don't have much reason to prosecute." But he seemed almost to be struggling to convince himself.

"Lindsay, will you go for the police?" pleaded Julie when Jack had subsided.

"Nobody's going for them!" croaked Jack. "They're not coming in here! I won't answer their questions!"

Rice saw that he was about to be involved in an argument. He didn't think he could be of any help with things as they were, he informed them both; and since only silence met this remark, he let himself out into Ferris Drive. Rossiter plunged determinedly under the sheets; Julie began various domestic actions and left each for visions of what might yet happen to Jack. But as the night progressed, emotion dulled in the semi-detached.

Next morning Rossiter threw off the bedclothes and declared he was off to the office; he eased himself upright, crossed the carpet jauntily, reached the landing—and ran into the bathroom barely ahead of a rush of vomit. All his odd determination could not carry him to work that day; nor the next, for it was Saturday. But by Monday he was sufficiently recharged to leave for Harrison Avenue after a tentative breakfast. The frosty air twinged his face; his footsteps on the arctic pavement sounded close and flat. From the front door Julie called "Do you feel all right?" but retired inside as he glared at her.

Somewhere a car engine was refusing to start. Two hundred yards ahead a red bus bound for Brichester appeared and vanished at the junction with Thornhill Road. Around the left-hand corner was his stop. With a glance at his watch, he hurried along the right side of Ferris Drive, glanced left and right some yards further on—the glistening road was deserted—and strode toward the opposite pavement. He was not halfway across when a figure appeared in a right-hand driveway and threw itself toward him. Turning, Rossiter glimpsed the rusted lid of a tin can a second before it slashed open the right side of his face. Gasping in agony, he was easy to trip so that his mutilated cheek and forehead ground into the gravel of the road.

Julie fainted when she swung open the front door to reveal Jack, his face gashed and blackened and pouring blood. He staggered back down the path, half-blind with pain, and gripped the thin painted bars of the gate. The nearby car was finally persuaded to start, pulled out into Ferris Drive and drew to a shocked halt level with him. Rossiter felt hands which he saw only as pink blurs help him into the car's back seat, heard a voice: "Christ, what happened? No, don't talk—don't *touch* it! I can't do anything for you—try to hang on, I'll get you to Mercy Hill hospital . . ." He managed to gasp out something about Julie lying inside the open house, and the driver clattered away up the path. His footsteps returned accompanied, and Julie's cool hand gripped Jack's. The car door chopped shut and the vehicle jerked forward.

The doctors at Mercy Hill met his mutilation with all the calmness of efficiency, and surprisingly soon one of them informed the waiting Julie that she might visit her husband. He was propped up by white pillows before a colourless ward wall, and his complexion toned alarmingly with the surroundings. A shocked expression was thawing from his face. There was nothing he wanted, he replied to her anxious questions; she should go home and get something to eat. "The doctors will do all that can be done," he reassured her. But she lingered until their conversation lost all impetus; and even while she descended the antiseptic stairs, she was convinced that Jack had had something urgent to communicate, something lurking just below his trivial words and strained expression.

No doubt it was this which, two hours later, made him throw back the sheets, drag on his shoes and clatter down those same stairs, knocking an unwary nurse and her tray down ahead of him. A doctor who raced after him but stayed to aid the sobbing nurse noticed that Rossiter was yelling something, apparently intended for anyone within earshot; and purposeful as his flight seemed, his words were definitely "Stop me! For God's sake, stop me!" But he was outside the hospital before the doctor had decided to obey, and by then it was too late.

The new vacancy was filled before the almoner had time to notice. A bruised and bleeding taxi-driver was discovered in an alley near Mercy Hill's taxi-rank, where he had been overpowered from behind and kicked unconscious by an unseen assailant. It transpired that it had been his taxi standing outside the hospital when Rossiter rushed out; the taxi into which, according to a doctor who had watched from the ward window above, Rossiter had slid or been dragged by the hands of someone unseen. Then the car roared away without leaving its number with any alert onlooker, and was found hours later—empty, of course—on a slum street at the edge of lower Brichester.

Julie Rossiter insisted on returning home unaided when she recovered from the hospital's latest bulletin; but this was only because she refused to break down in anyone's presence. She controlled herself as far as the bus shelter on Thornhill Road, but tears began to trickle as she made her way up Ferris Drive against an icy breeze. The house

lock blurred before her, and she had to squeeze her eyes shut before
the key would fit. The carpeted hall was dumb and unsympathetic as
she hung her coat on a squealing hanger, and hence she heard the
footsteps on the floor above. Fear of the unknown made her tiptoe
upstairs with a heavy poker poised for action.

The surgical dressing that turned toward her as the figure straightened up from the bedroom mirror was looser and grubbier than before,
but she recognised its wearer readily enough. "Jack, why did you run
off? Where did you go?" she cried, and he replied in a strained voice
"Why do you want to bother me in my condition?" interspersed with
several words she had never before heard from him. She blamed his recent experiences, however, and continued "Are you going to Mercy Hill
to have your face seen to, or shall I get in touch with the doctor?" to
which he responded "It doesn't need a doctor! With what they've already done, it'll heal by itself!" again tricked out with foul adjectives.
Julie felt too unsettled to survive any more of this, and when she had
cooked a meal for her husband she left to contact Lindsay Rice.

Rice was perhaps more disturbed by the change than she was, for
he felt without knowing why that it was not so inexplicable as it
seemed. He was unable to persuade the hostile man before him into
hospital: he soon left, apologising to Julie and shamefacedly assuring
her that all would right itself in time, with obscene directions still ringing in his ears. Early to bed, he was prevented by speculations from
sleep for some time.

All the rest of that week Rice did not speak to Rossiter on the bus.
The other remained at the back of the deck and never glanced up
when Rice passed; sometimes his hand was pressing that revolting
bandage against his face. Robbed of companionship on the downtown
journey, Rice returned to the world outside and within the window. It
was Thursday when a daily view down an alley to slum waste ground
took on a beckoning air, and Friday before he determined—for no coherent reason—to explore.

After all, he thought as he boarded the bus the following morning,
he was going to Brichester anyway. Half-an-hour's delay was negligible.
Not that he expected to discover anything specific; he was merely exploring. The more one knew about one's town the better. And he got
down at the Farriday Avenue stop just ahead of the alley.

A few grimy children splashing in the gutter and numbering the pavement for hopscotch contributed a questionable life to the dingy street. Back several buildings, he saw a draper's next to a fish-and-chip shop, its windows opaque with grease. On the corner of the alley hung a torn and pencilled cinema poster, two weeks out of date. He turned the corner. Alternate wooden doors in the walls hid back yards from intruders. A black cat pounced down, saw Rice approaching and hurried ahead of him, paused before the end of the passage and leapt aboard the wall again. Rice overtook its point of departure and reached his destination.

The waste ground fell away into the urban valley of a disused railway cutting; the ideal playground in the eyes of the local children, Rice would have thought—but none played here. Grass and broken bricks choked the rusty tracks. Houses walled in the rectangular cutting, all dilapidated, some disused; the left and right walls had once been undercut by the railway tunnel, but now the right-hand opening was sealed, though that on the left still gaped. There seemed to be nowhere else to go, and Rice clambered over the debris and into the mouth of the tunnel. It faded into darkness round the bend. The grass thinned and the sharp stones became infrequent, so that he was able to reach the darkness quickly and then feel his way, half-lit by a cigarette-lighter, along the cold wall. There was no sound except the occasional clatter of a kicked brick.

Around the curve, a collapsed roof blocked his progress. He touched the join of this accidental seal to his guiding wall and wondered what to do next; cross to the other wall and work his way back, he supposed, since the lighter did not reach across the tunnel. Halfway across the roof-fall, he came upon a gap above him; he pulled himself up to it—which proved easier than he had expected, since the heaped debris had formed into steps level enough to be constructed—but his eyes declined to penetrate the darkness within. He jumped down again and continued toward the wall.

When the lighter's aura included the further corner, it picked out several objects: most notably a man dressed entirely in red, lying against the wall. Rice approached cautiously, anxious not to wake the sleeper—presumably more poverty-stricken than the average local—and in the silence of his approach he thought he heard a sound; something stirring into wakefulness. It was not the figure in the corner; he felt it came from the blocked-off portion of the tunnel. His lighter preceded him and glistened on the sleeper's skin. The red was not something he wore, after all; the man was covered in red paint. Rice leaned closer before he jerked away and began to vomit.

He stood just inside the cool mouth of the tunnel, and wondered what to do. The police must be informed, but then they would question him—and how could he explain his presence there when he was unsure himself? At last he made his way up the bank of the cutting, down the alley and out again into Farriday Avenue, glancing to right and left as he emerged. The few passers-by were intent on other matters. He sneaked into a telephone box beyond the cinema poster and dialled BRIchester 1000. At that moment a downtown bus appeared on the street's horizon; Rice hastily described his find and its location, rang off, and ran.

The rest of it he read in the newspapers. The body was totally unidentifiable; the police surgeon stated that a knife, a broken bottle, and a heavy iron bar had mutilated the man at length, but neglected to say which had been used on a living man and which on a corpse. Julie Rossiter read the account in a horrified tone across the breakfast table, and was met by callous indifference. Over his own meal Rice examined the report, and recalled a glimpse of crimsoned glass and iron bar in the tunnel. The uncertain light had also shown several curved fragments of white material that could have been eggshell, but in that case the reconstructed shell would have been half as large as Rice, and what could hatch from such an egg? In any case, no light on this anomaly was reported in the newspapers.

Rice ignores Rossiter these days on the bus, and avoids the Queen's Restaurant; so that Rice has little chance to contact Julie and tell her of his surviving unease, always supposing he could coherently describe his feelings. Julie is still nervous, too; but Jack's voice is less strained than it once was, she assures herself, so he must be recuperating. The bandage is off now, leaving a long ugly facial scar. So Julie pursues married life as though nothing has happened and patiently waits for her husband to regain his old self; and Lindsay Rice searches the columns of each *Brichester News* and *Camside Observer* for a Ferris Drive address and the report of an occurrence whose nature he will not admit even to himself.

The Void

I stared at my right hand as it gripped the arm of the chair: the whorls of the knuckles, the wrinkles of the veneer. Nothing else in the room or outside seemed solid. A second ago I was born, my mind wiped clean, instantaneously inheriting however many years had cultivated hair on my arms, whatever actions had led to this room, the silver leaves of the wallpaper, the wind trapped in the chimney like a weak ghost behind the frame with its chemist's qualifications. I knew that in that second I'd been staring at my hand. When my wife entered I remembered everything, and my mind turned red and raw as litmus. Gradually I neutralised the colour. I thought of Edna.

But my wife was waiting. "Yes, Jo," I said. Such a tone I might have used to one of my girls at the chemist's, I knew, but I wanted to be alone, to sink into memory.

"You called out." She was about to sit on the arm of the chair, though oddly uneasy; already her fingers were stroking my hair—if they probed too deeply they might find Edna.

"Did I? I don't remember." It must have been before I'd been born. But I could see she wasn't satisfied. "What did I say?" I asked wearily.

"It sounded like 'chemically possible'. 'It must be chemically possible', you said."

"How strange." Independent of anything I knew, my right hand was tight on the arm of the chair. I felt it as frail; in a moment the whorls might burst.

"Tim, what did you mean?" Her face came round to mine and gazed in. "Tell me." I knew she could see, not Edna, but my memories. As at the bottom of a microscope she saw magnified a tiny frantic scene: the wet blinding road, the wheel that whipped through my hands like rope, my hand clutching air, the star which leapt from the windscreen jagged as pain—

And she stroked my hair. "I wish I could stop," she said. "You want to be quiet, I know." As she determined what was trapped in my mind I wondered what was passing through hers: frustration that she hadn't been in the car that night to share my suffering as the first cold drops of rain fell in my wound? Whenever she probed too deeply she was miserable, then bravely oblivious. I wished she wouldn't see so clearly into the depths of the gulf between us. If only once she'd forge ahead as if it were not there and leap across. If only there were something to bridge it, to fill it: children.

But now I must convey to her that I was ignoring it. "Jo," I said. "You're helping me, you know that." I appreciated her efforts, even while I wondered at the terror that I sensed she was trying to conceal.

"If only I could be sure."

"Why don't you make the tea, and I'll help." I was sure now that I'd achieved the right prosaic intonation, the correct suggestion that this was the answer, that nothing else mattered, that I didn't feel her terror growing.

"You sit quietly. I've only to set the table." Yes, she was responding. "And afterwards, I'll leave you alone if that's what you want," she said.

"You know I don't." Gently I traced the curve of her cheek. Her face didn't change. Only her legs trembled. And when she rose I knew she wouldn't shudder until she was out of the room, when she could blame herself for her terror. If only I could ask her what was wrong. I knew only that I'd known five minutes ago. I'd known what must be chemically possible.

As soon as I'd switched on the television I leapt up and turned it off. I must not avoid thinking; that was fatal. Briefly, as I sat down, a square of light dwindled within my reflection and expired. Somehow, I felt, Edna could help. Yet though at the thought of her the walls turned to cardboard, she wouldn't form. She seemed tenuous as a memory that might have been a dream. Where had we met? Chilled, I realised that I didn't know. Perhaps because of this frustration, I sweated with the certainty that our meeting was the key; if I could remember where then I'd understand. As my mind strained to clutch beyond its boundaries, my hand regained its grip on the chair-arm and trembled till I thought the wood might snap.

When Jo appeared in the doorway, striding down the hall, impelled by her determination, I was moved. She'd commanded herself not to falter, not to betray her terror. If I hadn't sensed it then perhaps she might have reclaimed me; but with this new unasked perception, this sense of viewing us both through a spyhole or projected on a screen, I could feel only how absurd all this was, the terrors which eroded us both yet might be destroyed by discussion which neither of us had the courage to force upon the other. "Come on, Tim, nourishment," she said.

The table was laid in a pattern I hardly liked to disturb: almost a symbol protecting the permanence of the house, the room, the walls, our life. Such thoughts led nowhere; I'd never been a mystic, I couldn't imagine who had infected me with such deathbed musings. Jo picked up her knife and fork and gave mine a hopeful glance. "How was the chemist today?" she asked as, with a clumsiness that shocked me, I gathered the first mouthful.

"Fine. Much as usual." Her words were a code of references which I had to translate back into a shared past. Startled, I realised that I'd forgotten nine hours of customers, admittedly alike as the ranked bottles, barrel bodies, smaller barrel heads, all outside whatever had been swelling inside my brain until tonight it had burst and blinded—except for one, somehow a key among my lost set, who'd been so grateful for a quick prescription that he shook my hand. Enraged, I knew that the chemist's too was charged with hidden meaning. Chemically possible. "How was the chemist today?" Suddenly I was jarred by what might be Jo's terror. But immediately I dismissed the idea as melodramatic; Jo hadn't spoken out of suppressed fear that I might clear the way for Edna. She'd never heard of Edna. She had merely been observing the teatime ritual.

"And how were the girls?"

Was one of them Edna? No, I knew that much and could compose a likely answer. "Still too much makeup. At least, Miss Latimer has seen my point, but Miss Trent, the unhelpful blonde you met, she still seems determined to paint herself a new face." Out of control, I'd overrun; robbed of memory again, I had absolutely no idea whether I'd invented everything I'd said. But Jo was clearly satisfied. The figure on the screen was sure of his lines even when my attention wandered. Cold, I wondered what shared implications I had touched of which I know nothing—as I looked down and found that while I'd been away, my independent hands had fed me, cleaned my plate.

"Shall we have coffee in the lounge? More—" I saw the words pass through her mind: cosy, intimate—but finally she said: "It'll be warmer in there." She couldn't approach what she feared. When she gave me the cup her fingers withdrew before my hand had time to find hers. We'd passed the point of touching to tap the sexual current; our touches communicated an awareness of security. Yet now I yearned in an agony of desire to touch her. Which was why Edna had to be.

If she had to be. I wanted to come home to Jo and sit and exchange thoughts through smiles and make love, even the cautious economic love we'd made somewhere on the other side of the splintered windscreen. I could regret all this without remembering its loss. I refused to be thrown together with Edna, whoever she was, whatever she signified. I made room on the couch for Jo. "Sit by me," I said.

She sat, uneasy as a virgin. I kissed her and she replied, but I could feel her braced for something yet to come. My first caress was strangely tentative, as if I'd never touched her, and with it the walls thinned, our eyelids darkened the room, we seemed surrounded by a void quietly chaotic as the wind in the chimney, a space at whose centre we floated fixed to the points where our bodies met. Then, as Jo sprang upright as from cramp, the void rushed out, to give place to the other which filled my mind, the void whose edge I'd been approaching. "I'm sorry. I'm sorry, Tim," said Jo on the brink of tears. "I do try. I can't help it."

"What's wrong?" I asked, feeling hysteria close. "What's wrong with me?"

"There's nothing wrong with you. Oh, Tim, please don't start thinking that. But—I don't know how to say this so you'll understand—please give me a little time."

And of course I didn't understand. As I looked back I saw her shoulders shaking and knew I couldn't touch them. I passed the front-door pane, solid with night, and went upstairs. Instinctively I entered the room furthest from the landing. A single bed, first for the child we might one day afford, then for guests, now for me. My removal to this room had been my decision, not Jo's. Why could I remember only ironies, as if I were my own disinterested observer? Such as my chemist's shop coming soon after the accident, allowing us the child we would now never have, not when the child might be in the car next time I crashed. No, that was rationalisation. We had sold the car. The reason lay elsewhere, close to Jo's plea for "a little time" as if I'd known her only weeks. Another key, and it came to me instantly that Edna knew. Edna knew and I'd forgotten.

I sat down on the bed, among the furniture with which we'd tried to hide the emptiness. Jo was silent: only the wind moved formlessly. I lay back and sought Edna's answer. My eyes sprang open. My husband filled my eye, bearing down toward me, and I twisted out of reach. I thought I'd fall, but it was a double bed, doubled again by a mirror over a dressing-table on which lay a separated loop of wire. If I could pull free of the pillow I'd scream. But my voice said only "I can't, I can't. Please, Eric."

"You know it makes no difference," he said. "I don't even notice it now. You're still you, Edna." But he must have seen my mouth gaping outraged, my eyes wide as the void expanded. He picked up the wire. "I'll see to the light," he said.

Like electricity, I thought. My mind had fled the horror, leaving me imprisoned.

When I heard Jo's footsteps I blinked away the nightmare and leapt back from the single bed. My hand, clenched on the sheet, tore it free with the fury of a husband discovering adultery. I had to scream, but as myself: I shrieked every obscenity I knew into the void, to destroy that hidden threat of femininity. But when I turned I saw Jo in the doorway, her face clenched by misery. As I took a step toward her, she whirled and ran to her room.

I stood trembling, my nerves scraped bare, my mind clutching space and slipping free. I didn't dare to lie down. Chemically possible. Like electricity. I battered the walls of my mind. Where were *my* memories? Who was I?

When I awoke nothing proved that I was not still asleep. Outlines were treacherous. I'd twisted and turned all night; now, as I tried to find form in my carefully defined movements about the room—a hand through a shirt-sleeve, a knowing grope, the other hand—my mind refused to be still. Beyond the window it was dark: that dark which creeps and crowds across the eye, a vision of the transient chaos which was my blood. I disowned my mind; let it probe and suffer, I wouldn't listen. I emerged onto the landing. Half-seven and still dark; everything seemed directed against me. Jo's door was closed; I imagined her huddled beneath the blankets, shutting out the world and me for a few short hours. In the kitchen I found the sandwiches and thermos which she'd left, a mute reproach.

Drops of dew hung at the cracked tips of leaves; against a thin dark mist the spokes of cobwebs glittered, intricate yet communicating only horror. Last night I'd been tired; I must have dreamed Edna. But I knew that she'd confirm the mirrored bed, the length of wire that seemed the seed of revelation. A boy with a sackful of newspapers cycled by, his cough muffled by a scarf. Shivering, I strode faster to the bus stop, between the houses that were blocks of darkness seeping into random yellow rectangles of light. All was veiled, beyond my comprehension. I had to be helped. Yet Jo had hidden. Suddenly I thrust the sandwiches into a clammy hedge and emptied the thermos down a drain. I'd call Edna. Whatever she could tell me, it must help.

On the bus everyone was coughing out his own mist. A good day for tonics, I thought—but somehow it wasn't my thought. Above the street a few neon signs flickered feebly against the murk; three silent men shouldering dustbins emerged from behind the shops and vanished. As I reached the door I glanced up at the plastic lower-case lettering: *dawsons chemists*. So that was my name.

Grey as planes of mist, the windowpanes hung before the bottles and cosmetics and smiling cardboard girls. My hand gripped the key as it might have a lifeline, and at my heels gaped the void. I folded back the gate and unlocked the door, to be greeted by a scent of antiseptic cold as the gleam of a scalpel. For a second I was on the edge of memory. I hung up my coat and pulled on my white overall. In the shop I switched on the heater; the careful displays, encased in glass as if in ice, rejected me. I opened the cash-drawer. The last time I'd met Edna—I shook bags of change into the drawer. When had I last met Edna? When and where had I met her at all? What did she look like? I must have glimpsed her, me, last night reflected shocked in the unexpected mirror, but there lurked madness, the void. I slammed the cash-drawer and strode into the dispensary, my right hand reaching out toward the telephone.

When I heard the shop door open my hand sagged and I hurried back to the counter. The sharp discoloured air had rushed into the shop, edged by Miss Trent's perfume. She and Miss Latimer had arrived; they glanced at the clock and relaxed. Behind them the door closed itself wearily, fitting my name into its niche, as it had done with increasing reluctance for weeks. I waited while they said "Good morning, Mr Dawson."

"Good morning. Close the door, please, Miss Trent," I said and examined the prescriptions that the night-letter box had collected. On the edge of my concentration I noted an exchanged glance. "Before you came, Liz," Miss Latimer laughed, "that door used to behave itself."

"I should think that's true of more than doors," I muttered. I shouldn't have; I wanted to ignore them and find myself. To shut out the world, which seemed determined to lure me into situations that I couldn't handle, and search within. I'd just thought of Jo, pulling the blankets back on the cold morning alone, perhaps relieved.

As Miss Trent approached, my right hand trembled. I couldn't look up; I saw something monstrous on her face, her false eyelashes starting from her eyes like insect legs from dark holes of mascara. This falseness, those alien objects like parasites on her face, were somehow the source of the terror that surrounded me. "We read the newspaper on the train, if you'd like to read it," she said. "I'll make a cup of tea if there's time. You must be as cold as we are."

"I scarcely think there'll be time for that," I told her, turning over the last prescription. "We open in seven minutes. Tea break is at ten, Miss Trent."

Before I could come to terms with Jo, Edna, the nightmare of last night, they'd returned. They couldn't have had time to say much behind my back, I reflected. "Gosh, isn't it horrible out. The sort of day when you like to be working," Miss Latimer said.

"I had hoped I was not alone in finding all days much like that," I replied. I was facing them; they couldn't glance their comment. I had some power over them, then; it gave me courage for the phone and whatever lay beyond. "Miss Latimer, I'll need you in the dispensary. Miss Trent, I trust you're capable of handling the counter without help?"

"I'll give you a hand if it gets too much for you, Liz," Miss Latimer said.

My power was weakening. "If you have time to spare, Miss Trent," I called over my shoulder, "the floor could stand cleaning."

The bottles were cylinders of fluorescence; on the dispensary wall the black telephone gleamed. When she'd applied for the job Miss Trent had seemed efficient, but in the weeks she'd worked in my shop the eyelashes had crept onto her face; at first merely absurd in their independence, they seemed lately to have changed her subtly into a coquette. Or was she gradually revealing herself? I neither knew nor cared; these were not the memories I sought. The white walls, the antiseptic; there was a memory, but I chilled. I idled back to the shop for the prescriptions, waiting for the weight of memory to press through into my consciousness. At the door I halted and listened.

"Was he like this before it happened, Jackie?" Miss Trent whispered.

"No, he used to be awfully sweet. Keen on his job but because of how it helped people, you know. I may be wrong, but perhaps now the job is all he's got. Maybe his wife—"

"I feel sorry for her. She was so on edge when she came in. I couldn't understand what she wanted."

"I feel sorry for him too, though. Never mind, love. You've got Kenny and I've got Dick, and we won't have to put up with all this for much longer."

What could I say? Miss Trent, I'm sorry but you're the sort of girl who reminds me that I'm betraying my wife? I strode into the shop and caught up the prescriptions. Next to them lay the newspaper. "When you're ready, Miss Latimer," I said coldly, "I should like to deal with these." Then I saw the headline: *New Hope for Heart Transplants.* Before I knew, my right hand had ripped out the words as a dog tears cloth. I glared up as if to see the truth at last, but I was confronted by Miss Trent before she looked away. "Miss Trent," I called, and my voice rose to a shout. "For God's sake, will you wash your face!"

When they both stared wordlessly I weakened. I needed my strength for the phone. "I'm sorry," I said wearily. "I've had a bad night. I'm not myself."

Handing me the bottles from the dispensary shelves, Miss Latimer was silent. So you've seen what I'm capable of, I thought. If your disapproval is so painful, how much more so would Jo's be if she knew about Edna! But the phone hung at the edge of my gaze. I needed Edna to reveal what was surfacing in my mind. I scribbled on the label of the last bottle and emerged into the shop. A motorcyclist slowed outside the window, exchanged distant kisses with Miss Trent, and roared away. "If you and Miss Latimer would like to go for break I'll hold the fort," I said, avoiding her eyes. "No need to hurry. There are biscuits."

I'd had to wait until I was sure that Edna's husband Eric would be out, mending fuses, tending wires. Now, every time I was ready to face the phone, the shop door opened; the world held me back from the truth. I was pulled back and forth behind the counter, from display to drawer to window. When the girls returned I was weak again. I wavered toward the tearoom. Then, desperately, I turned and caught up the phone.

The line mused sibilantly; the space of which it spoke was chaos. Only the throb of the bell and the click and the waiting breath were fixed. It was a woman's breath, which elsewhere I'd heard quick and harsh. "Edna," I said.

"Tim. Oh, thank God. I thought it might be Eric. He was hopelessly upset when he went out. Last night—"

"Edna, I haven't much time." Not last night, I yelled.

"Please, Tim, let me talk. I must tell someone, and if I can't talk to you—" Tim was silent; perhaps he wasn't listening. I gripped the phone as if to force my way through to him, my lover, to whom I was inextricably bound. "I thought I was going mad. Last night Eric was so miserable I felt I had to. I tried, Tim. Oh, God, I tried! He says I haven't changed for him but I can't forget." My eye ranged about the hall, as if in fear of Eric eavesdropping; it found the fuse-box up to which he'd once hoisted me while he explained how it worked. "But—oh, how can I make you feel it—as soon as he began it was as if I were someone else. Someone was watching us, and it was me. If he'd made love to me then it would have been rape," she said harshly, and fell silent. She was waiting for me to comfort her, but I was gasping, drowning in terror of madness. If she spoke again I'd be lost somewhere in the void which united us. It was like turning to stare into a camera and at the same time seeing oneself on a screen turn and stare. I clutched the receiver so hard it might have melted. "Tim, you're still there?" she cried.

To see her would be to preserve my identity with an assurance of her own. "We must meet," I stammered. "Today. For lunch."

"Oh, Tim, I can't," she said unhappily. "Eric may be home."

"You must," I forced out, beating my knuckles against the white wall. "Leave him a note. You know you're closer to me than anyone else could ever be, and you know why," he said. But I didn't know; I knew nothing, not even the varnish on my nails like surfaces of blood, not even the screwdriver lying on the hall table as if amputated. "Meet me at the station. I'll be there at one," he said. "Someone's in the shop. I have to get back to the counter," I said, and slammed the phone down.

My right hand hung trembling against the white wall. Suddenly the horror burst from me; I roared inarticulately. In the shop a murmur was instantly truncated, and glass smashed. I rushed out of the dispensary. Miss Trent was wide-eyed above a pool of medicine jagged with corners of glass. She saw me and ran forward. "Mr Dawson, are you all right?" she cried.

"All right!" I shouted. "You're trying to destroy me then, are you? Are you?"

I knew I was right in a sense. Something was trying to destroy me.

When I left the shop the sky had cleared from grey to glass. I'd spent the rest of the morning arranging displays in intricate patterns, chilling my fingers on linoleum, resolving the reality of my hands against sharp glass, even once, alone in the dispensary, dropping a bottle when I felt threatened. I hurried down the street. Figures emerged from ringing doorways and battled the wind for their coat collars. I wondered whether Edna had left; then at once I tied my thoughts to my stride.

As I crossed a shopping street, above which hung the first few plastic Santa Clauses, a car skidded on a lost patch of ice. Its grille reared toward me like a toothed mouth. Within three feet of me, it regained control. Gripped by a fear that was not that of death, I ran and plunged into an arcade. The lights were warm yellow, but I was striding forward into terror, cold as the insinuating wind. I pushed through the crowd, hoping to be trapped by bodies, held down by flesh. For a moment, as the faces pressed past, I invoked Jo. Perhaps she was smiling desperately in a supermarket, buying food for tonight; perhaps tonight we could sit down face to face and each confess to what obsessed us. But I couldn't look to her for help in her betrayal. For even as I shrivelled, emerging from the arcade to realise that the station was two streets away, my body strode ahead of me, inexorably drawn.

Below the bridge the lines spread out to align with their platforms, the signals seemed to point to the station like signposts. I dragged my fingers along the parapet as if to erase their prints, but already I was turning from the pegged magazines above the bookstall to search for Tim, starting as a platform gate clashed back and passengers welled out. I mustn't think of Edna. I ground the grime of the parapet into my fingers and fastened my mind on whatever presented itself; the train lines sketched into the faint distant mist to suggest an invisible union; a crushed shoe abandoned in the gutter; the Station Hotel, too close to book into with Edna; a tortured metal gate; long white echoing corridors where drifted terrifying anonymous smells; a bright blank light, a close blurred face and suffocation; a tilted lawn, white cane chairs and watchful figures on the gravel walks; Edna passing on someone's arm, turning her head, her guide delighted by the coincidence as she introduced us—I knew I was on the edge; I accepted. Receptive at last, I hurried across the bridge. Whatever happened now, my feet were set in their course.

The departures indicator shuffled like a pack of cards. I looked away from figures disconsolately turning from an empty platform, and saw Tim striding through the crowd, halting as a chain of trailers clattered ponderously before him like a noisy funeral. I thrust away the last and ran forward. My right hand clutched Edna's. "The waiting-room," I hissed.

Below the pale green of the dusty wall lay a fringe of darker green, like a precipitate in a test-tube. The bare bulb hung above a single street gypsy, asleep beneath newspapers against a cold heater. I saw a headline I knew and clutched Edna. We kissed as if to bind ourselves together through our mouths. And at once I was flung out to hover, impotent, bodiless, watching. Their mouths separated. "I want to say I love you," she whispered. "And yet I feel as if I'm being driven. Or drawn. Like magnets. Electricity."

"Even if it were chemically possible," he said, "you know that's not all that's brought us together. His hand—"

"And his eye," she finished.

And at last I knew who I was. I remembered the bent point of the front gate that one of my children had swung out of shape.

"I must have you. Tonight," he said.

"Yes. Whatever happens," she responded. Her eyes lifted to him, one a fraction slower than the other. "But somewhere else. We can take a train to the sea."

"It will give us three hours," he said.

I struggled without moving, clawed without substance at their skulls. Take me back to my home! I shrieked. Back to my twisted gate! And then, How can I be both of you? I was as helpless as the dust that swarmed above them from the ancient leather of the benches. I forced myself feebly between them, to destroy this shocking schizophrenia, and was caught. "Somehow I want to turn and run," she told me. "And yet I know I'll stay."

"Your magnets are turning," I said, and raised my hand toward her face.

From the corner of my eye I thought for a second that his hand was clawed to tear my cheek like paper. But he lifted my hair back, and we kissed. "We can't risk more. Tonight at six," I told her. "I'll tell Jo something or other. You leave first. I'll give you a minute."

As she hurried from the station I seemed to be stretched, wrenched apart in an agony without pain. It must be love, I thought. I had a brief image of a twisted gate; we must have met there once. Then I pushed open the glass door, signed in grime, and began to walk back to the chemist's. There was something I wanted to scribble down before I forgot, about a gate. Perhaps it was the gate across my shop doorway: it might need oiling. Tonight I could ask Edna; she might know. Otherwise, tonight would perhaps bury in the depths of my mind whatever had begun obscurely to trouble me again.

Or perhaps, as I rather hoped, it would simply cease to exist.

The Other House

One morning, after a weekend in Birmingham, I stood for an hour at the motorway entrance and thumbed. Dawn hung suspended, diluting the night, on which a distant line of telegraph poles asserted its blackness; rain weighted the beams of headlights and was flung out like sparks by whirling wheels. Across the roundabout a girl shielding herself with what remained of an umbrella caught my eye. "I may have a scrap of shelter left," she called. "Come and join me." Her name was Joan. Her eyes were black and bright; her face drew in to concentrate upon her mouth, and she smiled at least as often as her long legs shifted. She was hitching back to Brichester after a performance of *Othello*. "I should have had a lift back to St John's Wood," I said, "but they broke down." We talked until four nurses in a Mini skidded up to us and made room for her. "You have this," she insisted, moulding my fingers to the handle of the skeletal umbrella. "I can get another from the buses' Lost and Found." A few minutes later I attracted a car and, after crumpling the umbrella into its ring, sat knees drying before the heater and dozed. Only the edge of a thought was needed to recall Joan.

Two months later, since I still glimpsed her face between realities, I wrote to her. "I have an empty week to fill," I lied. "I've heard a good deal about Brichester." Well, I'd once encountered the name in a library book, whose title eluded me. "Do you think I might take up your invitation?" Five minutes more and she might have invited me; I felt that her invitations were frequent and sincere. "Love"—no, "luv"—yes—no, "thanks in advance!" The next day she replied. "Of course you must come and stay! Tell me when and I'll meet you." I told her of likely trains and she confirmed. When I'd carried my suitcase out of my flat, I returned to assure myself that the gas was locked up, the windows tight, the library books unable to overstay their welcome. Beyond the window, a concentrated sun eased itself above the roofs.

By the time I reached Brichester the back of every seat was spread with hot discarded jackets, hung with ties like nooses. In Brichester Central Station commuters waddled moistly or, panting, weaved their way like disturbed insects within the ribs of the dome. I felt that my hand could rust the handle of my suitcase. I'd decided to greet Joan: "Come to think, I don't believe you actually invited me but since you mentioned where you live—" She was waiting beyond the grille; she shook her hair down her shoulders where it rippled, black, on orange flowers and paler orange cotton. "Are you hungry?" she said. "We can eat at the Union."

"I had lunch on the train, thanks."

"How about a beer before they close?"

"I think I'd prefer coffee. Good for the pores, you know."

"Could you survive long enough for us just to pass through the Union Bar? It's only round the corner from my place. Someone I want to get hold of should be there."

We caught a bus into Lower Brichester; Joan pointed out artists and poets entering pubs. More pubs and Bingo halls, tufts of triumphant grass glimpsed down alleys, tall houses with iron balconies, a cramped park laden with factory girls, a formless stretch of waste ground bristling with the tubular tent poles of a market. We walked along Milton Street. As we passed a Victorian corner house like four grey monoliths set together to form a stone pillar, Joan glanced up. At the end of her gaze a window framed a sample of staircase. She pointed down Keats Street opposite. "There's your bed for the week," she said.

At the far end of Milton Street squatted the Students' Union, a long low concrete box with dazzling glass doors. We passed the notice board, Judo and horse-riding clubs, "Kill a Commie for Freedom Debate", "Challenge the Toothbrushing Champion for Oxfam", and stepped over a wizened balloon and two tankards into the bar.

"I'm not a student," I hissed.

"Nor am I," Joan said.

The bar was full of froth-specked beards and tall thin girls like spring onions in tiny skirts. The barman was poising his towel; Joan ran forward and bought two beers before I could forestall her. She half-emptied her tankard and surveyed the bunched faces. "Amos!

Come and met Amos," she told me.

Amos has a high shoulder over which his hair trailed as he peered round eagerly at me. "Is he here?" Joan asked.

"Sorry, love, no. I can't produce him."

"Did you hear him in the studio today?"

"No again. But then I never do. You have a nameless friend, I see."

"Sorry, I'm not usually so low on manners. Amos, this is John and vice versa."

My hand was caught and engulfed. "This is my first half-hour in Brichester," I said.

"Then there's a great many people for you to meet, and the best way to get to know them is at a party," Amos said, pouring down the last of his beer and collecting his strewn limbs. "Which is an oblique invitation for tonight."

"A party?" Joan demanded eagerly.

"Not one of mine, love. There's one tonight somewhere, though. You're sure to find it, and you can let me know where it is."

The barman began to shout and collect glasses. "Listen, Joan, why don't you come over and see if he's in the studio," Amos said. "I owe you a meal, anyway. You can eat when you come down. Then you can meet Natasha."

Joan looked at me as if to communicate something. "Your girl-friend?" I asked.

"Good God no. Only my lover."

We emerged from the Union into close immobile almost tangible walls of sunlight. I felt cut off from the others; there were too many movements beneath the largely opaque surface of the conversation. "I've already eaten, so I won't watch," I said. "If I could just drop this case at your flat, Joan, I'll explore a little Brichester."

"I've got a key for you," Joan said, producing it from a flowered handbag.

"I'll see you about five, then."

"Say six," Joan said.

As I turned up Keats Street, I looked back and saw them entering the monolithic house on Milton Street. The sun was high; the house was one with its shadow. Joan's house was false Regency, part of an undivided line whose perspective was truncated by a pale clay waste. Her flat was on the second floor, a large room and an afterthought crowded with bed, wardrobes, cups of coffee, the nipple of a cucumber. I made my way into the main room, trying not to tread on scattered sleeveless records. Propped against the open record-player was a note in Joan's writing: "TRY THE STUDIO!!"

I splashed cold water on my face. Finding no towel, I stood on the woven ironwork of the balcony and gazed across the baked brown chimneys to the green foreheads of the fields beyond. On Milton Street the grey porous house still absorbed the sunlight. If Amos was closer to Joan conversationally, at least I was here in her flat with my own key. I slid the records into the few sleeves I could find, locked the door and began to walk back through Lower Brichester.

The infrequent bookshops seemed to stock mainly *Private Eye* and *Rubber News*. Children threw tyres on a pale orange fire on a bombsite. Two girls carried piles of records into a second-hand shop. An old man swayed beneath a bottle on a doorstep. A couple embraced in a cemetery, watched by a movie camera and a bored clapper-boy with a Coca-Cola. Halfway down a street of disembowelled houses, I read a pencilled sign in a curtained window: "We still live here."

When I returned to Joan's flat she was lying on the couch in a dress whorled with lime and lemon; *Also Sprach Zarathustra* exploded and gathered again. At least it was the complete work, I thought, not the soundtrack record. "I'll make coffee," she said. "Christ, if I can find a clean cup."

I sat in the single armchair. "Brichester's varied, I'll say that," I said. "Did you meet whatever her name was, Natasha?"

"Oh, God, John," Joan said. "I don't know how old she was. I don't want to know. Amos set out to see how I'd react, that's all. He likes to create situations. She's only the latest of a series."

"Then why did you go?"

"I was looking for someone in the studio above," she said forlornly.

She was silent as she hunted for the elements of a salad. We ate standing up on the balcony before the heavy sun. Somewhere a clock struck eight with bells that sounded waterlogged. Joan caught my hand. "Come on, John, I'll buy you a drink," she said.

We turned left on Milton Street, away from the Union. I was sure that Joan waited until my attention was elsewhere before she glanced up at the grey house. Sensing her strategy, I waited and looked back. Within its outline the shadowed side of the house was formless, but the window which framed the staircase was lit. For a moment I thought I saw I the colourless form of a figure standing on the staircase, staring back at me.

All I could see of the pub was the stained-glass windows; inside was a press of flesh, faces, smoke, from which struggled glinting tankards and fragments of conversation: "She's stopping people in the street for the newspaper now and asking them whether they think Guy Fawkes should be abolished"—"To preserve his self-sufficiency he relies on other people." This time I beat Joan to the bar. We forced our way into an inner room and found a mantelpiece. "Remind me in the morning, I'm modelling at the art class," Joan said. "Hello," she said at intervals, and watched the doorway.

"Is that your source of income?"

"Well, I'm not completely a kept woman," she told me.

A Negro thrust between us and threw a butt into the fireplace. He stood up, his denim jacket tightening on his arms. "Do you smoke?" he asked me.

Feeling vaguely menaced, I took out a packet of cigarettes. "No, man, do you *smoke?*" he said.

"Oh. No, I'm afraid not."

When he'd elbowed his way out a Negro at a table touched my arm. "I shouldn't tangle with him," he warned me. "Last one who did, he set his Alsatians on him one night."

"I don't wonder you were put off," Joan whispered. "But if you're thinking of buying, I can introduce you to someone."

At twenty-five past ten the faces were closer, there might have been a blazing fire behind me. "Look!" Joan cried. My responses were muffled, but my eyes darted in pursuit. Two couples were bearing cans of beer toward the door. "They augur a party," Joan said. "Let's arm ourselves with a bottle and follow."

We finally managed to obtain a bottle of Californian Chablis with a paper collar, offering a decanter in exchange for a slogan. "God, what a bodega," Joan complained. The couples we had glimpsed were out of sight; we tramped up side streets, listening beneath lighted windows, demanding of passing groups "Are you going to the party?" "No, where?" they said. At last Joan despondently regarded a red and furtively active Morris Minor which we'd passed ten minutes earlier. "I would have liked a party," she said. "Still, we can take the bottle out on the balcony and feel superior to people."

As we came in sight of Keats Street I found myself glancing up at the massed black house. From nowhere came a shiver. I blinked and peered closer. I felt too mellow for it to matter: yet on the square of staircase a silhouette leaned on its hands and stared down. I looked at Joan. She too was staring at the house, but at a group brandishing bottles on the doorstep. The first-floor window was alight and crossed by sipping shadows. "There's the party," Joan said. "It's at Amos's. Do we really want to go? Oh yes, let's."

We showed the bottle and were admitted. The staircase was unlit, which seemed somehow wrong. I groped my way upstairs. My fingers, exploring rough wallpaper, encountered a cold perhaps wet patch of bare wall and recoiled. I tried to deduce whether we should by now have passed the window that overlooked the corner of the street. I stumbled and fell forward. There was no stair, only darkness through which I was falling, watched by an unseen figure that had snatched away the stair. Joan clutched my arm tightly. Of course there was no stair; we had reached the landing. The beer was thinking for me.

Amos opened the door; he wore a Japanese silk jacket, his eyes were bright and fascinated by something inside me. "I thought you'd found the party," he said.

"We thought we had too."

"No, these are just the people who couldn't find it."

Joan pushed past him and searched the faces. Behind them Popes screamed, a miniature lighthouse on the mantelpiece displayed combinations of colour. "I'm afraid the glasses have all been assigned," Amos said. "I'll decant this decadence into bottles for you."

Between the conversations trains shunted. "Listen to that closely," Amos said, returning with our Chablis in beer bottles. "It's a sound effects record. Rhythmically very subtle once you become attuned to it."

"Where's Natasha?" Joan asked.

"Over there." He pointed to a girl in one corner; her young body was mostly bare, her face might have been thumbed into shape from a lined pink tablet of soap. She was gulping wine and sucking at an amateur cigarette.

"She's fine. I promised I wouldn't give her a child on acid," Amos said to Joan. "I can't offer you food, I fear. However, I can offer you a sugar-cube if you wish."

"I don't think so," I told him. Joan gripped my hand.

"Well, just as you like. But do let me point out that once when I had a wholesale stock of sugar-cubes I had some people try to bring the house alive. That's the sort of thing you can do, you see. Once you know that everything lives and life is one, you're equipped to reach out to individual lives. It's the only way. I tell you what, let me build you a cigarette."

Joan's grip relaxed. "Just one, then," I said. "I'll share it with Joan."

Amos disappeared into the kitchen. "He's a pretentious bastard," Joan said.

I waited and tried to learn from the faces. I felt it would be difficult to reach out to them; there was a sense in which Lower Brichester was secretively massed, defensive, perhaps menacing. Several were crowded about the lighthouse, eagerly awaiting its next beam like the answer of an oracle. Another group endeavoured to compose with the notes of their stroked glasses. Some danced and stared away over the thrusting bodies of their partners; there was no music. I glanced at Joan. She was intent on the ceiling; her mouth was open, perhaps hopeful, perhaps fearful. "Do you hear anything?" she whispered.

"No, Joan," I said. "I don't."

Amos lit the cigarette for us. "Tell me what you feel," he said. "I always like to know."

At the first inhalation the room seemed to snap alert; my body abruptly sat down. I held the cigarette to Joan's mouth; her lips moved on my fingers; she closed her eyes. I inhaled again, feeling for and holding down the faint taste of spice. "Very little," I told Amos. "A slight gain in clarity, that's all."

Amos nodded indifferently and moved away. Joan took the cigarette and fitted it to my lips. I closed my eyes.

Around me the conversations were linked by a complex rhythm beyond my power to analyse. They massed and rose above me, and my head tilted back. Beyond my lids lay the ceiling, on which a huge form was dormant. No, not dormant; it was insubstantial as smoke yet lethargic and heavy as sinking mud; it was the essence of the house, of the gabble about me, of Lower Brichester. Its passively accumulated weight was pressing down toward me; it was trickling down the walls, merging with them, surrounding me, its nerves within the walls alert for Joan. My eyes sprang open. "What are you looking at?" Joan demanded.

"Nothing," I said. "What makes you ask?"

Joan took a last puff and ground out the cigarette. "John, if you don't mind, I have to get up early," she said. "You stay if you want to, of course."

On the stairs as we descended, Joan took my arm. If I could have found her in the dark I'm sure I would have kissed her, but I was afraid we might fall into the darkness. We crossed the road into Keats Street. Neither of us looked back.

In her flat I made coffee, while she laid blankets on the couch for me. "Would you think me terribly unsociable if I drank this in bed?" she asked.

I held my hand beneath the tap and perceived the transparent ragged leaves of water that sprang from my fingers. Prickling on the couch as the heat gathered, I closed my eyes. A car flickered by. Almost asleep, I became aware of a man with an undefined face. I knew his kind from delirium; he was composed of innumerable infinitely thin layers; but at some point that I failed to locate, his layers became those of a tall house. I turned over to dismiss him, but he lay on my eyeballs, waiting. In the next room Joan moved uneasily in bed and was quiet.

When I awoke it was past noon. Behind my head the long windows were high; lunchtime footsteps and petrol fumes drifted up through the mesh of the balcony. There was something I had to remember. I struggled free of the clinging blankets and saw on the boards of the floor a pair of gym shoes, the left one sprayed red. Yes, of course: I had to wake Joan; she was modelling. I knocked and entered her empty bedroom. Next to a ring of coffee on the floor lay a note in her handwriting: "TEA, EGGS, OCTOPUS TENTACLES." In the other room I fried myself an egg and spread bread. I wondered whether she had watched me as she painted her shoe.

Half an hour later I emerged. On the burning pavement opposite a couple walked barefoot, mystical stoics. The bedraggled bells tolled; the last note sounded like a glass dropped inadvertently: two o'clock, perhaps. Beyond the tower the grass on the hills had been quiffed up by a now suffocated breeze, but I turned toward Lower Brichester; I might encounter Joan.

I couldn't see her in the windows of the house on Milton Street. I strolled on, perceiving the textures of expanded brick, the spotlighted shiny tin of red sports cars. When I touched my cheek it felt like hot moist rubber. The sun had focused on the back of my neck; there was a sensation on my spine like the tactile equivalent of a dark shape on the edge of vision.

I came to a grocer's shop and entered. Perhaps Joan had intended her note for me. In the cool vegetable twilight between the lettuce leaves the shopkeeper was watching someone through the doorway, but I could see nothing.

I left my carrier bag of tea and eggs at the flat. As soon as I returned to the street the back of my neck was threatened again, but as if the dark sensed shape were moving closer—I might be able to lure it forward and then spring the trap. The heat was rising; my shirt would have to be flayed from me. I hurried away from Milton Street, up Wordsworth Lane and past a fish and chip shop to a pub. Among the locals a harassed girl scratched her ear with her circular spectacles and scribbled notes. The barman glanced frowning behind me; I caught myself, triumphantly crafty, searching the faces behind mine in the mirror. For a second I wondered if I was being pursued by last night's marihuana—but no, that was equally naïve.

At the end of Wordsworth Lane I stepped onto waste ground. A road of sorts led uphill across the wrinkled soil, its boundaries chipped and erased by chunks of rubble. On my left a lone house hung suspended in its last seconds of form as it burned; smoke and tatters of ash rose shrivelling into the sky. Two workmen kept watch, leaning on an iron bedstead; beyond the heat their faces fluttered like paper masks. The house coughed darkly, and one workman pointed behind me, his arm rippling, uncontrolled as a papier-mâché snake. I turned sharply, and the back of my neck carried its attendant menace with it. The road was empty of all but its own leavings.

At the top of the hill I found a road bordered with trees and a railway line. I paced along the road, trying to massage the threat from the back of my neck, to a bench with its back to the city. Brichester spread out beneath the hill, instantaneous blocks and intricate vertical designs of colour, denied shadow; the silver line of the Severn formed the top of the frame, but the grey repressed bulk of Milton Street refused to participate in the metaphor. I sat on the bench, which smelled of stripped paint. Sunlight was fitted like glass between two trees on the edge of the tracks. Through this I could see the hills, unreal as a reflection. Not so the landscape behind me: Milton Street had gathered itself together like a stone battalion and surged silently forward. I could feel its heat on the back of my neck. One more leap and its rough burning mass would crush me.

I twisted about. The landscape was too still, too innocent. But I thought I could feel the shadow behind me pale and move away. When I turned back to the road, Joan was approaching. Her eager eyes acquainted her with a passing train, then caught sight of me. "Well, that's the unpleasant part of the day lived through," she said. "Hello, John."

"Did you model."

"Euphemistically, yes. It was Amos's art class."

"Why, was Natasha there?"

"Hardly. She works in a cake shop downtown. No, it was just Amos. The bastard. He thinks everyone's a puppet. I was supposed to be meditating. He kept coming up and pushing my legs apart."

I wasn't sure that given the situation I wouldn't have done the same, but I said "He probably didn't mean it that way."

"No," Joan said bitterly, "you're probably right."

We stared at the dust struggling in the air above the railway lines sharpened by light. "I got your note," I said.

"I didn't leave one," Joan said, then reconsidered. "Oh, John, you shouldn't have!"

"Well, I have."

"Thank you ever so much."

I felt safe in taking her hand. "There's no need to be so grateful."

"Sometimes I think it's gratitude that keeps me going." She watched the last weary particles of dust sinking to rest until the next train. "Did you get octopus tentacles?" she asked.

"Not even squid."

"Neither did I. A negative coincidence!" Briefly she squeezed my hand. "The only kind I know," she said, and stood up. "Let's go and eat some of our food," she said.

As we started down the broken road I said "I had the feeling earlier that I was being followed."

"I wish I was." She stared down the hill, past a lamppost balanced on the stump of its standard like a limbless dwarf. "Why, there's— Oh no, it isn't. I must have been mistaken."

"You must have been," I said. "There's nobody in sight."

After we'd eaten omelettes at an uncertain six o'clock Joan said "Would you be suffocated if I played my Debussy?" She lay back on the couch. I glanced at her often, but her face was calm and closed as the shifting disloyal ruses of *Jeux* passed beneath it. Among the records shovelled into a corner I found a Stockhausen, and played that. The dabs and points of music fell together into an intricate pattern, like a kaleidoscope. For some reason, however, I thought of the desperate accumulation of detail that supports unrequited love.

Abruptly Joan sat up. "I must run round the corner for a minute," she said. "I won't be long."

At eight o'clock I left the flat. Habituated, my feet made for the Wordsworth Lane pub. Then I thought of the Union, and turned back. I was determined not to look up at the house on Milton Street, and I restrained myself until the last second. Then I hurried onward. I had seen a light extinguished on the staircase. That was all, I told myself. The light had gone out, and this had caused the effect I'd seen: a silhouetted figure that had suddenly expanded and blotted out the entire window.

The Union still retained a semblance of end-of-term life: in the film society students were tittering, catcalling and stamping at an Ingmar Bergman film. In the bar one group was playing cards with frequent cries of "Harrison!", a concrete poet was intoning "Norman's nose", a middle-aged man in a leather jacket was selling copies of *Black Dwarf*. I forced my way to the bar and gasped halfway through a pint of beer. "Alone?" Amos asked.

"Briefly."

"I'd like to wish you luck," he said, "but I honestly don't know whether I can."

"I'll try to do without your luck, then," I said. I finished the beer and made my way out, past the first overturned stool of the evening.

On Milton Street I felt hungry again. As I passed the grey Victorian house the door opened. I refused to look. Footsteps hurried down to the street as I reached Wordsworth Lane. I joined the queue inside the fish and chip shop. A minute later the door juddered open and Joan entered, throwing a Kleenex into the gutter as she did so. "I'm sorry you're hungry," she said.

"I always have supper at this time."

"Twenty to nine?"

"My God," I said, "I thought it was eleven. My watch must have stopped last night." I tried not to betray how disturbed I was. "Will you have something?" I asked.

"Not for me. Not now."

I ordered chips from the Cypriot owner. Folk music played on a tape recorder: notes harsh as plucked tin, a tenor voice flapping in trapped anguish. Over the mirror behind the bar of the potato-slicer hung a calendar portrait of a soulful girl. Joan stared at her; squares of light lay flat on her eyes. "I wish I had her face," she said.

"Why? You're singularly attractive as you are."

But her eyes were still mirrors of the mirror. I couldn't project my sincerity; I had the voice of a television interviewer, I knew. Once when I'd heard myself on tape I'd been depressed for weeks. "I'm not trying to be tactful, however it may sound," I said. "You appeal to me, I know that."

She disengaged another Kleenex from the sleeve of her lime dress. "I'm going back to the flat," she blurted. "I think I've got a cold."

When I returned to the flat she'd made coffee. Her eyes were red. I emptied the chips onto a plate and passed it to her, but she shook her head. She poured coffee and sugared it for me. I ate the chips and washed the plate, recoiling from the thick heat which bulged in through the open window. I sat down opposite Joan and she looked at me for a long time. "I won't ask what happened," I said.

"Gil." She waited. "He has the studio above Amos," she said.

"You'd better tell me everything," I said, "or nothing at all."

"When did you last feel there wasn't any point in going on?"

"Recently."

"If only I had a choice," she said. She stared out of the window at a footstep, stared as if its owner might pad up the wall and balance on the windowsill. "There isn't much that isn't cliché," she said. "I met Gil two years ago. That was when he was depressed. More than usual. He told me I might be able to help with his paintings. He paints as if he's operating on himself. Without anaesthetic. He wanted to do an exhibition to sum up Lower Brichester. He said I could help him sum it up. I still don't know how, but he did paint me. Not that it looked like me. It was so beautiful. I remember, that first night I was posing he came up to me and hit me because I moved."

"But tonight you got tired of it," I suggested.

"No, you're utterly wrong. That first night I realised he was dedicated. He knew where he was going. I fell in love with him."

My expression of disquiet must have struck her as one of interest. She went on: "About six months ago he left. It was Amos. Gil said he couldn't live so close to what he was trying to express. It confused him, he said, and something else—he said that Amos was spying into regions he wasn't equipped to come to terms with, Amos was surrounding him with chaos. We had a great scene in the middle of Milton Street. I said he couldn't—oh, couldn't leave me, you know. But he just hailed a taxi that was passing and never gave me his address."

She fumbled for a Kleenex. "They say this is good for you, don't they? Like going to the bog." She screwed the Kleenex into a ball. "Then just after Amos had this let's-all-make-the-house-come-alive acid party, Gil came back. About a month ago. I was walking past the house thinking about him and there he was, in the window on the stairs. He must be keeping out of Amos's way—that's why Amos never hears him in the studio. Although even to me he hardly seems tangible, he hardly seems there since he's come back. Yet everything around him suddenly comes so sharp, so immediate—oh, I can't explain. I think at the moment he's terribly depressed. But I know something must come of it."

"And tonight?"

"I saw him for two minutes."

"I'd have said two hours."

She stared at me. "I only said: 'I have someone staying at the flat, would you like to meet him?'"

"And he replied?"

"'No,'" she said, and sobbed.

I leaned forward and took her hand; she couldn't have seen my hesitation. "What do you get from all this?" What are your feelings on the present political situation?

"It sounds so simple to answer." Her hand was limp but pulsing.

"Can you say that you're helping him?"

"Not any more." Her hand moved in mine, then gripped.

"Don't you realise—for God's sake, surely you realise that you deserve a better relationship that this?"

"Sometimes." Her head drooped; she bowed forward; one more inch and we would touch. I stood and, lifting her to her feet, put an arm about her shoulders. "He never said I was beautiful," she said. I stroked her shoulders. Very slowly, we were walking.

But when her thighs gripped me like the rollers of a mangle I no longer felt desire; I hoped compassion would be enough.

It must have been past one o'clock when I awoke. Across the roofs wailed the crescendo of a siren. My legs were tangled in blankets on the edge of the couch; Joan hadn't wanted me to sleep with her. I raised my head at a scrape of metal. She was slicing lettuce over the sink. I dragged myself free of the blankets and she said "Just a second and I'll leave you alone."

She bit mouthfuls from a lettuce leaf and picked up the percolator through her handkerchief. Balancing my plate on the edge of the sink, I watched her. Head bent, she filled the cups. At last I took her wrist and laid my arm along hers.

"No, John," she said, not looking up. "I'm torn enough as it is."

We stood separate, poised; outside the window footsteps chopped the padded air like sharp dropped rocks. Joan thrust one leg onto the balcony and peered down. "Amos!" she called to a silence.

"Perhaps he doesn't want to hear," she said, returning. "I'm going across to speak to him."

"Shall I come with you?"

"I suppose so."

Amos was arranging shirts to hide a matchbox at the bottom of a drawer; behind his head the lighthouse stroked the wall with pale pink gleams. "I thought you might be over," he told Joan. "I heard you calling but I couldn't see you."

"Is Natasha here?"

"She's out hunting for food."

"Listen, Amos," Joan said. "Let her go. She's young yet, she isn't in deep enough to be caught. She doesn't have to stay."

"But she wants to stay," Amos said.

Joan glanced at me, appealing. I was mute; I wondered what I would have done if Joan had been ten years younger and I'd lived here.

"Perhaps I'll see her later," Joan said. "Amos, would you let me know if Gil comes in, please? Though I suppose you still won't hear him."

"You're wrong," Amos told her. "He kept us awake half the night. It felt like a storm overhead. As if the house was closing in."

"Is he here now?" Joan cried.

"No," Amos said. "Listen, when he left I understood he wasn't coming back."

"Well, now he has."

"Apparently."

Back at Joan's flat we discovered that neither of us had a key. "Oh, break it down," Joan said.

I butted the door with my shoulder to weaken the lock. About to attack it in earnest, I discovered that I'd already torn the entire lock free. Dismay at its weakness left me open to depression: Joan had relied on me but smashing the lock had made me feel an intruder. "I can't repair it," I said.

"Why should you? Lower Brichester is one big room."

I watched her roll up the blankets and sit on the couch. Two minutes later she said "I'm just going out." Before I had time to sort through the records she'd returned. "If you wouldn't mind, John," she said, "I have the beginnings of a headache." I took Keats from the bookshelf and opened *Lamia*. Joan stood up and leaned over the balcony, surveying the view from Milton Street to the churned clay hill. She turned, one hand on the balcony rail. "I'm sorry, I'm not going to be very good company," she said. "Why don't you go out? You haven't seen Brichester properly."

"I take your point," I said.

In central Brichester women stood and stared at clothed dummies, boys posted wads of Inland Revenue correspondence, men sold minute deflated versions of gigantic inflated balloons in clusters like pawnbroker's signs, polished glistening husbands carried their wives' shopping to long polished cars watched by traffic wardens. At six o'clock I dodged into a restaurant and ate steak in the shadow of plastic flowers. "Very good, thank you," I said four times, the last time choking. This was the sort of place where you dined on the first date.

The evening heat settled like steam on a bathroom wall. The cinema was cooler. At the end of *River of No Return* I was moved when Marilyn Monroe clung to Mitchum and escaped the river, time or life or whatever it symbolised. Yet could one escape? In reality she'd taken her place in the river now, a gentle rock, a small statue. She could never have trudged about with the crowd outside the cinema. And if she had created something, so did Lower Brichester. It might be as transient as the falling woven colours of a kaleidoscope, but central Brichester was no more than a loop of film. Joan wasn't, could never be, part of central Brichester. At least she had shown her willingness to escape.

It was midnight when I reached Keats Street, having walked in the wake of the last bus. Outside the house on Milton Street the streetlamp had failed. The window on the stairs was as black as the rest of the house. The moon urged the shadow of the building toward Keats Street.

Joan's flat was dark. I thought I would have to knock, but instead of a chair under the knob only a wad of Kleenex locked the door. The hall was full of Joan's faint breathing. I tiptoed into the main room. Moonlight slanted past the window. The blankets were spread neatly on the couch, but somehow I was reminded of a dustsheet. I caught up cold water to displace the stale air like breath that oppressed my face, undressed and lay down on the couch.

I couldn't sleep; all I could manage was a restless doze beneath the weight of air. My thoughts turned restlessly with me. If Joan could free herself of Amos's art class, of Amos—but that would mean climbing free of the whole of Lower Brichester. Gil? He was too shadowy for me to consider. I couldn't think. The heat was warping my brain. In delirium I'd often felt as if I were at the wrong end of a telescope with something vast peering down at me, its ponderous movements reverberating silently against my ear. Now it was beside me. It had awakened. The whole room seemed to spring alert. I struggled to heave off my thoughts as the night pressed down on me like a body.

When a breeze creaked at the window I started. My own heat prickled. The breeze should lighten the thick air. I lay waiting. The creak was insistent, and a cat moaned in the street. Suddenly I struggled upright, and the entire weighted crowded room tilted with me. What had creaked? Not the balcony, not the window. Had it been a cat that moaned? Around me hung the lightless oppression that awaits the first burst of thunder. I stared at the walls that separated me from Joan, from the sounds. I had a tense constricting premonition that the oppression might be split, that Joan would cry out. But around me delirium hung inert, stagnant and satisfied. There was nothing I could do. Five minutes later I went blank and fell asleep.

Again I awoke at lunchtime. Joan was washing her face at the sink. For a moment I decided that I'd been dreaming. Then she gripped the sink to support herself as she splashed her face.

"Give me five minutes," I said, "and I'll buy you lunch."

Two streets away we found a Chinese restaurant. By the door a businessman was sawing at a curried chicken leg amid an expanding pool of sauce. The menu offered six different preparations of pig's offal. Joan finished her sweet and sour and smiled weakly. I took a last gulp of saki. "Joan," I said, "about one o'clock this morning—"

She turned crimson and told her plate "I wish you hadn't mentioned that."

"All three minutes of it," I said harshly.

"It seemed longer," she said. I thought she was going to weep. I was mutely infuriated. None of this was our fault.

I knew she wanted to be alone. I took her back to the flat and left her. At half past five I drank among tired faces at the Union. Afterwards I walked, returning at intervals to Milton Street. There was no sign of life in the grey house. I remembered Joan confronting Amos.

At ten o'clock I strode toward Keats Street. If nothing else, I could buy Joan a drink. What could she be musing over, alone among the strewn records? I passed the house on Milton Street, and as I did so the street-lamp lit. I glanced up at the house, flat and bright as a cut-out against the darkened sky. Then the front door opened and Amos emerged.

As I ran forward I knew what I would say. "Hold on, Amos. I'm going in."

He blocked the door feebly with his arm. "Don't go in. Even I can't stand it any more. Natasha's gone home because she can't stand the feel of the place. For shit's sake, come on and I'll buy you a drink."

"I can't, Amos. There's something I must do," I said. "Sorry about Natasha," and I was inside.

The door slammed. Amos's head bobbed mournfully out of sight beyond the frosted pane. I made for the stairs.

When I couldn't find the switch I climbed the stairs in darkness. Halfway up the stairs, still vainly watching for the window on the street, I felt menaced. The house was too empty; it seemed hollow; the stairs felt like paper that would tear beneath my feet at the next step. I slammed my foot down, hearing the echo in a hollow room, and strode to the top. At the studio door I knocked. It swung inward.

I groped for the rusty insecure switch. The light blazed through dust. Dust on the floor, where footprints crossed like the marks of a bar fight in sawdust; dust on the single piece of furniture, a scrolled couch; dust on a confusion of easels, on a stack of paintings laid against the wall beside perhaps more wrapped in brown paper. From the uppermost painting Joan smiled radiantly at me.

I strode forward, kicking dust from my toes. I lifted the first painting and was about to turn its face to the wall when my fingers traced a piece of cardboard taped to the back. It was a photograph of a young morose bearded man; he'd signed across himself—"Gil". I laid down the painting and turned to the next. Joan looked puzzled. In the next she was uneasy, then downcast. In the last she was weeping. I gazed into her wet eyes, then glanced at the parcel in brown paper.

When it came to the confrontation for which I was determined to wait, I would have shown my strength. I picked the tape loose and un-folded the brown paper. As the corners parted like a curtain Joan peered out nervously. I stared at her and hurriedly turned to her next phase. Her eyes looked scared. There was one more painting. I pried into its hiding place and fell back. Joan gazed at me in naked terror.

I couldn't begin to think about the artist. Thunder was gathering; stifling air seemed to pour into the room. I squatted and examined the painting, but its age was uncertain. I was trying to analyse Joan's eyes out of my mind. When I glanced up they were wide, almost as if staring hysterically beyond my shoulder. Heat was pressing on the back of my neck. I grabbed for the next to last painting to cover up Joan's terror. As I did so I caught sight of a puff of dust creeping along the floor. Someone was behind me.

I whirled, off balance, and saw Joan.

As I teetered my hand came down on a corner of Joan's fear, which snapped. I looked down at it, then at her. There was nothing I could say.

"John," Joan said, moving forward: the heat and the suspended thunder crept forward with her. "It doesn't matter! Not to me!"

I half rose, confused. She ran forward and caught my hands, pulling me up and against her.

"Wait," I said. The boiling pendulous air lapped me; my thoughts were melting. "Let me take you back," I said. But she was pulling me toward the couch; our tracks cut deep into the dust, her shadow spread across the floor like a stain, absorbing my own. "Not here, Joan," I said.

"Yes, here! That's precisely it! Don't you see?" I disengaged myself; by God, all of a sudden she had the strength of a man. "*Don't* you see? Won't you give me this?" she pleaded.

I shook my head and tried to lead her to the door, but she sat down stubbornly on the couch. The thunder in the room was pounding my skull. I didn't intend to be used as a symbol. "At your place, Joan," I told her and hurried downstairs.

I stood on the corner of Keats Street and waited. The moon was cooling the night. Minutes later the door of the grey house opened and Joan emerged. No, it wasn't Joan; there was something wrong with her face. I started forward and realised that this must be another girl. But surely she was wearing Joan's flowered dress? Joan with a man's bearded face? I had reached the middle of the street when a crushed pain exploded like a storm in my brain and clamped my hands to my skull. When I opened my eyes I saw Gil in a sweater and jeans hurrying into Joan's house.

Joan's flat was unlit when I staggered upstairs. Their voices murmured briefly, then were silent. I battered at the door, but it held against my trembling shoulder. In the flat above I heard someone padding to the stairwell to discover the reason for the disturbance. What reason could I give? Suddenly afraid of the whole of Lower Brichester, I ran out into the street and stood in the pale night, staring up at Joan's window, black as a storm cloud.

At last I returned to Gil's studio, rammed the couch against the door and slept on it. It was the only victory left to me.

At nine o'clock next morning I brushed dust from my turn-ups and returned to Joan's flat. On the clay waste at the end of Keats Street a mechanical shovel opened its claw and dribbled clay. Her door swung open at a touch; the lock still hung dislocated. The flat was empty. The bed was shapeless; her painted shoes lay crushed in a corner; on the scattered records blobs of strawberry jam bulged like pimples. On the windowsill lay two rent books, Joan's and that for the studio. I packed my case, jammed the door shut with a Kleenex and left.

But in central Brichester, swept away by the suffocating crowds, I felt that I'd allowed myself to be carried away from Joan. I stood and pondered; the crowd eddied muttering around my suitcase. I caught up the case and made for the address on the rent books.

When I emerged I stood for a blinded minute, my case dragging at my hand like a restless child. My mind was burned bare as the sky. Then I began to walk very fast toward the railway station. The studio on Milton Street was rented to Joan. God knows where she found the money. Perhaps her acid-summoned incubus could make money appear. I was ready to believe anything, for the landlord had convinced me that although the studio might still be in use, nobody had lived in it for six months.

Broadcast

We were only fourteen years old, for God's sake. Only intermittently did we remember to try to think and act as adults. It was six years ago. I'd gone that evening to the Radio Brichester studio with Ste—with whom I lost contact two years later, when our attitudes to life began to sketch themselves in and clash. With a mixture of flattery and genuine enthusiasm we'd persuaded Mr Rolands, our art master, to allow us to watch him record one of his occasional broadcasts.

It was seven o'clock in the evening. In the street beneath the wide Cinemascope office windows above which the studio was hidden, the streetlamps were daubed with gold, and beneath our feet crunched like scattered breakfast cereal those clenched leaves that creep mysteriously into treeless urban streets. We took a silver-grey muffled lift to the fifth floor and the world was walled out.

There had been a fire at Radio Brichester the previous night; we were eager to see the damage. But the Reception foyer was empty of damage and of receptionist, although on the switchboard red paper crosses were pasted over some of the sockets. We disarranged the BBC leaflets on the low tables and Ste said "Shall we wait?"

"Nobody's here," I said. "Let's find Mr Rolands."

Ahead of us led a long white corridor reticently menacing as a hospital, inhuman as a dream of a papered maze where you shrink to an anonymous helpless point. However, we were growing up, and over the exit from Reception a speaker sang a pop song that we knew. We strode forward.

In some of the rooms we glimpsed effects of the fire. One office was stacked with grey dripping scripts and pamphlets, and tapes spilled onto desks from cardboard boxes. In one deserted studio the window over the tape decks had burst and framed an empty star, surrounded by tips of charred wood; we inhaled the stale stench of blackened plastic. The second studio was closed and full of gesticulating shirt-sleeved men. Before we reached the last studio we felt secure again, for we could hear Mr Rolands' voice. But two paces closer we made out his words.

"Come on, Mal," he was exhorting, "get that booze cupboard open."

"There's a good few local pundits available to us, not to mention eager," a light male voice reminded him.

"If you can open that cupboard to every nineteen-year-old who's able to smear paint on canvas within ten miles of Brichester—"

"I'll see whether I can find the key. After you've recorded the programme."

We peered through the pane in the door. Mr Rolands was standing by a tape deck with his tie thrown round the back of his neck like a rope, his hands hanging defeated. A young man in a pink open-necked shirt and fawn trousers was regarding him and turning knobs on a control panel. We knocked and entered.

"Why hello, boys," Mr Rolands cried in what we could see was manufactured welcome. "These are Adrian and Steven. This is Malcolm."

"Malcolm Hughes," the young man at the tape deck said, implying Mr Hughes.

"They'll be quiet, won't you, boys?"

We nodded. "Do you really want to use them in the programme?" Malcolm, as we'd determined to think of him, said.

"We'll see how the introduction goes," Mr Roland said quickly.

"Mike thought he might interview you on what art means to you," Malcolm told us. "He throws out all sorts of ideas on the spur of the moment."

Of course hadn't known; we were excited and terrified, punched unexpectedly in the plexus of our adolescence. "You can start as soon as you're ready," Malcolm said.

"Where do I start?"

"At the beginning."

"Yes, but I mean I've done the piece on sculpture."

"Unfortunately," Malcolm said, switching on a tape recorder: a smoked hoarse bass voice thundered, choked, burst out again.

Mr Rolands paled. "That can't be me," he said.

"It was until the fire," Malcolm told him. "You two stay out here. I'll turn on the overhead speaker."

We tried to look nonchalant on swivel chairs. Mr Rolands, still pale, gave us a forced grin and hurried through two doors like an airlock into the recording studio. Through a window over the control panel at which Malcolm sat we could see into the studio as into a private ward: Mr Rolands sitting alone at a circular table through which a microphone protruded. He took out a pad and leafed through it. "All right, Rolo," Malcolm said into his own microphone. "If you just run through your opening lines I'll check your level."

Rolo! We dragged our chairs back where Mr Rolands couldn't see us and spluttered, spinning wildly. Malcolm glanced at us wryly as he donned headphones like earmuffs. "Come in closer to the mike, Mike. That's fine," he said and Mr Rolands fell silent. "Sorry, by the way. I seem to have exposed one of your dark secrets."

"Well, that's journalism," Mr Rolands said harshly.

"There's enough room left on Janice's tape for you. Talk straight through if you can."

"I can," Mr Rolands said. "Let's get going."

"I'll give you a green in ten seconds," Malcolm told him. We watched the red second hand of the studio clock picking off the seconds; we couldn't see whether Mr Rolands was as tense as he sounded. In the foreshortened corner of the inner studio we saw a green light flare. Malcolm pointed his finger and pulled the trigger.

"Art in Brichester?" Mr Rolands said, falsely offhand. "Some of you may wonder where it is—" but somehow his voice exploded, scraping the microphone and jarring the studio. Malcolm grimaced and switched off the tape. "Don't overload, darling," he pleaded tightly. "I've told you I've just enough space on the tape."

"I'm not overloading. You took my level."

"Wait a minute and I'll check. Say something," Malcolm told him and exchanged wires.

"Such as what? There was a young lady of Bali, who took such a fancy to Dali—"

"That ought to be foolproof," Malcolm said, adjusting his headphones.

"It's a good job you stopped me there." We could imagine Mr Rolands composing his face, his thoughts and his voice. The green light flared. Mr Rolands cleared his throat. "Art in Brichester? Some of you may wonder where it is—" but now his voice rattled faintly like tin. Malcolm slashed his hands at the window in a cross, an exorcism. "It's the bloody mike," he said. "Hang on and I'll come in there. Mike trouble," he threw at us as he rushed through the airlock.

"Do you want to be interviewed?" Ste hissed at me.

"If Mr Rolands interviews us it'll be all right," I said.

"Rolo," Ste said and snorted uncontrollably. No doubt he would spread it all round the school, I thought.

We stared at the record covers in a cabinet until Malcolm returned; the studio lacked windows, the only light was blue as ice. "Mike trouble all the time," he complained and replaced his headphones. "Try it once again. I can't see anything wrong with the equipment."

"All these re-runs are liable to destroy whatever coherence I have," Mr Rolands said.

"It's hardly my fault. Green in twenty seconds."

When the light flashed Mr Rolands enquired wearily: "Art in Brichester? Some of you may wonder where it is—" and his voice was huge again; the speaker buzzed and snarled. "Dear God," Malcolm cried. "Keep talking. I'll bring Brian in to find out what it is."

He ran out. "Keep talking, indeed," said Mr Rolands' gigantic voice. "Don't worry about all this, boys. The perils of presenting yourself to an audience, you know, of making yourself presentable."

"I don't think that interview will transpire," I said awkwardly to Ste.

"He doesn't sound as if he'd be up to it, anyway."

Malcolm flung the door open. "Talk, will you, darling, for God's sake," he shouted at his microphone. "They think it may have something to do with the fire. I'm going out to find Brian. He's in the pub, they tell me. Keep talking, and these two can stop you if it rights itself. Did you understand all that?" he panted at us.

"Some of it," I said sharply, but he'd gone.

"All right, I'll talk," Mr Rolands boomed. "Are you listening? There was a young lady of Bali—no, I decided against that, didn't I. What would you like me to say? Well, I'll think of something, you'd better not touch that microphone. You can come out where I can see you if you like. No, on second thoughts don't, you'll only put me off. Let me see. If I can find my notes I'll give you a preview of tomorrow's lesson. Don't worry, I'm joshing you. What is there to talk about, in heaven's name?"

He was quiet for a moment. "I wouldn't like to have to do that," Ste said.

"He'll manage."

Mr Rolands returned, louder than before and very fast. "The studio in which I find myself is a pale green box. Around me are five deserted chairs encircling a table with a green felt top. I could play Patience. One hundred, no, one hundred and about ten degrees away on my left is a glass ashtray with rests for cigarettes, black as nicotine-tipped teeth. Ahead of me is a dead green light bulb on the edge of an only slightly less than square window through which I can see another pale green wall, an edge of the control panel and a rack of records. It's a painter's purgatory. Am I doing all right? Can I stop now?"

"Go on, tell him to go on," Ste hissed.

"He will. We don't have to tell him," I said, for I wouldn't have known what to say.

"Am I boring you? I'm boring myself. What can you talk about in this anonymous box? If I had a mirror I'd describe myself. Here I am, thirty-four years old and balding fast. Shall I lecture? I would if I gave lectures these days. I can't remember any. It's much easier to teach, you know, they can't contradict you. Don't repeat my jokes, will you, boys? It's my masochism talking. Ah, masochism. The only honest relationship. My God, it's impossible to cohere in front of this tin cobra!" A magnified thud fell from the speaker; Ste and I started. Mr Rolands must have thumped the table.

"All right, let's take the microphone. I'll get my own back, I'll describe it. It's like a disposal unit. It's draining me away. I don't know how much of me remains. The tape is carrying my voice away. It isn't my voice any more, it's a series of electronic impulses or something. I'm sure you know more about that sort of thing than I do. Myself, I can't fix a fuse without blowing a dozen more. Though of course one could think of circumstances where that might be exactly what was needed. Do you know what a girl said to me once? It wasn't once, it was last week . . . It's the tape, you see, carrying me away. You do realise out there that I'm joshing, do you? Only joshing. Come on, Malcolm, for Christ's sake where are you?"

"He can't be long," I said desperately.

"Malcolm darling, are you out there, you bastard? Come on, show yourself, you wouldn't want me to review you and the leggy telephonist. Ah, so you're not there. In that case I can talk. Are you a little shocked, boys? This doesn't sound at all like what the housewives thrill to, does it? You see, you never really know anyone. Least of all yourself. The things you do to get onto the air. Masochism again. Don't put your daughter on the studio floor, Mrs Worthington—"

He was singing. I glanced aghast at Ste, who was shaking and snorting.

"Enough of that. I'll close my eyes, perhaps I can keep hold of myself that way. And count to a hundred, if you like. Ah, it's warmer in here. Now, what was I saying that was worth hearing? Eh? Well, tell me, for God's sake! Do you see, we all need an audience to define ourselves. No, I don't need an audience, just one person. Perhaps she'll be listening. No, I'm rambling, this isn't even being recorded, it's just draining me away. I used to talk to her like this—no wonder she left. She'll hear the programme, though. What good would that do?"

There was silence except for his colossal breathing. "Where's that fellow Malcolm?" I demanded of Ste. "It's his fault."

"He'll be back," Ste whispered. "Shh."

"Where did he say Brian was?" Mr Rolands mused hugely. "In the pub, of course. I should be there now. By God I should."

Silence again. I wouldn't look at Ste. I stared at the blank wall and yearned for a window. Or anything to distract me from the silence.

Mr Rolands coughed; I leapt back before I'd had a chance to peer through at him. "You see, talking's meaningless unless you talk to someone. You need someone to catch what you've said and throw it back at you. Then you know what you've said. Otherwise what you say fades instantly and that part of you is gone. Until at last you've nothing more to say and you no longer exist."

The clock ticked like the drip of water the Chinese used. Say something, I pleaded silently. You must say something.

"If I die before the tapes, will they be me or not?"

Tick. Drip. Tip. Drick. I leapt up and pushed the door into the inner studio. I heaved at it. Perhaps it locked from the inside to prevent interruptions. "I'm going to find someone who can use the microphone," I told Ste. "Stay here."

I ran down the shadowless corridor. Through the door of the next studio I saw men gathered around a control panel; none of them was Malcolm. I wrenched open the door beneath the red light. Bent under headphones, one man twisted knobs desperately as a pilot diving for disaster, snatching forth music and voices and crackling static. I didn't know it then, but it was like those moments at a party when the people and their speech are no longer significant and only the mass of sound exists. One man half-strangled by the sleeves of a sports coat swung round to me. "Get out, you bloody child!" he cried. "Can't you see we're recording?"

I didn't realise that he'd given me the chance to talk; I bolted back to the other studio. "Has he said anything?" I panted at Ste.

"Not since you went. He's going round the twist!" Ste giggled.

"Listen, go and find Malcolm. He's in one of the pubs. You look older than me." Ste gaped. "Go on, go on! Tell him it's an emergency!" I shouted.

Ste still gaped. I shoved him out into the corridor. "Mad," he tittered.

The studio walls seemed to suck invisibly inward with Mr Rolands' breathing. I stood and swallowed my terror. Then I hurried to the control panel, to the microphone. The microphone was switched off; otherwise he would have heard me cry out. All six chairs around the table were empty.

I shut my eyes and shrivelled. Then, furiously, I opened them again and frantically searched for the knob Malcolm had turned. A switch looked familiar. I pressed it and shouted "Mr Rolands!"

My shout must have deafened him. He boomed weakly "I suppose so."

"Mr Rolands," I stammered. I didn't know him as a man, only as a teacher; I tried to forget what I'd heard. "Where are you? I can't see you."

"I don't know where I am. Am I at all?"

I couldn't answer; the knobs were slippery as onions beneath my palm. If only I could keep talking until Malcolm returned.

"What do you mean, you can't see me? My eyes are shut but yours aren't. Oh God." The entire speaker shuddered. "Don't tell me. I don't want to know. I don't want to talk any more."

He must have sunk onto the floor, I thought desperately. That's why I can't see him. Perhaps he's ill. "I mean I can't see you from where I'm standing," I said.

The speaker shook with coughs of laughter. "You'll grow up well, I can tell that. I was always fond of you, you know. When you were in my class. At least I can say that."

"I'm in your class!" I cried. "Hang on, I'll come round where I can see you. Yes, there you are, of course!"

"I wish there were more like you," the speaker said, and sighed. "All right, give me proof. God, how I need proof. There's my hand. What am I doing with it?"

I stared into the deserted studio; I realised I was weeping. My hands clenched on the knobs; I almost fled. I coughed. I tried to cough until Malcolm came.

"Come on, now," the speaker said. "A simple question. What am I doing with my hand?"

I swallowed and blinked. "Waving," I said.

And then there was only silence.

The Urge

I hardly know why I went into the coffee bar, except that it was close to the theatre where I'd just interviewed the cast, half in and half out of their togas and personalities, in a long low plaster dressing-room barred with spears and hung with masks. Just a jungle hut, I'd thought when an actor had screamed "Get out, puppet-master!" at the director. I'd strolled across to the coffee bar to translate my shorthand hooks into some sort of draft for the newspaper. Beneath the hasty murals of neon vistas and the hanging baskets of plastic flowers, the flattened mushroom tables were all occupied by couples and groups driving questions into one another. Trying not to appear patronising, I grinned at the owner as he served me. The coffee machine gurgled as he'd gurgled six months before when I'd interviewed him on the opening of the coffee bar, his answers as parched as the machine. I sat down at a table opposite a young man with long hair bedraggled as by rain, although it was a sharp dry February night. I sipped my coffee and reached for my notes, and he said "As soon as you sat down I knew I was going to dislike you."

I gazed at him: jeans and a black sweater with a pink glimpse of flesh at the elbow. Years of meeting disapproval and hostility had prepared me for this. "I thought you were supposed to love everyone," I said.

"Oh, you're one of those," he said wearily.

"Surely I don't look like one."

"My God, can't I ever miss out a step? You're one of the label-mongers. Don't you know any people?"

"People are my job."

He grimaced as he might have at a child's foolishness and stared out of the window on my left, at the sky. Perhaps it would have been simpler for me to find another table. But I detest retreating, and he seemed a challenge. "What exactly do you dislike about me?" I asked.

"That question, to begin with."

"Significant," I said. "It must be something within yourself. I'd advise you to analyse your reaction for your own good." I didn't realise that I was merely fighting back; I thought I was enjoying myself because for once I could probe deeper than the *Brichester Herald* allowed. But he was peering again through his hair at the sky. After a moment he glanced angrily at me. "All right," he said. "Look at the way you're holding your cup. Effeminate."

"Effeminate? I could introduce you to so many girls—" My hand had closed on the cup with a determinedly masculine grip before I grasped that his insult had almost succeeded in making me leave. I'd been shown the door and sat waiting with my next question too often to be tricked. "Of course we all betray ourselves at times," I admitted. "You, for instance. What are you so unsure of? Yourself?"

"Ha ha. No, wrong line," he said and completely bored, leaned back on his stool and let his eyes encounter the stars outside the window.

"I thought you hippies were supposed to have found a solution."

"I'm not a hippie," he replied abstractedly. "I'm me."

"In that case why are you chasing a fashion?"

"I was here first," he said. "I couldn't care less if it's long or I'm bald. I don't like to be touched, that's all. People touching me drag me down. Like they were hanging weights on me."

"You like to look at the sky," I perceived.

"Yes."

"And the stars. Like holes in the sky."

"No, not like holes in the sky," he mimicked. "Like stars."

"You don't respect style?"

"I don't respect anything people have invented. I use the words I'm stuck with. As few as possible."

"You don't believe in communication?" I began to see a way to break him down. Briefly I hesitated: perhaps he needed his defences. But no, nobody needs dishonesty. Losing one's defences is the first step to maturity, I've always told myself when those I've interviewed have cried or shouted. "You must have something to communicate," I said. "Surely you feel you're worth communicating."

His head jerked up. "To whom? Show me someone who's worth it. Look at them! You still holding your cup like that, him over there pulling his beard out and sucking it, that girl with him, look, propping her mouth shut and trying to look like a psychoanalyst in love— Puppets, all of you, acting out your idiosyncrasies as if they make you individuals. You interrupt the universe. Like that window." Like the sky, his dark eyes glittered yet were tranquil, I noted uneasily. "Out there is reality. No more acting."

"Then you should go out there," I suggested. I was sure I'd brought him down to earth.

"I shall," he said. "I climb."

"Climb," I repeated.

"Trees and roofs. I use cough syrup for fuel."

"I see."

"To get back out there."

"Back?"

"It's where I came from. It created me. Everything man creates is propaganda for himself. What's your defence?"

"Against what?"

"Everything. Must I use clichés? What do you do, as your aunt would say."

"I work for the *Brichester Herald.*"

"You mean you reduce people to columns of instant print. How many editors does what you write go through? If people can be brought lower, which I'd have thought was impossible, then people like you do it."

"I thought you were too contemptuous of people to care."

"I was one myself once."

"Aren't you now?"

"I'm determined not to be. Not what you think of as a person, anyway. Come on, show me what you claim in that paper."

I disarrayed the *Herald* on the table and found a headline: *Fire Kills Three.*

"Three what? Okapis? Kangaroos? Why do you expect me to assume they were human beings, why should they have exclusive priority? As if it mattered anyway. But God, it annoys me. Listen, that headline's evidence enough of how desperate you are to interest people in people! Show me one way man can prove he's not an animal!"

"He thinks."

"Thinks? What does that mean? Sets up defences?"

The owner of the coffee bar gripped the table and leaned between us. "Sorry to interrupt your discussion, but last orders, gentlemen."

"Coke, please," I ordered sharply and watched his quick inadvertent nod. My companion, if that was what he was, caught my eye and grinned faintly. "You may make it sometime," he told me, "if you ever use your contempt for people as a beginning. Surely I can't be the only one to see."

The waitress brought my Coke. Had it not been for the effervescence on my tongue, the strings of rain which had begun to melt on the window, the hypnotic jerking miniskirt of the waitress, perhaps I might have made that blind leap which leads to revelation. But what revelation could cough syrup offer?

"What would you do," I asked, "to make people see?"

"I'd persuade them to stop eating, drinking, depending on others. That would be the first thing, to evolve beyond this biological and psychological machinery which we all think's so wonderful. Then I'd have everyone sit alone and think for the rest of their lives. No, not think. Absorb."

"And then?"

"And then they wouldn't be able to. Why? Because they'd be weighed down by one thing: knowing someday they would die. That's the whole point. Not to notice you've died, because it's not important."

"But your perceptions would change."

"Balls, if you think that's an objection," he said. "From perceiving the universe you become the universe. Your body and brain cease to be obstacles. That's true perception."

The owner began to scurry between the tables, coughing and pointing out the time. "Listen," I said hastily. "If I could prove I was serious, would you agree to an interview? Not for the *Herald,* of course. For an intelligent magazine."

"I couldn't care less. No, I won't have the time. Anyway, show me an intelligent magazine. Anyone intelligent would have found out everything I've told you by himself, and he wouldn't bother reading magazines. My God, you don't imagine I'd let you reduce me!" Abruptly he stood up and, before I had a chance to speak, had left.

I folded the *Herald*. I couldn't write about what had happened and yet I felt it was imperative. All at once I let the *Herald* slip to the floor and hurried out.

Beneath the streetlamps sheets of rain ballooned and deflated. Halfway down the street, between the irregular patterns of light from high Victorian windows, I saw him. Head down, he strode into the angled silver rain. Once he halted, threw back his head and drained a small bottle. I hastened in pursuit.

Where the rain rushed bodily across a block of waste ground, he turned left. Surrounded by sucking pools of mud and dark rain indistinguishable from flat stones, a deserted tower stood protected by a circle of iron spears. Yards ahead of me he plodded, squelched, dripped, but never faltered or looked back. A path of slippery planks conducted me past the tower, so that I was almost at his heels when he reached the gate in the railings.

As I stepped into the hissing mud one plank resounded against another. He vaulted the gate and, as I reached it, glanced back. I raised my streaming eyebrows for approval.

"You don't think I'm waiting for you," he said in disbelief, and started up the path of swimming pebbles towards the tower.

Furious, I leapt over the gate. I would watch his failure. My hand caught in the black grinding chain wound through the padlock. I wrenched it free and confronted the tower. A streetlamp splayed out beams around its silhouette; dark scales of ivy overlapped on the stone. For a second I couldn't see him. Then my waterlogged eyes made out a ladder climbing the silhouette, and a figure humping upwards like a caterpillar. I almost laughed. Instead I moved closer.

He was thrusting his shoulders upwards through the rain, as if surfacing for air. Curving away from him, the tower was a cylinder of rain. I approached until I was beneath him. A pebble rattled, and his head turned a fraction.

At once the rung on which he was standing snapped like a bone, then the one beneath, and the next, leaving his legs suspended between the sweating uprights, his toes trembling towards the earth. I couldn't look up. I dreaded to see his neck snapped, his chin askew on an upper rung. Then I realised his absurdity and that of my idea. His absurdity—but he lifted one hand and dragged his body upwards as if it were someone else he was pulling to safety. Perhaps what had happened didn't matter.

But how could he descend? That didn't matter either, I told myself, and turned towards the gate. I took six parallel steps. My hands weighed in my soaked pockets. Before me I saw my shadow on the pebbles, my arms like the handles of a cup. I pulled out my hands and let them go limp as my hair. Something he'd said I should have realised was a revelation, some point at which I could have communicated with him. I turned back towards the tower. It and the ladder were deserted.

He couldn't have come down the ladder. If he had fallen inside the tower I would have heard. I stared about for a sign. Perhaps there was one that I couldn't interpret. But the sky was closed off from me, the stars blotted out by a churning mass and replaced by plummets of rain. For a moment I thought: imagine all that must be beyond this.

I dragged at my ear. Five minutes later I managed to control my hand and hold it restrained against the sky. At least I can write, I thought. That may help.

The Sunshine Club

W ill this be the last session?" Bent asked.

I closed his file on my desk and glanced at him to detect impatience or a plea, but his eyes had filled with the sunset as with blood. He was intent on the cat outside the window, waiting huddled on the balcony as the spider's cocoon like a soft white marble in one corner of the pane boiled with minute hectic birth. Bent gripped my desk and glared at the cat, which had edged along the balcony from the next office. "It'll kill them, won't it?" Bent demanded. "How can it be so calm?"

"You have an affinity for spiders," I suggested. Of course, I already knew.

"I suppose that ties in with the raw meat."

"As a matter of fact, it does. Yes, to pick up your question, this may well be the last session. I want to take you through what you gave me under hypnosis."

"About the garlic?"

"The garlic, yes, and the crosses."

He winced and managed to catch hold of a smile. "You tell me, then," he said.

"Please sit down for a moment," I said, moving around my desk and intervening between him and the cat. "How was your day?"

"I couldn't work," he muttered. "I stayed awake but I kept thinking of how it'd be in the canteen. All those swines of women laughing and pointing. That's what you've got to get rid of."

"Be assured, I will." I'll have you back at the conveyor belt before you know, I thought: but there are more important fulfilments.

"But they all saw me!" he cried. "Now they'll all look!"

"My dear Mr Bent—no, Clive, may I?—you must remember, Clive, that odder dishes than raw meat are ordered every day in canteens. You could always tell them it was a hangover cure."

"When I don't know why myself? I don't want that meat," he said intensely. "*I* didn't want it."

"Well, at least you came to see me. Perhaps we can find you an alternative to raw meat."

"Yes, yes," he said hopelessly. I waited, staring for a pause at the walls of my office, planed flat by pale green paint. Briefly I felt enclosed with his obsession, and forced myself to remember why. When I looked down I found that the pen in my hand was hurrying lines of crosses across the blotter, and I flipped the blotter onto its face. For a moment I feared a relapse. "Lie down," I suggested, "if it'll put you at your ease."

"I'll try not to fall asleep," he said, and more hopefully "It's nearly dark." When he'd aligned himself on the couch he glanced down at his hands on his chest. Discovered, they flew apart.

"Relax as completely as you can," I said, "don't worry about how," and watched as his hands crept comfortingly together on his chest. His sleeves dragged at his elbows, and he got up to unbutton his jacket. He'd removed his hat when he entered my office, though with its wide black brim and his gloves and high collar he warded off the sting of sunshine from his shrinking flesh. I'd coaxed his body out of its blackness and his mind was following, probing timidly forth from the defences which had closed around it. "Ready," he called if we were playing hide and seek.

I placed myself between the couch and the window in order to read his face. "All right, Clive," I said. "Last time you told me about a restaurant where your parents had an argument. Do you remember?"

His face shifted like troubled water. Behind his eyelids he was silent. "Tell me about your parents," I said eventually.

"But you know," said his compressed face. "My father was good to me. Until he couldn't stand the arguments."

"And your mother?"

"She wouldn't let him be!" his face cried blindly. "All those Bibles she knew he didn't want, making out he should be going to church with her when she knew he was afraid—"

"But there was nothing to be afraid of, was there?"

"Nothing. You know that."

"So you see, he was weak. Remember that. Now, why did they fight in the restaurant?"

"I don't know, I can't remember. Tell me! Why won't you tell me?"

"Because it's important that you tell me. At least you can remember the restaurant. Go on, Clive, what was above your head?"

"Chandeliers," he said wearily. A bar of sunset was rising past his eyes.

"What else can you see?"

"Those buckets of ice with bottles in."

"You can't see very much?"

"No, it's too dim. Candles—" His voice hung transfixed.

"Now you can see, Clive! Why?"

"Flames! F— The flames of hell!"

"You don't believe in hell, Clive. You told me that when you didn't know yourself. Let's try again. Flames?"

"They were—inside them—a man's face on fire, melting! I could see it coming but nobody was looking—"

"Why didn't they look?"

His shuddering head pressed back into the couch. "Because it was meant for me!"

"No, Clive, not at all. Because they knew what it was."

But he wouldn't ask. I waited, glancing at the window so that he would call me back; the minute spiders stirred like uneasy caviar. "Well, tell me," he said coyly, dismally.

"If you were to go into any of a dozen restaurants you'd see your man on fire. Now do you begin to see why you've turned your back on everything your parents took for granted? How old were you then?"

"Nine."

"Is it coming clear?"

"You know I don't understand these things. Help me! I'm paying you!"

"I am, and we're almost there. You haven't even started eating yet."

"I don't want to."

"Of course you do."

"Don't! Not—"

"Not—"

Outside the window, against the tiger-striped blurred sky, the cat tensed to leap. "Not when my father can't," Bent whispered harshly.

"Go on, go on, Clive! Why can't he?"

"Because they won't serve the meat the way he likes."

"And your mother? What is she doing?"

"She's laughing. She says she'll eat anyway. She's watching him as they bring her, oh—" His head jerked.

"Yes?"

"Meat—"

It might have been a choke or a sob. "Guh! Guh! Garlic!" he cried, and shook.

"Your father? What does he do?"

"He's standing up. Sit down! Don't! She says it all again, how it's sacrilegious to eat blood— He's, oh, he's pulling the cloth off the table, everything falls on me, everybody's looking, she comes at him, he's got her hair, she bites him then she screams, he smiles, he's smiling, I hate him!" Bent shook and collapsed in the shadows.

"Open your eyes," I said.

They opened wide, trustful, protected by the twilight. "Let me tell you what I see," I said.

"I think I understand some things," he whispered.

"Just listen. Why do you fear garlic and crosses? Because your mother destroyed your father with them. Why do you want and yet not want raw meat? To be like your father who you really knew was weak, to make yourself stronger than the man who was destroyed. But now you know he was weak, you know you are stronger. Stronger than the women who taunt you because they know you're strong. And if you still have a taste for bloody meat, there are places that will serve it to you. The sunlight which you fear? That's the man on fire, who terrified you because you thought your father was destined for hell."

"I know," Bent said. "He was just a waiter cooking."

I switched on the desk-lamp. "Exactly. Do you feel better?"

Perhaps he was feeling his mind to discover whether anything was broken. "Yes, I think so," he said at last.

"You will. Won't you?"

"Yes."

"No hesitation. That's right. But Clive, I don't want you hesitating when you leave this office. Wait a minute." I took out my wallet. "Here's a card for a club downtown, the Sunshine Club. Say I sent you. You'll find that many of the members have been through something similar to what you've been through. It will help."

"All right," he said, frowning at the card.

"Promise me you'll go."

"I will," he promised. "You know best."

He buttoned his coat. "Will you keep the hat? No, don't keep it. Throw it away," he said with some bravado. At the door he turned and peered past me. "You never explained the spiders."

"Oh, those? Just blood."

I watched his head bob down the nine flights of stairs. Perhaps eventually he would sleep at night and go forth in the daytime, but the important adjustments had been made: he was on the way to accepting what he was. Once again I gave thanks for night shifts. I went back to my desk and tidied Bent's file. Later I might look in at the Sunshine Club, reacquaint myself with Bent and a few faces.

Then, for a moment, I felt sour fear. Bent might encounter Mullen at the Club. Mullen was another who had approached me to be cured, not knowing that the only cure was death. As I recalled that Mullen had gone to Greece months before, I relaxed—for I had relieved Mullen of his fears with the same story, the raw meat and the garlic, the parents battling over the Bible. In fact it hadn't happened that way at all—my mother had caused the scene at the dining-room table and there had been a cross—but by now I was more familiar with the working version.

The cat scraped at the window. As I moved toward it, the cat's eyes slitted darkly and it tensed. I waited and then threw the window open. The cat howled and fell. Nine storeys: even a cat would scarcely survive. I stood above the lights of the city, lights clustering toward the dark horizon, and the tiny struggling red spiders streamed out from the window on threads, only to drift back and settle softly, like a rain of blood, on my face.

Writer's Curse

I looked up from the last line of handwriting, which was tight and nervous as a tongue between teeth. Dunn was conscientiously bubbling ink into and out of his pen beneath the theatrical gesture of the pink desk-lamp, but I saw that he was impatient for my comments.

"You have an undoubted ability," I said, "for involving your reader in the situation."

"Thank you very much," he said to the bookcase in front of him, but his eyes expected more.

"But," I interrupted. I'm never too kind to apprentice writers: the illusion of achieved ambition stunts them. "But. You pile so much into your stories that the tension breaks. And vivid as it is, it's derivative."

"Oh?" His head snapped up with his voice. "From whom?"

"Well, your white figure hopping along the beach has hopped out of M. R. James. Your faces in the sea you've fished out of Hope Hodgson. And your faces on the wind are someone else's story."

"Whose?" he demanded, turning his back on the cartons of magazines crowded against the pipes that bulged beneath the paper roses of the wallpaper.

"Mine, as a matter of fact."

At that he withdrew into the shadows beyond the downcast circle of light. I knew he had no answer now, but saw no reason to lend him one. A warm breeze which smelled of the cooling grass of the bowling-green fingered the curtains and let them droop. Dunn slumped mute, faceless, his shadowed hands struggling in his pockets, and a butterfly which should have been asleep flickered on the lampshade, blushing translucently. I listened to its frail questing patter on the shade, and without warning Dunn flung out a disembodied brilliant arm and crushed the butterfly in his fist.

"Nor have you much feeling for beauty," I said sharply, shocked.

"I'm not a moth at anyone's flame," he shouted. "You don't need to tell me I can write!"

"I've told you so several times, and it wasn't a moth," I said. "Look, you want an editor's opinion, not mine. I've given you enough addresses."

"And I'll try them, don't you worry," he said harshly.

"Good." The hairs on his arm on the lamplit desk were blurred bright wires; I felt bound to try to stop his trembling. "Look, I've told you that your stuff is vivid," I said. "Sell a few and then you'll have time to concentrate on discipline."

"Discipline," I heard him mutter as I left. When I'd picked my way over the tangled carpet in the hall, past the shattered patch of soiled plaster next to the disembowelled pay phone, I was glad of the summer night. I doubled back beneath Dunn's window, along the privet hedge painstakingly whitewashed by the moon, and made my way across the bowling-green to the pavilion. Its windows were boarded, but a few boards had been prised away and replaced by long strips of darkness. The railing of the veranda gave beneath my elbows as if jointed, and I gazed into the trees of the park, brushed together by warm shadow. Then Dunn leaned from his sill. "I shouldn't stand there," he called. "You never know what might be in that pavilion. Faces in the dark." I supposed he had to shape his material from something, but it was as I'd said: he had no feeling for beauty, no ability for form, no sense of peace.

A fortnight later, since I hadn't heard from him, I returned to his flat. The front door was open. The hall was a battle of sound; the landlady's kettle shrieked, dogs struggled over my feet and into the sunlight as the landlady scooped them out of her rooms with a frying-pan. "Out with you, the lot of you. And you make sure your friend goes out too," she bellowed at me. "Sitting inside on a day like this! The idea!"

Dunn was hunched over his table, constricted among the cartons and bookshelves, much as he'd gathered himself protectively around his notebook, patched elbows thrust out as a warning when first I'd met him in the pub. It had taken time and beer to convince him that my interest was genuine. Now there was no reply in his eyes to my greeting. But I didn't intend the day to be dimmed; I threw up the freckled window and watched for a moment the bowls rolling about the green, trying to dislodge indelible dabs of sunlight from their backs. When I turned to Dunn, two frowning slits were watching me beneath the black rim of his spectacles.

He slapped a letter down on my side of the desk. "I've had that story back," he said.

I might have written the editor's letter myself; I'd said it all two weeks ago. "Well, I did advise you," I pointed out. "Never mind. Most people start out with more rejection slips than manuscripts. I'm sure you can still make this story work."

But he was staring at his finger, on which he was balancing an ink-bottle drained pale. "You don't know that editor, by any chance?"

"He's had a couple of my things."

"You wouldn't have written to him about my story?"

"Good Lord, no." I laid my hand on the desk, a gesture of honesty. "Why on earth should I have done that?"

He clutched the bottle like a grenade. "Because you said I'd stolen your ideas! To get your own back! I know my story's good!" Before I could retreat he hurled the bottle. It shattered close to my fingers, and one fragment flew like a tiny jagged hatchet-blade to bury itself in my wrist. Furious, I pulled it out, and it rocked back and forth in triumph on the desk, a thin thread of blood settling like a ruby in its curve.

"I'm sorry," Dunn said. "I apologise. That didn't do any good."

"Your talent for observation is developing," I said sourly.

"She's got Elastoplast downstairs." As he hurried away, he seemed preoccupied.

In the hush, bowls clicked distantly; a cloud fluttered at the sun and fled. When Dunn returned, disappointed that I wouldn't let him place the sticking-plaster, he said "I've just had an idea for a story."

"Really."

"Well, you know," he explained apologetically, "ideas don't choose their time to introduce themselves. Would you like to read it? I think this one might get through to you. And after that I won't need to trouble you again."

I had myself had fits of uncreative fury in the face of obstacles; I edged toward forgiving him for the ink-bottle. Besides, he'd become overwhelmingly eager, and I hoped for an impressive story. "So long as you keep your hands off ink-bottles this time," I said.

"Don't worry," Dunn said. "I won't even let you see the ink."

The following week I had a card from him, rather like an invitation to a private view. Beneath a moon nibbled by fat clouds the pavilion half exhibited and snatched back its shadow, and I wondered in passing whether Dunn had shrugged off his obsession with the place. His window was a square of dim pink light, pasted like a square on the house. He let me in, smiling broadly—"She's at her Bingo"—and ushered me upstairs.

A chair stood ready for me at the desk; the desk-lamp bent its head over the first page. Dunn led me by the elbow to his story. "I think you'll lose yourself in this one," he said, grinning. As he took his place in an emaciated armchair facing me across the desk I glanced about, perhaps irrationally, for pens, ashtrays, bottles, any objects which might forswear their domestic calm and prove their loyalty to Dunn. His head ducked puppet-like beneath the rim of light; his gaze fastened brightly, eagerly on me. I closed the pink cone of light about me and sat down to read.

"—He sat down to read. Around him the room gave a mute cry of warning; the cartons of magazines seemed on the point of mounting to barricade the window, the frame of the window itself tensed as if to contract and wall out what he ignored beyond the pane. Moonlight sucked back like a misted breath behind a cloud—the edge of inexorable darkness. Now the park would be a single massed suffocating blot, he thought, and then the nerves of his ear strained toward the window, for outside he could hear the footsteps of a crowd. Running. A crowd running on boards. No, they weren't running; rather they were milling about, confined, like horses terrified now they had been plunged into darkness. But the terror was not theirs; it was soon to be his—"

"You've certainly improved," I said. "Why, I can almost hear—" and my mouth let the words drift away, for Dunn had vanished.

I twisted the desk-lamp toward the room. Shadows lifted and stretched from cartons; shadows drew out the arms of the armchair like rubber, pulled them to snapping before they slumped back. But the room was empty. Outside, across the bowling-green, I could hear quick overlapping footsteps. While I had been engrossed, Dunn must have slipped out, grinning. It was a good joke; it proved the power of his writing. I crossed to the window to call him back, and threw the sash high.

The bowling-green was an abstract expanse of grey, squared off at the pavilion. The green was bare—yet out there, close to me, the footsteps continued.

The joke was more sustained, then; perhaps a shade obsessive. Dunn was hidden somewhere nearby, tramping rapidly on the spot. Well, I would turn the joke. I picked up the desk-lamp and led its flex to the window.

The circle of light fell into the garden, which was deserted, and moved outward. On the black privet hedge, favoured leaves sprang up green. From there a stain of darker green spread across the grass, dimming and unfocusing as it approached the pavilion. Surely there wasn't just one set of footsteps; had Dunn brought his friends with him? The faint blurred oval of light drifted off the bowling-green and, when I strained my eyes, lent the pavilion a faint brown tinge. I steadied the lamp to coax back the light, and at the pavilion something pale moved.

Ah, Dunn. Even when the light lay inert on the bowling-green I could see the white egg of a face framed between two boards across a window. I lifted the light toward the building. I had barely time to think: if he's inside the pavilion how did he get through the boards over the door?—when the light framed the building again and as if on cue half a dozen pale featureless eggs clustered into the space between the boards.

While I watched, unbelieving, more of the eggs crowded into the space. I thought distractedly of those myriad eggs one finds in dead trees. But I knew these were faces. Paralysed, I imagined the unseen bodies piling over one another in the dark.

I was still staring when the first pale shape squeezed forth like a drop of poison from between the boards and dropped struggling to the ground.

Four more had burst forth before I realised what drew them. I clapped my hand over the lamp and threw it on the desk. Around me the room swayed drunkenly with shadow, but I knew what was solid; I leapt for the door. It was locked.

I wasted three blows on it before I felt that something higher and heavier than I had been pushed against it from outside. I didn't shout; the landlady was out, and there was little point in wondering where Dunn was. Perhaps I could jump from the window.

My shadow was flung helpless across the green to the pavilion, and the shadow teemed with life like a carcass. Within it white shapes massed; some still boiled forth from the pavilion, innumerable others scuttled across the green, throwing out their arms and dragging their legs forward, humping along like grubs, all their featureless heads turned up to me. They were too close. Even as I glared down into the garden the privet hedge creaked and gave way in a shower of black leaves.

I heaved the window shut. Then desperately I switched off the lamp, but it was too late; they already knew where to find the light.

I stood numb in the middle of the room, staring out at the piled sky. A minute later a white object bobbed into view, groping over the outer sill. One corner of the desk dug into my back like a weapon. Another blurred shape groped, and a head rose into view. I couldn't see the face, but what might have been hair straggled high, like cobweb drifting from a moon. A second head edged into sight, and their hands thudded against the pane, softly as children patting mud.

So softly that I thought I knew what to do. I threw myself forward and wrenched up the window. The pale heads recoiled; then the mass of them cascaded plumply down the wall, like a dislodged pile of rotten fruit. Blocking my breath with one hand, I peered down into the garden. Before I could see more than a struggling chaos of soft moonlit bodies, two arms reached damply down from above the window and softly, stickily, pulled at my neck.

I clawed at the fat hands, but my fingers slipped. In the garden bodies slapped clammily together and a mass of faces like weighted white balloons climbed towards me. The arms at my neck were strong as rubber. I clutched at the sill as I was lifted. All meaning had been betrayed; I was at the mercy of nightmare. How could the thing have climbed above me?

I cried out. It couldn't have. "Rubbish!" I cried. "A lousy loose end!"

And Dunn leapt out of the armchair as my hands on the window-sill clenched on the manuscript and tore it into shreds.

He rushed to the desk, snarling in fury and fear. I saw his hand clutch toward a drawer. I threw him aside, and caught up the bottle of ink within. I squinted into the bottle. On top of the ink floated a curl of crimson. I strode past him as he clawed at my arm, and poured the ink out of the window.

"Next time you want to write in blood," I shouted, "use your own!"

Yet on the stairs I almost went back. For halfway down I was halted, one foot in mid-air, by the fear that somewhere, sometime, talent will succeed.

Property of the Ring

When Alan Swift awoke he felt cold and attenuated as a sheet of tin. One finger of his right hand was constricted; he coaxed his hand from beneath the sheets and found a ring he'd never seen before. His head aroused, startled, but the room didn't roll; the party had left no trace. Ah, the party—that must contain an explanation. Around him he saw the walls of the flat were flayed and grey. In a second or so he remembered why. Sunlight poured effortlessly from a blue glass sky, and he lay back in the light and tried to account for the ring.

The events of last night toppled over one another, merging and obscuring, like spadefuls of earth collapsing back into a pit. Chris had been working; Alan had finished the children's novel at last, though he wasn't satisfied, and she'd taken the manuscript to begin work on the illustrations. Then? A pub, several students he knew and envied for their apparently untroubled vitality and instant casual humour, a party, a girl and an hour of that hasty snatching conversation with which one attempts to store up a friendship or more against the morning after. No, a friendship, nothing more—Chris was more. In fact, he was sure that it had been the girl who'd approached him. At one point she'd seemed pretty yet hollow as china; at another she'd brightened and throbbed—perhaps after they had exchanged rings, to touch as one tries at parties. His initials had been etched on his ring; with no trace of himself in his wallet either, he had felt anonymous. And now he couldn't remember her name or her face or her voice; straining, he managed to disinter just four words, voiceless and impersonal as though in quotes: "property of the ring."

He lay. He wasn't hungry. The June day streamed down on him, requiring no participation. He saw no reason to break the spell. But he glanced again at the ring, at the obscure shape of the band, like a snake

or perhaps like convoluted vines, at the unclear emotionless face of a
girl, less eroded than embryonic, in the setting of the ring. Surely she
hadn't said "I took it off my boyfriend, I didn't want him to have it"?
That must surely have been an overheard fragment. But he was troubled, dissatisfied, awake. Wearily he stood up and padded to the sink.
Automatically he pulled off the ring before washing. It hadn't, after all,
been so successful a party. Besides, he should have known he didn't
need parties now that he had Chris.

As though sunlight had exploded within him, the swirling faces of
the party paled and billowed back. He thrust his finger into the ring
and hurried out.

Chris never said "hello": rather it shone from her. Above the square
where she waited, lithe in a white blouse and slacks, cars sped downhill
like gleaming coloured beads slipping free of a thread and crushed together smoking beneath a fresh white statue. "Hello!" Alan shouted.

"Are the walls waiting?"

"They're bared to us."

Her blonde hair streamed behind her in no wind as she caught his
hand and led him beneath glittering frantic leaves to the shops beyond
the corner of the square. "Holidays," she said. Her voice was unself-
conscious as a stream. "I thought of Ibiza. Sun in the wine and rainbows on the hippies."

"It's later than you think, you know. Two months."

"But we aren't going to be packaged. No tinfoil buses, no brown-
paper hotels."

"True, yes."

His words echoed dully in Alan's mind. Usually, lit up by Chris, he
sparkled, even crystallised; now his responses seemed dredged up like
shards from mud. "I'm not awake," he apologised as they came in
sight of the shop owned by—what were their names, Tom and Adri-
enne? And at once a memory awoke, from the first disorientated hour
of the party. It hardly seemed worth mentioning now—they were almost at the shop—but rather than talk about the ring, he said "I had a
glimpse of another novel last night."

"Well, once the flat is bright and I move in, we can work on the
next novel together."

Dutifully Alan said "It won't be bright until you're there."

In the shop angular cardboard birds fluttered mutely in flocks; glass deers vital with light reared beside red white and blue mugs; a sitar leaned against a Peanuts poster and a snuffbox picked out bars of a Mozart concerto. "You know Ted and Arlene," Chris said, "and you two couldn't forget my fiancé Alan."

Ted shook back his hair and unrolled a strip of wallpaper on the counter; eagles swooped across the mysterious glow of an evening sky. "Oh, Ted," Chris cried. "How long did it take you?"

"About a week. Slightly longer than usual, but we wanted it to be special. I did the sky and the eagles are Arlene's."

"Oh, Alan, look at it," Chris gasped.

"Yes, it's fine," Alan said. "It certainly is."

"We're going to put it up today," Chris told the others. "Could we have some almond paste to improve that awful glue?"

"Here's something I kept to show you," Arlene remembered. She steered her wheelchair through the maze of shelves to the window. As Arlene pointed, Chris gazed into a blue glass egg in which a treasure of light was trapped. Tiny inverted passers-by climbed up its curves and vanished.

"It's so beautiful," Chris said. "It's the most intense image I've ever seen."

"It's more than that," Ted interrupted, wrapping the wallpaper. "It's perfect because it is its own single thought."

"It's a creature," Chris said.

"There's a difference," said Alan, "between a creature and a creation."

"Well, it's more than an image," she insisted.

"What does it think with?"

"Why, us, of course," Arlene said.

As Alan opened the door of the flat Chris asked "Where's your signet ring?"

His hand twitched and, twisting the key, fled behind his back. "I gave it away at the party," he said.

"Well, it doesn't matter. You're you, not a ring. But what's that?"

"Just something I got." The rolls of wallpaper swung before him like stretcher supports, and he hurried through the living-room, past drooping posters of Dick Bruna bunnies and scraped plates of scraps on a low table, into the bedroom. There he threw the wallpaper among the ridges of the bedclothes. Chris was unpacking the glue and washing out a plastic bucket. "We'll make coffee in a while," she said, "but first let's stir."

In the bedroom she hung an odd square of wallpaper off the centre of the wall, like a window or a block of amber within which the eagles hovered. "We'll build from that," she said.

Alan stood up from the bed with an effort, trying to draw on the vitality of last night, the leaps and surges of speech. "I'd concentrate on what we'd see from the bed," he suggested.

"Of course you would. Of course we shall."

Eagles rose across the wall in an irregular stepped design. "That paste makes me ravenous," Chris said.

The paste was cold yet the room was almond-scented as a bakery. "Look, that wall will be full of sunlight in an hour," she said. "Let's eat now."

"At this time?"

"I'm hungry."

"I suppose that's a good enough reason."

Sunlight sprang from a corner of the low table. Chris had cooked a mild curry; her piled fork sped from the plate on her lap to her mouth. Alan ate with his left hand; his right hung open at his side, having recoiled prickling from the texture of the couch. He felt the rice in his mouth like a handful of swollen pills; the meat passed through his throat like a slow roll of boulders clogging a stream. However slowly he ate, he knew that eventually he must join Chris in the bedroom. To stick paper on a wall, for God's sake! But no, Alan thought heavily, there was nothing else he would prefer to do.

As Chris had predicted, the bedroom wall was brimming with sunlight. At the foot of the bared plaster lay overlapping brown shards of old wallpaper. Alan felt an intuitive almost undefinable sympathy for the plaster, as if the glue and paper would stifle the wall. "Remind me to look for some cufflinks for you," Chris said. "There's all sorts of marvellously strange things in the antique shops these days."

She glanced frowning at him as he lay back on the bed. "Are you ill?" she asked. "You're not usually as quiet as this."

Alan shook his head on the pillow like a boulder rolling in treacle. "Just a bit tired," he said.

"Come on, have a bit of paper. It'll wake you up."

Alan watched as she picked up a rectangle of colour that curled into the air, turning a slimy snail-like underbelly, flapping once like a broken bat-wing. As she smoothed the glued surface across the wall, he shivered. "Come on, Alan," she said without turning. "Please."

Alan propped himself on his right hand and stood, although the hand was reluctant to leave the bed. He swayed above the bucket, but his hand flinched back; he imagined being coated with the glue from head to foot, drowning in a marsh. "That corner isn't clean," he said. "I'll do that."

At the first scrape of metal on plaster he dropped the tool, trembling. His bones seemed to shrink in anguish. "My head," he groaned.

"Are you hurt?" Chris cried, leaping up from a strip of paper.

"I'll do it," he said indistinctly, and staggered into the living-room.

After ten minutes he levered himself away from the couch; in the sunlight he burned like a black statue. He leaned against a shady corner of the room. The walls stood solid in mutual support. In the other room Chris patted paper onto the wall; her pats were like soft unbearable slaps on his forehead. She shouldn't. The wall was white and hot. She should leave it alone.

In a while she came to him. "Alan," she accused. Her sounds visibly rippled the air. Her face moved frowning across his eyes, then its strata shifted. She was puzzled, anxious. He closed his eyes as his fingers worked uncontrollably at the sight of the frantic changes of her face. "Are you all right?" she demanded.

He nodded; the boulder toppled into the treacle.

"Would you like me to make some coffee?"

Now his lips had to move, to rid him of the need to think. "Up to you," he said.

Shrugging her whole body, she filled the percolator. Glass flashed warm and vanished. He detached himself from the wall and tramped leadenly into the bedroom. At the foot of the bed he leaned back and fell inert on the sheets.

"Alan, whatever's wrong," Chris called, "don't be melodramatic."

His feet and knees pressed together; his hands moulded to his sides, and his eyes closed.

"I don't mind if this is just a mood," Chris said. "I'm not the one to talk about moods. But you hardly spoke to Ted and Arlene, you didn't want to discuss our holiday. It doesn't matter about Ted and Arlene. It doesn't matter, but you do. It doesn't matter if you're quiet. Only if you worry about it, and I'm beginning to. Are we going to be able to talk? If not, why go on?"

She came into the bedroom and looked on the bed. "Oh, Alan," she said. "Don't I matter?"

Its lips moved but it didn't speak; where its brain had been there was a stone.

"I didn't hear you," Chris said. She knelt on the bed and gazed down.

It felt a thin material brush its upper section, material similar to that in which it was needlessly encased. Then a warm soft appendage moved across its top, rhythmically returning. Above it an orifice opened and closed, within which a piece of the soft substance moved, striking vibrations.

"Alan, I know it's not me that's wrong."

The vibrations troubled it. They must stop. It poised to move for the last time before achieving peace, timelessness in which it could meditate again, and the soft appendage closed around one of the extensions moulded to its sides, still unmerged.

"Alan, look at the ring! Oh, Alan, look at the face!"

It struggled to move, but its peace had trapped it. Nothing mattered.

She wrenched at the ring, at the hand. It was immovable. Furious, frantic, she prised the finger free and tore at the ring. It shifted a fraction, and blood trickled down the finger. She gripped her wrist with her other hand and heaved. Skin tore and the ring threw her backwards onto the floor. As she struggled upright she brought the ring to her eyes, and almost could not recognise the face.

"Alan?" she called desperately, sunlight coating her eyes. "Alan?"

Blood streamed down the finger. The blood was moving, hot in the sunlight. His blood was moving. He was moving.

The Shadows in the Barn

That's decent of you, son. I'll have a pint of bitter, if I may. Just one thing, though—could you ask them not to give me a tankard? I have my reasons. A pint glass will be fine.

I hope you didn't mind me sitting here listening to you. Some people think if you sit with your hands in your pockets you're a layabout. Well, I didn't think you would. I used to work, you know. Believe me, I wish I still could.

You can't guess? Didn't you see me watching that trick you did with the coins on the tankard? That was a good trick, and I know what I'm talking about. Yes, you're right. I was a magician. I could show you some tricks. But I'd rather not, if you don't mind. These days I don't like to use my hands.

I suppose you think I'm being mysterious, not wanting a tankard and so on. It's not something I care to talk about generally. But I don't think you'd laugh. It might upset your girlfriend, though. God knows it upset me.

All right, I'll tell you. You notice how I'm drinking, putting my hand back in my pocket as soon as it leaves the glass? It's not my hand I don't want to see, it's—well, listen.

It all happened many years ago. You'd think I'd have forgotten, wouldn't you? I was on holiday, or as much of a holiday as I ever used to take. My father was a magician before me, you see, and he taught me most of what I had to know. He always used to wear a black top hat covered with symbols, and I can remember him sitting with his feet on the stove in our caravan, telling me that the most important thing was to get the measure of your audience. And that you should never leave your work entirely, even when you were on holiday, in case someone else should learn new tricks and force you out. He was always there to help me when I was rehearsing in the caravan, even after he died.

Eckhardt

So I say, I wasn't entirely on holiday. I'd promised myself a couple of weeks to drive through the Cotswolds. Yes, I had a van then. Now I walk, or slouch as they say. But I'd advertised ahead in some of the local papers of the Cotswolds, in case anyone could use me. I only had one answer, asking me to perform for a Sunday school party somewhere outside Berkeley. It was to be on the second day of my holiday, but of course I accepted. I didn't know that it would be the end of my holiday, and of everything else as well.

I started out early in the morning from Birmingham, where I'd had to spend the night. Birmingham wasn't as bad then as it is now, but those dead buildings were already beginning to rob the place of all its colour. I can still remember driving into the Cotswolds. As I left Birmingham I seemed to see nothing but grey and gouged earth, lopped trees—and then as I got nearer the Cotswolds grass began to spring up, the stumps grew into trees, hills rose: it was a kind of resurrection. Yet now I think about it there was something primitive as well, as if time were turning back: all the deserted barns, the stubbled ploughshares, the stone walls that seemed to follow the hills forever, had been abandoned by man because they didn't need him, only the earth and its forces.

Anyway, I reached the village by mid-afternoon; Camside, I think it was called. I know there was a river, because people were leaning on the parapets and watching the sunlight. The first thing I did was to find a little hotel. The vicar had said I could stay at his house, but I decided not. I'm not much for religion; there's something more than us, I know that, but I don't think it's friendly. It's up to us to make what we can of life. The woman who ran the hotel—a huge woman with an apron like a postage stamp stuck on her belly and a great melon smile—wanted to see some magic, of course, so I showed her some tricks with cards. If I'd known, I'd have left it at that.

Well, I had a meal and went across to the Tithe Barn about half an hour before the show was due to start. I hadn't been able to get in touch with the vicar in the meantime. I felt happy, I remember: passing all the red stone houses which didn't jangle as cars went past, strolling along the main street where stall-holders were unpacking their stalls, looking up at a village clock whose hands were clasped together at noon or maybe at midnight, walking through the churchyard where sparrows were singing among the headstones. I felt I'd have an easy night.

The Tithe Barn had one of the steepest roofs I'd ever seen. There wasn't much else to notice, just an entrance with a few church posters pasted on it. So I went straight in, and I was nearly blinded. God knows where they'd got their spotlights from. They'd built a stage at one end of the barn—for plays and so on, I suppose, because there were a couple of makeshift dressing-rooms behind it—but all I could see at first was a blaze of light with two shadows fluttering above it under the roof, and I told you how steep the roof was. Eventually I made out the vicar and his wife fussing about on stage, and realised that theirs were the shadows that looked like a pair of hands grappling under the roof.

Of course I told them I wouldn't need all that light. But apparently the local rep put up with it, and the vicar's wife was quite upset. "We had an appeal to buy them," she said. She had pale skin and a pale dress that was supposed to be pretty; she was one of those fragile women whose weaknesses you mustn't notice, the same way people would be afraid to say anything about a cup of tea at the vicarage. "All the villagers contributed," she said. "My husband bought them." Well, he was a long black pole with a head like a shelled egg stuck in a cup, and I could understand the spotlights, but I wasn't going to put up with them. Eventually I persuaded them that I could make do with one. That must have been when I lost my chance to stop what happened.

Then the vicar said to me "Thank you very much for offering your services." He had some knack of suggesting more than he said; I felt that he was telling his wife off for being unchristian and trying to remind me of my place. So when he said "I hope the children will enjoy it," it sounded as if he was saying that they might be difficult and that he didn't know whether I had the talent to win them over. I didn't quite tell him that I'd show him, but that was what I felt.

I had a look around the barn. They'd brought in rows of hard wooden chairs, which weren't going to help. Then I went into one of the dressing-rooms, which was more like a packing case. I took my time setting out my props, because I was determined not to go out again until the show was due to start. Well, I knew when that was easily enough, because all of a sudden I heard a chorus from Handel's *Messiah* coming from out front, which they'd put on a gramophone for the children. Follow that, as you'd say these days. So I gathered everything up, went out and told the vicar's wife to take it off—for which she glared at me as if I'd dared to hurt her—and strode straight onto the stage.

For a moment I thought I'd come out early, because even when the music stopped there wasn't a sound from the audience. And with the spotlight in my eyes I couldn't see whether anyone was there. So I arranged my props on the table they'd given me, to let my eyes adjust a little. Then I turned round and had another look.

At first all I could see were eyes glinting at me. After a while I made out that there were four rows or so of them, but it took me longer to work out what was wrong: they weren't talking, they weren't scuffling, they were simply watching me.

You know, this unnerved me so much that I almost muffed my first trick, a simple thing with coloured streamers. While I performed, half of me was trying to get the feel of those children. I gave them half a dozen tricks and there still wasn't a sound, not a laugh, not a mutter. Not a head turned. There's a bad audience that every magician knows, where half of them shout out how it's done and you have to find a trick that'll bring them up on stage and dazzle them. This wasn't that kind of audience. They were soaking me up and giving nothing back. Do you know, I found myself changing style halfway and turning it into a comedy act in the hope they'd respond. But they didn't twitch.

Well, my eyes were getting used to the light by now, and I was just about ready to give up when I saw two boys whispering on the back row. Now, they weren't like the rest: they were from some country house outside the village—their clothes were crisp as a fiver. And beyond them I could see the vicar and his wife just slipping out. When I think about it I suppose they were just going out for a word with some of the parents, but at the time all I could see was that they and those two brats on the back row weren't interested. So I thought, I'll show you. The wall behind the stage was panted white and perfect for a shadow show. But it wasn't going to be like any shadow show they'd seen before.

Of course I've thought about the whole thing since. You would too. I've hardly thought about anything else. And over the years I've worked out what was going on. I think those children were scared; I think those two boys had told them I was a real magician, in league with the devil or something like that. Remember, they wouldn't applaud me when I came on stage—looking angry I suppose—in the middle of the record, because it was church music. They may have thought I was the devil, in my father's hat and cloak; you see, they would have been more terrified not to believe if they'd been told it was so. Not that I knew this then. I was simply out to get through to them somehow. But all I'm saying is that what happened wasn't entirely my fault. God knows I wouldn't have wanted it to happen.

So I turned to the children and said something like "Watch very carefully now. I'm going to show you some ghosts."

Well, the silence somehow grew sharper. I told you, I didn't know they were scared. But I must have destroyed my last hope when I said "If they frighten you, scream and I'll make them go away."

The first thing I showed them was a kind of skull with a big silly Mickey Mouse grin. There were some little girls, you see, so I thought I'd better ease into it. I could move my fingers a little and make the eyes peer round the audience. I was standing side on to them and watching for any reaction, but there wasn't one that I could see. I broadened the grin on the skull and crossed its eyes, but they didn't make a sound except for the two whispering at the back. All right, I thought, you've had your chance. Now we'll break the rules.

I glanced at the entrance to make sure the vicar hadn't come back, and then I sent a spider with unequal legs hobbling up the wall and into the roof. You don't know how pleased I was when I saw all their eyes turn up to watch it. Some of them even moved in their seats. So when I'd got the spider over their heads I clapped my hands. And they all jumped and stared at me. I was nearly clapping for excitement; I was completely carried away. I produced another spider, an even bigger one, and it crawled up painfully, falling back every now and then, to where I'd left the other one. I don't know how many I sent up to the roof—a dozen or so. It was only when I paused for a moment that I stopped. Because the two boys on the back row hadn't made a sound since I'd started the spiders.

I was just congratulating myself when I thought of how the children might feel. Well, I'm not completely stupid. After all, think of them, sitting there waiting for all those spiders to fall, not daring to move. So I said "Well, did you like that?" Let's remember, now, that I hadn't reason to think they'd all been won over, since I didn't know they'd been scared all along. "Tell me what you'd like to see now and I'll see what I can do," I said to them. And then I noticed that the boys at the back were staring—not at the place where I'd left the spiders, not at me, but at the wall behind me.

I looked round and saw a face on the wall. I'll be honest with you; my heart jumped. It wasn't a pleasant face. There was grass sticking out of it, more like grass than hair, at any rate; one eye looked as if it had slipped down the cheek, and there was grass growing between its open lips. In fact, it looked like my father must have looked after he was dead. Well, I saw in a second that it was the shadow of the streamers that I'd crumpled on the table after my first trick. So I said something like "Well, that's an extra one," and knocked the streamers off the table.

And the face stayed there on the wall.

Now you can't think in a situation like that; you act. I threw myself in front of it and, even though it cost me a year or two, turned my back on it. I looked at the children, and I could see they knew. I could see something else, above my head, but even though inside I was one long deafening scream I stood sideways again and let them see my hands in front of the face. "There," I said. "That's how it's done," and before they could see my hands had nothing to do with the face I stood over and blocked it for good.

But then I had to watch them and feel their fear coming up in a silent wave, and see what was above my head and out there in the barn.

I didn't dare to look up in case they might look up too. It didn't seem as if that would matter, though, because I knew that any minute someone was going to see the humped shapes that were hobbling down the walls and clawing themselves across the floor towards the children. They'd be lost then. But I could see that my own shadow, which had been up under the roof all the time like a three-fingered claw, was moving and spreading like a stain until it reached above the rows of seats and began to close. I knew what was drawing it; it was their fear.

So I said "Well, that's all for now. You'd better go out to your parents, they'll be waiting," and I was shaking so much they must have noticed. But the claw didn't quiver, and the children didn't move. I looked straight at them, willing them to look straight at me, and I saw that the claw was almost closing, the other things had almost reached the seats.

And then the vicar appeared in the doorway. I shouted to him "We've finished now. Will you turn the lights on?" and my breath came out almost in a cry as they all turned to him, away from the shadows.

I couldn't believe it when he called back "If you could give them a few more minutes while their parents arrive I should be grateful."

Well, what would you have done? I screamed at him "God blast you, turn on the lights!"

There isn't much more to tell. Just too much. The vicar gave me my fee in the entrance as if it were a Christian gesture to help me redeem myself. I left my props in the barn; I intended to go back for them in daylight. Then I followed the children and their parents, who kept trying to lose me, back to the village street and the hotel. I wasn't much of a drinker; I asked the woman at the hotel for the strongest cup of tea she could make.

She brought it and when she saw I wanted to be quiet, she went away. But she must have heard me scream, for she came running back. I think she took me for a drunkard; I know she wasn't pleased when I kept the light on in my room all night. But she didn't see what I saw when I picked up the cup of tea. She didn't see a huge black insect with an odd number of legs scuttle from beneath my hand and into a corner of the room.

Well, I lived with them. I had to. After a long time, when I hadn't used my hands, I saw them less often. But once in a while, when I least expected it, something would move at the corner of my eye, and it wouldn't be something I'd want to see. I could show you what I mean, but it mightn't end there. The claw might come back. I know I wouldn't see what would happen if it ever closed. And do you know, I don't think I should want to.

Night Beat

Almost exactly three weeks ago, Constable Sloane had visited the exhibition. Now, as he stood outside the museum at midnight, his thoughts were elsewhere. Streetlamps marched up the hill on which he stood, their lights padded by mist; cars laboured up the carriageway, reached the summit and sped away—but he hardly noticed their speed or their numbers, for his thoughts had returned to the murder.

It has been the night of the day on which he had visited the exhibition. What mattered, though, was that it had been his first month on a beat, and it mattered more that when his radio had called him to view the corpse, thrown broken among the bricks of a disintegrating alley leading from one of his main roads, the older policemen who had discovered the body had had to drive him back to the station, where he had sat white and shaking, gulping cups of tea. Of course his superiors had been sympathetic: he was young, he had never seen death before—they had even excluded him from the investigation which would be concentrated on his beat, and insisted that he confine himself to the calmer city centre for a while. He had barely been able to persuade them not to give him a companion, for he knew that it had not been the corpse that had left him shaking, not the mutilations or the blood. When he looked back on that night, he felt that he had been shaking with shame and fury: for he could have led them to the murderer.

And he had been furious because he knew that they would never have countenanced his method. Intuition was no part of police procedure. Yet ever since his childhood he had been able intuitively to sense sources of violence. He felt profoundly what his superiors wearily accepted: that violence surrounds us all. His first beat had led him through both suburbia and slums; and if each broken bottle outside a pub hinted terror to him, equally he felt the presence of violence in quiet suburban

131

roads behind the ranks of sleeping cars, knew instinctively which set of patterned curtains concealed shouts of rage, the smash of china, screams. Sometimes he was honest with himself, and admitted that it was the violence buried in him that recognised these sources, reached out to them. But now this was forgotten, for never had he felt the imminence of violence so powerfully as here. When they'd moved him to the city centre neither he nor they had realised what they had done. Last night he had passed the museum and had come alert; tonight he knew. Within the museum lay the source of that murder.

His radio hissed and spat. For a second he thought of calling Central for help, but then he half-smiled bitterly: he had no evidence, they would only think that the murder had unbalanced him completely. Yet he was determined to act; once he had conquered his fear of the surrounding violence he had become obsessed with the suppression of violence—and as well, this murder had stained his beat. He thrust the radio into his pocket and started up the steps to the museum.

When he knocked on the doors the glass panes shuddered. They were a meagre protection against the violence within. After a minute Sloane saw a light bobbing closer through the wide dark foyer. As the light found Sloane and held him, a figure formed darkly about it; a face swelled from the shadows like a wrinkled half-inflated balloon. At a childhood party Sloane had dulled and grown more taciturn as the evening wore on; tired of trying to rouse him to play, the other children had buffeted him with balloons. "What's all this about, son?" the caretaker demanded.

Now that the doors of the museum were open the sense of violence seemed stronger; Sloane could scarcely remember his lies. "A routine check, sir," he said.

"What routine's that, son? What's up?"

"We've had a few robberies around here recently. I'd like to look around, if you don't mind. Just to check."

The watchman hawked and gave Sloane room to pass. The foyer was high, reaching above the light; Sloane felt the cold arch of the ceiling. The walls were walled by darkness; painted faces glimmered dimly in the void. "Can we have the lights on, please?" Sloane asked.

"You'd have to ask the curator for that, son. But he'll be home in bed." He was obviously triumphant. Sloane frowned and the man came closer, nipping Sloane's arm with his fingers and apologising with a lopsided alcoholic smile. "You can have my torch for a few minutes if you ask nicely."

"I'm sure you don't want to obstruct the law. You seem a bit unsteady—perhaps you ought to sit down."

"You can't have it unless I've got a spare battery." The caretaker sidled into his office behind the marble staircase and rummaged in the drawers of a dark table. Above the table a white lampshade was bearded with a single strand of cobweb; on the table, next to a sagging moist rectangle outlined in rum, lay an open copy of *True Detective Confessions.* "You're lucky," the caretaker said, passing Sloane the torch.

Sloane felt violence massing in the room. "I won't be long," he said.

"Don't you worry your head about that, son. I'll come round with you."

As Sloane emerged from the office the torch's beam touched a globe of the world standing at the entrance to the Planetarium. Above the globe a moon was balanced on a wire; a dim crescent coated its edge. Sloane crossed to the staircase and the crescent expanded. At the same time the caretaker moved behind him. Sloane flexed his shoulders as if to shake off the violence which he felt looming.

The staircase climbed through a void across which their footsteps rang. The marble was slippery and sharp; Sloane glanced back at the caretaker and hurried to the top. A finger on a marble pillar pointed to THE HISTORY OF MAN. The torch-beam led him through an archway and fastened on a crumpled yellow paper mask inexpertly smoothed: a mummy's face.

"These are their specimens, here," the caretaker said behind him. "This is where thieves would be hiding, son, among the bodies, eh?"

He can move faster than I thought, Sloane realised. He peered at the man behind him, redolent of alcohol, one hand on a case containing the dark handle of a Cro-Magnon jaw. The air was thick with inertia; even the violence hung inert, and the caretaker seemed embalmed as the mummy. "Not here," Sloane said.

As he crossed the marble landing, his heels clanking like boots of armour, Sloane felt the violence swell to meet him. He halted, afraid. "I'll show you this room, son," the caretaker said. "It's where I take my pride."

The torch-beam splayed out beyond the figure of the caretaker, a star of darkness shone from his limbs; Sloane moved aside to see at once what was beyond the second archway. As the light plunged in, moons sprang up in glass cases, slid from the blades of swords and axes. "Tell me those aren't good as new," the caretaker said. "They can't say I don't keep these clean, son, that's a fact. I'd be in here like a shot if I heard a thief. Take his head off quick as that, I would."

Aggression stirred. "You wouldn't need me, then," Sloane said.

"When you've seen as much as I have, son, then I'll need you."

Although he could feel the violence mounting Sloane half laughed: here they were quarrelling among the ready naked blades, yet no word was ever worth a blow. And as the violence ebbed from him, he located its source at last. It lay beneath his feet. "I haven't time to argue," he said, and ran.

The void beyond the staircase clanged about him; the caretaker shouted; Sloane's radio crackled and called out; in the shaft of light paintings, pillars, stairs leapt and swayed. Sloane's ankles trembled as he landed on the marble of the foyer. Then he ran past the moon on the globe, which vibrated and began to swing as he rushed by, into the Planetarium.

The arc of the torch-beam streaked across the false sky like a comet; on the ceiling stars sparkled and were gone. Beyond the ranks of benches leading down to the stage, Sloane saw a glass case. At once the air snapped taut. Within the case violence was trapped. Outside, in the foyer, the caretaker swore and clattered closer. Sloane switched off the torch and felt his way forward down the aisle.

He had never been afraid of darkness; it had been the moon that he had feared in childhood, never more so than on the night of the party. But now the darkness seemed a mass of weapons, any one of which might mutilate him. His entire body prickled; each nerve felt the imminence of some poised threat. He could hear faint footsteps, but the room was full of echoes; his pursuer might be at any distance on either side of him. Sloane had failed to count the benches. His hand groped forward from what he had assumed to be the last bench. His fingers touched another, rose and felt the darkness. Moist breath clung to them, and they recoiled from a face.

As Sloane fell back, struggling with the torch, the beam sprang between his fingers. He was close to the glass case, and the caretaker was inches from him. "I thought you'd be here, son," the caretaker said. "What's the game? Trying to twist an old man?"

The caretaker moved in front of the glass case. His face came at Sloane, nodding like a balloon. Instinct leapt and Sloane struck out, punching blindly as he had the children at the party. Gasping, the caretaker fell beside the case. And Sloane saw the sign that the man's body had concealed.

He had seen the sign before, on the day of the murder. Before his mind was overwhelmed he had time to remember and realise. Last time had been in daylight; the sun had helped him for a few hours, but they hadn't won. Already the sign was meaningless; all meaning was contained in the grey stone within the case, beneath the sign LUNAR ROCK.

Sloane felt his mouth forced open from within. His skin ached as if a million needles were being forced through. But they were hairs; and his shoulders slumped as his hands weighed down his arms, formed into claws, and dragged him at last to stare down at the unconscious caretaker.

The Precognitive Trip

Nobody heard the lecture until it had finished, of course. Like the rest, Berger was gazing at the film of the moonlit silver sea unfurling on the wall of the main hall of the Centre. His body assimilated the speech as his consciousness sailed. Then the sea faded and he heard what had been said.

"We are a threat," Rowe had been saying. "If you don't believe me go out and ask someone what's in this building. Evens they'll say witches, Satanists, psychic voyeurs, something they detest. Remember these things if you forget everything else: we could be the next persecuted minority. Make sure we aren't. If you don't wield your image it'll wield you. You have to be a benefit to society and make sure society knows it. But remember also, the majority of us don't choose our talents, they choose us. It's our job to meet their standards."

As the shadow of the Centre peeled back and Berger emerged into dust and sunlight, he realised with a shock not unlike that of precognition that he would probably never enter the building again. The great white walls that had bounded his vision for months were gone. He felt their loss more deeply than the loss of his fellow students. But at the same time he felt vertiginously free.

Rowe came out, his permanent frown cutting a path for him, as Berger and the other precognitives were exchanging a last intricate hand-dance. The dance meant: these movements have no resonance, they can't cause a future, they're neutral. A few people watched as they passed, laughing loudly, shrugging, shaking their heads. "Don't presume to control your future," Rowe said. "You can only ride it. And don't ride too fast or too far. Remember, your body is now."

Berger unlocked his car from its berth, folded the clip into the slim oval body and got in, feeling the single seat embrace him. As the car skimmed the spiralling ramp into the open air above, he wondered whether Helen would be home yet. Probably not, if her new formula had proved itself in the laboratory. So, good: they could ease into the evening and enjoy a leisurely meal now his nine months' term was over. Sometimes the mere attempt to precognesce would leave him drained and ravenous; sometimes, as now, he felt as if he bounded all time. His first, intensely vivid, memory of Helen's flat tingled through him: cool flat dry colours that touched him as she usually did, calmly and precisely; then the not entirely pleasant shock of his encounter with the bedroom, its glass roof unshuttered and open to the night sky, the rich black shiny surfaces of the material she'd synthesised looking moist and, in the context of the flat, secret. Words she'd spoken tumbled through him, somehow linked. "You may not be a poet but you're the next best thing"—"I'm trusting you with our future"—"Compared with you I'm blind but I think perhaps I'm glad"—"Sometimes I think you've seen something you won't tell me."

Ahead three youths drove, their cars clipped together laterally, one more than legal. A police truck swung around Berger's car, its grapples rising before it. Berger's car snaked around the arrest almost vitally; his fingers seemed hardly to touch the controls, nor his mind to touch his fingers. His mind felt borne on currents of time. Yes, he thought: and Helen anchored him.

He was relaxing into his seat as the car settled into the long straight towards the edge of the city when he saw Helen. She was walking on the side of the barriers nearer the traffic. A thrill that felt like surprise and joy passed through him. He had time to think—what's she doing here?—before he saw that he was walking behind her, that he was hurrying to catch her up, that his foot had slipped, that his hand shooting out to grab the barrier had overbalanced her, that she had fallen in front of a car that scooped her up then trampled her.

He flooded back into now. His mind clasped tight and immobile, he guided the car into a transient berth. Then he glared at the empty stretch where Helen had fallen, swept by cars. The road and everything around him looked and felt dull, as if on the other side of a thin almost invisible plastic sheet. For a moment he tried to convince himself that it had been a false precognition. Some of his fellow students had claimed an ability to distinguish the occasional inevitable fake; he never could. But as he regained contact with his senses, realised he was hear-

ing the swish of traffic and smelling the dust, he was sure that it had
been real. He could still see her rolling and jerking beneath the car.

He felt adrift in time. His shock had given his mind no chance to
structure a time or even a date into the vision. Suddenly he realised
that the thrill he'd felt on seeing Helen had been that of precognition.
He clung to that insight. Gradually, stabilised by it, he began to draw
back a little from his emotions. If his feelings for precognition and
Helen were indistinguishable then surely he didn't need both. He hurried to a nearby tc booth, but there was no reply from the flat. He sat
for twenty minutes, gazing at the place where she'd fallen. Then he
grabbed a handful of mud from the edge of a roadside fountain and
used it to blind the tc lens before calling.

"Something's wrong with the link," Helen said. "I can't see you."

"I saw my future today."

"Is it good? Am I in it?"

"No," Berger said. "That's why I'm calling."

"At least come home so we can talk about it."

"No," Berger said. "If I do that it might change. I don't know
when it starts. I'll send you my address when I know where I am so
you can have my things flown. I'll send you money for that and you
can keep whatever's left. But please don't try to see me. Goodbye, and
thanks for being understanding."

As he emerged from the booth he glimpsed a familiar imagined future dwindling, Helen, the flat. A shudder of emotion passed through
him. It faded, leaving him drained and feeling weightless and feverish.
He walked slowly back to his car. Beyond it he saw the bare road
where he'd seen Helen. Suddenly the significance of its continuing
bareness overwhelmed him. He had grasped the present and controlled
the future. Now snapped back into focus, and the road, the sky bluer
than the domes of the buildings around him, his car, everything became dazzlingly real and immediate. He gasped.

He slid into the car. More! He hadn't destroyed a future, he'd released himself into an infinity of them. He remembered the first time
he'd experienced precognition, eight years ago at the age of fourteen: his
instantaneous perception of each moment as the centre of an explosion
of possibilities, and a glimpse of some of their effects. He'd lost that intuition and now it was back, more intense than ever. Why? He slipped

the car into the stream of traffic. Perhaps Helen had been restricting him. He'd felt defined by their relationship but she'd cramped his future, domesticated his talent as she'd domesticated the night sky. Just imagine, having to predict what children they would have, having to map their futures day by day, draining them and him too of potential, pressured into coming up with fakes! No, he thought, leaning back in his seat and increasing speed. He felt himself exploding with futures. He let go of the controls and hand-danced wildly for a moment, laughing.

It occurred to him to wonder where he was driving so fast. This road would take him ultimately to the southern motorway. Then he remembered that some of the others from the Centre were going south to join research projects, which were including precognitives in their teams experimentally. That was where he was heading. His mind knew what it was doing, he only had to trust it. He recalled how he'd thought of Helen as an anchor. In the sense that she'd weighed him down, perhaps. As their future had been forming he would probably have ended up as a policeman, a good dull job anticipating crimes and, absurd still popular word, accidents. He hadn't needed her to anchor him. He was now.

The sky flickered between trees coursing by on either side of him. He eased himself into the rhythms of the road and the car. As the car rode a hump over a stream he glimpsed a car ahead, concealed from him by the top of the rise. Car from side road: brakes fail momentarily: too far out across main road: crash. His hands anticipated on the controls and he sailed around and past the threat without touching now.

He drove on, laughing freely. Everything around him looked refreshed, luminous with futures. His hands in particular seemed magnificent, guiding the car and him at a touch. Rather than fatiguing him, the latest precognition had filled him with a sense of power. They were collaborators, he and the future.

"You can only ride the future." Rowe had said that, and he should know, even though he wasn't a precognitive. Then I will, Berger thought. For a moment he struggled with his mind to recapture the easy precognition he'd just experienced. The sky and the fields began to look heavy, weighed down with the present, encumbering his mind. Then he relaxed his struggles momentarily and his mind slipped him the answer, a simple trusting calm.

The car passed a NO SMOKING sign fixed to a tree. The sound of the engine and the slight deliberately alerting vibration of the car faded into irrelevance and were gone. The car passed a NO SMOKING sign fixed to a tree. Berger's consciousness was dragged back into its socket. The sense of passing everything twice was more disturbing than he'd anticipated. A clatter of birds rose from a field; for a few seconds there seemed to be twice as many, exchanging roles as object and image. Berger's hands tightened on the controls for reassurance. Then he realised that he didn't need continually to check the present. All he needed was calm. It was only like entrusting yourself to a computer pilot in flight. The whole of him smiled broadly, amazed by the simplicity of it. Immediately his mind shifted into a light precognitive trance, and precognition locked into control of his hands.

His mind felt full of drifting ideas. Rowe had been right, you can ride the future, he thought, allowing thoughts to touch him gently as they passed. He remembered how Rowe had encouraged him after Berger had had his psychological, how Rowe had made sure that Berger was given his favourite music over the earphone while he absorbed the lectures and explored his talent, how pleased Rowe had been to hear that he was living with Helen. Well, everyone makes mistakes, Berger thought.

He remembered Rowe saying "We could be the next persecuted minority." He saw him saying "Even I don't like to be as right as that."

Berger's mind reverted, striking the present with an almost tangible blow. His hands clutched the controls. Again he hadn't had time to date the precognition. He tried to hold onto it as it faded, already separated from him by haphazard layers of time. Rowe had been, would be in his office, talking to someone Berger's mind hadn't found significant. The office was redecorated, which implied some way ahead in time. Rowe looked older, and his frown wasn't that of habitual telepathic strain, but an expression of heavy defeat. That was all. When? Why?

For a moment Berger's mind was pure despair. If Rowe looked like that it was hardly worth going on. The sky and the fields streaming by were pressed against his eyes, flat and lifeless and immovable. Then he realised that he was merely denying the future and dooming himself. There was time before Rowe's defeat, time beyond it. Nothing could neutralise the future.

He let his mind seek forward and take the controls. It could have been a fake that his mind had created to provide symmetry. And if not—if he could trace it perhaps he could avert it. Nothing's worse than respect for the future, he thought, that's the worst sort of superstition. He drove faster to give himself confidence and calm. Hedges whipped by like streaks of green paint, the snouts of cars winced back into side roads. His mind wove expertly between possibilities and Berger lay back laughing, alert for the drifting future.

The road began to descend towards the great pale star of an intersection among the fields. Cars scurried across it like a nest of painted ants, entering and leaving the motorway. Berger felt as if he were being borne gently from the sky to the star on the ground. Of course I don't need to take more control, he rebuked a stray thought. I'm a better driver this way, much better. Far better than most of them down there, that's sure. If they're going to persecute us I can see why. Incomprehension and envy, that's what persecution's made of.

He wondered if the others had discovered how well they could drive and saw two of them, several years later, saying goodbye outside a dilapidated tenement. "One day perhaps they'll let us mind freaks drive cars again," one said. "They can't steal all the future. Don't do that, not out here," he said as the other began a hand-dance. "Someone might see us."

That was about the same time as Rowe, Berger surmised as his car flashed between two others at the intersection. Two's more convincing, they confirm each other. I need to go back a little. But mind freaks, when do they start calling us that? He felt the beginnings of despair tugging at him; he smiled deliberately and let the emotion spread and calm him. Can't switch in the middle of traffic. Then—not a drifting precognition, not the easy control that was driving the car, but a shock that overwhelmed his whole mind—he saw a car plunge into the sudden convergence of two cars at the top of the motorway approach ramp and explode immediately, hurling a file of notes high among the fragments. It was his own.

Convulsing, his hands almost braked the car. The sounds and sensations of the intersection crashed back into his brain, so hard as to numb him and to rob themselves of meaning. The cars ahead hadn't converged, and they were further ahead than he'd seen them. It hadn't happened. It wouldn't happen. Berger felt as if everything around him, the speeding ovals, the sudden manoeuvres, the light like sharp blows, the juggled colours and hectic white dust, were piling up uninterpreted inside his brain, yet somehow his hands were still guiding the car. He was suddenly terrified that if he tried to examine how he had kept control then he would lose it.

His brain displayed the crash insistently, as if imploring him to see. He let it focus and establish the calm it required in order to persist. The file was sailing through the air to fall by the side of the intersection, its pages flapping feebly and then subsiding. As cars halted in disarray around the crash, someone ran to pick up the file. On the ramp ahead two cars were converging. I've seen that once or is that now? Berger thought, snatching at the man leafing through his file. No, this can't be what I saw. I haven't reached the end of the precognition yet, it can't overlap with now. The man called the other drivers to look at the file. My God, of course! Berger shouted, and crashed.

"Look at this," said the man with the file. "Here's your explanation. He was one of those mind freaks."

"Mind freaks," someone said. "That's a good word for them. A bloody good word."

Murders

One

All right, Mounth," I said. "I hope you're ready to die."
The point of my knife pursued him as if he were magnetic north. Light touched the edge, then spilled across the blade. Mounth had retreated towards the back of Holoshows Studios until an angle of the wall arrested his shoulders. As he made a timid attempt to scurry free I closed in, and he was crucified and quivering against the walls, and I felt the knife light on my fingers as it sailed forward for the first easy incision, and I noticed that the white walls against which Mounth was pressed were vividly lit. But it was supposed to be night. I tried to ignore the error, but my sense of it wouldn't let me alone. Maird, I swore, and began to reconceive. Without distractions I would have just about enough time.

"All right, Mounth," I said. "I hope you're ready to die."
He was squeezing himself back between the walls. It was dark, and darker within the angle, so that I couldn't see his face. Maird, I thought, maird. Then I heard Thaw getting into his car behind me. Its beam wavered a little, then snapped into place as a frame around Mounth. Thaw sat watching, appreciatively smiling, as I began to open Mounth up with the knife. Mounth's squeals urged me on, but his blood seemed too bright, no doubt because I'd seen little of the real thing, and there wasn't much of it, though my mind would have rejected profusion: indeed, had done so. I finished murdering him and stepped down from my throne, feeling rather disappointed, a minute before they switched off the power.

I stood in the centre of my apartment, gazing at the pastel rainbow whorls and curlicues of the walls, wondering whether Mounth knew I'd been killing him. Probably not, since he was involved in the first of what he'd assured us were the most important shows of his career. Anyway, I didn't care. I glanced at the holocast receivers pointing down into the corner of the room and thought of finding out what Mounth was saying. But I wouldn't; I kept my nights free from Holoshows completely free. And all because of Mounth, I thought. He was the latest and by far the worst of our troubles.

I switched off the windowframes. Activating them had been the product of habit; nobody was ever burgled on the fifteen-mile level, few people were burgled at all. But the government insisted we made ourselves safe during thronetime, so that nobody could accuse them of promoting crime. Nobody except Mounth.

I gazed from the window. At night you might as well be on the viewless ground level as on the fifteen-mile, and even during the day you could seldom see as far as that. I looked down towards the windows of the ten- and twelve-milers, bright discs and polygons set in implicit unseen planes of darkness, their total composition occasionally shifting minutely. I wondered how many people had felt compelled by guilt or fear to watch Mounth's holocast and to forego their thrones. I wondered again if he'd felt me murdering him. I would know tomorrow. I felt vulnerability and triumph swiftly mingling, and my mind retreated to the time before Mounth.

Not that Holoshows had ever been free of troubles. What is? Even the initial advertising of the new experience had fumbled somewhat, largely because the board hadn't wanted the public to dismiss Holoshows as just another disappointment hiding behind the images of an advertising cartel. Tridi was losing huge amounts of cash and credibility to its image, and the inevitable rise in fees was losing it subscribers by the thousand. Holoshows didn't intend to go that way, and we had created our own advertising. But for a while that threatened us as much as it sold. Except you can't touch it, it's solid, we said, and the tridi newscasts grabbed themselves interviewees who said they could see their apartment floor through a perfect holocast—but only by concentrating on one spot for more than an hour, as we eventually discovered and pointed out. If you walk into it you'll harm the holocast, not your health, we said belatedly as the tridis began interviewing mothers who thought their children were being lured into a deadly laser beam (instead of our harmless-for-half-an-hour variety). Our holocasts can't talk but you'll never know, we said to the people the tridis prompted to complain when they found they had to buy speakers as well as receivers and holostage cube. But: she's young, she's pretty, you can't touch but she doesn't mind what else, we said and had a rush of censorious good taste only just before the government did.

I shouldn't say "we" about that period, but I feel it. I was working for tridis then. When their sniping at Holoshows became embarrassing, and the ridiculousness of their attacks clear to everyone but themselves, I went to direct for Holoshows. I'd worked out new techniques of tridi editing and camera handling, and now I translated these into holocast terms. Ego break: until I came they hadn't even thought of taking the holocameras 360° around anything, let alone how. But my experiments were all formal. They didn't risk offending the government.

The government: they were our main trouble, or more accurately threat. They were teetering between the extremes of their two parties. They would touch an extreme and spark off a bill, then a year later to nobody's surprise they might ratify an almost direct contradiction. Work together, hurt nobody and the rest of your time within your own walls is your own; improve yourself, improve the worlds for your children, without help the future's always worse than now. Of course there was more than that to the parties, but it was often impossible to see what. Which made it especially difficult for Holoshows.

It sometimes amazed us how much we achieved. Our more blatant victories owed all to Thaw's strategy. Thaw was resident lawyer at Holoshows. Like most successful lawyers he'd been trained as a psychologist, and there was a whole psychological method in the way he used his stick as pointer, hinted threat, symbol of imminent victory, distracting pendulum as well as a third leg. But his gaunt frame and almost bone-tight skin, refusing wrinkles, were the emblems of decades of experience. It was Thaw, for example, who meditated a compromise on the holocasting of violence. Not that the majority of the government felt that the emulation of holocasts was consistent enough to be legislated for. No, the psychological effect we were accused of producing was subtler: a sort of vague domestic schizophrenia in which people felt dimly caged by apathy, the effect of violence transmitted so persuasively that it became indistinguishable from the real within one's walls. No use our asking why violence, nor our pointing out that the squirts of always slightly unconvincing studio blood vanished in mid-air (accurately, at the surface of the holostage cube). All we could do was transmit a bright coloured outline to the cube itself when violence was imminent and wait for cancellations to arrive from, in the literal sense, disillusioned subscribers.

"If you can stand realising your best isn't always good enough," Thaw once said to me, "you'll survive anything life can throw at you."

He might have been talking about the violence box, as we called the outlined cube, but in fact it was a year later and we'd had worse trouble: indeed, our earlier trouble in purest crystal form. The wife of the Minister for Media had left the room during one of our drama holocasts, and had returned to find a yard-high slightly drooping breast squatting in the corner of the room, the vision of a young holocameraman turned briefly avant-garde director. Arriving home minutes later to find his wife in hysterics, the minister called Emergency Power Control and talked quietly and coldly until they'd cut the domestic entertainments supply for hundreds of miles around the capital. Then: a commission of inquiry, threats of prosecution to half the staff at Holoshows.

Thaw took one glance at the robed bodies of the elderly women who were more than half of the commission and said that the holocast had been meant to express the director's sense of beauty. But meanwhile the minister's wife had wobbled on the edge of a breakdown, and (perhaps from an alarming and astonishingly single-minded sympathy) the majority of the government had upheld the minister's action. Tridis had embraced puritanism and sunk, but we were doing little better as our subscribers relinquished a medium that could be put out of action at whim. Everyone at Holoshows, even Thaw, was chasing the tail of depression.

Then Mounth arrived and offered a telepath show.

Telepath shows had been briefly in fashion some decades ago. They'd been burdened with titles such as the Tridi Telepath Talkshow, but these weren't the main reason why they'd died. So you could watch a perfect tridi of someone talking to guests whose evasions he could read: so? Hardly anyone became involved enough to sue. And when someone did, the law established that while unauthorised telepathy was still illegal, assuming the user was stupid enough to make it obvious, anyone who appeared on a telepath show had authorised telepathy by so doing. That decision was worth a few seconds at the end of a tridi newscast, and when the telepath shows were quietly faded soon after, it was generally agreed that what they'd needed had been far more purpose and force. Mounth had a great deal of both.

I was at Holoshows the day he was interviewed. I saw him stride into Reception, smile warmly but without familiarity at our receptionist, sit his lumberjack frame like a clear-cut sharply pointed statement on one of Reception's stools, hold his open alert face up to anyone who passed, eager to be called to speak. It was then I was convinced for the first time that the old sour belief about telepaths was true: that they adjusted their image each time they felt someone's opinion of them until they'd perfected it. I didn't see him go in, but in another corridor I met the interview board on their way, their faces saying last resort, try anything, what have we come to, and Thaw reiterating his favourite maxim that you can't afford to lose hope until whatever it is has been proved hopeless. He held up a lazy finger to confirm we would talk in an hour.

In fact it was closer to two, and while Thaw was telling me the interview was already becoming legend at Holoshows. Especially Mounth's final speech: "You, sir, you're wondering if the people can identify with a telepath, even one who's fighting for their rights," he said. "I think they can if he's fighting as hard as I will. And you, sir, think that I couldn't keep it up for long. But there's a lot wrong with our world, and I think we should give people the chance to see it all. And you suspect my motives because I used to earn so much as a salesman. But I had to earn money before I could do what I should be doing, if only to give my parents a real home. And you" (who was Thaw) "think I can influence you into hiring me. I can't, I'm not that sort of telepath, which is why I have to be honest. I can't avoid reading what you think about me but I could have avoided admitting it to you. I've been honest and you can show me the door if you wish. But there's no use my avoiding honesty and truth, because they're what my show will be based on if you let me have it. You've said yourselves that today people won't let advertising play with them in any way. I'm sure you'll agree that it's still truth that sells."

"That man's trouble," Thaw said to me. "There's no way of telling them that without looking as if I'm trying to cheat Holoshows of their last chance. But I for one shall be watching him very carefully."

Two

Watching the early, weekly, editions of Truthlight I began to feel that Thaw had allowed himself to be piqued by Mounth's reading of him. That was the period in which Mounth was challenging cartel bosses. He eased in his chat, probing gently and levering open his victim all the way back to a tiny original motivation, perhaps buried deep in a disowned childhood episode, which Mounth would pull forth writhing, shameful and banal. Only then would he slam in the errors that he'd known his victim hoped he wouldn't mention. "See you in six months," Mounth would say. "I know then you'll be able to talk to me and the people as friends."

"There's nothing you can't reduce to an origin that is trivial or disgraceful if you try hard enough," Thaw said to him after one Truthlight show. "It seems to me the point is what's achieved, not where it came from."

"I know appearances are your job," Mounth said, "but they're not the same thing as truth."

I was inclined to agree with him. In the six months he gave them, most of the bosses improved things for their subsidiaries, their employees, often for the public too. Most of them now always masked themselves with secretaries, but that was surely a small price for them to pay. A few improved nothing and blustered publicly about attempted brainwashing; but they were the first to discover that those who refused Mounth's invitations were announced on each Truthlight until they gave in. No use anyone saying he had nothing publicly significant to disclose, as Mounth listed the investors, and the investments began to be hastily if apologetically pulled away by vaguely threatened consciences. "If it's me you object to," Mounth said into the holocamera as the names he was addressing snapped into a frame behind his head, "I imagine the government would arrange for you to be examined by a social telepath." There were smiles of appreciation in the studio at that, and one of them was mine.

I was particularly pleased when he took on the social telepaths themselves. Yes, I knew that the reason he could line up four of them to interview in the studio was that the government didn't dare forbid them to appear; Mounth was already as powerful as that. "Don't look so uneasy, Thaw," I said. "The government never did much for us." But he was frowning at Mounth addressing the telepaths from within his almost invisible protective cube, on which a few of his interviewees had thumped wildly.

"Of course we all know that the only thing we mustn't do within our own walls is harm," Mounth was saying. "And we know that one of your jobs is defining and preventing harm. It's a difficult job and I know we all admire those who do it well. But outside our own walls it's up to us all to be vigilant. Now I gather a few of the poorer people not a hundred miles north of here have been soliciting. It's quite illegal, of course, and I'm sure we'd agree with the government that nobody's so poor that it's necessary. It's the sort of thing that might make a sentimental person disobey government rules," his gaze settling on the trapped expression of a telepath that the holocamera didn't catch, "but I shouldn't be surprised if I didn't even have to mention it again."

"I've seen the people on the north side," Thaw said to me, "and even when Holoshows were at their worst those people made me feel like a millionaire."

Me too, but I didn't say that; I said "I'll admit he could have carried his economic redistribution a bit further before starting this."

"One of these days you'll die of moderation. He'd have to push it a long way further before it took."

"If Mounth were as dishonest as you want me to believe," I said, "the last people he'd challenge would be telepaths."

Soon Mounth's contract came up for renewal. He didn't want more money; he wanted five shows a fortnight, and he got them. He also wanted me to direct. Most of my work was finding itself in the violence box. I'd felt Mounth's slight pained disapproval and had been distressed, because I respected him enough to identify achievement with his esteem. I agreed to direct Truthlight.

Then he began to extend his range from popular targets and the socially crucial to the accepted and applauded: gardeners, architects, tribalist percussionists. Not that his approach had ever been inflexibly hostile, of course; some of them came out smiling, perhaps even inspired. But more came out gripping their expressions as if they were the only part of them left unshaken, and probably they were.

The worst case was Clement, the lightpainter. "And this is a copy of your most famous work," Mounth said to him. "It's been manufactured frequently. I'd like you to take another look at it with us. This long thin beam going in between these two round pink areas: now what are these? They have a kind of soft rather motherly quality, wouldn't you say? And why does this little jagged ray keep trying to escape? I'm sure you can tell us, but let me help."

After that it became unbearable, and at last Clement walked out of the studio with nobody behind his eyes. Mounth saw my disquiet or perhaps he felt it, for he was looking at me when he said "We mustn't be too ready to call things beautiful. Real beauty's beautiful all the way through." I stopped my head nodding and determined to wait until I knew how Clement had been affected.

Others were quicker to condemn Mounth. Although, or perhaps because, Truthlight had the highest ratings in the career of holocasts or of tridi for that matter, every show was pelted with calls and letters of censure, anger, hatred. Mounth ignored the anonymous but often read out and answered the most pointed of the rest, complete with names and addresses, after his interviews. Then one accusation began to recur: that he was extending the range of his interviews so as not to run out of targets rather than from honest feeling. This time he was hurt and he asked me to help him answer.

We took the holocameras into the north side. Exteriors were still appallingly expensive, but Holoshows agreed this once. Mounth stood among the rubblegardens that the gardeners had constructed to unify the environment. I had the holocameras watch some children collecting plastic bottles and cans to build a rubbush outside their five-miler, then turned them back to Mounth.

"When I lived here it wasn't a garden," he said. "We didn't build with rubble, we hurt each other with it. Over there is where I broke someone's hand with a stone because he wouldn't share his beer with me. And just there under the five-miler is where I thought I'd discovered what sex was about, all sweat and blood and haste and sharp bits of stone. I'm better than I was but I've a long way to go, and I want you all go there with me. Someday I'll get married, but not until I'm worthy to. Tell me my feelings don't make sense, then tell me what else does. We all want improvement, it doesn't matter what our politics are. That's why I do what I do." As the holocameras returned to the children waiting for the adhesive on the bush to set I realised that Mounth hadn't been using his body or his image at all. He had answered with pure honest faith.

For the rest of his answer we took the next Truthlight to see his parents. We began at their front door. Everyone has a personal front door and a lift behind it, of course, but few have their own maintenance man living on the next level down. I posed Mounth's parents against the window and a clear twenty-five miles, and I was about to instruct the holocameras to track when I saw Mounth looking at me, and I realised that if anyone was falsifying to make a point it was I. "I'm disappointed and a little hurt," he said. "You still don't quite believe my answers."

Maird, I said silently, and effaced myself and let the holocameras gaze at his parents: chafing a little against each other but largely calm and self-contained, somewhat bemused by all the technicians, a little bewildered still after two years by their new demandingly clean and tidy home. "This was the first thing I wanted to achieve, and the easiest," was all Mounth said.

But it wasn't long after that I first looked up and frowned. While the attacks on him became more vicious, the letters and calls of support multiplied. More than one pleaded with him to interview the only group he'd consistently avoided, the government. "I've pledged myself not to interfere in politics," he said. "To do so would be to interfere with democracy. So I can't lead you in that area, at least not directly. But I hope I don't have to. I hope" (and Thaw mirrored my frown and nodded) "you've learned from me."

Then, almost as if responding to Mounth's implicit challenge, the government produced thrones.

Perhaps their inventor was a government man. If he wasn't he must have been shrewd, for he forestalled any battle with the government's arbitrary puritanism by selling the throne direct to them. Which meant monopoly; but since the throne wasn't a medium in the strict sense the government couldn't be accused of using it for dictatorial purposes. What the throne was, nobody outside the manufacturing process knew. The workers were gagged by the secrets act; the thrones were on hire to subscribers and mustn't be tampered with on pain of prosecution; the power source was concealed and government-controlled, switched on for a quarter of an hour each evening and otherwise apparently dormant except as an alarm system to betray those who tried to dismantle their thrones. We were reassured that the thrones were physically and mentally harmless. After initial widespread distrust we confirmed the statement for ourselves, and discovered what the thrones did.

Imagine: anything. The thrones made that both an offer and an equation. Sit in your throne, pull the crown forward on its arm and cap your skull with it and there it is, surrounding you and solid: your imagination. It's as though all your senses have become eidetic, and that's as close as you'll come to understanding what you're doing. Don't drift, because if you lose control you'll only be disappointed; construct your quarter of an hour toward a climax and you'll feel enriched, not disillusioned, when you take off the crown. Don't look for advertising; listen to your friends who've tried it.

So we did, and the government thrived, and Mounth disapproved. "If you want to ignore what's wrong with the world now's your chance," he said. "Don't change it, just make a world for yourself. But that world's a selfish world and you shut other people out. I don't even want to think how many people must look at their wife or their husband wearing a crown, and wonder. You won't let yourselves be seduced by advertising, haven't you the will not to be seduced by yourselves?"

I'd been one of the first to hire a throne; I knew Mounth believed what he was saying, but that didn't mean he was right all the time. This was too large an issue even for him, I thought; he would have to content himself with comment and with the support of those who agreed with him.

I didn't delude myself long. First we fought the thrones for ratings. Holoshows would have asked him if he hadn't suggested it to them, and so Truthlight was moved to overlap both sides of thronetime. Somehow Mounth arranged for the first set of ratings to reach him before anyone else saw them, but we all knew what they showed when Mounth strode out of Holoshows, looking at nobody. Not all the audience he lost when the thrones were about to be switched on even bothered to return to Truthlight when thronetime was over.

Then he seemed to resign himself to the attitude I'd predicted, though from the first I was disturbed by the way he did so. On the next Truthlight he didn't have a victim; he read out attacks and answered them, and seemed to be dawdling until thronetime. But there was a tension, a sense that he was delaying for some reason. A minute before thronetime he began to stare silently at the chronometer. We and the holocameras gazed at him. Thronetime clicked into place and he turned to the holocameras.

"Now I can talk to all of you who believe we have free will and that it's worth having," he said. "Now the others aren't listening. I think they must be the ones who tell us no murder is premeditated."

"And he's talking maird if he contradicts them," Thaw said in my ear.

"Well, perhaps they're right and we've taken care of that problem," Mounth said. "Let's leave aside those of you who are old or alone and wouldn't care if they were premeditated, shall we? And let's look at something everyone seems to have forgotten. If premeditated murders became common, if murder became an everyday activity, then the tension that produced them wouldn't be high enough for the social telepaths to track down. There'd be only one way to stop them, as there used to be, and that's the death penalty. Don't say anything yet," he said. "Think about it. And if you think this is just a fantasy of mine, I may surprise you."

"All the evidence shows there are fewer murders now the thrones are channelling tension," Thaw told him when he'd finished. And the social telepaths prevented most of the rest, reading emotional tensions unauthorised, by one of those inconsistencies without which no society functions. It was a job in which they could use their talents, and one in which they could feel disliked for what they did rather than what they were: preventing violence by talkouts based on telepathic readings, and if necessary by hypnotic sessions involving a panel of four, popularly regarded as the evil tamperer and the others not seeing, hearing, admitting what he was about. I suddenly realised that Mounth's faith in himself had borne him above and past that sort of work without a glance.

"Fewer murders, are there?" he said to Thaw. "In that case you needn't worry how my hypothetical murders are punished."

In the next few days his method began to pay off, perhaps even more spectacularly than he'd anticipated. Letters and calls of support mounted and toppled off his desk, and all from people who'd been crowned during Truthlight but now were angrily demonstrating their free will. Mounth smiled slightly each time he returned to his desk from reading our files on the government. I had no idea what he was planning, and I wasn't sure I wanted to be involved.

Three

When Mounth acted nobody had a chance to anticipate. I was just one of the audience, gazing and gaping as he listed the ministers, all the most personally unattractive members of the government, who'd been murdered by their secretaries and aides during the past fortnight's thronetimes.

"I hardly need to be more honest, but I shall be," he said. "I watched most of these murders happen, and I had no authority to do so. But our government has never punished unauthorised telepathy when it's been used in the service of the law. If I misjudged and must be punished, then I accept. But," he said with wide-eyed innocence to the holocameras, "in that case our government must accept that these murders are the purest harmless fantasy and do nothing about them."

When some of those he'd named were demoted he ignored them; he was sure of himself. Once our reporters had established that three of the aides had been dismissed, Mounth pounced. "I was going to suggest that these people could be examined by social telepaths, but now it seems I needn't," he said. "The government lawyers say they want to talk to me about my behaviour. I've said of course they can, here on Truthlight in front of us all. I believe there's a question we all want to ask them. Something on these lines: if these murders aren't a serious matter why have these people been dismissed? If even the government's as worried as that, what are we supposed to do? Not knowing if we've been murdered, is that supposed to reassure us? Do they want us to say never mind, it isn't real? Haven't they been telling us it's absolutely real, isn't that the whole appeal of it? Then where's the law in all this? Is it pretending not to notice? We can't dismiss our murderers, haven't we ordinary people the right to demand protection?"

At the side of my eye Thaw's face turned and loomed at me. I met his expression, for we both knew that Mounth was taking an extraordinary chance in describing himself that way. I saw in Thaw's eyes, and felt moving uneasily in my mind, a sudden conviction that he would succeed.

"Aren't we entitled to ask that these murders are stopped in the only way that works?" Mounth said. "Are you thinking you don't need protection? How do you know? I can't be sure, can you? Wouldn't you rather know you're safe? If you agree don't call, don't write. Think it to me. Think it now." And in millions of rooms his smile slowly grew and warmed and embraced his audience.

I didn't direct the first of the Truthlights on the law. A trainee director took over on my free nights, and was overwhelmed by the chance to handle such material. Before the show began I wandered into the studio to make sure no technical disasters were threatening. Thaw, whom Holoshows had self-protectively asked to mediate, was making his way to the stage. I was wishing him good luck when a reporter looked in to give us the news. Mounth had foregone his protective cube as a gesture to the lawyers, and was waiting at the back of the studio to walk on and face the panel.

We closed in on him. "Clement, the artist you broke down," I said. "He's killed himself."

"He would have in any case. He had a death wish."

"I don't think so," I said.

"It was in his work and I read it in him. He destroyed what he couldn't bear. Truth does that to some people, I'm afraid."

When I arrived home thronetime had just started, and I sat in my throne and murdered Mounth.

And next morning I was entering my office when Thaw caught up with me. "Someone murdered Mounth last night," he said. "At least, they did until he felt them doing it. It's all recorded. Come and see."

I followed him, not caring. I thought he was being unnecessarily oblique in breaking the news to me, but perhaps he hoped to convert me to his view of Mounth. If so he hardly needed bother; Mounth would have me dismissed in no time. I sat on a stool in the playback room, beneath the first words of IF YOU VISITED MILLIONS OF PEOPLE YESTERDAY DON'T YOU THINK YOU SHOULD SEE HOW YOU LOOKED, and Mounth opened from a bud of light in mid-air before me, melting a little at the edges until the recording stabilised. Long before the murder I was watching numbly, knowing Mounth had won against the lawyers.

"If you murder someone and a clone is immediately produced with the identical personality of your victim and total continuity, you're still guilty of murder, not attempted murder," he said. "That's not a hypothesis, it's a preventive legal precedent that was established to anticipate the event. If you killed the clone you would be guilty of murder in that instance too, that was also established. But this means that in law if you kill something indistinguishable from a human victim you are guilty of murder. And the whole point about the throne experience is to make it indistinguishable from reality. If that's the case it must be so in law as well. I suppose it's too late to ask the government to switch off all the thrones and repossess them. But the least they must do is retrain the social telepaths to be sensitive enough to anticipate these murders."

"Where's he getting all this?" I said.

"Look at his face, look at the strain," Thaw said, poking his stick at Mounth's nose. "He was using us on the panel as a pool. There was nothing we could have done about it short of getting up and leaving, because if we'd challenged him to quote the references he'd been reading he would simply have picked them out from behind the question. Now look, here it comes, the murder."

Mounth was staring directly at me, smiling with a triumph so confident it hardly bothered to smile. "Excuse me a moment. There's someone out there getting ready to murder me," he said. "A young man called, now let me find his name, Harri Sams. Why is he doing that, I wonder? Ah, because his mother watches Truthlight and because he's heard me saying he won't be able to do exactly what he likes. I don't think he's going to succeed. No, he's off the throne. Thank you, Mrs Sams, that's right, you keep him away from it. Sorry I had to bring you the news, but I'm sure you can handle it."

Thaw was watching me. "Nothing occurs to you about all that?" he said.

"No, nothing."

"Good. Then do me just one favour. Don't think about it. Wait and see."

I didn't intend to think about it; I was too busy thinking of anything my mind could grab that didn't relate to Mounth and the possibility that he'd felt me murdering him. I had a grim suspicion that he might make that revelation and my dismissal one of the high points of tonight's show. Or maybe he'd been too preoccupied with Sams. Taking the hint from that hope, I preoccupied myself with explaining to last night's trainee that the secret of directing Truthlight was to be unobtrusive, even static; he'd been so drawn to Mounth's enthusiasm that toward the end of the show Mounth's head had swelled and sat decapitated in millions of homes, addressing an invisible panel. Then I filled myself with setting up tonight's show and with the fact that since last night's had been more successful than even Mounth had expected, this one would be merely a rerun for the less intelligent and for those who'd been crowned during last night's. Mounth rested in his office and read the response of his supporters. I'd heard that the simplest preoccupations were the best proof against telepaths.

Tell me that day lasted less than a year; the clock told me so but I didn't believe it. Every so often I felt rising to the surface of my mind like the threat of a deafening belch the growing desire to go and tell Mounth I knew he knew I'd killed him, and I would chatter faster and louder to the technicians until it went away. We set up the holocameras so as to contain Mounth and the panel, and placed another pair on standby in case we should need to cut to an emergency set-up (always disconcerting in a live holocast: a sudden blurring into a cube of light, then behind the walls of light the figures have shifted). Then the panel began to arrive, and we waited for Mounth.

Mounth strode onto the stage as the Truthlight theme rang out, a two-bar determinedly rising theme on baritone steel drums, and we knew what sort of show it wasn't going to be. As the lawyers had taken their places I'd hoped they might have produced some answers overnight, but their expressions were those of a cast repeating a dismal rehearsal. Only Thaw had his keep-hoping look, and I felt this had more to do with his philosophy than with the situation. Everyone in Holoshows was watching the show, but they'd already accepted there would be no surprises. This was just a recapitulation before the lawyers were called in to talk by the government, then Truthlight would abandon the theme unless Mounth's arguments were denied. The audience which had been persuaded by last night's Truthlight switched this one off after the first few minutes.

"Even within your own walls you mustn't do harm," Mounth was saying when I began to hear the Truthlight theme. Bom bom, bom *bam*. At first I thought it had crept into my head uninvited, then as it grew a little less faint I realised it was somewhere in the building. Perhaps someone was playing back last night's Truthlight to catch Mounth in a contradiction.

"They try to tell us there are fewer murders with the thrones," Mounth said. "But we can see that exactly the opposite is true." He was ignoring the Truthlight theme, which was repeating like a cramped recording loop and growing louder, loud enough to be picked up by the holocast. One of the off-duty audience moved towards the studio door.

"On the contrary, people who would never have thought of murder are now being encouraged to try it and take it for granted," Mounth said, and I suddenly realised that the theme wasn't only growing louder, it was actually approaching. More than that, an aggressive rather desperate quality was gaining on it, betraying that it was the sound of a human voice. As I realised that, the studio doors were thrown open and in he came, singing.

He was a young man, fashionably bald head shining, his eyes gazing at Mounth and brighter still. He strode up the studio aisle, roaring the Truthlight theme. An oddmind, I thought, struggling to squeeze my face shut against laughter. Let someone else throw him out, I'm the director. I signalled the cameramen not to cut. As I did so Mounth shouted "Sams!" and grabbed Thaw's stick and hurled it at the young man.

The heavy end of the stick whipped round and struck Sams between the eyes. He fell. And I'd turned to call cut when I saw Thaw's face as he leapt.

He'd levered himself painfully but swiftly to his feet behind Mounth. And as if his face were a frame three expressions fell into place just separate enough not to be simultaneous: astonishment, comprehension, decision. Sams had fallen just within the transmitted holostage, but only his back as far down as his hips would be visible to the audience unless they were morbid enough to crawl round for a closer look. Thaw launched himself from his stool and fell short of Sams. He dragged himself rapidly across the stage on hands and knees—I'd never seen him move so fast—and slipped his hand beneath Sams' chest. "He's dead," he said, and his hand came out displaying a knife.

"He had a knife," Mounth said.

"We've all seen that," Thaw said before Mounth's lips had finished moving.

"He was singing to cover his thoughts. He was going to kill me."

"Were you in his mind?"

"Only just in time."

"Were you in anyone else's mind?"

"What? No, of course not."

"Not in mine?"

"Why should I have needed to be?"

"If you weren't," Thaw said, and his words were following Mounth's so closely they seemed to be attached and Mounth's mind couldn't move ahead of or through them, "how did you know my stick was behind you to reach for?"

A cameraman gestured to me for authority to cut. I shook my head furiously, and Thaw pulled himself up with his stick. "Why did you throw my stick?" he said, riding the pause and forcing the pace faster.

"I knew he had a knife."

"So did we at the time you mentioned it."

"Only because you were so quick."

"Weren't you a bit quick to kill him?"

"To stop him killing me. I know everyone else can see that."

"Remember Clement?" Thaw said, and I wondered how long he could juggle faster than Mounth could follow.

"Of course I do."

"The artist you said killed himself because he had a death wish?"

"That's true. He had."

"I think if anyone has a death wish you have."

"I can see what you're doing!" Mounth cried, and suddenly so could I, but Thaw's voice was on top of him. "You spend weeks arguing for the death penalty and then you commit a murder that certainly looks premeditated to me. You didn't have to look for my stick. You knew it was Sams coming to spoil your show and you got ready to murder him. It's a complicated way to fulfil your death wish but that's what it sounds like to me. What does it sound like to everyone else? Do you think he's been trying to get himself executed? Think it to us. Think it now."

Maybe you've been in a room where someone hates you. Possibly you've experienced a roomful of them. Try to imagine almost instantaneously becoming the focus of millions of people, many of them hating you, many believing that your whole career has been directed at achieving your death, and the rest simply bewildered. That's what Mounth must have felt, for when Holoshows tried to investigate nobody came forward to say they'd supported him. Imagine it, and try to feel it as if you're built on belief in yourself and everyone else's belief in you. Mounth did, and that was why he snatched the knife from Thaw. And then went weak or stumbled? Maybe. And fell on the knife.

And that was when I called cut.

Before the governors dismissed him Thaw told them "I didn't think he'd do that. I was being ironic and yes, I wanted him to experience his role turned against him. But whether or not you like it, Mounth's death wasn't the important point. If Sams would have killed him that proves that if you inhibit thronetime murders you promote the real thing. We have to decide which we prefer. And that's what I'm going to tell the government."

Now Thaw works for the government. We still meet sometimes, when he holds the government and Holoshows apart. He often insists to me that he didn't intend Mounth to die. Of course persuasion is his job. At any rate, we agree on one point. The ratings showed that as soon as Mounth fell on the knife almost everyone switched off and didn't wait for me to cut. The experience Mounth had offered was over, and his dying was too realistic and banal. For once we were glad that we hadn't started a trend.

Point of View

I'd just entered the staff area, whose open plan was laid out in the sunlight, when I felt that it was going to be turned inside out. But I had no time to look at that notion, because beyond the half-partition I could see Roy and Ken fighting in the Domestic Science area. Roy had managed to grasp Ken's hair and was banging his forehead against a shelf, like a tough egg. "Now come on," I said. "What's the problem?"

They raced each other to me. Their faces looked rumpled. "He said I had nits," Roy said, whining.

"Well, you did six months ago," I said. Since then puberty had made him fastidious; he washed his hair every second night and was anxious to tell me so. "He hasn't now, you know," I told Ken.

"He hit me first."

"I seem to remember you used to hit someone who called you a nigger," I said. "But you've both got over that. Do you see this is the same sort of thing? Now then, I take it you were in the Domestic Science area meaning to make us some coffee. So how about getting on with it and trying not to break anything. Particularly not each other."

They went behind the counter between Domestic Science and the staff area, their elbows recoiling in an exaggerated don't-you-dare-touch-me. I feared I'd only talked the situation into hiding for a while. I suspected I'd seen merely the surface. Gazing from the window at the warren of grey siamesed houses that surrounded the school, strung on their narrow corridors, I could imagine that the situation was rooted deep and far. But I found myself gazing at the bright still blue sky, which seemed fixed and on the verge of growing brighter; fixed as if to give me a chance to find the point from which everything would be turned inside out. I couldn't, because I felt fixed myself, like an object being scrutinised. I turned and saw Cox watching me.

He was standing at the far end of the counter. When I turned his eyes widened quizzically, and I frowned slightly to tell him that if he wanted me to understand his comment he would have to speak it, and he moved his eyebrows negligently to indicate that if I didn't follow it wasn't worth continuing, and I saw the lines around his eyes which were scratches his wife's sarcasm had made. We stood at either end of the counter with our faces shouting at each other, and when someone had to speak Cox jerked his head at Roy and Ken. "Coddling them again," he said in a tone that meant I was a fool if I thought it was a question.

"No," I said partly to make him shrug and go away, partly because I felt arguing might give me a hold on my mind and on the odd things it seemed to be doing. Of course he didn't shrug, but he turned a shoulder to me.

"I hope you know I may have you next year," he said to Roy and Ken. "If I were you I'd take time off fighting to think about that. You won't know yourselves by the time I've finished with you, but if I were you I wouldn't want to. Then again, if I were you I'd be standing staring with my mouth open instead of pouring coffee."

"Thanks for the coffee. Maybe you ought to be heading for assembly," I told them. "No doubt," I said when they'd gone, "they were standing still out of respect. And I had the situation in hand, thanks." Then I sat against the Arts half-partition and hid myself behind a science fiction magazine while I tried to consider the behaviour of my mind.

But by then it had stopped and all I could retrieve were impressions. Such as a vague yet intense feeling that everything around me had been about to shift into a new pattern, rather like an op art effect, so that my mind had ranged about searching for the point at which to make the optical turn. That was a general impression, so general as to be false: it hadn't been optical, particularly. For example, there'd been my sense of being an element in the process, an object—not of Cox's stare, I decided on reflection. I was still trying to define what had happened when Cox stood up and I, having given him time to be out of sight round a bend, followed to assembly.

Roy and Ken and the rest of their class looked eager to get to the laboratory. "Are we going to do an experiment today?" one of the Lo twins asked. When I said yes there were so many cheers and smiles I had to give at least the latter an echo, but it was no more than that.

The head gave us a daunted therefore angry glance as he made his way to the stage. At least they might enjoy the lesson, which would please me, since chemistry was the one science for which I had virtually no enthusiasm at their level. It was all dull foundation that had to be learned before you could build, and they knew, which only made it harder for me to communicate enthusiasm. Still, they can look forward to next year, I thought and stopped, wondering if I'd scored over Cox at the expense of his classes.

The head appeared on stage and there was the usual scattering of might-have-been-sneezes of stifled laughter. Beneath the screen which the community film society used he looked like a cinema manager determined to quell a Saturday morning audience, but none of us ever had the courage to tell him why he shouldn't wear a bow tie. He made a slightly drooping shelf of his folded arms and began to peck at the silence. "You're all here to get ready to take your places in the world your parents have made," he said, and I knew most of the staff and who knew how many of the kids were thinking: oh, that one again. So long as he didn't try to convince us. I tried again to look at what had happened earlier.

Suddenly I thought I'd found its context. After all, what I'd felt had been a perception growing so intense that it had to break through to intuition. I'd had a similar experience several times on both trips I'd taken, with Laura of the English Department—trips which, as she'd said, were about the most contemporary way apart from science fiction to unite the two cultures. So perhaps what I'd felt had been an acid flashback. In any case, one thing I'd learned from tripping had been that you couldn't regain perceptions by forcing them. I relaxed inside myself. "We're all here to work," said the head. Fair enough, I thought, and I haven't done much yet today. Enough introversion.

"Are we having crystals?" one of the Lo twins asked.

"Not today, er Marie," I said, hoping she hadn't noticed the er. "Today it's chlorine."

"Gases are last," Ken complained. "Why have we got to do chlorine?"

"Because when you come to do your exams," I said, "we think you'll probably be asked about chlorine. Now come on, let's get the background over with and then we can look at the real thing."

I talked and gazed out at the kids among the laboratory benches full of glass tubing and beakers and flasks. Their faces had formed into listening masks, and they looked to me rather too much like shelves of plates. I resisted the urge to hurry in order not to lose their attention, because even if I'd lost it that never helped. This kind of teaching is an act of faith, I reminded myself, if you need to be reassured that they're responding you shouldn't teach. CHLORINE IS, I squeaked on the board, and said "Does anyone know what chlorine is used for? Do you, Ken?" to stop him before his pen, poised on the edge of boredom, touched the bench. But his eyes just widened, and everyone else's stayed that way, until to break the stasis before I went to absurd lengths to evoke a reaction I said "It's a bleaching agent," A BLEA(snap!)CHING AGENT.

"Isn't that interesting," someone hissed.

"No, it isn't especially interesting," I said. "Not now, at least. But someday you may find yourselves using chlorine, and it may be useful to you to know exactly what you're doing." And what an interesting job you'll have, my mind was already answering back on behalf of the kids. Just think, bleaching for a living. "Now look and I'll show you how it happens," I said, picking up the stub of chalk.

But I hadn't been writing long when the murmur began, the eddying wind that doesn't even sound as if made of words and that whips into silence when you turn to it. I wrote the first equation and said "And when that happens," but the murmur didn't make way for me. I was turning when my mind changed.

I wasn't turning fast to catch the murmurers. On the other hand, I wasn't turning slowly to give myself dramatic stature. Yet I had time to watch what was happening to my mind as I made the turn. It had become an object through which I was perceiving. Just that: it was a transparent thing of no particular shape between me and the world. What disturbed me was that it was solid to the touch of one of my senses, maybe more: which one I couldn't tell. It had been the intangible me for a good many years and now here it was, insisting on being felt.

No time, I told it, because the kids were watching me and waiting for me to speak; I had the advantage. But now my mind was nearer turning things inside out for me to look at. Except that as we came nearer I could see that it had nothing to do with turning things inside out but something quite different, so different that I'd had to produce that approximation to comfort myself. It was something like fossils.

Only although this obviously meant something to me I couldn't, now that I examined it, see what. I stared around the laboratory, and the kids stared back at me, and I began to feel vaguely that my surroundings were fixed in some kind of stratum, that the objects around me were closely surrounded by a material, apparently invisible and certainly indefinable so far as I was concerned, that fixed them like fossils. Particularly the kids—because they were alive; that was the reason, I felt instinctively if incomprehensibly.

I'd no idea what game my mind was playing, but thinking of the kids enabled me to run a short circuit back to my job. I realised that they were still gazing at me because they thought I'd been waiting for them to shut up. I grabbed the speech I'd had ready as I turned. "I know this is pretty dull," I said. "But you know perfectly well that if we did the experiment now we'd still have to go through all this and you wouldn't have the experiment to look forward to. So let's get on."

I turned to the board, but it was worse to feel the undefined fossilisation going on behind me, where I hadn't even the chance of making out what it was. If it's a retrip you can ride it, I shouted at myself, and wrote the second equation to prove my control. But I wasn't explaining as I wrote, and I could hear my grip weakening.

Weakening on Des. "I saw your gran last night," he said to Roy.

"So what," Roy said, but it was it more violent than indifferent.

"Thought your dad didn't let her out by herself."

"You fuck off."

Apparently my filing system was still working, because I remembered it had been Roy who'd said that about his grandmother. If he was objecting now it meant something was wrong there. But even as I built on that, some of the material on which I'd built my teaching and which I'd thus concealed began to tumble into my mind. Something was catching me wrong, maybe a mood, and I was thinking how all I could give a kid like Roy was a little mental leverage, which I couldn't force him to use: all I could do was give it to him again if he fell back. And again. But wasn't this merely an answer I'd invented to satisfy myself? Wasn't I trying to avoid the truth that these kids weren't important in themselves, that they were functions of a process, simply a step out of the vicious circle of illiteracy, probably far less than one step per generation? Maybe, I shouted myself down. But shut up.

"Now listen," I said, loudly because of a mounting suspicion that my mind had any number of tricks still to play. "If anyone would like to come up here and take over, fine. Otherwise let's just hear me talking until we come to the experiment. The more stops I have to make the less enjoyable this morning's going to be."

By the end of that my voice was quieter and hard and controlled, and the kids had taken on a kind of chastened stillness. But despite their reaction I hadn't been angry, I'd simply been trying to restrain my mind again, because it had been watching my behaviour with an amused slightly patronising fascination. It was rather like the glimpse of my role-playing I'd had while tripping, except that there was no impetus to drop the role in order to catch myself unmasked. I was still trying to shrug all this off as a failed flashback perception when it drained away of its own accord. For a moment I felt that the viewpoint which had been affecting me had now actually physically withdrawn from my mind, and I snatched at that idea, then I let go in the determined hope that it had gone for good. "And these are the other uses of chlorine," I said somewhat hastily. "Now I'm going to set up the apparatus and I want you to do the same in your groups. After break we'll do the experiment."

In the staff area I glanced rather apathetically at my science fiction magazine. I felt a little as if I were a character in a science fiction story, one that was perhaps still being written. That's what you get for reading Pirandello, I thought. If someone knew the ending I wished he'd tell me. I sat down and read a story about a man who didn't know he was a programmed robot.

The kids were lined up outside the laboratory when I arrived. "Call that a line?" I said. "I've seen monkeys draw better lines than that." I said this largely to distract Roy, for Des was saying to Ken "Isn't his dad going to have his gran put away." I could understand if this were true, because since Roy's mother seemed to do little except procreate his grandmother had become the maternal head of the house, though her mind was long past such responsibility. Which all led to arguments, fights, threats, insomnia, and to make Roy's situation worse he was fond of his grandmother, probably because she didn't keep begetting rivals. "We haven't got the manganese dioxide out yet," I remembered gratefully. "Roy, you be mother."

I watched him doling out the chemical. My mind felt fragile, delicately balanced, glad not to be called on immediately. Fragile in the same way as the kids, in fact. Fragile like a punch in the face, my mind scoffed, becoming a bluff child-hating oldster for a moment. Don't let them kid you they're tough, I retorted. When you had to handle them so carefully lest you crush them against the cages of their childhood while trying to help them at least to see out, what were they if not fragile? Yes, I thought, fragile like Roy, and he was only today's problem. "Pardon?" I said.

"Will Mr Cox be taking us next year?" Susie Lo repeated.

I should have noticed that there was depression drifting like a fog between the groups, making them tense and restless. "I don't know, Susan," I said. "He may be."

"I hope he doesn't," she said, and to loudening agreement, "I wish we could have you again."

"If Mr Cox does take you," I said, "I think you'll find if you try hard enough to get along with him he'll get along with you. Life's like that, you see." Christalmighty, my mind said, disgusted. "Now," I said, turning to the apparatus on my bench. "Don't anyone do anything yet. Watch me first. Here we have a round-bottomed flask" (nudges, giggles) "fitted with a rubber bung," (snorts) "*bung.*" I was glad to hear them laugh, glad enough to smile instead of pretending I didn't understand the joke. "Here's the manganese dioxide, at the bottom, here's the thistle funnel and down this very carefully, very carefully, goes the hydrochloric acid."

I'd begun pouring with almost exhibitionistic care when my concentration seemed to blur. Here was a glass thing like a little fat vase, here was liquid dropping into it, but they didn't mean much to me. It wasn't quite that my eyes weren't focusing, more that their information was coming through confused or that I was meeting it with a so what? or even a you must be joking! But mostly it felt as if my sight were menaced, and my mind was worried and was casting about for a means to give my sight back its conviction. It was like searching for the angle that explains an op art effect.

Then I looked at my hand, pouring the acid.

For a few seconds I didn't know what I was seeing. It reminded me of the effect that occurs if you stare at an object long enough: its shape settles on your retina, blazing up when you blink. Except that in this case it wasn't just one shape; it was the outline left by each movement my hand made. I'd seen episodes in films printed in a slow motion so extreme that you could watch each position a figure occupied parting stickily from its predecessor. This was like that, but the previous outlines didn't fade. It was as if someone had slowed down what I was doing in order to examine it.

What made it more distracting was that it wasn't actually visual. It was so intense that it seemed to be threatening to make itself visible, which no doubt was why my sight had felt menaced. If it had been out there in front of my eyes it might have been easier to deal with. Inside my head it could insist that it had priority over whatever my hand was doing out there. But I knew what my hand was doing; it was pouring concentrated hydrochloric acid, and had been doing so for I had no idea how long—not long enough for the kids to become restless, apparently, nor for the acid to brim over. I thrust away a recurring amused fascination. It was my hand and if I couldn't control it nobody could. So, forcing my mind to catch hold of my hand's most recent movement and to keep pace with it, I did.

"And there it is," I said. "Now let's see you try it. If you're not quite sure of anything, don't be afraid to yell." I was glad when nobody did, and gladder not to hear the hushed disagreement which meant that a group was determined to risk resolving a doubt for itself— encouraging in theory, but not where burners and concentrated acid were involved. I stood behind my bench, reassuring myself by the duplication of activity each group maintained. Around them their movements effloresced.

So this is what it was all leading up to, I thought. So long as it doesn't overstay its welcome I'll cope. I knew that the worst response to an acid flashback was paranoia, because that was self-perpetuating. If you rode the experience it would fade away eventually, integrated. But it was a year since I'd taken a trip; once I'd discovered the extra perceptions I'd set myself to learn to recapture them unaided, and to some extent I'd been successful. I'd felt my teaching was a discipline that would enable me to master and integrate these experiences, as well as being helped by them. It annoyed me that this belated pointlessly elaborate perception should suddenly appear unasked. At least it explained everything by cumulation: the impressions of an optical effect, the amused fascination, and I supposed everything did seem fossilised within the persisting movements. But this isn't it, a querulous intuition seemed to be insisting. This is only a stage on the way. Oh shut up, I told it.

"Go on, Roy," Susie said. "Don't mess."

I'd been trying to avoid doing more than glance at the kids, since when I looked away their accumulated outlines faded. I'd been glancing most often at Roy, because I knew his tensions hadn't been released. I looked at him now. He was about to pour the acid. "Who's messing?" he said. I couldn't tell if there were real tension between him and Susie. I started across to the group, trying to be unobtrusive, as reminiscences of their movements bloomed around them.

And my mind arrived where it had been heading.

Maybe it hadn't been able to take the whole thing at once. It had worked up to it by easy stages. Not easy enough so far as I was concerned, though, because they gave no idea of how it was going to feel.

It was the accumulation of outlines, fanning out wilder and faster. It was the slow-motion film, speeded up without eliding any of the visible quanta of movement. I realised that it was my mind, not time, that had gathered momentum, and at once I was lost. Because my mind was blinded by the intricately overlapping webs of movement, and I no longer knew where the present was. Given the speed with which the ripple of outlines had been impressed on my mind I knew that they had overtaken the present; that was surprisingly easy to take, maybe because I'd been timeless on trips. My nagging intuition compared it all with an impatient reader flicking pages, but I didn't see how that helped. Not unless it helped me to feel I'd been hypnotised by the movement of the pages, because I'd halted, hemmed in by impressions that my mind refused to accept.

I was gazing at Roy, because I'd been making for him. There was something about him that communicated to me even through the enormous complicated cocoon of movement which was my mind's version of him, something simple enough for me to grasp. He was afraid.

He'd seen me advancing on him and suddenly halting in the middle of the floor, staring wordlessly at him. That might have been the explanation, but Roy would more likely have turned sullen and tough. Somehow I didn't think any sight of me was enough to scare him. I thought it was something worse, and I had the sudden dreadful notion that he was feeling what I felt. On a trip your most powerful experiences can often reach other people directly. Perhaps the effect on nearby adolescent minds is all the more immediate and irresistible. I was sure that Roy was suspended helpless and bewildered in the accumulation of his movements, as in amber.

"Stop a moment, Roy," I blurted as if to hold him still while I searched for his present. And, glowering a little because I'd betrayed him to Susie, he did.

So perhaps I was wrong. Or perhaps he was glowering because I'd interrupted him when he was trying to ignore the disturbing behaviour of his mind. Or perhaps that and Susie too, because kids' minds, the same ones that can be harmed by the most minor sort of carelessness, can sometimes effortlessly hold paradoxes and complexities of feeling that would half pulverise mine. All I knew was that I could see Roy again, that I'd traced him back through his movements to the point at which he'd halted for me and there he was, solid and with the acid in imminent danger of spilling on the bench. "No, it's all right," I said. "Go on. Watch what you're doing." And I didn't mind that he resented my interruption; in fact I was glad to see Susie agree with his puzzled shrug.

"Now listen, everyone, I've got a headache," I said, closing my eyes because I couldn't bear the sense of their outlines of movement filling and emptying progressively as they turned to me. "I'm going to sit at the back while you carry on. If anyone thinks I'm needed for anything call at once, all right? At once."

"Shall I get you an aspirin?" Marie said, and "Shall I see if someone else'll take us?" said someone else.

"No thank you, or we won't have time to finish," I said, noticing that they all looked rather bewildered, perhaps because of my behaviour rather than because they were sharing my experience. I made my way between the benches, which since they didn't move seemed aggressively solid within their outlines. "I'll be back here looking something up," I said. "Don't worry."

I sat with a textbook of parapsychology that one of my predecessors had left in the hope of broadening our minds, but the amused fascination began to mount so fast that I had to turn to the blank flyleaf before I started laughing out loud. After a while I was able to look at the kids and watch the extraordinary silent whirring of movement redescribing the patterns already impressed on my mind. I rather hoped nobody would need me, since the entire laboratory seemed to be looped and crossed by the paths the kids would follow at the end of the lesson. My mind felt transparent and empty, merely a medium, and my heart felt like a fist clenched hard and frequently. I watched and clung to the present and trusted the kids.

When the bell rang they'd cleaned up and labelled their gas-jars proudly and left them by the window for next time. They sped through their paths, erasing them as they went. I sat at the bench and gazed, just gazed. My mind felt scoured.

It was so lightened as to be sensitive to the slightest touch. I sat and let my eyes gradually recover my surroundings, and I felt the drifting feathery touch of a thought on what seemed to be the very edge of my mind. Leave him now, it said.

I didn't respond, I was still gazing. After a while a thought floated towards the first, barely emerging from the other side of my mind, or close and so low as to be a whisper, or so far in some other direction as to arrive delayed and faint. He's all right, it said. We haven't left any marks.

He knows, you fool, said the first in diminutive rage.

How can he, the second scoffed. Nobody could that far back.

Then why is it forbidden? I knew I was right. We shouldn't have.

Look, back then they couldn't even conceive what we're doing now. They thought there'd be some sort of machine that would take you back physically.

Then why did he behave the way he did?

I'm not saying he didn't feel us reading through him. But he'll never know what it was.

But that proves what the law says. No matter how far back you go, there was never anybody you can use as a neutral point of view.

That's not what it means. He may think about what happened for the rest of his life but he doesn't have the concepts. So it doesn't matter.

Then what does?

Let's say he was a good deal further forward, nearer us. Then he might be able to realise that anything he does is fixed, predestined as they called it then, because it has to lead to us. I mean, we're here, that can't change, so nothing that leads to us can change, that kind of paradox doesn't exist. But he mustn't know that, because that means he knows everything he does leads to those who destroyed him, that's us. Destroyed him because either he thinks himself into complete apathy or he goes wild trying to do something that isn't fixed, but of course both ways he knows he's doing what he has to do to lead to us. That's the paradox but it affects only him. But we're talking about someone much further forward. This one is open or we couldn't have used him as the point of view, but he's ordinary otherwise because that's what we wanted to read, an average day. It's beyond his comprehension, don't worry. He'll find some other explanation to satisfy himself.

But suppose he can hear us?

He can't when we're not reading.

You can't be sure! The law doesn't say!

Oh all right, we'll leave him. I think we read all there was to read, anyway. I didn't think it was much. I don't think reading's worth it.

Fading rapidly, and I had to add the last word. I sat at the bench a few minutes longer, but my mind was silent. Meanwhile, before my gaze but unremarked, reality had fallen back together for me. I locked the laboratory and made for the stairs.

I sorted out the crucial elements from the morning and earlier. I'd been preoccupied with the kids' futures and the way they were cramped. I'd been reading science fiction. These elements and the belated effects of acid had constructed this intricate symbolic statement. I was glad that it had reached what I hoped was its final climax, and unsure what it meant, but not entirely sorry that I'd had the experience. At least I'd had a useful glimpse of my mind's tendency to emblemise.

Two flights down I could see Roy and Ken in the doorway to the yard. I thought of trying to discover whether Roy had shared my experience to any extent. I shook my head. The only certain effect that would have was to make it more difficult for him to store and perhaps forget.

"Up you, you nigger," Roy said.

Right, I thought. This time I'm going to find out what it's really all about. Then maybe I can work on it. From the window on the stairs I saw Cox striding across the yard, bearing down on them. I hurried downstairs. At the back of my mind a doubt was nagging fretfully: surely I didn't think that my mind was capable of producing so complex and subtle an experience as I'd had? Why couldn't I face the possibility that it had been real?

I reached the bottom of the stairs. So if it had been real, I thought, what? I couldn't do anything about it, could I?

"Now come on," I said.

The Grip of Peace

If my wife and I hadn't argued before our first hyperflight together this world would still be haunted, but in quite a different way.

That sounds like a shipman's tale, and I'm sure you've had your fill and plateful of those on your way here. But don't put this pamphlet down. I'm not shipping you, be sure. It means what it says on the cover: WELCOME TO HAPPYHOME. Someone will have welcomed you when you left the ship's boat, but they'll have left the welcome tale to me.

I hope you didn't expect me to use a telerecording. We're not much for next best things here. We're personal contact people, and we don't like to undermine that with telecommunication. I may be dead by the time you read this, and I wouldn't want you watching a ghost that's going dim with information decay.

If I'm still around we'll meet at the ragefest tonight. It'll be in the honour of new arrivals, but if you're tensing up for it, don't: that's exactly what you don't need. Just relax and let me tell you my story. My name is Tid Frobes. I'm a doctor. I hope you can read my handwriting.

When I came out of hyperflight my wife Luli was staring at me. The cabin screen was telling us we'd been hyperflying for three hours, and we were one and a half real hours out of Happyhome. You must have been through it to get here if they still do it that way, so you know how it feels—as if you've nodded off for a moment and the screen has awakened you, except that all your senses feel on edge and clutching for something just out of reach: the nagging notion that you had a glimpse of some enormously important concept while you were out, what the shipmen call the Unremembered. I had to cope with that and more, because Luli was glaring at me as if I'd fallen asleep while she was speaking. I might well have. We'd been arguing up to the moment of hyperflight, and whatever those activities are that we know the brain performs in hyperflight, they might well have been three hours' marshalling of arguments so far as Luli was concerned. "You didn't want to marry me," she said. "You just wanted a nurse you could work with."

"I wanted to take you out of the group," I said. They may well still group back on Starnose (yes, the red planet that joins its neighbours in making a beery face of its parent body when you catch the orbits right). You could join any group if you knew someone in it, and once in you shared everything, including each other. "You said yourself you needed more real demands made of you."

"But I didn't say I wasn't happy in the group." People matured from one group to the next; sometimes couples married. It's surprising the number of people you meet again in different groups; Luli and I had met in two, though we weren't consciously pursuing each other. You were never asked to leave a group, but the married tended to drift away. "I think you signed for this flight just so I'd have to leave," she said.

"But you didn't have to. No torture or hypnosis was involved." We're doing well, I thought bitterly, for seven weeks married. I'd hoped to persuade the shipmen to perform a timebonding ceremony, their marriage ritual that's based on a shared sense of the way the ageing of the rest of the universe speeds up during hyperflight, but we'd hardly been in the mood. "If you'd waited for the next traderoute ship we'd have had a few years to think about marriage," I said. "Maybe we'd have been better suited then."

"Maybe you should have left me behind your time," she said, her eyes furiously moist.

I wondered if we could be heard in the next cabin, where our travelling companions, inventors of the peacecube, were berthed. "I'll tell you what we're really arguing about," I said. "Not getting married, and not where we're going either. You were the one who couldn't wait to breathe open air. No, you're frightened of remembering the Unremembered. You were frightened before we went into hyperflight, you can only be more so now. I don't know why you can't just worry that the automatics might fail, like I do. Not that they have for centuries."

Her eyes said I was right, but the way they focussed past me showed I couldn't have handled my understanding worse. Her mouth was moulding a cold grin around a retort when she was interrupted. "Engineers Pefa Bain, Hodd Tangam, Doctor Tid Frobes, Nurse Luli Frobes," the screen called.

"See," I said, hastily unstrapping myself from my couch, "we're separated already."

"All please report to the communal area to discuss urgent message from Happyhome," the screen said. Only it didn't say Happyhome, since the world was then described and located by a mass of symbols only a computer could pronounce with conviction, or want to.

"Maybe we are better in a group than with each other," I said. "Let's see."

I was glad to leave the rounded-off cube of the cabin, for it made me feel quarantined—which of course I was, along with anyone else who wasn't shipborn. Loudly silent, we walked along the imperceptibly curving corridor to the dining/viewing/recreational area. Pefa was saying "Engineers indeed," and Hodd said "What else are we?"

Ahead through the viewport, Happyhome was a pale apple patched with two giant paralysed amoebae of water, slowly filling with glints as the world turned. "So what do you think is urgent?" Pefa said. "Too much good air, too much fresh food?" I tended to agree with her innuendo: there couldn't be any cause for alarm on Happyhome. We four were heading there not because we thought medical staff were urgently needed, but because we were attracted. Even the local microbes had ready-found answers in the Starnose antibiotics laboratories, and otherwise Happyhome was a world of bright airborne insects and mostly edible vegetation, scattered with all the periods of architecture of a long-gone race like a planet-sized archaeological exhibit.

"I suppose it would have been too much to expect the ship to transmit the message direct to us," Hodd said. "We might have breathed germs all over the transmission."

A disapproving shipwoman's face jerked into frame on the screen beneath the viewport. "Message from [Happyhome] follows," she said. "Unidentified local effect has caused breakdown of colony structure and of many individual personalities. Be ready to conduct psychological stabilising of thirty-one cases. Remaining eighteen colonists have also requested permission to board."

"That's not in their own words," Hodd said.

"That is an accurate digest of the message received," the ship-woman said. "We were unable to record."

"Can we tell them we'll be ready?" Luli said to me.

"We shall transmit your assurance," the shipwoman said, interrupting my nod. "Since we are only an hour from arrival, we have not the time to convert your screens for transmission. You would of course need bridge permission to use the main transmitter, as well as lengthy sterilisation."

"I would just love," Hodd said, sitting forward with a vicious smack of her heels on the deck, "to go and sneeze over the lot of them."

"All cabins in your section will be made available," the screen said. "Five extra couches will be supplied for use in the communal area. We are trying to determine whether your home world will fund our return there with your patients. . . . I am now informed that Starnose has taken responsibility for this deviation. We shall orbit [Happyhome] for three days to allow you to prepare your patients for hyperflight."

"There's a lot that's unremembered on this ship," Hodd said, "such as human feeling." But the screen was blank. "God's bowels."

"I know, but never mind," Luli said. "Let's make sure the couches are ready."

"At least we'll be able to give the peacecubes an optimum test," Pefa said, looking slightly worried.

"That reminds me," I said. "I just went Pefa and Hodd to explain to me exactly how peacecubes work."

"Well, good. Good!" Luli shouted and stalked away, trailing a promise of the next instalment of our argument.

"We'll hurry," Pefa called after her, and Hodd shrugged. When I caught up with them they were already unpacking the foam-lined carriers in their cabin. Hodd lifted out one of the three-inch cubes in its heavy metal sheath and handed it to me with what I immediately discovered wasn't delicacy but controlled strength, for the weight of the cube was considerable. "Forty-eight cabins," she counted. "A cube in the eighth, the twenty-fourth, the fortieth, and one in the communal room."

That was the cube with which they explained. The rim of Happyhome had swelled and was touching the frame of the viewport. "Once it's unsheathed," Hodd said, "the cube is triggered by any form of suffering and goes to work on soothing it, which it does by one of a number of methods that the trigger selects. Redirecting the patient's preoccupation, intensifying memories of pleasure, focussing on any positive philosophy the patient may have, and so on. It's a little like the old anaesthetics."

"Nothing of the kind," Pefa said. "It's a substitute for telepathic nursing. If there hadn't been so little need for practical nursing on Starnose we wouldn't have had to invent this."

Two young shipmen, sealed from head to foot in sterilised snapsuits over their clothes, were setting up extra couches around us. "Maybe," Hodd said. "Anyway, you can see that's a lot of work for something this size to do, even today."

"Now hold that," Pefa said. "The telepaths who imprinted the cubes did all the work. It took a lot of discipline for them to produce universal responses."

"You don't need to envy them," Hodd said. Luli was trying to help the shipmen as they dodged around the other side of the couches. Her violently silent back was turned to us. "We're going to need to educate the nontelepathic medical profession to use cubes. I mean, we don't want doctors operating with a worry somewhere in their minds and inadvertently getting high on a cube."

And so on, chipping away at each other's ideas. That must have been the way they worked on inventing the peacecubes, I thought, and they succeeded then. The shipmen fled. Pefa unsheathed the pale green crystal cube for a few seconds but I didn't feel anything, perhaps because I didn't feel I was suffering. Pefa said to Hodd "I wish you hadn't made that remark about the Unremembered. It's basically a religion, you know." I went to find Luli, but she snapped a couch cocoon angrily at me.

Yes, all this has to do with the haunting of Happyhome.

If you think we might have been insufficiently prepared for the cases that were boated up from Happyhome an hour later, you're right. We'd expected the kind of fraying of personality that may develop in a small closely dependent pioneer group, the casualties of authority conflict, a few cases of world shock for variety. We weren't ready to meet a biochemist cradling the ghost of her second miscarriage. Nor a nutritionist who had to be ferried separately from an ecologist to prevent his breaking the latter's jaw again. Nor two engineers, transport and electrical, both laughing harshly until one burst into tears and the other followed, until either led back to laughter. All we could do was persuade everyone to lie down, the worst cases nearest a peacecube, and unsheathe the cubes. Then we wandered among them, feeling our concern dimming as the cubes took hold, then flooding back like adrenalin as we moved beyond them. The boat went down for the rest.

Even those we theoretically weren't treating were lying down. All except the correlator of the group, a psychologist called Hald. If it hadn't been for a sense of tight unrelenting control, as he consciously preselected his every movement, you might not have realised he was from Happyhome. He stood in the entrance to the communal area, beyond the radius of the cubes, groping for memories. "It was a model colony at first," he said. "No arguments, no conflicts, total community. Then gradually things went wrong. Some of the most placid of us began to lose their tempers for no reason and commit spur of the moment violence. That was five, six years ago. We called for aid but of course you were on your way in hyperflight. Things became so bad nobody could bear to be touched, they were sure to have a flash of violence. So the colony moved apart. There were no children, only miscarriages. What happened as people were left alone you can see."

His lips didn't move like a talking mouth, they looked as if he were operating them from behind with his fingers. "Whatever it is, it isn't chemical. It isn't in the food or the atmosphere. It isn't microbiotic. And I'm sure it isn't world shock. All I know is it can't be perceived, not even when it's working on you."

The people lying in the communal area were stirring and muttering uneasily; I knew I should go to them, but Hald was staring at me as if he'd fitted his fingertips within his eyeballs. "There was one thing," he said. "People dreamed. I did myself lately. You know a good deal of the local architecture is still standing. No records of the race, those must have been destroyed or decayed. Just the architecture. The more recent it is, the simpler it's become. The early building is complex, then there are things like spiral shells, and the last forms of all are spheres. There's only one place they're found and that's near the colony. They're about a thousand years old. We never knew what they were for. But people dreamed about them. Every night."

His eyes were full of what he thought that meant, but he wouldn't tell me. I might have asked if one of the others hadn't swung himself off his couch, shouting "There it is! That's what's doing it!" and pointing at the peacecube. They were all shouting and pointing. I could hear it spreading into the cabins. The doors were opening and they were all converging on the nearest cube.

Hald stepped within the radius and shrank back. "You mustn't use that, whatever it is," he said. "Not on these people."

That was all he could or would say. Pefa and Hodd sheathed the cubes, looking morose and baffled. Luli and I injected the patients with soporifics. I wondered what we might have to use when they came out of hyperflight. Hald refused his injection and went from couch to couch, gazing down at the sleepers. "It's what I was for," he said.

In the morning—which is to say, when the viewport had to be dimmed because the light on the larger sea was spilling in and searing our eyes—they were all still asleep. We'd given them the maximum dose; if they hadn't improved when they awoke, one more would take them up to hyperflight. Hald awoke on a couch, glaring about with a vengeful look for the thief of his consciousness, as Pefa and Hodd arrived to begin their shift. I heard Hodd begin to ask him something, but Luli and I were trudging away to sleep.

Later, as a timid snapsuited shipgirl brought us food, averting her eyes for fear of having to watch us eat, Hodd explained why she'd consulted Hald. "We stick it up our noses, if you want to know," she called after the girl, and told me "Evidence is that whatever broke up the colony takes years to accumulate and works only down there. I'm assuming brief contact with it won't affect us later. So we're going down."

"We need an inkling why the peacecubes don't work," Pefa said.

"Certainly," Hodd said. "And I can't say I'll mind upsetting the shipmen, either. You know how they dislike the idea of leaving the ship for a nasty unhygienic world. I wonder why. Maybe it makes them feel there's too much universe for the Unremembered to control after all."

I shared the urge she was trying to hide: to prove herself superior to the shipmen, who had mastered and built a philosophy upon the vertiginous clutching of the mind after hyperflight. We four needed to dissociate ourselves from the shipmen, for Starnose had been a closed environment too: exhilarating gravity, tracts of vegetation and integrated architecture, everyone's favourite hydroponic foods, but domes pressed down over it all to keep out the killer atmosphere. We'd needed the outward call of Happyhome; we'd been settling into the stasis of a disinfected perfection. "How many do we need to look after the patients?" I asked Luli.

"The soporifics have twelve hours to run. One can manage for the rest of the day."

"We'll draw lots," Pefa said.

"Don't bother. I'll stay."

"Are you sure?" I asked Luli. "Wouldn't you like to go in the open?"

"I've said no, haven't I?"

"We'll be away for a couple of hours, no more," I said. "There's no danger. Don't worry." But she'd turned away, almost colliding with Hald, who was frowning anxiously at us.

When we landed the shipman pilot hardly gave us time to clear the field. I felt as glad as Hodd that he would have to brave the world again in two hours to retrieve us. We stood at the edge of the colony and gazed about. After the controlled and unchanging illumination of the ship, what overwhelmed me was the sunlight. A yellowish sun sailed in the blue-tinged sky, brushing off occasional white clouds, and as they slid free the light welled up intoxicatingly. The pale green grass, the fifteen-foot vegetables that clustered nearby like a gathering of melting pink spoons with lowered heads, the squat round flat-topped white buildings of the colony, all swam in the light, piercingly clear. "Let's get the transport," Hodd said.

We'd borrowed a map of the colony and its surroundings from Hald. As we walked through the colony I glanced up at the railed observation roofs. I imagined colonists gazing out on their landscape. When this hospitable world had been discovered, so near in hyperflight terms to Starnose, all we specialists in the minutiae of our world had looked up from our microanalysis and outward again. I remembered my joy at the promise of being able to practise rather than theorise. I was sure that if this world proved uninhabitable it could only add to the suffocating apathy back on Starnose. I gazed up at the empty railed roofs. A few grains of dust sifted down.

One groundcar had been driven into the edge of the parking bay and left there, buckled. We took another car and headed for the oldest of the nearby groups of surrounding architecture, at Pefa's suggestion. Since the colonists must have performed all the obvious analyses, she felt we needed to be intuitive. We left the flexite cover turned back and listened for sounds above the drone of the car. The pale grass stirred in a breeze, as if ruffled by cloud shadow.

Our first sight of the buildings was of a series of irregularly spaced stone loops rising over the horizon. Half a mile separated the furthest apart. The nearer we approached the more bemused our eyes became. Eventually Hodd, who was driving, had to halt the car. The loops were only the highest tips of an intricate filigree structure, formed of intertwining coils and arcs of multicoloured stone. Some arcs were covered with rung-like protrusions, others bulged like a sated snake and were living quarters, to judge from the openings they displayed. The whole was over fifty feet high. "I'm surprised it wasn't this the people dreamed about," Pefa said.

We walked closer but didn't venture beneath the structure. "Look at the foundation," Hodd said. "The whole thing was carved from a single block."

I suddenly saw that the structure looked like a nest of inextricably ossified rainbows. "If we knew anyone as aesthetically obsessed as this race must have been, we'd be treating them," I said.

We were glad to drive on, spreading ripples through the fields of grass, which stirred like the fur of a sleepy cat. The stone maze sank beneath the horizon. "I'd like to think it was back there, but no," said Hodd. "Hold said they went over it thoroughly: nothing. Not all of them visited it, so it couldn't have been a psychological effect. And besides, that wouldn't explain why they dreamed of the other area."

Soon the next set of architecture was mounting the horizon. As Hald had said, they were like spiral shells, revealing themselves ring by coiled white ring as we approached. Each of the forty-nine buildings was composed of seven rings and a topmost point. They were arranged in a square of seven ranks. Grass stirred feebly at their bases as if crushed, and clouds of insects faceted with colours flickered swiftly between them. As I gazed at the cloning of massive cones I became aware of Pefa, who had frozen, listening intently.

"I'm trying to get hold of a feeling I've had since we landed," she said. "Have you ever read what it was like in the eye of a cyclone? A kind of uneasy calm. I suppose it's just so quiet after the ship."

I remembered the call-notes and the whirs and creaks of energy, and listened to the hushed breath of the grass, and nodded. Hodd had entered the base of a cone. As we followed I was counting the narrow viewslits in each ring: seven in the topmost, fourteen in the next down, and so on. We looked through an open exit from the spiral hall into the first room. The ceiling reminded us gently to stoop. The cones were clearly a simplification of some of the forms of the multicoloured structure, but still I felt raw with unease. It wasn't the desertion, for the abandoned colony hadn't bothered me. It wasn't the unfamiliar functions of the seven-slitted room, with its oddly scooped stone benches and its hornlike carvings protruding from the wall. What I found intensely disturbing was the formalism of the place. It made even the clinical life of shipboard and Starnose seem preferable.

I was glad when we left the cones below the horizon. We swathed our way towards the colony. Before we reached it we would encounter the last construction the lost race had made. Pefa was staring ahead, dashing her hair from her face. The grass hissed by and leapt from beneath our wheels, scattering in our faces.

At first I didn't realise I was seeing the spheres. Something was gleaming like trapped stars through the grass. As we came nearer the grass sank like cloud from the lights, leaving them suspended within a faint circular presence. They were manufactured spheres of transparent crystal, at whose centre a steady light was contained. There were five of them, set unequidistantly along a straying line. We stood in front of the central sphere and the light gazed at us.

"They're the lost race," Pefa said suddenly.

"What?" said Hodd sharply, then her eyes widened.

"The light in the crystal. That's where they went, that's why there's no trace of them. They simplified themselves and their environment until they had psychic control. They must have been preventing everyone from realising, it's too obvious to have been overlooked otherwise. Yes, and it was the struggle to realise that made everyone dream and eventually crack."

"We must tell them," I said. "Once they know they may be able to return to the colony." I was full of ideas, spilling them. I pulled aside a long blade of grass that was obstructing my view of the sphere, and tried to grasp an idea about Luli that was staying out of reach. Yes: I realised the way she'd manoeuvred to let me come down here, although she would have loved to visit an open world. We have a fine marriage, I thought, despite the superficial turbulence. "We won't have to leave," I said. "I know we won't."

I was still secure with my thoughts behind a smile when the boat returned. Only when Hodd began arguing with Pefa did I rouse myself, and then only to nod. "You're going to have to force a lot into your explanation," Hodd said. "Such as why any race would leave itself so exposed and vulnerable. You'll agree they would be. The fact that you spotted them at once proves that."

"It's a cumulative effect, remember. Maybe there are some minds their defence mechanism doesn't work on."

"Such as yours? What you'd like to believe is seldom valid science. Ask Hald if they analysed the spheres. I assume you aren't saying the spheres could persuade them they'd run a thorough analysis?"

"I don't know," Pefa said furiously. "Maybe they could."

We'd hardly docked when she was running to the passenger quarters. I'd followed her closely enough to be within earshot of her question to Hald when Luli rushed up to me, crying "What happened? What have you done?"

I glanced down at my hand, directed by her gaze. The skin between the fingers was black with blood. There was a long deep cut in the palm. "It's all right," I said, wanting to know what Hald had replied, not wanting Luli to see my disquiet. "I'll see to it." I hurried to my equipment in the storage area.

When I'd finished examining myself I slumped. The cut wasn't anything antibiotics and a bandage spray couldn't handle. I'd realised by now that I'd cut myself on the blade of grass I'd moved from the sphere. No doubt there'd be no more to feel than the sly tickle of a razor blade, though I couldn't remember even that.

Pefa appeared, looking disconsolate. "Hald says they took one of the spheres into the colony to examine it," she said. "The light is just sunlight, they blocked it off easily. There's no energy in the spheres. I thought they were something like peacecubes, but they're just objects."

Then I remembered something, but before I could tell her Luli looked in. "As I thought, just a cut," I called. "I'll take over now. You catch up on your sleep." I didn't mean to sound as if I were dismissing her, but after a glare she flounced away.

"You ought to try and see her more," Pefa said. "No, not more. Better."

"You could be right," I said. "But look, there's one question we forgot to ask. Let's go and see Hald."

By now he'd loosened up somewhat, relaxing at least until he caught himself at it. I was afraid he mightn't answer, but he did. "I dreamed the same as everyone else," he said. "I suppose it was like having a blind spot, only you knew there was something hiding behind it. I'd be standing between the spheres and I'd know there was something besides them and the grass. But every time I was on the brink of becoming aware, the awareness was—turned off, I suppose. That's all. It kept repeating until I woke up."

"You and Hodd think," I told Pefa. "I'll think too. It's there somewhere." But all I heard them arguing about was Pefa's image of the eye of the cyclone.

"There's no surrounding violence down there, so where's your cyclone?" Hodd was criticising. It took them long enough, I thought.

I dreamed, not surprisingly, of the spheres. My mind ran through the afternoon's encounter with them. I awoke convinced we'd overlooked something while we were at the spheres, not necessarily anything visual. I lay awake for a long time, pondering.

In the morning the patients were stirring. We gave soporifics to anyone who wanted them, which was everyone except Hald. I hoped we weren't creating a psychological dependence. I was becoming more anxious about the effect of hyperflight on these cradled minds, beginning to dread the risk; it had no precedent.

"I want to go down again," I told Luli. "You can manage for a couple of hours."

She almost dropped a needle, then caught it and herself. "I'll be all right," she said. "I hope you find it, whatever it is."

When Pefa and Hodd had slept we went down. "We told him two hours," said Pefa as the boat fled. "Let's leave the car and walk, try to feel the place. We'll still have an hour at the spheres."

For a moment I disagreed, then I thought her intuition might be useful. We walked away from the colony. Today there were no clouds, and the sun burned within its rim etched on the glassy sky. The light gave the pink spoons and the grass a luminous glaze. Our feet passed through the grass with a faint snap and a hiss.

Gradually the silence that surrounded the sounds, isolating and displaying them with what seemed unnatural precision, began to take on a presence. It felt as if the tranquil dazzling field of grass was in the grip of peace. "I know what it is," I said suddenly. "It's a kind of world shock after all. It's the silence, it's stifling. That's what they couldn't stand."

They stared at me, then their mouths opened and they both nodded solemnly. "Let's go to the spheres anyway," Pefa said after a while.

As we neared the spheres I was thinking how the silence could be tamed. I'd rejected the idea of artificial noises, the piping into the colony of music or natural sound. But we could plant for real natural sound. The calm lights of the spheres seemed to brighten with my mind. We could import some of the Old Earth trees that we dutifully grew on Starnose; we could set the threshing of branches and leaves against the silence. It would be the first time we'd heard those sounds. It seemed right.

We stood gazing at the spheres. Now I could see them for what they were: repetitions of the same statement of aesthetic perfection, the final result of their creators' formalism. There was a poignancy about them; they could only symbolise beauty, and achieved that only by excluding a great deal. They'd been like the peacecubes after all, but perhaps they'd become a way of life. I felt pity for the race that had died gazing on them. The lights hung steadily against the grass like the core of the planet's peace.

At first I didn't register what Pefa was saying. "Suppose the people at the colony were trying to understand the architecture," she said. "We couldn't stand the first set ourselves. They must have gone walking outside the colony, and where else would they go? And the harder they tried to get hold of the progression of the architecture the less they'd have been able to keep their own cultural balance. That's the kind of world shock it was."

Hodd frowned at her, then her face cleared. "My God," she said. "I think you're right."

I stared at them both. Hodd must be joking. It was a total contradiction of my own— My own what? I couldn't remember. I thought, It's just ridic— And this time I felt, for barely long enough to be aware of it, something reach into my mind and deftly snatch the thought away.

That awareness itself felt threatened. All I could do was think about something else. The time. "Time to get back," I said.

"We've a few minutes yet," Pefa said.

My mind was flinching and crying We must get away! "I'm exhausted," I said. "I'd like to slow down on the way back."

Now I'd committed myself to walking slowly, as if I'd chosen a nightmare. The sun flooded down, the field of grass flexed its muscles, the pink spoons nodded slightly in the breeze, and I felt as if I were trying to creep out of a room unnoticed, unable to see whether I was succeeding. Except that it was worse, because I was trying to creep with my mind. It was a long hot trudge, but I didn't feel hot at all.

When we reached the colony the boat wasn't waiting. We should at least have been able to see it leaving the ship. We sat on the edge of the circular landing field. I closed my eyes to contain my panic. All I could see was Luli. If my mind didn't make it to the ship I would never be able to resolve— What? As the insight was instantly suppressed I realised that I couldn't remember our arguments. Pefa called out, and I saw the boat beginning its descent.

Halfway up I felt my mind slip free. "Tell Hodd your theory again," I said to Pefa.

"Don't bother," said Hodd. "I think it's utter nonsense."

"Then why couldn't you say so before?"

I saw a barrier give way within her eyes. "My God," she said.

We found Hald in the communal area. The sharp lines of his face kept collapsing into weariness, then twitching back into the mask. But we surrounded him and insisted on talking. Around us the ship buzzed softly in its sleep and the colonists snored. Luli stared from the viewport. Happyhome turned slowly in the frame, reeling in our time before hyperflight.

"I'm beginning to understand the lost race, I think," Hodd said. "You can see them in their architecture. They grew so obsessed with perfection that they became intolerant of anything else. Presumably that might have included interpersonal conflicts."

"And they managed to leave the effect behind them, haunting the planet," Pefa said.

"Which explains why you couldn't argue," I said. "But it isn't only overt conflict of that kind. There were things I couldn't think about. My image of them was forced to be perfect." Luli looked at me. "I think any potential for conflict is censored. No wonder your people disintegrated," I said to Hald.

"It does explain a good deal," he said. "The tensions must have built up until they had to be expressed somehow. And even the violence was over almost before it began; it must have just slipped through. I never felt it myself, though. I mustn't have had any conflicts. Except being unable to help, and even that didn't seem to matter after a while." He shook a finger at Pefa. "I don't go for this idea of haunting, though," he said. "I'd accept that the race left behind them some kind of physical force, even if it can't be traced."

"How do you know they aren't still there?" Luli asked.

I think she enjoyed our silence. She let it hang before she went on. "You know that something was controlling your thoughts," she said. "Why shouldn't they be able to censor your sight as well? You never found evidence of what destroyed them. Why shouldn't they still be down there, gazing at their spheres?"

Imagine our hours of argument for yourself. But the more we argued the more tempting the hypothesis became: a race that had pursued idealisation and simplification in terms of themselves as well as their architecture, until they'd achieved total control and sensitivity at the price of drastic exclusion. "There is only one answer to that kind of sensitivity to hurt," Hodd said; and amid another silence Pefa said "The peacecubes."

There was one way to test the hypothesis: determine whether the solution worked. "Luli, you and I must go," I said. "I felt the effect most strongly." Besides, since we had the most violent arguments we should be more able to feel the cubes distracting and appeasing the censors, if they had any affect at all.

In the boat down I said to Luli "Try to feel the tension between us."

"I don't have to try," she said.

But as soon as we stepped onto the field she said "I can't feel it now. I don't like it."

The boat was trembling impatiently. "Come on," I said, hurrying her off the field.

We walked, because I wanted her to become familiar with the sense of censoring. Now I had an explanation it didn't seem so terrifying. Shallow hollows were blown through the grass. As we walked Luli kept trying to frown, then smiling as if someone were dragging at her mouth. Tears were struggling to leave her eyes. I put my arm around her shoulders.

We had four peacecubes, one for each gap between the spheres. We placed them in the centre of each gap, then moved back beyond their radius. Everything's fine, I thought, knowing that meant it wasn't at all. I returned to my first cube, moved it a fraction, retreated and tried to feel. Then Luli did the same. It was exactly like trying to tune an invisible musical instrument, except that we were unable to perceive any pitch until it was perfectly tuned.

The sun was sinking, the fields were stubbled with shadow. I'd managed to beg a ship's communicator to call the boat; I'd known this would take time, but not so long. Maybe I'd been wrong to assume the spheres were the significant area. Maybe the human telepathic imprints in the cubes weren't sufficiently universal. Maybe our whole theory was wrong.

Exhausted, I saw Luli returning to move her cube as I moved mine, instead of waiting her turn. "Do you want to wreck this whole thing?" I called. "Just try to contain yourself until I've finished!"—and then I gaped at her. "We've nearly got it!" I shouted. "It's weakening!" It felt like a chess player's flood of inspiration. Two more tiny shifts of the cubes and we felt the clinging presences fall away.

And Luli was staring at me, all her emotion brimming over. "You brought me down here to use my feelings!" she cried. "Just to be sure this worked."

"Your feelings!" I shouted. "My God, it's you who use your feelings. You expect me to share your moods as a matter of course, and when I don't you use that as an excuse not to communicate!" Then we had the most violent row either of us had ever experienced. All the poison burst forth at once. We yelled, pummelled, struggled in the slashing grass.

We fell silent only because we were exhausted. In the silence we heard the soughing of the world. We suddenly realised that we'd made it ours. We gazed at each other and saw how quickly we'd become mutually blind. We shared all this wordlessly; then we made love on the grass, beside the dimming spheres.

And that's really how Happyhome began. It was Hald's idea to bring the colonists back down. The shipmen resigned themselves to what they obviously believed was the total insanity of their passengers. Even we weren't sure Hald was right that the new Happyhome was the most convincing form of therapy, not even after he'd been down himself and stood roaring in the fields for half an hour, looking absolutely at ease when he rejoined us. But hyperflight seemed more of a risk, and you can see now he was right.

We've fenced off the spheres, of course. We don't want anyone moving the peacecubes. But it's useful in some ways to be haunted; we're never likely to have an immigration problem. Sometimes I wonder if our solution wasn't like stuffing a baby full of candy to shut it up. But then I think no, they had their chance and made their choice. Now they have to be satisfied with what they wanted. After all, they have perfection.

At least that's my opinion. There are people who disagree and can argue all night. Still, that's what makes a ragefest. Just let your emotions come as they will and don't bother who gets them in the face; they can take care of themselves. We started the ragefests to make sure the cubes were working. But apart from that, they seem to help us get on very well together the rest of the time. We know you will too. As well as Luli and I.

Only the Wind

There's just one more thing I want you to see," Truman called to Hope. "Over here."

As Hope walked toward the edge of the roof the wind caught him, rushing him forward. Truman was standing at the gap in the railing at the edge, holding onto the railing at either side. He'd waited for a strong gust, but it was almost too strong; it was fumbling to pluck him free and send him over the twelve-storey drop. He was just able to yank himself out of the gap as Hope came hurtling towards him, sliding on a patch of rain.

Truman shouted inarticulately, still dragging himself along the rail. The inspection party looked up in time to see Hope fall, a whirling helpless doll, a spreading splash at their feet. Truman stared across at the next multistorey block, crumpled by a gale six months ago. He tried to ignore the peremptory thumping of his heart. The wind carried sounds of dismay up to him like an accusation.

But when the case reached the court, the accusations weren't aimed at him. The police had found documents in Hope's safe that betrayed his accomplice: Price, a stooped man with wistful eyes whom hardly anyone knew outside the city council chamber. The multistorey block that had collapsed had been let down by inferior materials, and the documents showed that these materials had been supplied by Price from his builder's yard. Clearly Hope had kept the documents to protect himself. Price was sent for trial, and the court forgot him. At least he hadn't tried to kill Truman.

"I took Hope on the roof and told him that all the evidence pointed to him," Truman told the court. "I thought that seeing the damage he'd done to the other building might spur his conscience. I'll be frank: I chose the day the buildings were being inspected so as to have people nearby in case he did anything impulsive." His speech was carefully prepared, but he was becoming distractingly hoarse through having to shout over the rattling of the windows. Even when an usher closed them the March wind continued to rattle them viciously.

"I saw him coming toward me and stepped back instinctively," Truman croaked. "I didn't know whether he meant to push me or to throw himself off. I prefer to think the latter. He may have yielded to temptation once, but he wasn't essentially a bad man." He made way for the chairman of the inspection party, who confirmed that Truman had been nowhere near Hope when he fell. Not that anyone was suggesting anything else. The windows shook as if with a fit of rage.

Truman read the newspaper reports as they appeared. No, he'd told a reporter outside the court, he didn't think there was any further corruption among his fellow councillors, but he would be the first to lead a committee of inquiry if corruption were suspected. The interview never appeared, since the reporter's notebook had blown away during it, down a grid. Price pleaded guilty and was sent to jail, which was reported at length in the national newspapers, as Hope's death had been.

The national publicity worried Truman. He barricaded himself behind his work as chairman of the housing committee. But the letter was waiting on his hall table one night. It was from his brother Mike. Please come at once, George. Bernadette knows. I am sure you would prefer to keep our discussion as private as possible. In the morning Truman packed a bag and told his housekeeper he hoped to return the following day.

He drove out of the city, past the collapsed building. Nobody had been killed; the building had been evacuated in time. Homes had been destroyed, of course. But what homes, Truman thought. More like filing cabinets, those buildings. His committee had recommended them reluctantly, only for reasons of speed and cheapness. I'd have been glad to see the last of a home like that, he thought.

On the motorway he relaxed. No need for haste. Mike wouldn't do anything until they'd talked, even if his wife Bernadette urged him to. Driving easily, Truman thought back.

Hope had approached him one day to confide his suspicions. A man had left Price's yard to work for Hope, who had deduced from hints that Price had provided disguised inferior materials for the multistorey block, supplying the original materials to someone else. Hope had wanted Truman to help him find out who that was. Truman wondered whether he'd realised at the end. Even though Hope owned a builder's yard, which had seemed to confirm his guilt in court, he couldn't have known that Truman's brother owned one too.

The hills beside the motorway smoothed out. A wind swooped over the fields, grabbing Truman's car, nudging it out of its lane, shaking it violently. He curbed the wheel. A few minutes later the first of a series of flyovers closed about him, warding off the wind, and he relaxed again.

He'd paid Price to plead guilty and to name Hope as his accomplice. The man would in any case have gone to jail, he'd been pathetically grateful that the money would be waiting in trust for him. He'd been as grateful before, when Truman had promised not to reveal Price's sexual life if he'd help in a deal that would pay him as well; and later, when Truman successfully nominated him as chairman of the committee to investigate the building's collapse. Mike had been grateful too, for his yard was failing, even though he knew Truman had added the materials into a council contract in order to pay for them. Perhaps he was still grateful. But as for Bernadette—

A gust of wind seized the car and hurled it into the fast lane, into the path of a lorry. The lorry blared, slowing hardly at all in the fifty yards between it and Truman. But he'd wrenched the wheel over and had fled back into his lane, almost skidding with haste. The lorry swept past enormously, flourishing a tiny fist.

When he reached the service area Truman parked to let his heart quiet. It shook him like a great soft gong. He couldn't understand; he'd been deep in the flyovers, there'd been no gap for the wind to enter. But it had. He drove the rest of the way gingerly, never freeing his mind to think.

When he reached Mike's yard it had been dark for hours. Nobody was about. He climbed onto the roof of his car and over the wall. Two hours later he climbed back panting, kicking away a crate and lifting his coat from the topping of jagged glass. Near the car the April wind was raising a small cloud of brick dust, like someone stamping as he waited for a meeting. In a minute Truman had driven to Mike's house.

Bernadette opened the door. Behind her, ranked neatly on the stairway wall, Truman saw miniatures she'd taken from a friend of her mother's, having contested her mother's will. "Don't bother talking," she said. "We've made up our mind."

"Let him in," Mike said. "He's still my brother."

Bernadette set out dinner, every movement sharply proclaiming that she felt obliged to do so. They ate timidly, embarrassed by their sounds. Truman felt surrounded by her taste: her decor, her arrangement of the house. He and Mike had been brought up by relatives, indifferently; he'd always helped Mike, advised him, supported him, given him things. Now she'd replaced him.

After dinner Truman talked. He told them he hadn't realised that Price's stock was so limited he would need to make the substitution. In fact he hadn't realised, to begin with. "I was only thinking of you," he told Mike.

"That's what we're doing, Mr Truman," Bernadette said. "But we're doing it like normal people."

"I'd be glad if you'd call me George."

"You must have done some good, Mr Truman," Bernadette said, "or you wouldn't be a councillor. But you have to pay for your mistakes in this life. I know that embitters some people, but I have a feeling about you. You defended your friend in court, you could have said he meant to kill you. I think when you've paid your debt you'll find you want to do all the more for people."

Truman gazed sadly at her. I'll do for you, he thought, that's for sure. "Have you any of the materials still? Then at least let me take them away," he said to Mike. Bernadette frowned, shaking her head. "If you help me load the lorry I'll got rid of the materials," Truman said. "Now, while it's dark. You come too, Bernadette. I don't want you to think I'm getting at Mike behind your back."

In the end they persuaded her. Pursing her lips, she went upstairs to dress. "She wants to tell the police," Mike said. "I'll stop her, though. I'll talk to her after you've gone."

And lose, Truman thought. They heard her open the front door, silently rebuking them for keeping her waiting. A moment later the door slammed violently as the wind forced its way in. Glasses chattered on the sideboard. The wind was still coming, out of the dining-room, chiming through the hall chandelier, dwindling but still coming, nudging open the door of Mike's den. It fell just short of Truman's face. "We're coming now," Mike called.

Truman drove them to the yard. "I'll park and meet you at your office," he said.

When he'd parked he sat in the car. He didn't want to enter the yard until it was over. He fought an urge to call Mike back. If there had been only Mike this wouldn't have been necessary. It was Bernadette's fault. Truman cursed her.

Mike's office was built into the back of one of the two store-houses. It was approached by a path between the two buildings, along planks laid over mud and rubble. Earlier, Truman had substituted thinner planks. They would beneath the weight of two people, and the bricks that he'd piled precariously to a height of seven feet against the walls in the middle would topple inward on them both. If they were only stunned Truman would have to finish the job. He hoped Bernadette was only stunned.

At last he began to walk toward the gate. He'd heard nothing from inside the car. Silver light from the streetlamps veiled the sockets of the surrounding derelict houses, lay flat on Mike's yard, dimming almost to darkness on the path to the office. It took time for the eyes to adjust to it, but Mike knew his way without looking.

Inside the gate a dilapidated lorry huddled beneath a long tarpaulin. Piles of timber and brick stretched away into dimness. Truman began to pick his way over the ruts. Then he heard a rattling of brick between the storehouses. He began to run.

He had almost reached the path when Mike called "Come and see what someone's done."

Truman would have run for the gate, except that this was his last chance. When his eyes adjusted to the dimness of the path he saw that the bricks had fallen, but not on Mike and Bernadette. They had nearly tripped over them. "Someone had thrown all these down here," Mike said.

A wind was bumbling between the walls. It was the wind that had thrown the bricks down, Truman realised. It had helped him on the roof, but not here. He strode toward Mike and Bernadette. It was his last chance. "Look there!" he cried, pointing behind them. As they turned he picked up a brick in each hand.

And something hurled him forward, face down on the toppled bricks, thrusting him down among them. They cut into him and bruised him as he struggled onto his back to face his assailant. But there was nothing, although it was crushing him, pressing into his eyes and ears until all he could see was the inside of a ringing crimson mask. He opened his mouth to cry out and it rushed in, feeling as if it were wedging down his tongue, forcing his jaw wider like a too-large gag. It had filled his nose too. The crimson mask was being hammered into his head, growing blacker now, squeezing him out of his body. He had one last glimpse of Mike and Bernadette pressing themselves against the walls, staring down at him and trying to make out what he was struggling against. But it was only the wind.

Morning Call

As soon as the phone rang Craig jerked awake. Green blotches hung beside his eyes. The clock face. Four o'clock. He groped for the light cord and pulled it, then he lifted the receiver.

The phone was still ringing, slowed down and rustily painful, in his head. "Yes?" he said feebly. At four in the morning he could think of nothing else to say.

The line sounded like a beach. There might have been breathing mixed with the static, but he wasn't sure. He was about to replace the receiver when a voice said "Is that you, Peter?"

It was faint and sexless. It sounded like someone talking in sleep, or under a drug; it seemed to strain to hold onto the words and get them through. Perhaps the caller was mentally disturbed; Craig had had enough such calls in his time. "Who do you want?" he said.

"Don't you know?" the voice said sleepily. "I thought you were supposed to be clever."

"I think you have the wrong number."

"Then I've had it for a year." The voice had grown harsher. Craig could hear it was a woman's, but so strained it didn't sound like any voice he knew. "May you be damned," it said. "That's all I wanted to say. Just thought you'd like to know that you've killed me."

While the silence challenged him to reply, Craig replaced the receiver. That's all I need, he thought, something like this. As if I'm not asked to do enough during the day. All I need is something like this to drag me in and knot myself up with the rest of my life. I can't even see where the knots are any more.

He debated leaving the receiver off the hook. He was sure that wouldn't be the only call. But he couldn't; he didn't know who else might ring. He lay back and tried to relax. He'd just begun to sink into sleep when the phone rang again.

"You don't believe I'm dying, do you?" the voice said at once.

Craig sank back on the bed as if the weight of the receiver had pulled him down. He recognized only too well the sort of hysteria that was mounting at the other end. If he cut the woman off it would only grow worse. But he knew from experience that far from being able to calm it down, he was likely to become infected by the hysteria himself.

"Can't you say anything?" the voice said. "Hoping I'll forget you're there? Don't you worry, I'll remember you until my dying breath. And that won't be long, you swine. Don't you even want to know why?"

"Look, I'm sorry," Craig said. "If you're really as you say you are, you should call a doctor immediately."

"But that's what I am doing! Or have you decided to give up your, what did you pretend it was, your vocation? Are you being honest at last? Come on, you dirty little swine, stop hiding. You were always good at that, hiding behind your job, pretending you cared about people. I know it's you. What's the matter, afraid to hear—"

The voice faded, squeaking, as Craig dropped the receiver back on its hook. He lay, eyes closed. This was too much. All his sense of being burdened weighed on him; he felt helpless, unable to move. When the phone rang he lay counting the peals, wondering when it would tire. Thirty. Forty. He grabbed the receiver and immediately slammed it back.

A moment later it rang again. He cut it off at once. Then began a game of reactions, of Craig interrupting the bell almost as soon as it threatened to sound. Once, in the tiny gap between lifting and replacing the receiver, he heard a thin wordless scream at the other end, a squeezed cry of frustrated rage. He started and let the receiver drop. He gazed at the bottle of barbiturates next to the phone. No, not those either. I can't knock myself out, in case someone needs me.

He'd lost count of the number of times he'd silenced the phone when he realised that among the repeated calls, someone else might be trying to reach him. He had an idea. The next time, he answered. "Hello," he said, hoping he sounded like a policeman. "Who is this?"

But she didn't even bother to taunt him about his ruse. Her voice was dull; she sounded stunned. "I can't move my fingers," she said. "You didn't tell me it would do that, you swine."

For the first time he felt that she might be more than hysterical. "Hoping I wouldn't be able to dial, weren't you?" she said. "But you forgot the operator. I can still pick up the phone and rattle the hook.

You've left me that much."

"Then the operator must be incompetent," Craig said. "If she weren't I'd advise you to call a hospital."

"In other words, anyone but you? You know I wouldn't do that. Because you wouldn't really like it, would you? I'd have to tell them what you gave me. And how you made sure I'd read what it said in that book you left lying around, how you're dead in two hours when you've taken as much as I have. You're supposed to fall asleep before that. That's what you must be hoping I'll do. But I'm going to keep talking until I die. You won't stop me talking."

Craig sighed. He still wasn't sure whether the woman had simply been taken over by some insomniac hysteria. Perhaps she might say something by which he could tell. He didn't know what to do except listen. That wasn't too taxing, after all. He closed his eyes, which were rough and burning. "Go on, then," he said.

"There it is, the bedside manner. You think that makes people think you care, don't you? It certainly worked on me, for a while." Her voice was beginning to falter occasionally; she was shouting—to wake herself up, he thought. "You put it on when I told you how my husband used to treat me. But you should have seen your face then, when I told you what he was really like as soon as you'd closed his eyes. You did your job well, though, I'll give you that. Don't you worry, you said, I'll help you in any way I can. But I don't imagine that your medical association would approve of some of your ways."

She seemed to be trying to winkle him out of his silence. He lay inert, the receiver at his ear. This early in the morning I don't help people, he thought. Not this morning, anyway. Not strenuously, at least; I'm listening. Her voice kept jarring him awake.

"You really were absurd sometimes," she said. "When you used to pretend I was pestering you when you visited me. You thought I believed you. Until the day I took you upstairs. You didn't mind that so much, did you? You didn't mind—"

Craig gazed at the receiver. She'd lost control completely, he thought. Well, let her run on. It doesn't matter whether I'm listening. He stuffed the receiver into his pillow. Her voice mumbled on, as if battling suffocation. He found the noise even more unsettling. When he could no longer stand it he put the receiver to his ear.

"—drink so much, don't smoke so much. You didn't want me to do anything except put up with you. You made me feel as if I'd dragged you into bed, as if you weren't a poor lonely little swine. We couldn't even be seen together, because of your job. That was always more important than me. You thought I was demanding, didn't you?"

Can you wonder, Craig found himself about to say.

"But you didn't mind having me. That was all right, until the baby came. Just a poor little baby that might have given you away. Of course you didn't say that, you said it might harm me to have it. Do you remember telling me that the one thing you always respected was human life? I wonder what you called that. Maybe there wasn't enough of it to be respected. I don't suppose you even looked at it. Something to be thrown away."

She snarled back a sob. "But even that wasn't enough for you. You had to make me so I'd never have children. Oh, no, of course that wasn't you. Just an unavoidable complication, wasn't it? And of course it wouldn't do for me to ask for a second opinion. That would have given you away. So you gave me this stuff to calm me down. To shut me up, you mean!" She was shouting; her voice was rawly distorted by the microphone. "You thought I didn't know why you wanted to shut me up. I could lose you your job, but that wasn't it. That wasn't why you hated me. You hated me because you'd had to betray your ideals. And that had to be my fault."

Her voice picked at Craig's ears like a rusty chisel. He moved restlessly, his fingers working on the receiver. She had to run down soon. She was saying anything that came into her head.

"I've decided," she said suddenly. "Talking isn't enough. I want you to come here and see what you've done. I want to watch you see what your ideals have accomplished. You've got time. If you don't come I'm sure the police will. Especially when I tell them your name."

Craig's eyes opened, and he glanced at the clock. "You said that whatever you've taken took two hours to work," he said. "You rang me at four. It's six now."

She was laughing, a dry rattle. "You lying little swine. You'd say anything to avoid me, wouldn't you? I've got my watch in front of me. It's five o'clock. Better get a move on. I'll give you half an hour, then I'm calling the police."

Craig switched on his bedside radio. After a minute the six o'clock news began. "You heard that," he said.

"Oh dear God," she said. He heard her start the plunge toward death. He'd never heard death quite like that, the death of someone falling wide-eyed and unbelieving into darkness. "You've done it," she said. "Are you proud, Doctor Peter Craig, you swine?"

"All right, Kathleen," he said. "Yes, it's me. There's nothing either of us can do now. Close your eyes. Just close your eyes and I'll talk to you."

But he didn't know what to say. In any case, there was no response from the other end. Even the static had been swept away, and there was only a gaping silence. "Kathleen?" he said. Still silence.

He was about to replace the receiver when, distant but unmistakeable, he heard the door of her room open.

It was impossible. Something on the line. It couldn't be Kathleen, she didn't have a housekeeper, she could hardly have anyone else in the house now. Unless—unless the operator had noticed how odd her voice was—unless she'd been so troubled by it that she'd listened in—unless, having listened in, she'd called the police—

Heavy footsteps approached the phone at the other end. A man's voice said "I don't know who you are, mister. But you won't have time to make it difficult for us to find you."

Craig opened the full bottle of barbiturates. Quickly, abstractedly, he swallowed the contents. He lay down and closed his eyes. After a moment he opened them. Reaching out, he left the phone off the hook.

Pet

When I was old enough my father took me to see the market. I'd looked forward to it for years, because I'd had to wait until my body was old enough to keep me awake all day. I don't think I could have fallen asleep in the market, though. Everything made me want to run ahead and see what was on the next stall. I just kept running, even though people were laughing and pointing at me. I didn't stop until I saw Pet.

He didn't look much. I'd seen other things in the market that had made me dizzy, they were so beautiful. A black jewel the size of a big apple, which an exploding sun had made of a planet; when you picked it up you felt you were holding a world in your hand, and I felt so sad and uneasy I started to shiver and had to put it down. And time-record crystals that you gazed deep into, until you saw a world begin to form; you could watch the whole history of a world in a day if you wanted to, because the crystals speeded up your mind as they went faster. And dust-dancers that were a cloud of all colours of glittering dust, that would dance for you and make patterns almost too fast for you to follow, and go back in their box when you held it open, because they were thousands of tiny creatures that lived like that on their own planet, dancing for anyone who came near. But when I saw Pet I forgot everything else I'd seen, and forgot there was anything else to see.

He was the only thing left on the stall. He was half as tall as me, covered with a short smooth amber fur. His eyes were black and very big, and they looked as deep as I dreamed the night sky must be. Under the fur he had a little pink face that looked old and very peaceful. He was squatting on top of the crystal that made the field that kept him caged, with his legs crossed and his arms folded under his knees. He was looking at the sky. I'd never seen anything like him, and I thought he must be from galaxies away. I didn't know anything else about him, except that I wanted him.

When my father caught me up I said "Can I have him?"

"He's the only one on the planet," the trader said. "Maybe the only one anywhere."

"Then he must be far too expensive for me," my father said.

The trader named a price that sounded expensive even to me, though I didn't know much about those things. "There, you see," my father said.

He could see I was disappointed. He bought me an orchestra pipe instead, the kind that can both play a tune for you to follow and improvise along with any tune you choose to play on it, six different added lines at once. A little computer does that. But I kept running back to look at Pet.

The last time the trader was folding up his stall. "Can I touch him?" I asked.

He looked at me to decide whether I was going to run off with Pet, then he made the sign at the crystal to shut off the cage-field. I reached out and stroked Pet's head.

His fur felt like grass in the sun, only it was softer and finer and warmer. He didn't move when I stroked him. He kept gazing at the sky. Only his eyelids moved, blinking. "What's he looking at?" I said.

"He isn't looking," the trader said. "He's listening. Listening to hear if there are any others like him left."

I don't always remember when I dream, but I did that night. My father had brought some of his friends into our home-field, but that didn't disturb me; that wasn't what made me dream. I dreamed I could see Pet in his cage on the stall, gazing up. But he was gazing up at me, and his eyes said: please take me home. I told my father the dream next day, and he frowned and said "Not at that price."

After that, every time we went to the market I would run straight to Pet. Every time my father would say to the trader "How much is he today?" The trader would say a price that was a little less than last time, but my father would say "Still too much." Pet would squat there peacefully, gazing at the sky. He never seemed to have moved.

Once my father said "Why do you want him? He won't play with you. He'll just sit there."

"I want to look after him," I said.

Then, one day, we arrived at the stall just as two people were walking away with what they'd bought. For a moment I hated my father, because he'd let someone else buy Pet. But they hadn't. They'd bought a pair of silverspinners, the most valuable pets of all. Pet was where he always was. "How much is he today?" said my father.

The trader looked at me. "He's the only one on the planet. Probably much rarer," he said. "He's quiet and clean. He doesn't cost me anything to feed. But nobody can be bothered with him. I've had a good day. He's yours for half of what I asked last time."

"You'll get tired of him," my father said to me.

"No I won't," I said. "I promise."

My father and the trader began talking, about where Pet had come from, things like that. I wasn't listening; I was stroking Pet's head. He didn't look at me, but I knew he must be able to feel me. It was enough for me to know that. "You'll have to think of a name for him," the trader said, but I already had.

At first I couldn't see how we would take Pet home. I thought perhaps I'd have to carry him. But the trader took hold of one of his paws, which were like little furry hands, and drew it out from under his knees. Then he put the paw in my hand.

I could feel each of its fingers resting on my palm. I could feel blood pumping in the fingertips. It felt small and easily hurt. It didn't take hold of my hand; it just lay there, trusting me. Pet was waiting for me to lead him, as if he were blind.

When we started for home he walked along beside me, his legs reaching out so far in front of him that his bottom almost touched the ground, as if he were making up a new way to walk. People laughed at him; I did, a little. As he walked he gazed up at the sky.

He almost bumped into our home, and I had to pull him back. I jerked his arm rather hard, because I'd forgotten that he wouldn't be able to see our home even if it was visible. The jerk must have been a shock, but his pulse stayed steady. He was even more peaceful than he looked.

My father made the rapid movements of his hands that cut off our crystal's field. The movements are like birds dancing, so fast I could never copy them exactly, although I'd always tried. He always used to say that when I could copy them I'd be ready to use them.

I led Pet around our home. I somehow thought he might like it, because it's almost all natural unchanged. I thought he was like that. There's no furniture, except for the crystal at the centre, if you call that furniture. There are ridges of rock with natural seats to sit in, there are fields of grass to lie in, a stream running all the way through and bringing air in with it, though its gaps in our crystal-field. The crystal-field surrounds it all. The field is shaped like a dome, my father says, but completely transparent. "Put as little between yourself and the world as possible," he always says. But even he had a heating system built into the crystal's brain.

I might just as well have shown all this to myself, because Pet didn't look. He followed me, but his gaze never left the sky. The sun was two fingers' length above the horizon. One thing I'd overheard the trader telling my father was that Pet ate the light, took it in through his fur and made it feed him. I wondered if he'd fall asleep when the light went, like us. "No," my father said. "He never sleeps."

I took Pet up on one of the ridges. I thought that since he was listening for something from the sky, the higher he was the better. He squatted there, gazing. That was all he'd done during the half a day I'd had him. But I wasn't impatient. I knew he had feelings, and this was what he wanted to do. I sat very still and watched him. I wanted to see if he ever moved by himself. That seemed very important.

When the light began to slip over the horizon I tried to stay awake. I thought Pet might move while I was asleep. But of course I couldn't. Your body puts you to sleep to stop itself being worn out too quickly, like a machine. As you grow older your body lets you stay awake longer, until when you're very old you see the middle of the night. You can't trick your body—at least you can't at my age, though a good many older people, including my father, were trying to keep themselves awake to have more time to work. I was trying to keep awake, staring at Pet beside me on the ridge, and the next moment I was asleep.

The next thing I knew, I was awake. And it was night.

I was lying in my nest, which I'd made in the middle of one of the fields, using some of the grass. My father had carried me there. I could feel the grass, but I was blind. There was darkness close against my eyes. I knew it was only the night, and I lay quiet until my pulse slowed. Then I rolled onto my back, and I nearly cried out. The sky had gone.

There was nothing above me but blackness, that could have been as close as my eyes or so far away that I felt myself spreading into all the space between, as if I couldn't hold myself back. Then a tiny glint of light at the edge of my eye caught my attention. I stared directly at it, and after what seemed a very long time I saw it was the blink of a star. Now I'd seen one I could see others. There were six, there were a dozen, dozens. Perhaps Pet had come from one of them. That made them feel closer, less distant and lifeless and frightening. I let out my breath, which I'd been holding as if afraid that the darkness might hear me.

I turned on my other side to see Pet. My nest rustled. My father had called a small circle of light from the crystal, so that he could see to work. As the nest rustled he glanced up sharply from the calculations he was making. I held myself still, because I knew he would be worried or angry if he knew I was awake. After a moment he went back to his work.

Pet was squatting at the edge of the light. He looked as if he didn't care whether it was there or not. He was gazing at the stars. Suddenly I wanted him to come to me, to show that he knew I was there. I thought that, very hard. Sometimes, if you think hard enough at animals that know you, they'll respond. But Pet didn't move, even when my father kept glancing at him as if Pet were disturbing him. I kept thinking at Pet, until I began to dream I was doing so. Then I was asleep.

When I next awoke it was dawn. I could feel that without opening my eyes. You shouldn't be able to; you aren't supposed to be able to tell when the heating system gives way to the sun's heat. But I can. I like to feel the wave of light spilling over the horizon towards me. I opened my eyes. Pet hadn't moved from where I'd seen him during the night. The light was sweeping past him.

I didn't tell my father I'd been awake before. We ate leaf and flour pie, then I went to the crystal for my lessons. The crystal's smaller than my hand, but besides making our home it teaches me the history of the universe, and mathematics, and sciences. One day when I'm old enough it will teach me how it works.

It shows you things in the air just in front of your eyes, words and ideas and happenings in the past, then it asks you questions that tie all these things together. My father says it always makes learning a little difficult for you, so that your mind will grow. I try to make it teach even faster, so that it'll reach the point where it tells me how it works. But I can't make it believe I'm cleverer than I am.

Only that day I couldn't concentrate. I kept looking at Pet, sitting patiently near me, his head tilted back. The crystal was repeating my lessons, speeding them up so I'd have to concentrate. Finally it slowed down to let me catch up, and made a gong-note in the air to call my father. It had never done that before.

My father frowned at Pet, then he gestured to switch off our home-field. "We'll let him sit in the open," he told me, taking Pet's paw. "He might like that." But I knew he thought Pet was distracting me from my lessons. He left Pet near the edge of our home. Eventually I managed to concentrate.

Later my father took me walking, for the second half of the day's lessons. I always enjoy that part, because he shows me how to read the landscape, what you can eat, where it's easiest to walk and run, the best places to set up home. I'd asked whether we could bring Pet, but he said "Better not. He'll be quite safe in our field." So he was, when we came back; he was still sitting where we'd left him. But I felt mean, even so. I hadn't enjoyed our walk as much as usual.

That night I woke again. I'd already grown used to it. I was lying on my back, and when I opened my eyes I saw the stars, appearing one by one as my eyes took hold of them, like buds of light growing through dark soil. I wondered if this was what Pet saw.

Nearby I could hear voices. One of them was my father's; the others were friends of his. I realised that they were forcing themselves to stay awake. They'd decided that if you forced yourself long enough your body would have to give in and let you choose how long you wanted to sleep. I lay listening to them.

"He just sits there and listens," my father was saying. After a moment I realised they were talking about Pet. "Look at him now," my father said. "Sitting on top of our crystal. He can if he wants to. He isn't doing it any harm. I can control it without even moving him off it. But he's a distraction. I think it's the very fact that he isn't doing anything that's distracting. You find yourself waiting for him to do something, anything."

"You sound as if you want to get rid of him," someone said.

"Well, put it this way. If there were anyone who wanted to study him or would even look after him, I might. But I don't think there is. Sometimes I think we've become too interested in our own minds to bother about anything else."

I'd started, and my nest had rustled. "I think we've woken the child," someone said.

There wasn't any use pretending. I sat up. There was my father with six of his friends, in the pool of light from our crystal; I could see them between two of the ridges of our home. Pet was squatting on the crystal, but the light still spread around him, making his fur look like a halo. "Please don't sell Pet," I said.

My father came over. "You should be asleep, not listening," he said. "But I didn't say I'd sell him. That depends on how he's affecting you."

"We'd better go," someone called. "We didn't mean to keep anyone else awake."

If I'd thought I would have said nothing, but I blurted "It wasn't you. I woke up last night as well."

"Then there's only one thing that can have done it," my father said sharply. "We'll talk about it in the morning."

I knew he didn't want to take Pet away from me unless he had to. In the morning he decided that it was having Pet after wanting him for so long that had excited me. "But you'll have to get used to him soon," he said.

I led Pet away from the crystal and up on one of the ridges. My father switched off the field. Then I went to my lessons, and managed to learn faster than I had for weeks. On our walk I read a landscape all the way to the horizon by myself. My father was pleased, and so was I. I was pleased he'd been right about Pet.

Except that I woke again during the night.

I tried to go back to sleep at once. I tried to pretend to myself that I wasn't really awake, that it wasn't Pet's fault. But even with my eyes closed I could see the stars as I'd seen them before, and I could feel Pet listening, straining to hear through our field.

I tried to make myself comfortable, and my nest rustled. After a long time, when I still couldn't get to sleep, I moved again. This time I felt my father looking, and he looked for so long I couldn't stop myself moving. "I can't sleep," I said.

"Well, you won't be able to force your body to sleep," he said. I could tell he was angry that I couldn't, but he was holding himself back in case he disturbed me more. "Do you want me to talk to you?" he said.

"Yes please," I said, sitting up. "Tell me about Pet. Why does he sit on our crystal?"

"I'm not sure. He only does it when the field's on. Perhaps he feels that the field is making it hard for him to listen. There wouldn't have been anything like it where he came from. You know he isn't listening for a sound. He's listening for a call in his head, one of his kind sending a thought to tell him where they are."

"Are there others like him?" I said. I wanted there to be.

"I don't think so, or he'd have heard by now. Though it's possible they've forgotten how to send."

"But what happened to them all?"

"We don't know much about them. We know a little from other races who tried to trace their history. They had complete control of their minds, they could make their minds do anything, though whether they always could we don't know. They could stand on a planet and read off everything about it, its history, its geology, its place in the universe, just by standing there. So they say."

"Can Pet do all that?" I said, looking at Pet sitting on the light.

"No, not any more. They lost it, you see. They decided they could read the universe between them. They must have had space travel, because they scattered through the universe, one to a planet. They read the planets and sent each other what they'd read. But they were so busy doing that, they forgot everything else. They didn't have to eat, they could even stop breathing if they had to. They lived as long as ten of us, but because there was nothing for their bodies to do, they began to die out. There weren't any children. And as the ones who were left had fewer to call to, or to hear, they pined away faster. You can see why. This one must have been the strongest of the lot, and look at him."

"But why should our field worry him?"

"I don't know. But I think it does."

"Switch it off for a while," I pleaded. "They may be calling him, and he won't be able to hear."

"Just for a moment," my father said and gestured it off.

I gasped. I wouldn't have believed it could be so cold. As soon as the field was off the cold rushed in, as if it had been waiting to pounce. I felt as though I'd been covered in ice, so thickly that I couldn't feel my nest around me.

Pet didn't move. He was as still as the light around him. "Now you see why we need a field," my father said, closing it down again.

"Oh, don't," I cried. For a moment I'd felt that Pet was just about to hear his call. Before I knew it, without thinking, I'd made the gestures to lift the field, and the cold rushed back in.

"Now that is quite enough!" my father shouted, closing it down. "Just you go to sleep! And even if you can't sleep, I don't want to see your eyes open again tonight!"

It took me a long time to fall asleep, because I was afraid of what he might say in the morning. But it wasn't all what I expected. "I'm sorry I shouted at you," he said. "You're growing up faster than I realised. I was a good deal older before I could lift our field. But now you're growing up you must think as if you are."

I knew what he meant, but I said "I want to keep Pet."

"Don't you want to sleep?" he said. "It's the field that disturbs him, I'm sure of that now. And when he's disturbed he disturbs us— yes, me as well, though not as much as you. You found out last night why we need the field. So I'm afraid we're going to have to part with him. We'll take him to the market tomorrow."

I think my father was surprised when I hurried away to my lessons. I think he expected me not to be able to concentrate. But I needed as much time to myself as I could earn, so I made myself concentrate. When I'd finished I asked if we could leave our walk today, because I didn't feel like it. My father thought I wanted to stay with Pet for the rest of the day, and so I did. He let me stay. I took Pet up on the ridge and began to think at him.

I stroked his head softly as if to soothe him to sleep, and I tried to tell him I was sorry that he was the only one left. I told him I'd care for him, I'd think at him whenever he wanted to listen, so that he wouldn't feel lonely. He gazed up at the sky.

I stroked him and thought harder. If he wanted, I thought, he could listen to me as I learned. Then it would be like listening to one of the others like him reading a planet. I knew I wasn't as clever, I told him, but in time I'd be able to tell him anything anyone knew about our planet. And if he wanted to keep on looking at the sky I'd take him for walks and think at him everything I saw, then he could see it too. I'd do all this if he would just look at me once, so that I'd know he wanted me to.

I thought this at him hard, for a very long time. The sunlight was fading and I was beginning to feel sleepy. Once I thought his face moved. I jumped up, but it was only his eyelids blinking as he gazed at the sky.

I began to cry. I stroked him and cuddled him, and I told him that if he wouldn't stop listening to the sky and listen to me we'd have to get rid of him. Then he might be owned by somebody who'd be angry when he listened, and they might hurt him, or take him out and lose him. And all because he wouldn't look at me or let me care for him.

I was sobbing. My father looked up at me and frowned. The light was draining away over the horizon. "Please," I said to Pet, and then I began to fall off the ridge. Sleep hit me as I fell.

While I was asleep I dreamed about Pet. It wasn't a dream I should have expected to have. I was lying in my nest at night, and Pet was lying just outside, near my feet. His eyes were closed. I felt very peaceful, and so did Pet.

I woke at dawn. My father was standing by my nest, watching me. I couldn't read his expression. Because I couldn't, I felt panicky. "Where's Pet?" I cried.

My father's voice sounded surprised and puzzled, like his expression. "He's there," he said.

I looked down. Pet was lying at my feet, his eyes closed. He opened them and looked at me.

"He came here while you were asleep," my father said. "I caught you when you fell and put you here. He sat up on the ridge for a long time. Usually he goes and sits on the crystal as soon as you're asleep, as soon as the field's switched on. But this time he just sat up there. I believe he was thinking, if he still can. Then you started moving. I thought you'd woken up, but you were dreaming. And that was when he came and lay down here."

"Can I keep him?" I pleaded.

"Yes," my father said. "I don't know what you've done, but I think you can keep him."

I lay back in my nest. "I'll look after him," I said. "I want to find out everything about him, so I can look after him better. I want to find out all about his kind. I don't even know what they were called."

"You'll have a lot of work to do. I'll help you when I can," my father said, taking my hand in all of his. "But one thing we do know. They managed to trace what his kind were called. They were called men."

Hain's Island

Everyone watched the supply ship down, except the man it was intended to save.

Since they'd just finished battle drill, it had been an unusually eventful day. "Events are supposed to come in threes," Temeran said as they watched the ship. "What's next, do you think? Something uncommonly spectacular, I hope. Maybe someone will trip over, or sneeze."

When the ship had appeared, first in the scanner and then in the sky, they had tried to persuade Hain to watch instead of going away by himself again. But even Rads the doctor hadn't succeeded. "Just because they're bringing the stuff you want to pump into me," Hain had retorted, "doesn't mean I have to hang around until they show up," and he'd slumped away through the trees, back to the plants that had given him cancer.

Some of the watchers laughed as the supply ship came down. They were used to the sight of the six-hundred-yard trade ships standing off in the sky, sending down their boats; they hadn't expected this one to be so tiny. In fact it was owned by a private company from a nearby colonised planet. For speed in an emergency, and for the human touch amid their efficiency, they were preferable to the shipmen in their trade ships. Still, the watching colonists thought, nothing much could come out of a ship that size.

They were wrong.

When the ship cut its drive the forty-nine colonists converged on it. It squatted on the landing-field like an overfed beetle with a rounded head, twice the height and four times the length of a man. One of the supplymen emerged from its disproportionately bulging midriff as they reached the ship.

He looked rolled in his fat. He had the face of a petulant baby, but much of his weight was muscle. "He will help you unload," he said,

213

jerking his thumb at his partner in the cabin. "I'll try some of your local food."

If the colonists had been used to imperiousness they might have stopped him there. But all their decisions were made communally, and they'd grown unused to behaviour such as his. Besides, his behaviour might be normal for his culture and hence, in a way, privileged. He wouldn't be on their world long enough to do harm. Thus they let him through unopposed—though by the time they'd thought all this, he was already past.

Rads hurried after him, frowning, and some of the others followed. The rest began to unload the ship. Although much of the space was occupied by cabin and drive there was a surprising amount of supplies, ingeniously stored. Luice, Temeran's wife, took the supplies from the second supplyman and handed them down the chain. "Is your partner always like that?" she said.

"No, he isn't," the man said. "Only this trip."

He sounded worried. She was about to pursue the subject when he said "You all look healthy enough to me."

"Oh, you mean Hain. The man with cancer," she said. "He's down looking at the relays. Do you know about them, the relay plants? They're an indigenous species—of course, because we mustn't grow anything exotic—but quite rare. They each produce one seed, fertilise it and immediately die. Hain was studying the fertilisation. But they have defences, and one pricked him. That's what gave him cancer."

"The only danger on the planet," Temeran said. "Of course the observation satellite couldn't pick that up. It had to be one of us that found it, to his cost."

Luice could sense her husband's bitter frustration rising. "So that's where Hain is," she told the supplyman. "Only now he isn't so much studying the relays as blaming them. I wish he wouldn't. It isn't helping him."

"What can?" Temeran said. "He knows as well as we do that he's dead. Your supplies won't change that, friend, I'm afraid. Whatever the initial reaction was, all that's perceptible now is a runaway cancer nothing can head off. Rads knows that, but he has to try. At least the relays give Hain an interest."

They finished unloading and made their way to the communal

area. The afternoon was sinking into evening. Plants were closing the jaws of their pollen traps; one plant snapped a last trapful from the incessant gentle wind. The communal area was between the long wooden buildings of the colony: an open glade, since except when the rains swept over the land the colonists had no reason to shelter. Segmented trees nodded in the wind, the loose segments of the trunks working like pistons, quickening their sap.

Most of the colonists were at the trestle tables, eating. Hain had left the relays and was sitting near Tilp, the first supplyman. Their end of the table had been ostentatiously avoided by the rest. "There can't be much to learn from your relays," Tilp was saying. "I reckon you're wasting your time."

"The next one is always stronger and healthier," Hain said. "That's how they breed. It's not true of many things in this universe. Consistency like that is worth studying."

Luice sat near them. She could see that Tilp would depress Hain more unless he was interrupted. "We think all our work is worth doing," she said.

"I don't believe that," Tilp said. He pointed at the observation satellite, glinting in the whitish sky. "It seems to me that's doing all the work," he said. "You're just here for it to watch, to see how you and the environment interact. That's the purpose of this colony."

"That's part of it," Luice said. "But we're qualified to study the environment too, you know. We can do so in ways the satellite can't."

"I can see one way," Tilp said, looking at Hain.

Temeran gripped the table with both hands and leaned across to Tilp. "Shut up, you fool," he said. "You're not only a fool but a liar. You've done nothing but lie since I sat down here."

The nodding trees creaked. Everyone was gazing at Temeran, thinking that they'd been about to say exactly the same themselves. If he hadn't spoken they would certainly have massed against Tilp. But he had, and now it was too late. "I'm sorry," Tilp said at once, holding out his hand to Temeran.

Temeran clasped it brusquely. Then at once he thrust it violently away. After a moment Tilp stood up, looking dazed, and went to his partner. "I'm sorry," he said. "I don't know what's been the matter with me."

Luice gripped Temeran's hand, but he dragged it away. "I don't need you to patronise me," he said. Luice withdrew a little, hurt. She'd only meant to convey that she knew he'd silenced Tilp even though he agreed with much of what Tilp had said. She'd often had to distract Temeran from his bitterness; she'd learned to deal with that, but a cold rebuff like this was new, wholly untypical.

"What work do you do?" the second supplyman asked Temeran.

"I'm balancing the ecology."

"Well, you're going to," Luice amended, still upset.

He seemed to ignore her. "We can construct a perfect ecosystem here," he said. "I know we can. We can form a perfect symbiosis with this world. As for you," he told Luice, "I suggest you save your observations for your laboratory."

At the other end of the table Rads the doctor glanced up, frowning.

"I can see how to balance this system," Temeran said, "but this world keeps fighting me. It keeps tipping the balance."

"You know it isn't like that," Luice said. "Just keep trying. Thinking like that won't help you."

"You may be competent in your own field," Temeran said, "but if you've got time to poke around in mine then it's time you extended yourself beyond botany. Now shut up. You've got your flowers to mother, for God's sake don't do it to me."

"I certainly won't shut up," Luice said, and she didn't. The evening soughed around them, creaking. After a while the others began determined if subdued conversations. Hain trudged away to stare at the relay plants.

Rads gazed down the table, at the argument. This was wrong, it wasn't the way the colony worked. Conflicts were always resolved communally, without rancour. But there was something about the increasing violence of this argument that was exclusively private, that made it difficult for the others to listen, let alone to intervene. It was defiantly alien.

Rads felt obliged to lead an intervention. But he couldn't help feeling relieved when, while he was searching for an impersonal way to halt the argument, Temeran and Luice stood up and left, still shouting. Their argument faded into one of the dormitory buildings. Everyone relaxed. A few stray explosions of pollen drifted by, locked out of the pollen traps by the evening.

It wasn't long after that the screaming began.

It came from the dormitory building. Someone sitting near to it turned, tumbled clumsily off his bench and ran into the building. Others followed. Rads was faster than most, and urged aside those ahead of him in the pale green corridor. He knew he was needed.

The screams had turned to sobbing now. They came from Temeran's and Luice's room. Two men were throwing their weight against the door. It couldn't be locked; Temeran must be braced against the other side, for he was shouting "Go away! This is my room!" None of them had time to think how unlikely a protest that was for one of them to make, because the door had given way, and they could see in.

Luice was huddled in one corner of the room. Bruises were already darkening her face and arms. She was holding her right arm, flexing its fingers painfully, gingerly. Her right leg was stretched out awkwardly before her, as if she were afraid to move it. Temeran stood in front of her, blocking the way, looking defiant. For a moment everyone stared incredulously. Then two men pinioned Temeran's arms viciously behind him.

The violence was infectious, Rads saw. He had to halt it. "Leave him," he told them. "I'll deal with this."

They could see what he was doing, and let go of Temeran reluctantly; one of them twisted his arm before letting go.

"Come here," Rads ordered Temeran. After a moment he did so, slowly, shaking his head at himself. The others drew back warily. Rads took hold of Temeran's chin firmly and lifted his face, to examine his eyes.

But he hadn't looked into Temeran's eyes when he flung him violently back, banging his head against the wall. The others started anxiously, bewildered. Rads paid him no further attention, but went to Luice. "Now let's see you," he said.

He gripped her injured arm and leg rapidly. Luice winced and bit her lip hard. "Nothing broken," he said. "They'll ache, but you'll have to put up with that. Get yourself some ointment if you must, then get to bed."

"I'll get you the ointment," Temeran said to Luice. She gazed at him for a moment, then looked away and nodded. The others relaxed. The incident had been profoundly disturbing, but it was all right now. They could remember it and learn from it.

Rads strode out, and after a pause Temeran left too, looking at nobody. The others made comforting approaches to Luice, but because she only nodded and smiled shortly, abstractedly, they soon left her alone.

The night was quiet, disturbed only by the slow creak of the segmented trees.

Next morning the supplymen left. Rads led a small party to watch farewell. He seemed to feel it was his place to do so, though nobody had delegated him. "Do you know what was wrong with me? Was it a kind of space fright?" Tilp asked him, but Rads said "I couldn't put a name to it."

Most of the colonists had gathered in the communal area. Even Hain was there, for there was a general feeling that the colony's principles had been threatened. Nobody referred to yesterday's violence, but all felt that it had been the ugly result of inaction and frustration. They needed to act more.

Temeran and Luice sat together, listening. Luice was shiny with ointment, and the wind fluttered a little inside the improvised sling on her arm. She and Temeran glanced at each other warily.

Eventually all agreed that they should begin studying the sea. The colony was near the edge of a continent. They'd planned to begin submarine studies in a year's time, but all agreed they needed the activity now. Enough of them would always stay at the colony for the satellite to observe in those conditions. And if it didn't like that, they decided, glancing up at the glint, let it complain. Though they could have called a print-out map from the satellite, a group went to the field to ready one of the two flyers for a mapping flight.

As the discussion became more speculative Hain wandered slowly away, toward the relay plants. Luice watched him go. At the edge of the communal area he passed Rads, returning from the field. Hain didn't look at him, nor did Rads acknowledge Hain.

Luice limped quickly over to Rads. "When are you going to try to help him?" she demanded quietly.

"Hain knows there's no point in my trying to help him," Rads replied, loudly enough for Hain to hear. "I see no point in wasting time and supplies on him."

For a moment Luice was speechless. Then she said "Don't be stupid. It's your job."

"Then you must allow me to know how to do it," Rads said, and strode away to his laboratory.

Luice stared at the others. "What's happened to us?" she cried. When she limped after Rads, a couple of them followed her. Hain hung about the edge of the glade, looking half-embarrassed, half-amused.

Rads was sorting supplies on a bench near the door of his laboratory. At the far end, transparently screened, was the surgery area. He was examining and laying out a set of surgical knives. He didn't falter as Luice came in.

"What's wrong?" she demanded. Her tone was challenging, but her words were almost a plea; too much was suddenly happening that was unfamiliar. "This isn't you," she said.

"Then it should be," he said, not bothering to look up.

"You don't believe that," she said. "You could be cold when you had to be, but not like this. And you'd never let a patient overhear the sort of thing you said about Hain. I don't think you'd say it in the first place or even think it. There's something wrong here, and I think you know what it is."

"Then leave me to know how to handle it."

"It isn't as simple as that," Luice said. But he'd slipped half the knives into their case and was carrying it away, leaving the rest of the knives on the bench, by their case. "Don't you walk away," Luice said, and grabbed at him. Her hand missed, and she began to overbalance.

She'd almost regained her balance when her injured leg gave way. She clutched at the bench. Her hand, slick with ointment, slipped. She grabbed at anything, which was a surgical knife. The handle sprang from beneath her fingers, and the blade entered her thigh.

She fainted as Rads pulled out the blade and probed the wound. He fetched disinfectant and an instant dressing, and handed them to her two companions. But they stood watching him as he made a space in the surgery area for the cases of knives. "What are you waiting for me to do?" he said without turning. "That was stupidity. I'm not treating that."

"You're here to treat whatever you're needed for," one of them said.

"And I've done as much as I intend to," Rads said. "That won't kill her. I could stand it. So must she."

"If you won't do your job we'll have you relieved," the other one said.

"You mean the satellite will," Rads said. "It sees all, so when it prints out back home no doubt they'll send someone eventually. But you can't communicate with it, you know. Unless you want to write a message on the ground."

They were glaring impotently at him. "Or you could radio the world across the way. But if they can spare a surgeon I doubt he'll be as reliable as their supplymen," he said. "Go on. Take her away and put her on her bed. If she keeps still she'll be all right. You know where the anaesthetics are, see if you can use them. Better still, see if you can find some indigenous natural remedies to help her. That would be closer to the terms of this experiment. That's what we're here for."

They carried her to her bed, then they told everyone outside what had happened. A frown was growing on Hain's face. Before they'd finished Temeran was shaking with fury, holding himself back only to hear all. Then he strode into Rads' laboratory. "Help my wife," he demanded.

Rads was leisurely inspecting the second set of knives. "That's an ironic thing for you to ask me," he said.

"I know that. But I'm asking."

"And I'm saying no—or rather, that I've done all I propose to do."

"Then I'm telling you. And I'll make you if I have to."

"You should know there's nothing you're less capable of."

Temeran snatched a knife and held the blade near Rads' face. "I think I can make you suffer a good deal without making you incapable of operating," he said.

"Then please try. I can stand it." Temeran waved the blade, and Rads said "Do you really think you can do what you say? And do you expect it to achieve something?"

Temeran tried to outstare him, but couldn't. His hand slumped. "She's my wife," he said. "If she jerks her leg she'll tear that muscle more. Nobody else can make sure she doesn't." But Rads was slipping the knives into their case, was carrying them away down the room. Temeran trembled with frustration. At last he turned to go.

He had almost reached the door when Rads called "Wait."

Temeran whirled. Rads was staring at him through the transparent screen. "Don't even you know what's going on?" he said "You caught it from Tilp, I caught it from you. It's contagious. It's a disease. But you of all people should know that it feels fine. Better than you've ever felt before."

Outside, Temeran told them "He says it's a disease. And he's enjoying it."

Hain gasped. Everyone turned to him. They could see an idea forming in his eyes. "Yes," he said. "I think—" They waited eagerly. After a minute he hurried away, toward the relay plants. They turned away in disgust, dismissing him.

"I'll talk to Rads," one of the women said. In a few minutes she emerged, shaking her head in bafflement. Others tried, singly and in groups. Once those outside heard a crash of glass, and Rads' smooth voice: "Destroy whatever you want. It won't touch me." The party returned from readying the flyer and were told what had happened.

Temeran kept hurrying away to ask the women who were watching over Luice how she was. One of them had succeeded in anaesthetising her with an ampoule someone had brought from the surgery. The two women were holding Luice still, but every so often she tried to stir.

At last, when most of them had tried to persuade Rads, Temeran said "Get the battle weapons. Even he won't like what the lasers can do to him."

They stared at him, disturbed. They'd never used the weapons except in drill. They were hardly expected to be attacked. They'd been provided with the weapons and the drill largely to maintain their aggressive instincts at a healthy level. It was a game most of them enjoyed, but to play it in reality was altogether more disturbing. "Get the weapons!" Temeran shouted at the three who were keyed to the store.

Eventually they had all strapped on their power packs. They each coiled the leads around one arm and held the vicious needle-pointed tube in front of them awkwardly, as if embarrassed by it. They surrounded the laboratory in a disorganised way. They'd worked out their battle-drill places between them, and in a drill they would take their places without thinking; but now, with Temeran directing, they felt clumsy and incompetent.

"I'll go in first," Temeran said. "I'll get him out, however I have to. Then it's up to all of you to make him go to Luice. The more we can make him do, the easier he'll be."

"Wait a minute," someone said. "Here comes Hain."

"We can do without him," Temeran said, advancing on the laboratory.

But Hain was hurrying toward them, waving his arms. "You don't need that," he called, gesturing Temeran to lower his weapon. "Rads!" he shouted.

"That's no good," Temeran said, pushing him back. "We've tried talking. Now we're going to try my way."

Hain ignored him. "I know what's happened to you, Rads," he shouted. "And I'm equal to it. Come here and let me show you I am."

Temeran stared at him, confused. The others had already lowered their weapons, glad of the respite from threatened violence. Hain was gazing calmly at the laboratory door. Temeran let his laser-tube sink. The segments of the trees pumped, creaking; great bladders of fibre drifted by in clumps, bearing seeds on long threads; the pollen traps snapped. Many of the watchers saw the laboratory door move while it was doing nothing of the kind. But at last Rads opened it and stood waiting.

Hain was already striding toward him. Temeran thought he had the look of a man compelling himself into an action before he could regret it. He could imagine how that felt. Hain grasped Rads' hand as he reached him. Then he thrust him away, back into the laboratory. "Wait until I come out," Hain told the others, and closed the door.

For a long time the voices in the laboratory talked. Nobody outside could distinguish a word. At first the voices were calm, but later the doctor's was raised in protest. Hain's never varied in its calm, and eventually the doctor's seemed to sink into resignation. Outside, the others moved restlessly, avoiding each other's gazes. They looked up at the satellite sailing untroubled above them, considering them indifferently, betraying nothing to their receiver.

When the voices ceased, the creaking of the trees seemed to retard time. The door opened and Hain appeared. He was alone. They were starting toward him when he seemed to take their measure. He brought Rads forward around the door, urging him out with an arm around his shoulders.

"He's well now," Hain said. "He'll help Luice, then he'll tell you what's been happening. Believe what he says."

He hurried away, in the direction of the landing-field. Rads made a gesture as if he was only just preventing himself from calling Hain back. Nobody else noticed Hain's departure; they were staring at Rads. "I'll give you a stretcher," he said to Temeran. "Then you can bring her to the surgery."

He had just finished, and Temeran was relaxing, only now sure that Luice had been in no danger from him, when one of the men hurried in. "A flyer's lifted from the field," he said breathlessly.

"Yes, I know," Rads said. "That was Hain. Get Luice to her bed, then I'll explain."

When everyone had gathered in the communal glade he said "I was wrong. It wasn't a disease. It was contagious, and Tilp brought it here, but there was far more to it than I thought. I wouldn't be exaggerating if I said it was equal to the best of us."

"How do you know this?" Temeran said. "I must have had it, but I can't even describe it, let alone say what it was."

"It was an entity," Rads said. "That's all we know. There's a good many things drifting round in space we've yet to put a name to. Tilp picked it up on the way here. However it was composed, it was obviously capable of penetrating the cabin wall. Hain thought it was pure energy, a sort of spore of energy. Certainly it had to remain dormant until it encountered another entity, because that was how it grew."

"But how could Hain know that?" Temeran demanded.

"By looking at his relays, he said. Think of how the relays reproduce, each one stronger than the last. That was what gave him the hint what to do. He realised that it didn't migrate indiscriminately from person to person. I wasn't the first to touch you, Temeran, but it waited for me to pick it up. Because I had a stronger personality, you see. It was always attracted to the one who could dominate its present host. That was how it grew."

"Grew how?" Temeran said. "Why?"

"We can only guess. Hain figured that it matched the host personality, or at least its drive towards power. Only he figured that power had to be wielded externally to satisfy it, over others."

"So that was what made me hurt Luice?"

"It must have been." Some of the others frowned at that, and Rads hurried on. "The externalisation was crucial. Otherwise it wouldn't have needed to make us behave that way. It could have exerted its power internally, over itself—presumably, in that case, without using us at all."

"And Hain has it now?"

"Yes, he has." Rads gazed toward the sea, walled off by the trees. "He thought he might be able to turn the power inwards. I tried to make him see that in that case there was no need for him to go. But he said that even if he succeeded, someone else might challenge him and pick up the thing. So he's flown to an island. He says we can drop food in six months if he's alive, but he has a laser to stop us trying to go down."

"But how did he manage to take it from you?" Temeran said. "I don't think even you would have picked him as our strongest personality."

"Yesterday I wouldn't have," Rads said. The trees creaked sharply, but the others gazed at him, hoping for a resolution. "But even if anyone else of us knew they were going to die," he said, "would they deliberately do what he did?"

In a month the satellite began to print out ONE OF SUBJECTS HAS LEFT EXPERIMENTAL COLONY AREA. PLEASE ARRANGE HIS RETURN. Later it became less polite, but none of them would go near the sea; some were convinced that the force could reach to them from Hain through the water, like a gigantic electrical charge.

In three months a group of men with disapproving expressions arrived to rebuke the colonists, fly out to the island and bring Hain's body back. Tilp's broadcast testimony helped to vindicate the colonists' inaction. Then men acknowledged this disapprovingly, and took Hain's body with them.

The colonists waited for news, but none came. At last they accepted that Hain had been right in his unspoken surmise: that the entity would die with its host if it were unable to migrate in time. Luice had a permanent limp to remind them all that Hain had saved them. Some of them felt privately that the glint in the satellite's eye had turned suspicious, as it scrutinised them for traces of lingering infection. Beyond that they didn't care to think. They preferred not to realise that Hain had given them the chance to believe he had taken with him all that had threatened the colony.

Bait

That light is all that is left of your life," Lord Robert said, gesturing negligently towards the torch set in its niche in the wall opposite that to which Thomas was chained. "Though perhaps I should not be so niggardly. You would scarcely have time to savour the attentions of your new companion. Perhaps when you have had a taste of the dark, I may return to discover whether your thoughts are of your wife or of what will visit you."

He turned away. Then, as if inspired, he swung back and slit Thomas's forearm with his sword. A minute later Thomas heard the door slam stoutly, amid the new stone that walled off this extremity of the cellars. The torch flame streamed away from the gust, dragging its niche and part of the wall by their shadows.

Thomas slid down to squat on the damp stone floor. The short chains gyved to his ankles collected in a heap beneath his thighs, cutting dully into them, but he squatted unmoving. The wall before him panted with the flame.

The light reached out along the grey stone and fell back, unable to maintain its grip. At its farthest reach it snatched forward what Thomas had taken to be part of the darkness: a fissure in the grey wall, moist-edged as a wound. From its apex plopped a slow deliberate drip, mud-thick. Within the fissure, muffled and distant, Thomas heard an awakening scrape of claws.

Rats, he told himself. They must be the companions he had been promised. He hoped they would find him dead. He hoped death would come to him softly as sleep, and as quickly. He closed his eyes and let the plump drip pace his breathing, slow his thoughts. But the flame tyrannised his eyelids, demanding that he watch the light plucking nervously at the fissure.

Already the light was fading, unless a clinging shadow of sleep was gathering on his eyes. Deep in the fissure the claws scraped, growing bolder. He stared into the unsteady cleft of darkness and tried to coax its depths to draw him into sleep. The depths only filled with his memories, the hut at the edge of the forest, Marie.

Marie was crying. "Don't let him take me, I couldn't bear it. If he takes me I won't be yours." Thomas's friends were nodding their heads angrily. "He has no right," they said. "Someone must stand against him. We would have if we'd known. It only needs someone to tell him we know there is no such right, and he will never dare claim it again. We'll stand by you."

Marie was screaming, for Lord Robert had thrown open the door of their hut. Behind him at a distance, blurred and surreptitious in the twilight, Thomas's friends peered. Thomas stood before Marie, warding off Lord Robert. "There is no lord's right, no other lord claims it. You cannot have her. The other lords will come to our aid if you try."

Lord Robert did not speak. His sword, infamous for its sharpness that clove men as a scythe mows grass, trembled a fingernail's breadth from Thomas's eye. Through the doorway Thomas saw that his friends had retreated behind their barred doors. Lord Robert gazed at Marie and held his sword carelessly at Thomas's face until Thomas fell back.

Marie was screaming, no longer in terror of her husband's fate but of her own. She was hugging her breasts and pressing her legs together closely as Lord Robert's lips. Lord Robert threatened her with the sword, prodding her gently with it here and there, each time drawing blood. Abruptly he seemed to tire of trying to persuade her. In a moment he had deflowered her expertly with the sword. After a while he silenced her cries with the blade.

Thomas stood drained of all feeling, too drained even to impale himself on the sword. He waited for the blade to cut him down, but Lord Robert was speaking. "Since you desire a companion who will be yours alone, you shall have one."

The turnkey had led Thomas through the cellars, his torchlight glancing at huddles of chain and starved flesh. Behind Thomas, Lord Robert's sword was ready in its scabbard, a fang in a snake's mouth. When the turnkey had unlocked the door in the depths of the cellars, he'd thrust his light through the opening so sharply that the darkness had almost gulped it up. He'd held the light while Lord Robert fettered

Thomas; then, at a gesture from his master, he'd niched the torch and had fled beyond the new stone wall. Now Thomas wondered dully what that wall had been built to contain.

The torch was sputtering. The cellar wall gasped feebly as its light drained. Thomas was trying to determine how close the sounds within the fissure were, the sounds of something hard scratching faintly and stealthily against stone—he was trying to think how rats could make so measured and purposeful a sound—when darkness doused everything.

The chains bruised his thighs, which throbbed. He wished he had moved before. Now, if he moved, he would betray himself to the rats, which would fasten unseen on him. Unseen: that was the worst, as Lord Robert had intended. It denied Thomas the chance to fend them off before they reached him. It denied him everything save the sounds of encirclement, the tearing of sharp teeth.

He moved, spreading the chains on either side of him. Let the rats come, he would best them yet. Without the nagging of the iron links, he could sleep. Lord Robert was starving his body to weaken him, but had forgotten that he had already starved Thomas's soul. All Thomas need do was let himself sink into the void he had become. Not even rats could awaken him from that sleep.

But sleep hung back, its presence close yet impalpable as the dark. As Thomas tried to muffle himself in sleep, strove to calm himself so that it could take hold of him, part of him remained doggedly alert to the sounds within the fissure. He tried to judge if they were approaching, to satisfy the sleepless part of him, but each time he had almost grasped their distance the slow drip interrupted, distracting him. The hushed claws scraped in the dark. The drip prodded Thomas awake. Exhausted, he forced himself to listen. The drip pulled his mind down, down into sleep.

He awoke in the forest. Lips were moving timidly over his cheek. It was Marie. He opened his eyes gradually. Above him, swarms of leaves drifted gently over one another; pools of light rippled over him, soft as breath. He couldn't see Marie, for she was kissing his forearm shyly. If he raised his head he would see her. He awoke, and a tongue was lapping thirstily at his sword wound in the dark.

He roared and kicked out, until the fetters wrenched his ankles. Amid his terror was a deeper horror that his mind had accepted what

Lord Robert had given him in exchange for Marie, accepted it even if only in sleep. He thrust the thing from him, and his hand touched an arm. He felt bone and dust-stubbled wiry muscle that twitched his fingers away, but no flesh at all. Then the thing scuttled dryly back into the fissure.

Thomas held himself still, though the links bit into his thighs. The lethargic drip mocked the scurrying of his heart. Now he knew why the turnkey had fled, knew the extent of Lord Robert's cruelty. Thomas had heard tales of hungry cadavers that roamed from their graves at night, writhed where they lay impaled beneath crossroads, tapped stealthily at doors to be let in. Only Lord Robert could have made a pet of such a thing. Thomas's folded legs trembled, blazing with pain, but he held himself still, clinging to the silence.

When the hollow scrape of bone emerged from the fissure onto the cellar floor he began to roar like a beast in a fire, shaking his chains. There was nothing else he could do. In a moment he froze aghast, for his noise might have allowed the thing to creep to his side unheard.

But it was scuttling back into the cleft. He listened to the aimless shuffling of bone, and thought the darkness was deceiving him until he remembered how the thing had waited for the light to fail. Suddenly he realised why it had delayed until he had fallen asleep. It was as timid as anything else that might crawl from a hole in a rock.

It was less timid now that it had tasted its victim. The tentative dry groping retreated into the cleft when Thomas shouted and rang his chains against the stone, but each time it came closer to him. Soon it failed to retreat even as far as the wall. He roared and shook the chains desperately, but his noises seemed to be snatched away at once and muffled, scarcely echoing. They hardly stirred the air, which hung damply upon him, dragging him down into sleep.

He sawed his wrists against the gyves to fend off sleep. Then he clutched his wrists, gasping. He had almost drawn blood and offered it for feasting. When he touched the sword wound and found it moist, he plastered it with gritty mud from the floor. He hammered his elbows against the wall to keep himself awake. Nearby in the blindness he heard bone scrabbling towards him over the floor.

The dark nestled against him, urging the bony claws forward. It settled insidiously about his mind and held him more tightly than the gyves, imprisoned him outside time, choked off his furious sounds. It pressed faces of bone and working muscle against his eyes, jarring him awake. It flooded his mind entirely, while the thirsty bones crept closer.

Lord Robert returned to Thomas several hours after leaving him. He motioned the turnkey to precede him beyond the partition wall, then he took the nervous torch from the man and gestured him out. Holding the torch above Thomas, he gazed down at the slumped unmoving figure from which iron links spilled.

"You have days yet, perhaps weeks," Lord Robert said. "The last man to wear your chains lived for a month, for the others heard his screams. They found your new companion crouched over him like a spider, and you will know it has a spider's appetite. The wall was meant to help it hoard its attentions for those who most deserved them. I am glad they were kept for you."

Thomas did not move. "You are not dead," Lord Robert said, "nor yet so weak that sleep may shield you from me. Show me your face while I prepare you further."

Still Thomas squatted, huddled into himself. Lord Robert thrust the torch into its niche and stooped to Thomas, grasping his hair. The tip of the scabbard touched the floor.

As the hilt inclined toward him Thomas snatched the sword. His chains betrayed his movement, the hilt rang dully against the wall, but the razor-keen blade pierced Lord Robert's groin. The point glanced from bone and, slipping upwards, emerged beside his spine.

Though Lord Robert screamed and writhed heavily, Thomas held the hilt fast until his captive fainted. Presently the turnkey's scared face peered in. The door slammed at once, and Thomas heard the key turn.

Lord Robert found himself propped against the wall next to Thomas, impaled on the sword. His cloak lay across Thomas's knees. Thomas gazed at him while he moaned. "I shall call the turnkey," Lord Robert said, not daring to move on the sword. "He will free you and escort you unchallenged from my castle and my domain. None shall pursue you."

"The turnkey has imprisoned us both," Thomas said, lifting the blade. "Stand up. You will be my bait. We shall see if your sword will destroy your pet."

Lord Robert obeyed. He stood before Thomas, moving with minute delicacy on the axis of the sword. Sweat poured down his face. When Thomas withdrew the blade slowly until the point was flush with his captive's back, Lord Robert moaned but stood firm.

"Let him come now," Thomas said. Within the fissure an impatient desiccated rattling had ventured almost to the edge of the light. "He will have to come as many times as I need to impale him. We shall live until that is done."

Lord Robert was gazing down, seeking in Thomas's eyes some sense of what was to come, when Thomas threw the cloak at the torch and gave them both to darkness.

Snakes and Ladders

The shop was totally silent. Even the man who had beckoned Booth in managed to pad back to his place without making a sound. Thick curtains were tight at the window. The sole light came from a candle waxed to the table set in the middle of the floor, between the counters.

The woman who stood behind the table ignored Booth; so did most of the dozen watchers. But the old man lying on a mattress before the table, his knees drawn up by arthritis, turned his head painfully on its worn-out neck as Booth tried to tiptoe in. The boards caught Booth's footsteps, reverberating them hollowly.

When you enter Mrs Cooper's toyshop, you step into a world of faith and magic, Booth scribbled in his mind, defensively. But is the magic real?

At the table Mrs Cooper waited patiently for silence, waited for Booth's last movements to fade. She waited while the whistle of the ferry on the nearby river trailed away; even the lapping of the canal at the edge of the street was closed out by the curtains. Then she opened the drawer of the table and took out a doll, whose flat face she touched to the old man's forehead. She held it there for minutes, as if she were holding the taut silence still, challenging it to break. Even the candle's flame streamed up true. The old man's face wizened with intentness, and a tear squeezed out beneath one eyelid.

Without moving his head, Booth glanced at the watchers. An awkward red-faced girl, a middle-aged man leaning pugnaciously forward over a walking-stick, a woman weeping with hope; behind them dim chessmen stared palely through glass. The two people who had turned when he'd entered were still watching him.

One was an enormous woman whose breasts, sucked out of shape, had been forced into an almost colourless flowered dress, along with her belly and hips. Each breath strained at the dress above the swollen legs as if against suffocation, yet her eyes were alert. The other was a broad man, uncomfortably tall; above the lit chin his face was a dark blank that watched Booth steadily. Despite the atmosphere of the shop, Booth thought, you soon begin to suspect that you're meant to be impressed.

Mrs Cooper was holding the doll above the old man's glimmering eyes. Very slowly, tenderly, she straightened the doll's bent legs. The old man's hands gripped the edge of the mattress, trembling. His left foot began to quiver. It shook violently, straining to reach the end of the mattress. It worked within his shoe, nails scraping; it inched forward, quivering; it reached the floor. He was struggling to rise. The pugnacious man hurried to offer his stick. The old man stumbled limping on his left leg toward the weeping woman. At once, as if at the end of a play, the lights came on.

The shop was smaller than its darkness had seemed. It was full of the table, three glass counters full of toys and games, the dozen people clustering about the old man. Booth could hardly sidle his way to the table. Mrs Cooper was scraping drops of wax from the wood. "I'd like to ask you a few questions," Booth said.

"I'm sorry." Her voice was thin and high, not at all commanding. But her eyes held the conviction her voice lacked; her gaze was neither challenging nor defiant, but completely sure. "You've seen all there is," she said. "I can't add anything to that."

"I must have some background."

"There is none." She turned as the red-faced girl—clearly her daughter—whispered to her, and Booth knew he'd been dismissed.

The enormous woman plodded up, beaming. "She's a miracle, isn't she?" she demanded of Booth.

He glanced about at the chessmen, the board games, the dolls: all Mrs Cooper's work. There was a board game lying half painted on one counter. "She's very talented," he said.

"What are you going to say about her in your paper? Listen now, Elsie," she shouted to Mrs Cooper. "He'll tell you what he's going to write."

"I don't know yet." They had all turned toward him, even the old man, who gave him a weak smile of encouragement as if to win a favourable report. "I'm sorry," Booth said as the woman expostulated. "I don't know."

"She wouldn't let just anyone watch, you know. You were quick enough to come when we asked. It's only that she needs more people to come to her, so she can afford to send her Bernadette away to school. At least you can give her an idea of what you'll say. Play the game."

Though the October night was cold, Booth was growing clammily hot. The bare light bulbs, and the tin cymbals they wore, poured heat over him. In a minute he really would tell them what he intended to write, and damn Mrs Cooper's feelings. "I'll send Mrs Cooper a copy as soon as it's written," he said. "Now you must excuse me."

"Oh no," the enormous woman said, blocking his path. "You think she's a fake, don't you? Eh, don't you?"

This was unbelievable; it couldn't be happening. He tried to slip past her, but her belly trapped him, hot and soft. Her thick fingers gripped his shoulders. Mrs Cooper was helping the old man to hobble; the others watched Booth's plight, smiling, enjoying their triumph. He ducked out of her grasp, sweating, furious. "Let's say I'd have been more easily persuaded if I'd been allowed to bring a doctor," he threw back defiantly, nearly at the door.

The tall man stalked forward. "I'm a doctor. That man's legs were crippled, if that's what you're wondering."

"Where is your surgery?" Booth said, clutching the door handle for reassurance.

"I'm retired. But I haven't forgotten what I knew."

"Well, thank you," Booth said, nodding to Mrs Cooper, and pulled at the handle. The door rattled, but refused to yield. He tugged at the handle; sweat trickled over him, prickling. This was the last time he'd follow up a story phoned in by the public.

The door pulled free of the obstruction; but as it moved, fingers closed fatly on his wrist. "Not so fast," the woman said. "You're going to say she's a miracle, aren't you? The last one who lied about her found out what else she can make happen."

Booth's control broke. He threw her off and pushed her back into the shop. "I'll say nothing of the kind," he said viciously. "I'll say this looks to me like a fake, set up to exploit the gullible and desperate."

He wrenched open his car door and thrust the key into the ignition. As the engine started, he looked back. They were hurrying out of the shop a dozen yards away, running to close in on the car from both sides. The girl Bernadette had picked up a handful of litter and was poised to throw it at the car. Booth fumbled hastily with the gears. The girl's hand went back. The car leapt, accelerating wildly. His hand had slipped on the lever. The car was accelerating in reverse.

No, this wasn't happening. The girl Bernadette hurtled toward him in the mirror; she looked like a picture on a tiny screen, unreal. But he heard the dull thud, and felt the rear wheels buck. As he braked convulsively, the enormous woman stumped quaking past the car and stood in its way.

Surely she didn't expect him to flee. He pushed himself out of the car and peered down. The girl was lying beneath the car, her neck broken; she stared blindly towards him, slack-mouthed and drooling blood. Mrs Cooper straightened up from her daughter's body and gazed expressionlessly at him. Then she paced deliberately back to the shop, walking steadily, erect, purposeful. When she halted in the doorway, Booth turned to the others. Only his movement saved his hand as the pugnacious man kicked the car door shut.

"Now wait," Booth said. "It wasn't my fault. She distracted me."

Half of them were blocking the street behind the car, while ahead the enormous woman waited for him, arms spread. The old man leaned against the shop window, bewildered. The rest of them were closing around Booth as he backed away from the pugnacious man. The doctor strode slowly toward him, arms rising from his towering shoulders.

Booth saw escape, and leapt. He vaulted over the car's hood, skinning his elbow on the windscreen. He rolled over the metal, then was running. He reached the bridge over the canal beside the street before they could stop him. Ahead, beyond the warehouses, were the docks. Through the docks he could reach the ferry.

The railing of the bridge scraped between his fingers, shedding rust. On the cobbled pavement before the warehouses, he glared back. They hadn't followed him. The canal slopped over his feet. His pursuers had returned to the shop doorway and were conferring with Mrs Cooper. With a shock Booth realised that he'd left his key in the ignition. Still, they could have the car. He was too glad of his escape.

To his right the canal curved round at the end of the line of warehouses, leading the street to the ferry's landing-stage. There might be other bridges back to the street, but if he could reach them, so could his pursuers. He was sure his first instinct had been right: he must go through the docks. Ahead was an alley, a dark crack between the warehouses. He ran forward.

He'd thought the alley must be wider than it looked, but it was hardly an alley at all—more a gap. The dark cold stone loomed over him, almost touching his shoulders, blinding him at once. It was as though he were being led blindfold by captors that paced him relentlessly, close and alert in case he tried to flee. He ran, trying to outdistance panic, hands outstretched to save him if he tripped. Around him, against him, his footsteps clapped.

He made out a pool of light ahead, lying stranded on the floor of the alley. It had splashed up a side alley, which finished where it joined his. At the far end of the side alley he could see the canal; its light struggled feebly between the alley walls, trapped. He hurried on, faster now that he could see the next gleam ahead.

The dead girl's face hung in his mind. It was Mrs Cooper's fault; it had been her game. She could have called off her friend and let him go, she could certainly have called off her daughter. But it was all a game to her, he was sure. An ingenious one: he admired the way the old man hadn't been entirely cured, to make it more convincing, as though her results were only approximate.

He ran across the gleam; at the end of his path he could see the water of a dock. The old man must have been a considerable actor, and the weeping woman too. And why not? Out-of-work actors, that was all. The key to Mrs Cooper was the array of games that filled the shop. He found himself trying to remember what the half-painted game had been. But the walls fell back. He was at the dock.

The water stretched before him, dimly lit by glimpses of moon that squeezed out between grey clouds. It swayed sluggishly; in the middle he could see the moon, a dull whitish underwater movement. The water was penned on three sides by a warehouse, a single five-storey bracket-shaped building. A few hundred yards beyond the mouth of the dock, a ferry was tying up at the landing-stage.

Booth began to hurry along the pavement of the dock as fast as he dared. Water sprang up the stone with a flat smack, pooling toward his feet, draining away, glistening. He'd seen a bridge for vehicles linking the far side of the dock to the road near the landing-stage. There was no sign of pursuit. In any case, there would be people at the landing-stage; his pursuers wouldn't dare touch him.

He had reached the second side of the dock when he heard a wallowing like the sound of oars. Had they followed him by water? But there was nothing on the water; even the drowned moon had gone, though in the sky it had fought off the clouds. He must have heard fish. He hurried on, faster, faster, and almost fell through a gap in the pavement.

It was at least six yards wide, and as broad as the pavement. Dim water slapped the jagged stone. Peering, he made out a crane beneath the water at the side of the dock, quivering like jelly. It must have torn free, taking the pavement with it. Glancing desperately about, he saw that the dock was disused.

He couldn't cross here. He might try to make his way through the warehouse. He gazed at the thick walls, their massiveness merely accentuated by dozens of square lightless holes, and knew he couldn't. There was something about the place that made him dread the darkness within; something about the rocking of the dark water, the whitish gleams that swelled and thinned to threads beneath the ripples. He ran back to the alley.

He started uncontrollably when he saw, beneath the water near the alley, a length of piping as stout as a man, exactly the colour of the drowned moon. When he'd seen the moon moving underwater he had been standing here, yet there was no sign of it now. Distracted, he stumbled towards the alley. As he plunged between the walls he saw the ferry, smoothly riding its inversion across the river.

He halted, panting, on the first gleam. He stared down the side alley, but could see no bridge. He might lose himself time in searching for one. In fact, he thought, his pursuers might have headed that way. They certainly seemed to have lost him. Perhaps now he could reach his car.

He was between the gleams when he heard the wallowing again. This time it sounded like someone emerging hugely from a bath. He faltered, then hurried on; it couldn't be anything to do with him, any more than the sound he could hear now of something—an enormous sack, he thought—being dragged intermittently over stone. Someone unloading in a nearby dock, he thought: it must be the acoustics of the alleys that made it sound so close. He glanced down the second side alley, and gasped.

It was all right. Anything would be a shock in this dimness. But he was sure he hadn't seen it when he'd passed here before—a row of whitish tires at the far end of the alley, stacked together like a pipe. In the flapping reflected light they seemed to shift restlessly. He shook his head violently and ran to the end of the main alley, dragging the walls back with his hands. Three of his pursuers were waiting for him.

The enormous woman, the doctor, the pugnacious man: they were standing just beyond the bridge. They'd known he couldn't escape through the dock. They came alert when he emerged, but made no further move. Behind them, framed in the shop window, Booth saw Mrs Cooper sitting at the table, painting by candlelight. He knew at once she was finishing her half-finished game.

Her disinterest terrified him. He was being trapped on her behalf, yet she wasn't even bothering to watch. It was inhuman. But his pursuers, he thought, were human. "Listen here, doctor," he said, stepping forward. He fell back at once, for the gangling man had loped forward onto the bridge, arms spread eagerly, while his companions blocked the way behind him.

Frantic, Booth gazed down the canal. The meagre light from the street lay in it like mud; moonlight trickled over the ripples. The rest of his pursuers had reached a bridge for vehicles and were coming back along the cobbled pavement on his side of the canal. If he made a run in the other direction, even if there were a bridge one of the three people opposite him could head him off—the long-legged doctor, no doubt. He was trapped.

His fist clenched on an iron rung. As if she felt his terror, Mrs Cooper looked up and gazed at him over the empty street. The old man and the dead girl had gone. Keeping her gaze on Booth, she painted a last detail. Then she came to the shop doorway and stood watching. She had won.

The cold iron dug into Booth's palm, and he realised that the ladder led to the warehouse roof.

The roof was flat. He'd seen that from the dock. If the roof were whole, if the ladder held, if there were a ladder for him to descend on the far side of the dock, he could reach the landing-stage. It was his only chance. He heard the rapid clattering of his pursuers drawing close; somewhere nearby he heard the moist intermittent dragging make a final surge, and halt. He tugged at the rung. He braced his heels against the wall, and pulled. The ladder held. At once, silencing his fears, he began to climb.

A few rungs up, he twisted about to see what his pursuers were doing. Mrs Cooper was still in the doorway, gazing at him. The three at the bridge were approaching leisurely; the others continued to run. He almost lost his hold, and swung back, his blood throbbing wildly. But the ladder hadn't shifted at all. It would hold. He had won after all.

He climbed swiftly. He felt the ground fall away beneath him. There was nothing to fear so long as he held on. No doubt Mrs Cooper expected the ladder to part rustily from the wall. No doubt her friends were expecting that too, or perhaps they were waiting for him to lose his head for heights. Let them wait. He might have been nervous in the shop, but he had no time to be nervous now.

He was nearly there. He glanced up. The sky swam greyly; the wall sailed free in space. He closed his eyes, gasping, and the wind tugged at him, at the same time dragging at something on the roof. Nothing to fear. He'd seen the iron handholds at the top of the wall. Take it slowly. They couldn't reach him now.

He grasped the holds and rested for a moment, eyes shut. He wouldn't take the ferry. He would telephone the police from the landing-stage. Let Mrs Cooper try to blame him for her daughter's death then. The police might well be interested in her deceptions. She'd played her last game for a while, he thought, smiling. At once he remembered what the half-finished game had been: snakes and ladders. He hoped she'd appreciate how lucky she was to have had the time to finish it.

He was still resting at the top of the ladder when the moon-coloured fat-lipped mouth, puckered wide as its body and wider than his head, stooped toward him.

The Burning

Though crowds were making their way to the park, there were still bonfires in the streets. Patches of waste ground were heaped with flame; shadows jerked in gaping windows, made derelict houses flinch back from the creeping fire. When firemen arrived to put out the blaze, children began to stone them. Some of the crowds booed the firemen, some cheered a man who went for the children, brandishing a piece of wood and roaring. People haven't changed, Blake thought as he followed the crowds into the park.

What exactly did he mean? In the park he had no chance to think. At night, even in the open, he could hardly see his way; tonight the sky was a cave's roof of dark clouds overgrown by trees, the uneven ground was treacherous, disguised by fallen leaves. The park felt like rush hour in a blackout. He could only let the crowds bear him along.

Once he strayed onto what felt like a path—his eyes were still dazzled by the flames—where he almost stumbled into a small unlit bonfire. Around it several dim figures seemed to be awaiting a signal. He hurried to rejoin the crowds.

They weren't entirely reassuring. Apart from shuffling their feet, they made very little noise. Were they so eager for the yearly ritual that they had no time for speech? There were so many of them, crowding three deep for hundreds of yards along the fence that held them back from the display. Now they had begun to murmur, an impatient almost ominous sound, as undefined as the constant brooding of the city. He was beginning to wish he hadn't come.

Why had he come? Because it was Guy Fawkes Night, because he'd lost his job, because he had wanted to get out of the house—but those weren't answers to the question. He was here for the same reason as the rest of them: to watch a man burned to ashes.

Of course he wasn't a real man, only a guy—but there had been a real Guy, centuries ago, who had been bound to a hot stone until his flesh was seared. Perhaps Blake was just depressed, yet it seemed to him that while Halloween was supposed to be the feast of the macabre, tonight was altogether grimmer. How else could one describe a night when an executioner's victim was resurrected to be burned a thousandfold?

The display was beginning. Rockets flung out streamers of fire that glared red and blue and green on the clouds. Fireworks spat showers of crackling silver, juggled whirling balls of fire. The dance of light revealed the crowd, which was even larger than Blake had thought. The bonfire writhed with shadows. Above them the guy seemed to struggle.

The glare turned the faces of the crowd into bright cardboard masks. Perhaps it was the light that made the watchers seem restless, though they had reason to be, for smoke was flooding over them from the display. There was no need to suppose they were impatient for the burning.

Blake thought they were. People hadn't changed. The crowd that had waited to watch Guy Fawkes hung, drawn and quartered must have looked as mindlessly eager—but why was this crowd so eager now, as men bearing flames converged on the bonfire? Bonfires had been for burning heretics, and also for public rejoicing; how had the two become combined? It was as though tonight's ceremony was so ancient that nobody could recall what it invoked.

People were milling about now, trying to avoid the smoke. Blake's eyes were a jumble of after-images; when someone peered round his shoulder to scrutinise him he couldn't see the face. Were several people searching? Were their faces lopsided as masks that had slipped awry?

He started, and came to himself. For a moment he'd known how it must feel to be trapped in a crowd through which searchers were closing in. Now they had moved away, if indeed they had been there at all.

It was no wonder that he was thinking oddly, perhaps hallucinating, when he'd had so little sleep. Every time he managed to doze, the realisation that he had no job jarred him awake. There was no appeal against redundancy, nobody to blame, only the economic climate that also virtually ensured nobody else would employ him now.

"Remember, remember, the fifth of November," a man with a megaphone was saying, "gunpowder, treason and plot. I see no reason why gunpowder treason should ever be forgot." All at once, as flames scrambled up the bonfire and the crowd cheered more loudly, Blake saw no reason either. The man up there was evil, and deserved to burn. The men who had put Blake out of a job, whoever and wherever they were, deserved it even more. His roar of approval was the loudest of any.

When he heard himself he stopped, dismayed. That was part of himself he didn't want to know. Had the searchers returned, or was everyone nearby peering at him? Ashamed to look, he stared at the bonfire. The face above it was burning now, the arms were writhing; one fell from the shoulder, into the roaring blaze. He could hardly bear to look.

It was quickly over, at least for the watchers. As far as a live victim was concerned, it must have taken longer. A last flourish of fireworks spelt out GOOD NIGHT. He was glad when they faded, for their glare made the faces around him seem even more like masks.

In the dark the crowd seemed to have grown. As people began to disperse, the park sounded like an enormous playground. Of course he'd known that there were many children, but now the thought dismayed him. Had children sounded so excited on the way home from public executions?

He must avoid these thoughts out here in the dark. He was thinking too vividly of Guy Fawkes, tortured and executed centuries ago, only to be revived each year for entertainment. Blake had been thinking about death recently, since it seemed he was no use to anyone. Perhaps death was a kind of sleep—but what if you were jarred awake each year for further torments? The intervals between would seem less and less like sleep.

Suddenly he wanted to be home. At least his house was familiar, empty of surprises. He stumbled along in the midst of the crowd that filled the park. When he glimpsed people their movements looked jerky, tangled among after-images. Here and there flashlights lapped the ground, revealing fallen leaves sketched by frost. The pools of light wavered away from him. At least they were taking the children with them.

Trees closed overhead. They looked like after-images too, branded on the looming sky. He had little time to notice, for he needed to watch his feet, if he could see them. At least the crowd was thinning, though the people around him stank of smoke. The rustling of leaves underfoot was harsh, almost deafening.

Here at last was a path; his feet had sensed it, even if he couldn't make it out. He hurried recklessly, anxious to come in sight of the main road, the streetlamps. His insomnia was oppressing him; the rustling around him sounded harsher, the figures appeared to be moving stiffly as cripples.

He was in too much of a hurry. For the second time that night he almost walked into the unlit bonfire. That was the fault of the people who were crowding him and who had given him no chance to dodge. There were only a few of them; the rest of the crowd, he realised suddenly, had gone. They'd better let him through, or he would make them—he didn't care how rude he had to be.

He was turning away from the bonfire when they seized him.

They were moving as swiftly as he'd thought they were. They were rustling, though there were no leaves underfoot. Their gloved hands felt soft and lumpy, too clumsy to hold him—but before he had thought to struggle they'd twisted wire around him and stuffed a wad smelling of petrol into his mouth.

When they toppled him backwards onto the bonfire he tried to lash out, but his hands and feet were bound tightly. His shoulder caught one of his captors in the face. That paralysed Blake more severely than his bonds had done. Not only did the figure's head feel softer than jelly, but the face slipped awry, revealing a pale blur.

As Blake lay helpless on the bonfire, shuddering as though that would break his bonds, he heard a sound of scrabbling around him in the dark. They were trying to light matches. He threw himself back and forth, but that only sank him further into the bonfire; twigs scratched his face and hands. When he tried to spit out the gag, he began to choke.

A match flared, and another. He saw hands, or stuffed gloves, touching flames to the bonfire on both sides of him. Twigs and leaves blazed up. He could feel the heat through his clothes. He shrank, digging his arms into his sides until he ached.

The flames sputtered and died. The scrabbling began again, sounding vicious now. The depths of the bonfire gave way, engulfing Blake further. The snapping of twigs deafened him, so that at first he wasn't sure that he was hearing a voice. "Good God, what's this?"

All at once lights were darting about the open space, glancing at the masked figures that stood immobile around the bonfire. The flashlights converged on Blake. "God Almighty," said one of the men, the one who'd held the megaphone. "Who did this to you?"

As soon as they'd pulled out the gag and untwisted the wires, Blake fled. Even if the figures propped against the trees were still now, he couldn't bear to stay near them. As he fled, he saw the men lighting the bonfire and throwing the figures into the flames. Was it only the leaves he heard squealing?

When he reached the main road at last, he looked back. Then he ran faster, dodging traffic. The streetlamps had dazzled him; he couldn't have been sure of what he was seeing—yet he thought he'd glimpsed flaming objects across the park, hobbling toward him as best they could as they burned.

He ran down his street, past crawling piles of ash. Against a pink glow deep in one of them, he glimpsed a feeble stirring of charred sticks. He slammed his front door behind him, but couldn't keep out the stench of smoke. He stood in the empty house, wondering if anything was left in the street fires that might move.

A Play for the Jaded

A schoolroom. It contains a blackboard on whose ledge rests a stick of chalk. The room occupies half of the stage, which is divided by a wall containing a door. On the other side of the wall is a flower-bed from which protrudes a trowel. Between the schoolroom and the audience is a locked box with holes bored in it. Sounds of clawing and thumping as of something trying to escape are heard from the box.

The schoolteacher enters and chalks the name *Jack* on the board. On this cue, **Jack** appears from the rear of the auditorium and makes his way to the stage.

Teacher: "This is Jack."

The teacher writes *Jill,* and **Jill** joins **Jack** on the stage.

Teacher: "This is Jill."

Jack and **Jill** stand on either side of the box and face the audience.

The teacher chalks the word *owl* on the board and hands the key of the box to **Jack**, who unlocks it. **Jill** reaches in and produces an owl that she dangles upside down by its legs while showing it to the audience. The owl flaps and hoots, as should the audience.

Teacher: "This is an—"

Jack and **Jill** in unison: "Owl."

The teacher chalks the word *fowl* on the board.

Teacher: "The owl is a—"

Jack and **Jill** in unison: "Fowl."

The teacher chalks *howl* on the board. (The timing of what s/he writes and of what s/he then says ought to give the audience time to anticipate how the word is going to figure in the action.)

Teacher, speaking directly to the audience: "Shall we make the owl howl?"

Jack and **Jill** nod eagerly. **Jack** grasps one leg of the still inverted

246

owl while **Jill** keeps hold of the other. They pull in opposite directions, very slowly. The owl begins to screech.

 Teacher, in the tone of someone teaching an important lesson: "A screech owl cannot howl."

 Jack and **Jill** continue to pull. The teacher chalks the word *bowel*.

 Teacher: "See the owl's—"

 Jack and **Jill** are too taken aback by what they've done to respond. The teacher repeats the cue more loudly and raps the word on the blackboard while s/he stares at the auditorium. Once members of the audience have responded, **Jack** and **Jill** repeat the word as if it causes them some distress.

 Jill: "That bowel is foul."

 The teacher's expression makes it clear that the pupils are not supposed to anticipate words. As the teacher angrily chalks *foul* on the blackboard, **Jack** lets go of the leg he's holding, and the remains of the owl swing towards **Jill**, who cries out and drops the object.

 The teacher swings round and, having seen what's happened, paces toward **Jill.** When s/he's close enough to touch her s/he points at the mess on the floor, then returns to the board and chalks the word *trowel*.

 Teacher: "**Jill** must dig with a—"

 Jack, delighted: "Trowel."

 Jill trudges to the flower-bed and begins to dig. She grimaces at the audience.

 Jack, more delighted than ever: "See her scowl."

 The teacher turns slowly and stares at **Jack** with hideous menace, but **Jack** doesn't notice. *Scowl* is chalked on the board. **Jill** continues to dig until the hole is several feet long and a couple of feet wide.

 Jack, puzzled: "That's a big hole for an owl."

 The teacher shares an evil grin with the audience. **Jill** is standing in the hole and wiping her forehead with the back of her hand. The teacher chalks up *towel*.

 Jill to **Jack:** "Towel."

 Jack to audience: "Hear her growl."

 The teacher's expression makes it clear that if there had been any hope of a reprieve for **Jack**, there certainly isn't now. While **Jack** saunters offstage the teacher chalks *growl* and then, after a short pause, *jowl*.

Teacher to audience as if sharing a secret: "Is the towel for Jill to mop her jowl?"

The teacher's delivery ought to be sufficient answer in itself. If anyone in the audience calls out a response, the teacher may stare hard at them as if identifying them for future reference. **Jack** returns and takes a towel to **Jill.** It has obviously been pulled off a roller—it's quite narrow, but several yards long. He teases her, offering it to her and snatching it away, before she is able to grab it from him.

Jill mops her face and gazes after **Jack** as he moves away. He goes to the owl and grins wickedly at the audience. Squatting down, he separates the body from its contents. He doesn't notice that **Jill** is tying a noose in one end of the towel, which she then conceals in the earth at the side of the hole. The teacher watches.

Jill: "Owl."

Jack winks at the audience. He hides the entrails in one hand before picking up the owl. The teacher chalks up the word *yowl* on the board as **Jack** walks innocently up to **Jill. Jack** drops the owl in the hole and then stuffs the contents of the owl down **Jill**'s collar. He's so overcome by mirth at the result that he can't move from where he's standing—that's to say, in the noose concealed by the earth.

Teacher to audience: "Shall we make Jack yowl?"

This question may be repeated more than once. When the audience seems sufficiently enthusiastic about the prospect, **Jill** slips the noose over **Jack**'s ankles and pulls it tight. He falls on his back at the edge of the hole. As he tries to push himself upright, **Jill** wraps the other end of the towel around his wrists and pulls it tight before tying his arms behind his back. He's now lying on his side by the hole.

The teacher writes *bowel* on the board, and then *trowel.* He takes his time about this and about asking the next question.

Teacher to audience: "Shall Jill trowel his bowel?"

The teacher shouldn't be satisfied with less than full encouragement. When the appropriate business has been performed the teacher speaks again.

Teacher to **Jill:** "Feed Jack his bowel."

Jill sets about this operation. As **Jack**'s protests become less coherent, the teacher poises the chalk at the blackboard.

Teacher: "Jack, that sound is a—" [writing the word while speaking it] "—vowel."

Once **Jack** is gagged, **Jill** stands back to admire her handiwork. His struggles grow weaker and eventually cease, and she pushes him into the hole. Throughout this action the teacher waits at the blackboard with the chalk poised to write another word. When **Jill** has finished, the teacher gazes about the audience, locating those people who were vociferous earlier, and then chalks the word *prowl.*

Teacher: "Prowl, Jill, prowl."

Jill surveys the audience. Her experiences have obviously turned her brain. She advances towards one or more of the members of the audience identified by the teacher, then rushes at whichever of them first responded to the teacher's prompting. Flourishing part of her victim as she goes, she dashes out of the auditorium.

The teacher looks satisfied with a job well done, and calls the theatre staff to clear the auditorium. As the audience leaves, the teacher shouts after them.

Teacher: "Now Jill is on the prowl."

Acknowledgments

"The Childish Fear." First published in *Alien Worlds* 1, edited by Charles Partington and Harry Nadler. Copyright © 1966 by Ramsey Campbell.

"The Offering to the Dead." First published in *Necronomicon 2nd Edition Programme Book*. Copyright © 1995 by Ramsey Campbell.

"The Reshaping of Rossiter." First published in *Transactions of the Doppelganger Society*, edited by David Cowperthwaite. Copyright © 1990 by Ramsey Campbell.

"The Void." First published in *Two Obscure Tales*. Copyright © 1993 by Ramsey Campbell.

"The Other House." First published in *New Writings in Horror and the Supernatural 2*, edited by David [A.] Sutton. Copyright © 1972 by Ramsey Campbell.

"Broadcast." First published in *New Writings in Horror and the Supernatural*, edited by David (still missing his arcane A) Sutton. Copyright © 1971 by Ramsey Campbell.

"The Urge." First published in *Two Obscure Tales*. Copyright © 1993 by Ramsey Campbell.

"The Sunshine Club." First published in *The Dodd, Mead Gallery of Horror*, edited by Charles L. Grant. Copyright © 1983 by Ramsey Campbell.

"Writer's Curse." First published in *Night Flights* 1, no. 1 [*Myrddin* 5], edited by Lawson Hill. Copyright © 1980 by Ramsey Campbell.

"Property of the Ring." First published in *Arkham's Masters of Horror*, edited by Peter Ruber. Copyright © 2000 by Ramsey Campbell.

"Night Beat." First published in *Haunt of Horror*, 1, no. 1, edited by Gerard Conway. Copyright © 1973 by Ramsey Campbell.

"The Shadows in the Barn." First published in *Dark Horizons* 12, edited by Stephen Jones. Copyright © 1975 by Ramsey Campbell.

"The Precognitive Trip." Original to this collection.

"Murders." First published in *New Writings in SF 26*, edited by Kenneth Bulmer. Copyright © 1975 by Ramsey Campbell.

Printed in the United States
205487BV00002B/106-156/P

9 780979 380662